THERE CAME
A BIG SPIDER

Terry White

IndePenPress

First published in Great Britain by Indepenpress

All paper used in the printing of this book has been made from wood grown in managed, sustainable forests.

ISBN13: 978-1-907499-86-9

Printed and bound in the UK
Indepenpress is an imprint of Indepenpress Publishing Limited
25 Eastern Place
Brighton
BN2 1GJ

A catalogue record of this book is available from the British Library

Cover design by Jacqueline Abromeit

A sense of humour is a wonderful gift. I dedicate this book to my family and friends and all the other people who bring me laughter and happiness.

Other Marcus Moon books by the author

Trespassers Will Be Mutilated
Till The Fat Lady's Sung
The Horns of the Moon
With Gently Smiling Jaws

PROLOGUE

Eifrith, thane of Earl Kenet, lay curled up snoring gently on a pile of dirty straw in the corner of his watchman's reed hut. The remains of a roasted rabbit and an empty pitcher lay scattered round his recumbent form. He never felt a thing when the axe cleaved through his skull, splitting it down to his jaw.

'That bugger'll wake with an even nastier headache!' grinned the larger of the two Danes, a big burly man wearing a rusty mail coat over a stained leather jacket, as he wiped the blade of the axe on the watchman's ragged tunic. He gestured with his thumb to his companion and they moved silently back along the river bank to join the four longships that were holding steady against the current. The banks of oars dipped into the water and the boats resumed their creep up the river towards King Alfred's camp. Spies had reported that he was still there and had only a couple of hundred armed men, priests and courtiers to protect him.

The Danes had timed their move perfectly. At the agreed time, when the thin crescent of the new moon split the dark sky to the East, they were no more than twenty leagues from Alfred, cutting off the possibility of any escape down the river. It was planned that they would link up with the bulk of their army moving down from their newly established base at Cippanhamm.

Further upstream, Robert, the charcoal burner, groaned as his bladder called yet again for relief. He swore off his home-brewed firewater for the umpteenth time and staggered out of his hut in the grove of trees by the river. Fumbling his way to a convenient spot, he began operations. Still half asleep, the unusual movement on the river caught his attention. A ship – in the middle of the night? Rubbing his eyes to clear the film of mucus from his eyeballs, he looked again. Two ships – no, three, four! – with round shields lining their sides and terrifying carvings on their high prows and sterns. Now fully awake, he watched them wide-eyed as they glided quietly past.

Although he had never seen a Viking or one of their ships before, he knew about the fierce men from across the sea and he knew that they were enemies.

He crossed himself muttering a prayer, and hesitated for a minute. His instinct told him to flee deeper into the forest and then a thought struck him. There could be a reward for anyone who brought the warning to King Alfred. And so, hastily pulling up his drawers, he set off, running and walking along the deer path between the massive trunks of oak, beech and hornbeam. Taking a short cut to avoid a long loop in the river, he reached the castle well ahead of any boats.

Alfred's castle was more a fortified camp than a stronghold. A low earthen rampart topped by a stout wooden palisade sur-

tion where the treasure was buried, were tossed casually into the flames. Thus all knowledge of the whereabouts of Arthur's treasure was lost.

Although he didn't appreciate it, the roasting gave Alfred the extra time he needed to direct his followers westward through the forest so that they could make their way safely to a fort further west in the Sumorseate marshes close to the River Saefern.

History tells us that, using this as his base, Alfred set up court and regrouped his forces. He was eventually able to muster a West Saxon army strong enough to beat the Danes at the Battle of Edington and drive them back east out of Wessex.

However, when he returned to the King's Castle site there was nobody left alive who knew where the treasure had been buried. After months of fruitless digging, it could not be found.

No trace of it has emerged since.

CHAPTER 1

Wilf Davies was a contented man: everything seemed to be in full working order. Mrs Davies, or Gwyneth, as he liked to whisper in her ear at intimate moments, was on for a promise that evening and life seemed good. The furthest thought from Wilf's mind on this bright autumn morning was that he was about to become an entry in *The Guinness Book of World Records.*

What more could he want he thought to himself as he cruised steadily down the M4 towards junction 16a at Swindon. He had a lovely family – one of each, a good wife – and a responsible job. Although the traffic on the motorway was heavy he manoeuvred the huge lorry with the casual skill expected of the company's top driver as he headed westwards. The heavy showers had passed over and the sun shone between the white puffy clouds that drifted lazily overhead.

Mrs Davies had been given her usual 'see you later' kiss, and Maldwyn and Mivanwy their usual pats on the head and told to work hard at school and not get into trouble.

He had departed 'Yr Wylan', 43, Church Road, Reading, early that morning with a packet of sandwiches for lunch (his favourite bacon and tomato) and a flask of sweet coffee. Queen was playing on the stereo as he swung the huge 'artic' off the M4, eased it round the roundabout and on to the A399 Kingscastle road.

Wilf was a proud man; the juggernaut was one of the first of the brand new articulated lorries recently permitted by European Union regulations to be operated on British roads: twenty metres long with a load capacity of forty-five tons spread over six axles. The massive steel casting on the trailer, destined for Semmingborough Power Station, had been loaded over the Bank Holiday weekend and the tractor unit fuelled up ready for him when he arrived at the depot that morning. He'd checked the load, noting that it seemed closer to the rear axles than normal, but he assumed that was because most of the weight was in the front part of the casting. He signed off the paperwork and swung up easily into the cab. He wasn't aware that the regular loadmaster had been ill over the Bank Holiday and it had been one of the assistant managers out of the office who had supervised the loading of his cargo.

Wilf hadn't travelled on this particular road before, his area was usually eastwards to the Channel ports, but the satellite navigation equipment in the cab had given him a route that kept him either on motorways or 'A' class roads so, as he tapped his fingers on the steering wheel to the rhythm of Queen's music, he hadn't a care in the world trundling along at a steady thirty-five miles per hour.

Being the day after the Autumn Bank Holiday, there was a lot of traffic on the A399 travelling in both directions. On the opposite side were cars and four-wheel drives – some towing caravans or boats – heading back towards London and the Home Counties from the south-west at the end of the holidays, heavily laden with luggage, children and the reluctant knowledge that summer was over.

'Poor buggers,' he muttered to himself, thinking of the tail-backs he had seen on the M4 stretching way past Reading nearly to Newbury. They were in for a long hot day.

Although classed as an 'A' road and widened in parts, the A399 was still basically a Wiltshire farmers' cart track. Over the centuries the wheels of numerous carts and the hooves of equally numerous horses had eroded the surface so that the present tarmac road bed was at least a metre below the level of the surrounding fields in many places. In addition, high hedges of hawthorn and elder had grown up on the banks flanking the road. Overtaking on the A399 was a hazardous exercise at the best of times. There were a few passing places where a couple of cars had time to whip past a heavy lorry, but not today with all the returning holiday traffic on the opposite side of the road. The A399 was an important link between the industries of the East Midlands and the south-west ports. It was busy in both directions and traffic that day was nose to tail. After the extended weekend holiday there was heavy lorry traffic heading for the ports; container trucks, tankers carrying fuel and chemicals, general haulage vehicles, tour buses as well as the usual cars and vans. The quicker vehicles rapidly formed an ever lengthening queue behind Wilf's slow-moving juggernaut, unable to pass. Tempers were fraying, curses muttered and fingers given.

About a mile outside Kingscastle, Wilf hit the even slower moving queue of traffic that had backed up from the town's narrow streets. The queue wound round the rolling chalk downs and into the outskirts of the town. At least we're moving, thought Wilf as he watched the container truck in front of him gently manoeuvre its bulk round the tight right-angled bend from Fore Street into the Market Square.

There was a hiss of compressed air and a change of gear as Wilf applied the brakes to cut his speed; he eyed the corner apprehensively. It's a bit tight, he thought, but he was a skilled and experienced driver so at no more than five miles per hour he inched the big vehicle forward, keeping a close eye on his wing mirrors. He realised that to make the turn with clearance he was going to have to ride the tractor unit up over the kerb on the opposite side of the road. A helpful policeman stepped forward, held up the oncoming traffic and waved Wilf on. He could see in the nearside mirror that it was going to be a very tight squeeze, but he calculated that the corbelled overhanging first floor offices of Norfolk and Chance – Solicitors, with its half-timbered black solid oak beams, would just avoid contact with his truck, or rather it with the building. What he didn't allow for was the sudden tilting of the cab as the wheels mounted the high kerb on the opposite side of the road.

The outcome was spectacular. The whole rig tipped sideways with a sudden jerk, impaling the cab on the projecting oak beams and causing the heavy steel casting to slide across the trailer as far as its restraining ropes would permit. This put the trailer out of balance and most of the forty ton weight of the casting over the nearside rear wheels – wheels which happened to be resting on a large cast-iron manhole cover in the road.

PC Shayne Connolly was enjoying his third week as a fully-fledged police constable, boots polished and shoulder number gleaming. He was revelling in the authority he had controlling traffic in Kingscastle Market Square. His signal to hold up the oncoming traffic was precise and clear – perfectly textbook with an intimidating glare. His confident wave to Wilf to move forward was equally precise, and he was just congratulating himself when the tractor and trailer tipped. From his position at the end of the Market Square he couldn't see exactly what had happened, only that Wilf's vehicle had come to a sudden standstill. The sight of this blockage when he had taken the trouble to organise its safe passage annoyed him.

He waved Wilf forward angrily.

'You can't stop there!' he shouted. 'Come on, move it out – sharpish!'

At that moment the manhole cover cracked with a sound like a rifle shot, and collapsed in pieces into the town's main sewer. No longer supported, the nearside rear wheels fell into the exposed hole and the trailer slewed violently. The sudden force of the movement caused the huge casting to break free of its restraining ropes, it slid across the trailer with a scream of tortured metal and, with a crash of shattered glass, came to rest halfway through the plate glass window of the 'Mother Wouldn't Like It' boutique. The tractor unit twisted and rammed itself further into Gervaise Norfolk's private office, bringing down a shower of brick and plaster on to the small pavement beneath.

There was a stunned silence for ten seconds, then all hell broke loose.

Gervaise Norfolk, covered in plaster dust with spectacles askew, shouted angrily through the hole in his office wall that he would 'sue the pants off whichever lunatic was responsible!'

Ms Golightly from 'Mother Wouldn't Like It' clearly didn't like it either, with the best part of forty tons of rusty steel parked across her range of 'Knickers and Bras for the Imaginative Girl', and began to scream hysterically.

PC Connolly, forgetting all his training, grabbed his radio and gabbled into it, 'Christ, Sarge, we're fucked.'

And Wilf sat paralysed in total shock as Freddie Mercury sang 'Tomorrow could be worse'. Automatically he reached over and switched off the engine.

PC Connolly's radio crackled. 'Repeat again with more information,' said the cool voice of the dispatcher at Kingscastle Police Headquarters.

'We're well and truly fucked then – left, right and centre!' gabbled PC Connolly.

'That's not what I had in mind,' snapped the dispatcher. 'Is that you, Connolly?'

'Yes,' he said shakily.

'Well get a grip, man, pull yourself together and start again.'

Taking a couple of deep breaths, Connolly tried to explain the problem.

'Are there any casualties?'

'I don't think so.'

'In that case I'll send a car.'

PC Connolly looked round at the traffic piling up in the Market Square. Horns were being blown and voices raised. He assumed that round the corner on the other side of the trapped juggernaut the same thing was happening.

'A bike would be better; I don't think a car would make it through. I also think you're going to need more than that. A large crane and a breakdown truck at the very least, although how they'll get here defeats me.'

It was a very astute assessment of the current situation but nobody could have predicted the ultimate outcome. So although the dispatcher sent two officers on foot and a patrolman on a motorbike, by the time they arrived it was too late.

The road was now blocked to traffic in both directions. Those that could see the carnage on the corner realised that a major problem existed and tried to reverse or turn their vehicles round. Unfortunately large numbers of those vehicles were towing caravans, boats or trailers of some sort, and the drivers were not accustomed to reversing in tight spaces with such attachments. The result was a shambles of jack-knifed caravans, cars and vans rammed into each other at all angles, fists being waved, voices shouting and children howling. The outcome was a total blockade of the Market Square. Traffic began to build up nose-to-tail outside Kingscastle to the South West. Unfortunately this blocked a junction which could have provided the only escape route, had the drivers realised it.

On the North East side of the accident the situation was even worse. Within half-an-hour the queue of cars, lorries and buses stretched for two miles. Then a large chemical tanker containing sulphuric acid rounded a sharp bend to discover the traffic immediately in front of him at a standstill. The driver slammed on his brakes, skidded on the still wet road and jack-knifed his 'artic', ramming a large farm lorry and trailer containing over a hundred sheep on its way to Plymouth docks. The ruptured chemical tanker slid round and hit the high verge, overturning and spilling concentrated sulphuric acid all over the road. Dead, injured and maddened sheep spread into this mess and the ones that could run ran back up the road into the oncoming traffic, causing more accidents and chaos.

Six hours later the combined efforts of police forces from three divisions had managed to get some control over the situation and seal off the area. By then the M4 was closed in both directions between Swindon and Doddington, traffic jams stretched as far west as Bristol, as far east as Newbury and as far south as Salisbury. People who tried diversions down country lanes met heavy traffic coming the other way doing the same thing, and everything gridlocked in a thirty-mile radius centred on Kingscastle.

It was the biggest traffic jam ever experienced anywhere. The AA estimated that the best part of quarter of a million vehicles were involved. Police and Army helicopters ferried blankets, food and water to the occupants of the trapped vehicles. Working day and night, it took three days to extract most of the vehicles on the A399. A bulldozer made a temporary escape road round the chemical hazard before a large mobile crane could reach Wilf Davies' crippled 'artic' and two more days to move it and its load. Contractors were called in to shore up Norfolk and Chance's offices and replace the manhole cover so that the road could be re-opened.

At first it was just another item on the South West News. '*An accident in Kingscastle has caused tailbacks both ways along the A399. Motorists are advised to take alternative routes to avoid Kingscastle.*' But by then there were no 'alternative routes'. The narrow country lanes were now blocked with lorries and caravans with no room to manoeuvre even if they wanted to. The lucky ones pulled off the road into fields and set up camp there.

By the following morning national television had picked up the story and had chartered helicopters to fly over the chaos and film the carnage of jack-knifed lorries, crushed caravans, burning cars, blocked roads and hordes of angry fist-waving people. Air Ambulances were scrambled from all parts of the country and RAF and Army units evacuated the sick and old to hospitals outside the area.

The Kingscastle authorities, as well as the rest of the country, put the blame for the situation squarely on the shoulders of the government: in the case of the Kingscastle authorities, justifiably so. They had been lobbying heavily for a bypass to be built round the town for ten years without attracting so much as a flicker of interest from the Department of Transport. As for the remainder of the country, it was axiomatic that the government were automatically responsible for any cock-up or shambles that befell the worthy citizens of the British Isles, which again bore an element of truth in this case.

By midnight the first ripples of a political tsunami were heading towards Downing Street, and the Secretary of State for Transport sinking a final glass of a good port before going to bed, received a terse telephone call from Number 10.

'Graham, have you seen the late news? Is this thing at Kingscastle going to cause us a problem?'

Graham Preston, Her Majesty's Secretary of State for Transport and Communications, a well-fed, well-watered space-hopper of a man, hadn't seen the late news. In fact he had just got back from a good dinner at Grosvenor House for the Society for Building and Construction where, in his opinion, he had made a brilliant speech about how the Government had improved the road network, and were continuing to do so to ensure that business didn't suffer by traffic delays on major roads.

'By careful planning this Government has saved the country billions' had been his punchline.

The phone call twitched his political antenna; this was thinking-on-one's-feet time, or, in his case, lolling-back-half-pissed-in-a-deep-leather-chair time, trying to cudgel some cogent thoughts into his drink-befuddled brain. He didn't want to admit that he hadn't a clue what the Prime Minister was talking about, but appreciated that whatever it was it had something to do with transport, hence the phone call. Also it wasn't serious yet but could become so – hence the late-night phone call. A carefully phrased reply was called for and this was not going to be easy after two glasses of champagne, three quarters of a bottle of good claret and several ports. He had a vague memory of somebody at the dinner making a joke about a traffic jam

'I've asked my PPS to have a report waiting for me on my desk first thing in the morning, Bill. I'll call you immediately I've absorbed the detail.' He metaphorically crossed his fingers but it seemed to do the trick. The PM was apparently satisfied.

'Without fail, Graham. Without fail! I do not want you to let this get out of hand.' And the line was broken.

Preston scratched his head nervously at the implications of that last comment; somebody was going to have to do some work tonight and one thing was certain, it wasn't going to be him. He debated whether to ring his Permanent Secretary at the Department, Sir Joseph Storey, or his Parliamentary Private Secretary, Tom Froome. It would be better to let Froome handle it; he couldn't face the wrath of rousing the testy Storey from the warm bed of the formidable Lady Storey. He picked up the phone.

The next morning Preston rose early and watched the morning news on the television whilst he was shaving. He nearly did himself a nasty injury when the extent of the problem was revealed by the BBC helicopter overflying the area round Kingscastle. The roads and lanes were solid with traffic as far as the eye could see. He ordered his official car immediately and arrived at the Ministry, to be greeted by a haggard PPS and a remarkably fresh and spruce-looking Sir Joseph Storey.

Wasting no time on the walk to his office, he said, 'Right, fill me in.'

'You've seen the news, Minister? Apparently there's been some sort of accident in Kingscastle which has caused the traffic jam. We have a mixture of holiday and commercial traffic snarled up in the area.'

This understatement didn't sound too bad so Preston thought he'd lighten the atmosphere a bit; throw in a little humour.

'So nothing new then, a typical Bank Holiday Weekend: the British seem to enjoy being stuck in traffic for their holidays, they do it every year. Perhaps 'Visit Britain' should advertise 'Spend Your Holiday on the M6' as one of the attractions for tourists! Ha, ha, ha!'

Sir Joseph gave a weak smile. 'Very droll Minister, but I'm afraid it's a little more serious than that, the early morning papers are baying for the Government's blood, and yours in particular They say it's all a result of your failure to implement what they describe as the disjointed, badly planned, half-baked 'Integrated Communications System' that you promised at the last party conference. They're also reporting your speech at last night's Society for Building and Construction's Annual Dinner, at which you emphasised how well the Government was handling the roads problem, "saving the country billions".'

That wiped the smile off Preston's face.

'The police say that they have it under control now…' added Tom Froome.

'Yes, quite, Tom!' snapped Sir Joseph, irritated at having a distraction from the knife he was carefully sliding between the Minister's ribs.

'…and the Army had to get involved this morning,' continued Froome, only to be quelled by another withering glare.

Graham Preston's political and self-preservation antenna, being one and the same, quivered at the mention of the Army. To involve the Army meant trouble, big trouble. His piggy eyes swivelled round as his brain rapidly calculated on whom he could lay the blame, and locked on to his Permanent Secretary. However, Sir Joseph had long since resolved that if shit was going to be shovelled, it wasn't going to be shovelled over him; a quick analysis of the position was called for to remedy this situation.

'You will recall, Minister, that Kingscastle have lobbied heavily for a bypass over the past few years and your department has always turned them down. I recollect that our engineers recommended that funds be allocated for such a road as a priority project but it was felt…' He put his hand to his mouth and gave a slight cough '…that the money could be more usefully spent, in a political sense naturally, on the Gardale Bridge.'

He gave a thin smile and continued. 'The long bridge over

the Wharfe valley that links rural Garstone with your constituency in rural Lowdale. You will no doubt recall some opposition wag describing it as "the most expensive cattle crossing in the world".'

Graham Preston winced; he knew full well that it wasn't his department that had rejected Kingscastle's bypass, it was him. Garstone had had a by-election coming up and he thought the new bridge would swing a few votes towards his party and gain him some political kudos with the PM.

He brushed it aside. 'Yes, yes, never mind all that, what am I going to tell the PM, for Christ's sake? He wants a report this morning.'

Sir Joseph stroked his chin. He loved these situations when he had the Minister floundering about and panicking, not knowing which way to turn or what to do. It was bread laid up in heaven for some future situation if he was experiencing difficulty getting the Minister to act as Sir Joseph thought he should.

After a pause to build up the tension a bit more and give the Minister the impression that he was mulling over the situation, he said suavely, 'Well, Minister, I suggest that you tell the PM that it's a major problem but thanks to his policies of integrating police forces and the setting up of the Emergency Task Force, everything is coming under control. Also, it's unfortunate that the European Union imposed their new expanded lorry regulations upon us without giving us time to implement your vital new road programme – which contains the Kingscastle bypass as a priority item.'

'But it doesn't,' said Preston, puzzled.

'I think it does now, Minister!' murmured Sir Joseph with a grim smile.

*****

Ironically the only person to benefit from this traffic jam initially was the unfortunate Wilf Davies. Having been seized by PC Connolly as the perpetrator of all the chaos, the police had to let him go when he claimed that it was all Connolly's fault for waving him on when there wasn't enough room for him to get through. There were plenty of witnesses to this, and suffering parties, including Wilf's company, were likely to sue the police for all they'd got.

He became a celebrity overnight. An enterprising TV show hired a helicopter to extract him from Kingscastle and put him on TV that night. Max Clifford took over as his agent and arranged to syndicate his story in the world's press for a small fortune. Offers to appear on 'Hot Wheels', 'Hit the Wall', 'Celebrity Ding-Dong' and 'Masterbrain' flooded in. Wilf revelled in his new fame, quit his job, put a deposit on a new bungalow for his mum and dad, ordered a completely new wardrobe, had his teeth fixed, grew his hair long – and went bankrupt nine months later.

But his name lived on. *The Guinness Book of World Records* trumpeted 'The Man who caused the Biggest Traffic Jam in the World.'

Just about the same time as Wilf's finances hit the rocks, a wave-let from his earlier disaster washed against the shores of a small ground floor flat in a terraced house just off Wandsworth Common.

It was a cold wet day that Sunday, the rain beat against the windows of the flat, little trickles of water seeped round the dirty glass where the putty had cracked away from the window frames. They formed puddles on the chipped cream paint of the sills. Reaching for the sweater he had hung over the back of a chair, Ivan Masterland shivered as he sought some warmth against the chill of the late afternoon.

'Bloody Sunday,' he muttered to himself, 'I hate it! Why does everything happen to me? What have I done to deserve all this?' He slumped miserably in the old leather armchair as close to the fireplace as he could get and gloomily reviewed his life to date. The smokeless fuel fire in the grate struggled to emit a few calories from the damp briquettes he had collected from the bunker outside.

It could not be said that Ivan Masterland was a candle sent to light up the world. This was not a new or surprising condition. It wasn't an unusual situation either; indeed, happiness rarely entered his ethos.

Ivan was born with a sunless, doleful, suspicious nature. He had been miserable and infectiously depressing all through his childhood: what friends he had at the age of three he had lost by the age of four. It wasn't that he always wanted to be the leader, the top dog, in the children's games they played – he didn't. It was more that he didn't want anybody else to be more important than him, so he criticised and complained about everybody and everything, and when others suggested ideas and activities, he poured scorn on them. The chip on his shoulder that arrived with him out of the womb grew at exactly the same rate as he did, and he was big for his age. The only redeeming feature he had – fortunately for him and maybe the world in general – was that he was quite intelligent and thus the worst excesses of his aura of gloom and negativity were somewhat mitigated by his academic achievements.

Bert and Gloria Masterland found it hard to believe that a combination of their genes had produced such a depressing child and agonised over their past sins to try to see why some Almighty Power thought that they deserved him. Bert, who didn't believe in God, claimed it was Gloria's mother's fault, 'the wicked old witch of Worthing', and told her so – once too often.

When he could see out of his right eye again they took a more pragmatic approach and asked the maternity hospital to check its records to see if there had been a mistake and they had been given an alien baby.

Until Ivan arrived they had been a normal, loving couple, but the thought of having any more children like him drove them to extremes at the Family Planning Clinic, to such an extent that the surgical precautions they took to avoid conception at their now infrequent copulations became more like having a kidney transplant than an expression of love and affection. They prayed enthusiastically for the day when he could go off to boarding school and sunlight could illuminate their home once more.

So it was shortly before his ninth birthday that a young Ivan Masterland, rucksack on his back and wheelie case in his hand, was ushered by his smiling parents through the lofty portals of St Cuthbert's Preparatory School for Boys [Aged 8 to 13] into the hands of a welcoming Miss Morris, Assistant Matron.

And it was shortly after his ninth birthday that he was rapidly ushered the other way by a grim-faced Headmaster into the hands of his weeping mother and distraught father with firm instructions that he must never darken St Cuthbert's door again.

The first term had been barely two thirds of its way through when the letter from the Head hit the Masterlands' hall carpet, suggesting that perhaps Ivan wasn't cut out for communal life and that they *withdraw him at the earliest opportunity.* There had been *incidents,* unspecified, which had *led me to this irrevocable decision. The morale of the whole school had been affected.*

Gloria had hysterics and Bert sank a whole bottle of Glenfiddich before collapsing unconscious on the sitting room settee.

Strangely, Ivan himself was not unhappy at the school. Big for his age and quite bright, he gave back more than he got. There were a few attempts to bully and tease him by both boys and staff but after Mr Phelps, the Latin Master, was found face down in the school fishpond, having been eased off the bridge by an unknown hand one dark night whilst having a quiet smoke,

18

and Jenkinson awoke with his feet on fire in Dormitory Two, Ivan was left alone. Neither suffered any serious damage – the pond was shallow and Mr Phelps emerged wet but unharmed, apart from swallowing a lot of water and a small Golden Orfe. Jenkinson managed to blow out the matches that had been stuck under his toe nails, suffering only minor burns to his big toes. Nothing could be proved but the finger of suspicion pointed firmly at Ivan.

His gloomy aura and unsparing criticism of others above him hovered over the school like a dark raven. Morale began to crumble, Fennington, the Head Boy, kept bursting into tears and the school's rugby team, unbeaten for three years lost 17-7 to St Anselm's. For the Headmaster that was the last straw.

Similar stories occurred with the next two boarding schools so Mr and Mrs Masterland had no option but to send him to the local Michael Foot Comprehensive in the hope that his infectious negativity would be diluted by the fifteen hundred other pupils. To some extent they were justified and Ivan's gloomy aura got submerged in the hustle and bustle of a big school. He still wanted to be thought important and a success but the social skills to handle this were alien to him. The other children sensed that he was too self-centred to join in their activities and left him alone. He was too big and clever to be bullied and too nasty to be mocked. Anybody who crossed his path seemed to have unfortunate things happen to them and the pattern at the junior schools was repeated. Jeff Jones the woodwork master, who disciplined him for putting glue on Fraser's chair, found his car spluttering to a standstill on Station Road with half a bag of sugar in the petrol tank, and Mr Greenhalgh eventually discovered a potato stuck up his car's exhaust pipe the day after he spent half-an-hour trying to start it and he had to walk two miles home in the pouring rain without a coat.

At the age of eleven, Ivan's growth slowed and by thirteen had stopped. The others in his class caught up, and in most cases passed him in physical size, and so his gloomy misery, which he happily bestowed on others, was converted to introspection and introversion and his retaliation became cunning rather than physical.

Fierce ambition thrust him forward but only in a personal way; everything he did was for himself, never for others. He got grades good enough to be offered a place at university to read civil engineering and so, aged eighteen, Ivan departed Michael Foot with no regrets on either side.

Reading University was a big shock. The people there were as bright, if not brighter, than him and he no longer stood out from the crowd. At Reading he lodged in digs with a succession of formidable landladies whose hearts had been marinated in the juices of students' booze, fags, sex and drugs over the years, but even they couldn't tolerate the pall of gloom which descended on their establishments with his arrival. Other students began to give excuses and move away, so he was invariably slung out on his ear after a couple of months, with instructions never to set foot on their worn lino again.

He worked hard and humourlessly for three years and was rewarded with a good degree before launching himself on the jobs market.

At interview he soon found that his depressing and critical demeanour didn't go down well with the contracting side of civil engineering, but local authorities weren't concerned about his personality and he was able to secure a position as Assistant Road Engineer with South Hampshire County Council.

He was not comfortable in local authority work; he felt lost in a vast, inefficient, disorganised mass of people who didn't appreciate him enough. Notwithstanding that, he gradually established himself with his superiors as a reliable if unpopular road engineer. His companions soon realised that he was a miserable sod whether in the office, in the canteen at lunchtime or in the pub after work, and so he was left to his own devices.

After three years designing road junctions, traffic calming schemes and street widening proposals, an encounter with one of the principals of Sir Terence Darlow and Partners, consulting engineers for the County Council's new Traffic Plan, changed his life. It opened a new perspective on civil engineering.

Ivan now had a positive goal. He wanted to be a consultant. Having encountered consulting engineers, he realised that to be one was his target. That was where he would really be appreciated, a place where his talents could blossom and the respect he craved be duly accorded. Fortunately the County Council had some exciting and challenging road projects at the design stage and his reputation as a good engineer and planner increased, although his boss, the County Engineer, thought that he was lacking in imagination. The important thing for Ivan, however, was that the experience he gained, when dressed up and polished on his Curriculum Vitae, looked very impressive.

At that time there was a shortage of good road engineers and so when he spotted an advertisement by Consultant Design Services in *The Daily Telegraph* and sent off his CV, he was immediately short-listed for interview. As luck would have it, on the day of his final interview, the roads and bridges partner, Hugo Elmes, was struck down by a savage dose of flu and confined to his bed and thus the senior partner, Geoffrey Arbuthnot, who was a water supply and drainage man, and his colleague Ewen Jones, the industrial buildings specialist, were left to make the decision. They interpreted Ivan's gloomy demeanour as serious and sound, 'just the sort of chap we need to deal with our road commissions', and so he landed a job at CONDES.

This was, for him, a massive step; it had got him into what he considered the 'respectable' part of engineering. Now he needed to plan his progress upwards.

He quickly worked out that the ladder led from the design office, through one of the Civil Planning Teams to Associate, then to Junior Partner and finally Partner, and set about getting his foot firmly lodged as high up the rungs as he could and then climbing higher. He had no qualms about climbing over other people in his quest for recognition.

He was put into Roads 1 under a Team Leader who was a couple of years older than him; efficient but easy going. He was a pushover for Ivan. His neck provided the first useful step to help Ivan's ascent up the ladder and by toadying to the partners and slyly demeaning the work of his colleagues in Roads 1, he managed to get himself promoted into Civil Planning Team Two. The Planning Teams were the cream of the company.

This was a major boost to his ambitions.

At roughly the same time as he joined Civil Planning Team Two, Ivan's liaison with Agatha Harcourt commenced. She was one of the secretaries to the Civil Planning Teams and was plump and lumpy to his spindly and hairy. It did not start off as two hearts fusing as one, or even as an instant sexual attraction. In fact it could hardly be said to be romantic in any way. Apart from the absence of a sense of humour, the only thing they had in common was that neither had ever had a meaningful relationship with anybody of the opposite sex before. They had been forced together at the firm's Christmas Party when nobody wanted to sit next to either of them. When everybody got up to dance, Ivan and Agatha were the only two left sitting at their table. She felt embarrassed and self-conscious that she had been left so, to cover the fact that nobody wanted to dance with her, she grabbed Ivan by the hand and half-dragged him on to the dance floor. Ivan had never danced with a girl before and shuffled around like a guardsman with a poker up his bottom, body rigid and teeth gritted. But things began to happen to Ivan, things which he'd only heard about from Jerker Johnson at school, and that snotty bloke Partington-Pratt at Reading, who got sent down after two years for shagging the Warden's daughter. (In itself that act would not have warranted expulsion but they were doing it on High Table amidst the silverware, linen and glasses set out for the Annual Founders' Dinner, and were discovered when the lights were turned on and all the dignitaries and graduates in their hoods and gowns filed in. The Lady Mayoress had a fainting fit, the Vice-Chancellor apoplexy, and the practical Professor of Medical Hygiene insisted that the table be cleared and everything thoroughly washed and disinfected before he would permit a fork to touch his lips, delaying the whole proceedings by an hour.)

Having this warm female body twisting in his hands was opening up a new chapter in Ivan's dismal life. So whenever the music permitted, he clutched on to her, hands investigating various parts of this alien creature who was turning him on without him realising what was happening. She, on the other hand, with that unerring female instinct, was aware of this and decided that although Ivan was naive as far as women were concerned and not exactly film star material in the looks department, he was going places in the firm and might be her only hope for a future meal ticket if she played her cards right. Thus it was gratitude rather than affection which bound them together.

So, twelve months later, when Ivan eventually got her knickers off, he felt obliged to propose.

In Civil Planning Team Two, he soon worked out the strengths and weaknesses of his new colleagues. Des Doubleday was the

Associate, and David Nairn the specialist roads man. Doubleday he rapidly dismissed as a 'has been': an elderly man with vast experience but, in Ivan's opinion, no ambition to progress any further in the higher echelons of CONDES. He was content just to work out his time to retirement, doing only sufficient to hold his job, and he constituted no threat to Ivan's progress.

But David Nairn was different. David was also a roads man, and a clever and ambitious one as well. In addition, he was cheerful and well liked by his fellow engineers, including Ivan's managing partner Hugo Elmes. Ivan spent many fruitless hours racking his brains for a means of superseding Nairn. He was going to be a very difficult man to dislodge.

It had taken two years before the opportunity had arisen and it came when Ivan learned through his girlfriend Agatha that the firm was contemplating opening an office in the Middle East. Ivan did his research and learned that huge road building programmes were being undertaken by some of the Gulf States. Over a period of a few weeks he suggested to the various partners that somebody from 'Roads' should be sent out to establish a design office there, knowing full well that Civil Planning Team Two had the two best road engineers in the company, him and Nairn. Doubleday was out of the equation.

Both were interviewed by the partners to see if they were interested and Ivan, claiming that he was, also suggested that, although he was keen, his Jewish background might be detrimental to a firm struggling to gain a foothold in the Arab world and he wouldn't want to prejudice the firm's prospects by pushing himself forward if they felt that this could be a hindrance in any way. This was a total fabrication, but his swarthy face and black goatee beard did add credence to his statement.

So it was David Nairn who was sent out to Ajman to open CONDES' Middle East office. Ivan was commended by Geoffrey Arbuthnot for his honesty and self-sacrifice and took over from Nairn as project leader for the road design for the prestigious Kingscastle bypass project.

Ivan couldn't believe his luck. The way was open, his path ahead clear, a straight line up the ladder to Associate in maybe two, three years, and then onwards and upwards. A faint sense of pleasure illuminated a small corner of his mind and this made him uncomfortable. Was it too good to be true? Was there something in the wings he wasn't aware of; something lurking to spoil his plans? No, there couldn't be, he had covered all eventualities.

But there was, and all unknowingly and unwittingly, it was me!

CHAPTER TWO

The Frog and Nightgown was packed that Saturday lunchtime. England were playing a World Cup Qualifying Match against Poland at Wembley and the public bar had a large TV fixed high on the wall. The kick-off wasn't due for another hour at least but people wanted to establish their places for a good view. Tony Scales had managed to shoulder his way through the mob thronging the bar and secure us three pints of Ruddle's Best Bitter. Peter Smallwood and I waited expectantly in the corner by the back door which was wide open, giving access to the small garden. The leaden sky and the heavy drizzle precluded any thoughts of stepping out there for some fresh air.

Tony put the three pint glasses down on the fretted, cast-iron table with its chipped black paint, and wiped his brow.

'Christ, it's hot in here! It's bad enough by the door where we are, but back at the bar it's like a sauna.'

I picked up my straight glass and savoured the moment; Pete always asked for a glass with dimples and a handle, he said it made the real ale taste 'better'. Pretentious bollocks, we told him frequently, but he just grinned and called us Philistines. As I sank the first pull I studied my friends over the glass rim. Peter

Smallwood was a short, cheerful, tubby, dark-haired chap. Always smartly dressed, usually in striped suit, club tie and fancy waistcoat as befitted the Harley Street consultant he claimed he would become, although at present he was working his way up the National Health Service's ladder as an Assistant Registrar at Queen Mary's Hospital.

Tony Scales, on the other hand, was the complete opposite. A six-foot five-inch flank forward for Harlequins, flowing blond hair, drooping Viking moustache and casual polo shirt with an England Saxons logo. He worked as a dental surgeon in a South London practice and specialised in reconstructing malformed jaws of young children: a remarkably delicate task for someone with such huge hands, each of which could easily hold a rugby ball. The third member of the little coterie that constituted my closest friends worked for a firm of estate agents and had not yet arrived. The object now was to sink the first pint quickly so that when Bob Barclay did turn up he could buy the next round. He had phoned me on my mobile to say he was showing a client round some expensive houses in the part of Chelsea quite close to the small square that hosted our local pub, and would be there any minute.

'Ho ho! I see you miserable buggers haven't set me up a pint then,' he boomed, eyeing the three glasses that miraculously emptied as the crowd parted to allow his burly figure to view our corner.

'Four pints, Jessie!' he called to the barmaid over the heads of the throng. 'And a glass with a handle for Doctor Smallwood here, it's his upbringing you know, his nanny always made him hold the handle on his Tommy Tippee mug, it stopped him playing with himself.'

'For heaven's sake' shut up' Barclay!' hissed Pete. 'You know what it's like. If people find out I'm a doctor they always start showing me their revolting rashes and scabs and asking for advice.'

'A waste of time in your case then,' grinned Barclay. 'If it's not piles or balls you're out of your depth!'

These then were my friends.

'I start my new job on Monday,' I announced. 'With a very reputable outfit called Consultant Design Services. Their offices are on the river just across Albert Bridge, not far from here. It'll be a step up in salary; I was very lucky to get the job and I'm really looking forward to it.'

Really! I wonder if they are?' mused Scales. 'Do they really know what they're letting themselves in for with you?'

I ignored him.

They raised their glasses. 'Here's to Marcus' success, may he design many bridges and pull many birds without over-taxing himself.'

'Talking of birds,' said Pete, 'how're you getting on with Miss Horse Power?'

I chewed a lip thoughtfully wondering whether to come clean. Polly Power was a farmer's daughter from Lincolnshire. We had met a couple of years ago at a friend's party and gone out, off and on, since then. Admittedly she was a big girl who could win a tractor-pulling contest with her teeth without breaking sweat, but she had a nice personality and was a very willing and enthusiastic roger: an attribute which weighed heavily in the plus side of the Moon scales. Pete had christened her Horse Power because she had rather a long face. The boys in the Frog teased her unmercifully. One lunch-time she had turned up wearing an unusual necklace and Pete asked her where it came from. She told him she'd got it a horse show and Pete said dryly, 'Was it the first prize?'

I decided to tell the truth, not necessarily a wise move in the Frog and Nightgown but I couldn't see that I was leaving an opening for penetrating wit in what I was about to say.

'She's been pressuring me to go up to Lincolnshire and meet her parents and you know what that means?'

'She's pregnant?' Scales responded in an instant.

'They want some cows artificially inseminated and you've got the right genes,' offered Bob Barclay.

I sighed wearily. 'No, have another go.'

Pete said, 'Oh, I see, you're coming under pressure to *do the decent thing*? Well I suppose it'll get us all one day, you just happen to be the weakest link in the chain. I'll put in the order for the toaster on Monday.' He shook his head. ' Sad, very sad!'

Scales added, 'Just imagine what the children will be like. Will they have Marcus's blue eyes or those big brown cow-like eyes of Polly that roll at every word he says? Will they be tall and thin with tousled brown hair like a tired-out domestic mop or have shoulders like Polly that could easily fit into the Harlequins front row?'

'Alright, alright, you've had your fun. No, it's all off. I've told her as kindly as I could that I don't want to make any commitment at my age and that we should stay as just friends but go our separate ways. Naturally she wasn't overjoyed at losing a man of my calibre and charm…' I glanced down modestly at my finger-nails '…but I think she accepted the situation quite well.'

I forced a grin. 'Anyway, the Hi-fi was only a cheap one and when I extracted it from the television screen I think it can be repaired. The flat door will be a little more difficult; the hinges are badly bent and will have to be replaced. At the moment it's held closed with a bit of string but as she's wrecked the only two things worth stealing, it doesn't really matter.'

'You're kidding?' exclaimed Bob. 'She didn't really take it that badly, did she?'

I nodded mournfully and put my empty glass down in front of the other three as an obvious hint.

'It's your round, Moon,' Tony Scales said unsympathetically, and called out, 'Four more pints please, Jessie – on Marcus's tab.'

On Monday morning the first of May, scrubbed up and I hoped presentable, I sat on the back seat of the bendy-bus, wondering what the future held.

The present situation didn't provide much inspiration, jammed as I was between a very overweight woman eating a Cornish pasty and carrying a large shopping bag which she was no doubt intending to fill with even more calories for her eager consumption, and a black guy who would have had no trouble in passing himself off as the Heavyweight Champion of the Universe. It was hot and humid on London Transport's early morning service from Battersea to the Kings Road, and the smell of damp clothing and last night's takeaways permeated the close atmosphere.

The bus eased to a standstill opposite Chelsea Old Town Hall and, brushing off some stray pasty crumbs, I made my way through the standing passengers and stepped out of the warm fug into light rain. With shoulders hunched and umbrella up I made my way down Oakley Street and across Albert Bridge to the offices of my new employer, Consultant Design Services. It was my first day and I wanted to make an impression. A dark blue suit, a shirt without the usual creased collar, a striped pink tie, new shoes and a new black leather briefcase (a present from my mother: just the gear for an aspiring city gent, she told me).

The rolled golf umbrella, now unrolled to keep off most of the rain, showed its broken rib so I re-rolled it, fastened the clip that kept it rolled and, taking a deep breath, pushed open the glass doors and strolled nonchalantly into the marble-floored reception area.

There were three other people there, two girls and a stocky man with a weathered face and twinkling dark brown eyes. That was all I had time to register before the wet rubber on my 'Clearance Sale' deal from 'R. Soles', the local shoe shop in Wandsworth, had a friction problem with the polished marble and sent me skating round the reception area like Torvill and Dean on speed.

Eventually I slid to a stop at the feet of a pretty girl who dissolved into a fit of giggles.

With pride and dignity at low ebb, I scrambled to my feet, collected my now bent umbrella and scuffed briefcase and, mustering some semblance of self-respect, addressed the man. But before I could speak he asked concernedly, 'Are you OK? That was a nasty fall you had there. I think your umbrella cushioned most of it when you landed on it but it hasn't done it much good, has it?' He smiled; a friendly but enquiring smile.

'It was a bit of a wreck anyway,' I replied with a shrug, trying to muster some semblance of dignity. 'I'm a new engineer here. This is my first day. Can you tell me to whom and where I should report please?'

He held out his hand. 'I'm Hugo Elmes, one of the partners. Welcome to CONDES, I hope the rest of your career with us will be less dramatic than your entrance – for the benefit of both of us!'

I shook the proffered hand and smiled sheepishly. 'Me, too!'

He turned to the pretty girl. 'This is Sue, she looks after the Reception. Mr Geoffrey usually likes to see new engineers, doesn't he, Sue? His office is on the second floor, turn left at the top of the stairs.'

Sue nodded agreement. Hugo Elmes continued. 'Geoffrey Arbuthnot is our senior partner, you probably saw him at your final interview.'

I recalled the event. There had been three interviewers, a ginger-haired Scotsman in a tweed suit, a man who sprayed spittle around as he spoke and a rather austere cove in a high collar, club tie and dark pin-stripe. He said very little but listened intently to the questions the others put to me, and to my answers. One of them, the splutterer, was called Jones and the Scotsman looked more like a 'wee Jimmy' than an Arbuthnot, so the haughty silent chap must have been the senior partner.

Thanking them, I gathered myself together, handed the now defunct brolly to Sue, saying 'Can you dispose of that please', and hit the stairs.

By now more people were arriving and heading upstairs as well. Most of them, particularly the young ones around my age, twenty-five, wore T- shirts, sweaters, jeans and trainers. Only the older guys wore sports-coats and ties. I stuck out like a sore thumb in my suit.

'You new here?' asked a cheerful chap going up the stairs with me. I nodded. 'To see Mr Geoffrey?' I nodded again. 'The last door on the right.' He pointed down a corridor. 'That's Joanna his secretary's office. You should see her first.'

'Thanks!'

I walked down the long corridor; this was obviously the lair of the big cheeses with private offices holding anything from one to four people. There was a buzz of industry about the place even though it was relatively early.

The secretary's office door was open and I could see an attractive woman aged about thirty with long shiny blond hair and a neat figure ferreting in a filing cabinet. I tapped on the door and she looked up. 'What can I do for you?' she enquired with a warm smile.

'I'm Marcus Moon, a new civil engineer. I believe Mr Arbuthnot wants to see me?'

'Ah yes,' she said in a crisp accent that could only have been honed in the classrooms and common rooms of Cheltenham Ladies' College. 'We were expecting you. You'll share an office with Desmond Doubleday, one of our Associates, and Ivan Masterland, but Mr Geoffrey wants to see you first. You can leave that with me,' she said, indicating my shiny but wet briefcase with its nasty scuff across leather, 'and go straight through.

'Marcus Moon's here, Mr Geoffrey,' she murmured as she gently ushered me through another door and I entered into the presence.

I was right; the haughty silent interviewer was indeed Mr Geoffrey Arbuthnot.

'Come right in, Mr Moon, and take a seat,' he said in a brisk, nicely modulated voice.

He indicated a visitors' chair in front of his desk and scanned me with shrewd brown eyes set in an austere face. I put him at about sixty to sixty-five; I guessed he couldn't be far from retirement and there was a faint pallor to his face which could be an indication of poor health.

'Welcome to Consultant Design Services.' He glanced at a file on his desk. 'It seems that your previous employer was very reluctant to part with you. He serves on the same Institution committees as me and spoke very highly of your abilities.'

As I was basking in a small glow of self-satisfaction, he added, 'However, he also said you were of an…eh…how shall I put it, individualistic turn of mind. In a nutshell, an oddball!'

'Well, I wouldn't go so far as to say that, sir,' I spluttered.

'No, I'm sure you wouldn't but he did. However, don't let that worry you, we like oddballs here: people who think outside the box. That's why we have the high reputation that we enjoy. But just remember it takes years to build up a good reputation and a few minutes to destroy it by carelessness in word or deed.'

I nodded, somewhat relieved.

'Joanna has told you that you'll be sharing an office with Desmond Doubleday. He's one of our most highly qualified engineers: vast experience.' *And the laziest person on the planet*, he could have added, as I found out later.

I took that as a signal to stand up but Mr Geoffrey had two more maxims to bestow upon me and waved me down.

'I only have two rules for engineers: if you make a mistake tell your managing partner immediately so that we can put it right; and I will not tolerate sex in the office.'

I blinked at this last comment. With whom, I thought? Was he was worried about me and Desmond Doubleday, or me and him? Was Desmond gay or did he think I was? It must be that bloody pink tie I was wearing. My sister had given it to me for Christmas as a joke but it was the only presentable tie I had in my limited wardrobe. The other Christmas tie, the one that sang 'Jingle Bells' when you pressed Rudolph's red nose, wasn't appropriate for the first day in a new job in May and, I guessed, would not have gone down too well at my initial introduction with Geoffrey Arbuthnot. My only other respectable tie had been chewed by the family dog when I fell asleep on the sofa after too much champagne on my sister's birthday.

'Shall I repeat that? You seemed to drift away there.' Mr Geoffrey's snapping voice hurriedly brought me back to the present.

'No, no, sir! I've got the message, no sex in the office,' I hastily replied, and was aware of a quizzical look following me to the door as I made my way out.

Not off to the best of starts then. Joanna gave me a sympathetic smile as she directed me to my new home saying, 'Ivan's out today but Desmond's in.'

I noticed that she was wearing a wedding ring. I smiled, it was far too early to be thinking about that - although what was it Barclay said? "Nobody misses a slice out of a cut cake!"

It turned out that Desmond Doubleday was anything but gay. He was a portly fifty-five-year-old with a jolly face, a nose that looked as though it had smelt the inside of many glasses of vintage port, thick swept-back grey hair and a manner that oozed charm and bonhomie.

He greeted me extravagantly with a firm hand-shake and a smile.

'Welcome, dear boy, to the sweat-shop of the company. I'm Desmond Doubleday, you can call me Des; everybody else does. Do you like coffee?' And when I nodded: 'So do I, the best coffee comes from the machine in the structural engineers' office. Mine's milk with two sugars.'

And with that he put his feet back up on his desk and returned to reading *The Times*. I glanced round the office and dumped my briefcase on what I assumed was to be my desk as it was the one with an air of vacancy about it. It had a swivel chair, a PC; a complicated-looking intercom/telephone system and more cup rings than the Olympic logo imprinted on its stained wood top. Then, with another glance at an unresponsive Des, I set sail to find the structural engineers' design office and their coffee machine.

The coffees cost me fifty pence each and I returned to the first floor trying not to burn my fingers on the plastic cups.

'You should have used two cups,' grumbled Desmond as he took a sip. My fifty pence remained unrefunded. I sat down at my desk and sipped the coffee.

'OK, Des, so fill me in on what goes on.'

'Well, dear boy, we are what is known as Civil Planning Team Two. We come under one of the partners, Hugo Elmes, a decent enough chap and very clever, but a little too enthusiastic for my taste. It's our job to come up with bright ideas for the more diffi-cult design problems, and also examine some of the designs that the boys downstairs produce to see if they're practical and eco-nomical to construct. You can produce the most brilliant design going but if it's so complicated and unusual that it will cost an arm and a leg and take years to build, then the client isn't going to be very happy, is he?'

'No, I suppose not.'

'You suppose correctly.'

I looked at his pristine desk and more carefully around the room. A third desk stood in the far corner, with papers, books, a PC and a large framed photograph that slanted away from me at an angle, bearing what looked like the head and shoulders of a chimpanzee. There didn't seem to be a buzz of industry whirling at high speed anywhere in this office at present. In fact there didn't seem to be anything moving at any speed. If this was the sweat shop of the firm, I would have sold all my shares in deodorant companies instantly – if I'd had any. There were a few drawings pinned to a large board, three bookcases – one empty, the others full of a whole variety of engineering books, books on contract law, design handbooks, safe load tables and Institution Journals. The one nearest Desmond contained, in addition, *The Good Food Guide, The Michelin Guide for Great Britain and Ireland, Egon Ronay's book of Hotels and Restaurants, Pubs of England and Wales, Relais & Chateau, Knots and Flies for the Trout Fisherman, MacDougals Book of Malt Whiskies* and other similar guides to what I assumed were gastronomic watering holes.

He noticed me looking at them and said, 'You can use whatever you like as long as you put them back. The empty bookcase is yours.' As I glanced towards the third desk he added, 'Ivan is out on site today. You'll have the pleasure of meeting him tomorrow morning.'

Did I detect a note of irony in that remark? It was hard to tell and Desmond kept a perfectly straight face.

'Come on,' he said, 'I'll take you round and introduce you to everybody you need to know, the rest you'll pick up in time. You won't remember three-quarters of them but the important thing is they'll know who you are.'

He finished his coffee and got to his feet.

'The important people first, we'll start with Angela. She's the secretary that the three of us share and you'll want to keep on the right side of her.'

He took me down the corridor to an office containing three girls at work-stations with humming word processors and printers.

'Ladies,' he announced. 'May I present the one and only Marcus Moon. As you can see, he's togged up for the occasion, has his own hair, a good set of teeth, clean habits and, as far as I can tell, is single.'

He raised a quizzical eyebrow at me. I didn't respond. I was looking at the girls, wondering which one was Angela. This was quite important because two of them were attractive but the third one was clearly the chimpanzee in the photograph on Ivan Masterland's desk. Did one put a photo of one's secretary on one's desk? I wasn't sure.

I offered my hand to the nearest, a cheerful-looking, smiley girl with long brown hair tied back in a pony-tail. She was wearing a sleeveless blue blouse and a tight blue skirt which finished just above the knee. She shook my hand and with a nice smile said, 'I'm Angela. Des has probably told you I look after your office.' She turned to the chimp. 'And this is Agatha, she's engaged to Ivan. She works for Civil Planning Team One.'

Full face Agatha didn't look too bad, it was the angle that was deceptive; but she had a heavy jaw, big round dark eyes and a low hairline. She was dressed in loose-fitting clothes to hide what looked like a surfeit of beef-burgers, so her effort was only partially successful.

'Jennie there works for the Quantity Surveyors for her sins.'

I shook hands with both of them. Agatha had a grip like a walnut cracker and didn't smile; the elfin-faced blonde Jennie shyly shook my hand but didn't speak.

Well, that was a bit of a relief; Angela was certainly the pick of the bunch. Neither Angela nor Jennie wore a ring on their left hand. Agatha had an engagement ring which might have had a diamond buried somewhere amongst the built-up, encrusting platinum clasp, but if so it was hiding its brilliance from the world. Ivan was obviously saving his money for other things.

Des said, 'Right, dear boy, come on and I'll introduce you to Hugo, our boss. He's the bridge wizard in the firm. What he doesn't know about bridge design you could write on Agatha's diamond!'

She shot him a look that would curdle milk. So he had noticed that as well and clearly there was no love lost between them.

We went up to the second floor, to a bright airy office that overlooked Battersea Park. The spare scholarly man who had witnessed my Torvill and Dean entrance was standing by the window.

Des introduced me. 'Hugo, this is Marcus Moon; he's joined us in Civil Planning Team Two.'

The dark brown eyes crinkled at the edges. 'Yes, we've already met.' And turning to me, he said with a smile, 'So you're finding your feet and keeping them now? Well, after Des has given you the tour and you've settled in, come and see me tomorrow, I've got just the job for you to get your teeth into.' He smiled again. 'Geoffrey has passed me all your details, welcome to the team and don't be afraid to put your ideas forward. You'll soon get the hang of things here but if you have any questions that Des can't answer, come and talk to me.'

The rest of the day was something of a blur. I met a lot of people and couldn't remember who did what but they seemed a friendly bunch; I read the firm's Conditions of Employment from cover to cover and discovered that I was entitled to twenty-eight days' holiday a year and that anybody caught *in flagrante* in the office could be instantly dismissed. Obviously this had some historical significance but it didn't seem right to question it on my first day.

The rain had stopped and the evening sun shone in the Western sky when five o'clock came, and there was a slow drift out of the office to cars, buses, trains. I decided to take a walk through Battersea Park before heading back to my flat in Prince of Wales Drive.

Relaxing in my one and only armchair with the sagging cushions and slack springs, chewing a take-away Four Seasons Pizza and drinking a can of Heineken, I reviewed my day. In fact it turned into a review of my career so far and an examination of motives and intentions to work out what it was I was trying to achieve and what I wanted from life hereafter.

Success. Yes, we all want to succeed but what would be the price? Because for sure there would be one. At present I was inexperienced and reasonably well qualified, but that was just a way of getting a foot on the ladder in consulting engineering.

'Boring, boring!' chanted my sister when my father asked me what I was doing and what my job entailed. He was the manager of a small bank in York and measured life in fractions of a per cent. He knew farmers and farming, crop yields and livestock prices but I had sensed a frisson of disappointment when I announced that I wanted to be a civil engineer and read engineering at university. My mother, on the other hand, just wanted me to 'do well' and make a good steady living. She knew about Isambard Kingdom Brunel and Sydney Harbour's Bridge and I think she imagined that I would be famous like Brunel and that Sydney Harbour was a man who had designed a bridge somewhere.

My first job after graduating was in West London as a design engineer with CERAF Construction Limited. I worked for them for four interesting, happy years, avoiding any serious managerial responsibilities and cruising along at a steady speed, absorbing experience where I could. It was a nice life, Saturday in the pub with friends, then football or cricket in the park; parties, girls, weekend trips out with the 'boys'; no responsibilities and no stress. I was having a good time; I didn't want that to change, the future could take care of itself.

That was the situation when I saw the advert from CONDES. Everybody in construction knew of them, they had a terrific reputation for innovation and design skill, so I sent in my CV more in hope than anticipation.

I got a first interview at which I learned that they had had over two hundred applicants and I was in the last thirty. The letter inviting me for a second interview filled me with excited anticipation; maybe I was in with a chance.

The second interview was much more intense and I ended up arguing with one of the partners about the way to demolish a post-tensioned concrete bridge without the whole thing exploding. Not the brightest move of your life, Moon, I thought, you've blown it completely; and I mentally kicked myself for not keeping my big mouth shut. So it was with huge surprise that I got the phone call asking me to go for a final interview. This was definitely a suit and tie job, so it was in the white shirt, the smart tie before the dog got at it and the best suit that I presented myself at CONDES on the prescribed date.

There were just two of us for the interview. The other chap seemed very self-assured, he told me he had a first from Cambridge, had done two years in Africa for some engineering charity and won the Hawkes medal for being the most promising young engineer when he became chartered.

Sod me, I thought, this doesn't sound like much fun for a game of soldiers. I don't stand a chance against this paragon.

He was called in first and after half an hour came out with a smug expression on his face.

'Mr Moon,' said a secretary, and I entered the room with a sense of doom hanging over my head. This didn't lift when I noticed that one of the panel of three was the same guy I'd argued with at the last interview.

They indicated that I should take a seat and the elderly aristocratic gent who was chairing the panel pointed to the arguer and said, 'Mr Jones, would you like to start.'

Jones, who spluttered a bit, looked straight at me and said, 'Just because you were right about demolishing post-tensioned bridges doesn't mean you'll always be right, you know.'

'I know,' I replied, 'but that was something about which I'd had experience, since I'd been involved in the demolition of two with my present firm, and designed their replacements.'

He grinned. 'At least you stuck to your guns, young man.'

Bloody hell! He'd just been provoking me to see if I'd back down when he knew and I knew that I was right. A tricky bunch here, I'd have to watch my step carefully with these three. The tweed-covered Scotsman opened up next to ask me what I knew about large dams.

'Apart from the fact that they hold back a lot of water, nothing,' I replied.

'Could you design an arch dam, for instance?'

The questioning continued. I think they were trying to see if I would claim to be able to do something that I couldn't, and my answers were of the kind that said I wouldn't turn down anything, but if I couldn't do it I'd find somebody who could rather than turn work away from the firm. After all, a dam or

45

a nuclear power station has many other elements included in it that we could do, they didn't just consist of a big concrete wall or a reactor.

At the end of a good hour and a half they turned to salary. What sort of salary was I looking for?

As much as possible in my impecunious state had been my immediate answer, *but what were they offering?* In fact I didn't mind as long as it was at least equal to my present salary. I didn't add that part, of course, and waited whilst they had a chuckle at my reply. The senior man glanced at the other two, who nodded, and then turned to me and offered me twice what I was currently getting. I gulped, coughed and gargled out something which they took for acceptance.

'When can you join us?' The Scotsman asked.

I told them I was obliged to give my current employer two calendar months' notice and I felt that I should stick to that as they had been very kind to me in the past.

'Well, young man,' said the aristocratic gent, 'the job is yours. We'll send you a letter of appointment within the next couple of days.'

Hands were shaken and smiles all round exchanged, then the secretary showed me out down to the Reception. The Cambridge guy wasn't to be seen but I couldn't wait to get out of sight of the office, jump in the air and shout 'Whoopee!' at the top of my voice. Made it! A job in a top firm at twice the money.

Could anything stop a new master of the universe?

CHAPTER THREE

The next morning the sun shone strongly out of a cloudless sky, promising the making of a hot spring day, and the birds chirped in the plane trees lining Oakley Street as they crapped cheerfully on the parked cars beneath. More casually dressed today and carrying my squash kit for a match that evening, I pushed open the glass door to the office a couple of minutes before nine o' clock.

'Morning, Marcus.' This was said with an open smile. So the receptionist remembered my name.

'Morning, Sue, a more controlled entrance, you'll note – I'm not trying to make an impression today.'

'You didn't make much of one on the marble floor yesterday,' she grinned as I hit the stairs.

So there we were, off to a good start.

It didn't last long!

Des hadn't arrived yet but sitting at the third desk was a spindly-armed, hairy, dark-visaged man with a face like a cheese-grater. He had narrow dark eyes, a little black moustache and a goatee beard. He glanced at his watch as I came in. My boding was fore; it was one of those feelings where instinctively you knew that the chemistry wasn't going to gel. I judged him to be about twenty-eight, three years older than me, and his dark eyes seemed to regard me, and I suspected the world, with permanent suspicion. Clearly a little ray of sunshine he was not.

Having dumped my squash kit on my desk, I turned to introduce myself and greet him but he beat me to the draw.

'You must be young Moon, the new guy from...' he drawled, scrabbling amongst the paper on his desk but failing to find whatever it was he was looking for '... somebody or other.', And he reluctantly took my offered hand.

'Marcus,' I replied, 'and you must be Ivan. Not Ivan the Terrible, I hope. Ha ha ha!'

Well, it was worth a try; a small ice-breaker to loosen up the situation, but my laugh was stillborn in the face of a glassy stare of response from the flat dark eyes set in a pale, hairy face like an anaemic sporran.

'I do hope we're not going to be subjected to your feeble witticisms too frequently,' he growled.

There was no point in being confrontational unless it couldn't be avoided and I had no intention of being provoked. Maybe he was just nervous or had had a bad morning. I'd have to get to know the man first and work him out before establishing any form of a relationship with him, friendly or hostile, so I gave him a grin as though I had taken his comment as ironical rather than rude and said in a friendly voice, to try to loosen up the situation, 'I met your beloved yesterday. She seemed a nice girl.'

Now you wouldn't think that a bland, conversational, olive-branch like that would provoke anything untoward, but Ivan's brows beetled like electrocuted caterpillars, his teeth gnashed or gritted. I watched these dental machinations with interest. Did anything else 'beetle' or 'gnash'? I wondered; I couldn't think of anything offhand. Was a 'gnash' a sort of more meaningful chomp? And what about gritted? Roads were gritted to stop cars skidding in frosty weather but what had that to do with teeth? Strange: but whichever one it was it resulted in the tight clench-ing of his jaws so that the words he uttered sounded as though he was talking through a ventriloquist's dummy.

'Are you listening to nee, Noon? You gust keep your hands och her,' he ground out. 'She's engaged to nee.'

I blinked. Christ, he must be having a very bad morning if that was his reaction. Assuring him that my intentions towards Agatha were entirely pure, I hastily added, 'If I ever was going to have any, that is, and ny hands would never be laid och her nee, or any other part of her anatomy, under any circumstances.'

I turned back to my desk, trying desperately not to crack out laughing. Was he being serious or was he just winding me up?

Fortunately Des Doubleday hove into sight at that moment with *The Times* tucked under his arm and grasped immediately that all was not sweetness and light between us.

'So you've met Ivan I see, dear boy. Don't worry, he's like that with everybody!'

Ivan switched his glowering from me to Des and snapped, 'Late again, Des, what excuse is it this time, "leaves on the line at Clapham" or "truck derailed at Vauxhall"?'

Doubleday just grinned. 'Sod off, Ivan, just worry about your blood test!' Then, turning to me, he said, 'By the way, I bumped into Hugo on the way in, he wants to see you this morning to talk about Kingscastle.'

With that he propped his feet on his desk, opened up *The Times* and began to tackle the crossword.

'What's Kingscastle?' I asked him, ignoring the exclamation from Ivan.

'It's the proposed new bypass round the town of Kingscastle, you must have read about it in the paper? It was headlines last year for producing the biggest traffic jam the world has ever seen.'

I recalled it vaguely, I could remember the jam, it took days to clear, but not the name of the place.

'Wasn't it somewhere down in the West Country?'

'You've got it, dear boy. Well CONDES are appointed by the Department of Transport as the consultants for the design of the road and all that goes with it. Your predecessor, before he went off to higher things running our Ajman office in the Gulf, spent some time looking into various routes and eventually came up with a solution that the Department liked because it's the shortest and, more importantly, the cheapest. Unfortunately it goes straight through the middle of a Site of Special Scientific Interest.'

He waited for my reaction and was disappointed when he didn't get one.

'So?' I said.

'So.' he replied with some exasperation, 'so this will bring out all the greens, tree-huggers, bunny-cuddlers, tunnel diggers, tree dwellers, Basil Brush fans and other Save the Universe nut-cases in profusion.'

'Well they'll have a good point, won't they? After all, the Sites of Special Scientific Interest were established to protect Britain's countryside and wildlife, weren't they?'

Des snorted irritably. 'This is nothing to do with wildlife, it's geological. The proposed line of the road takes it over the Shering Valley and across a high chalk ridge called Hickling Edge – and Hickling Edge is famous for the fossils that are found in the chalk.' He paused, with a sly glance at Ivan. 'Hugo will give you all the details. Ivan was expecting to continue with the job but he's got too much on his plate at the moment with his problems, haven't you, Ivan?'

Ivan flushed angrily and didn't reply.

As I strolled to Hugo Elmes' office I wondered about that. What sort of problems could Ivan be having? It must be work or health. Or could it be his love life? Had he managed to impregnate Agatha across a desk in the office and was worried that Geoffrey Arbuthnot might find out; or conversely was he back-pedalling on his engagement to Agatha? Why would that interfere with his work? But what else could have prevented him from continuing with this project? Well, it wasn't my problem; I switched back to thinking about the Kingscastle bypass.

Hugo's door was wide open. 'Come in, Marcus,' he called cheerily, 'finding your feet today?'

Well he was my boss so I gave an acknowledging laugh at his feeble witticism.

'You wanted to see me, Hugo?'

'Ah yes. What do you know about the Kingscastle bypass?'

It didn't sound like a trick question so I told him.

'Not much. Des has given me a brief run-down but said you would flesh it out much better.'

He beckoned me to stand with him at the conference table in his office where there were some large-scale drawings spread out. Spreading his hands over the drawings, he began.

'We are appointed by the Highways Agency on behalf of the Department of Transport and Communications as the consultants for a new road to bypass the old market town of Kingscastle – you remember the traffic jam last year?' It was a rhetorical question so I just nodded.

'Well, your predecessor in Civil Planning Team Two, David Nairn, had all the surveys done and prepared three alternative routes for this road. He had to take into consideration cost, obviously, but also prime agricultural land, the general topography – rivers, hills, valleys, environmental aspects, etcetera. The final route that David came up with is the cheapest and the one that least affects the productive land around Kingscastle. It's the one that the Department prefers. Its advantages, apart from the cost, are that a large stretch of it passes through one ownership, and it's basically park land. Its disadvantages are that it will need a long bridge over the Shering Valley and it also passes through a Site of Special Scientific Interest. That's it in a nutshell. I know you're not a roads man, Ivan is handling the road design, but I want you to take it to the next step, which is to sort out a design for the long Shering Valley Bridge. Ivan did the preliminary costings but I want these worked up in more detail – and see if you can come up with a solution that minimises the effect on the Site of Special Scientific Interest. The other bridges will be just standard prestressed concrete beam and slab construction. Ivan will take back the road design when he's resolved certain personal situations.'

He turned one of the drawings round and I could see the draft route for the road marked on it, together with the estimated land take required to construct it outlined in red. There was a gap of about half a mile where the red lines were dotted. Hugo put his finger on that stretch. 'That is Hickling Edge, and that's the SSSI.'

I could see the contours were very close together on the Shering Valley side, indicating a very steep slope, almost a cliff, and the land flattened out more gently on the opposite side.

'It's a chalk ridge caused by some sudden geological upthrust eons ago and is a major feature in the area. The chalk is very hard but contains a profusion of fossils from the Late Cretaceous period – hence its status as an SSSI.' He gave me a slight smile. 'The draft route has recently been published to enable organisations and individuals to prepare their initial comments; we haven't provided any detail yet but we're going to have to do that for the Public Enquiry.'

It was the smile that produced the whiff of rat. So far everything he had told me indicated that the whole project had flowed smoothly to the stage when it was being handed over to me. I didn't know much, or rather anything, about the history to date of the Kingscastle bypass or Sites of Special Scientific Interest, except to appreciate that if that is what they were then somebody was not going to be too happy about having a motorway blasted straight through one. The last thing a reassuring smile does in these circumstances is reassure. My incredulity antenna twitched violently.

'Is there a problem about that then?' I enquired tentatively.

'Not yet,' Hugo replied, which didn't allay my suspicions one little bit.

However, I was the new kid on the block so it didn't seem tactful to pursue the matter further at that time – just to be careful.

He began to roll up the drawings.

'We've done a basic soils analysis along the proposed route but you'll need more detailed information for the foundations for that bridge, so can you arrange with the owners and tenants of the land around to give permission for our site investigation contractor to drill sample boreholes on their land? The Department of Transport have a standard document for the landowners and tenants to sign granting permission for the boring machines to enter their property, it covers compensation for any damage or losses. You'll have to spend a couple of days in Kingscastle sorting it out so get Angela to see if she can arrange some digs for you, the budget won't run to hotel expenses just for a short time.'

His lips twitched again, and I interpreted *'the budget won't run to hotel expenses'* as *'we don't want you getting pissed in a hotel bar every night and charging it up to CONDES.'*

I remained seated; there was one thing that puzzled me.

'You refer to it as the draft route for the bypass – isn't the route fixed then?'

Hugo looked a little sheepish. 'Well the answer is yes and no! It's fixed as far as the Department is concerned, and the Local Planning Authority have given it the nod, but, as I've said, the whole route has to be the subject of a Public Enquiry which will then go to the Secretary of State for his final decision.' He held up a hand. 'I know what you're going to say but that's where politics comes in, and the Secretary of State will decide whether it's a vote winner or a vote loser – particularly if there's an election in the offing. It's called impartiality! We will have to demonstrate that the route is feasible, economic and sensitive to the environment to help strengthen the Department's case to convince their political masters. David Nairn did a report on the back history of the project; it's in the files somewhere.'

He paused and frowned thoughtfully. 'By the way, have you got transport? You're going to have to spend some time in King-scastle, and journeying back and forth from here by public transport is tortuous and time-consuming.'

'Er, not at the moment but I'm looking for something,' I improvised hastily, missing the full import of his first comment. He nodded.

Hastily changing the subject, I asked, 'Is there a castle at Kingscastle? Because if so I've never heard of it.'

Hugo smoothed his chin. 'Apparently there used to be one back in the Dark Ages. It was Alfred the Great's headquarters for a while until the Danes made a foray into Wessex and he abandoned it to move to Winchester, I think. It was more a fortified camp than a castle but the name stuck. No trace of it remains and its exact site is unknown.'

I shrugged disinterestedly, that was one less thing to worry about. I took the bundle of rolled up drawings under my arm and wandered back to my desk in Civil Planning Team Two, thinking, *Bloody hell, that was an expensive meeting; they might have doubled my salary but I'm going to have to buy a car now, which is going to stretch the overdraft somewhat.*

Kingscastle, its history and Alfred were the furthest things from my mind at that moment.

Well, I'd been thinking about a car for some time but there didn't seem to be any necessity before. I'd have a chat with the guys in the Frog and Nightgown; they seemed to have fingers in many pies, no doubt one of the pies being the second-hand car trade.

Des Doubleday had finished the crossword and was now thumbing through *Recommended Hotels in Great Britain*. Ivan was hunched over his desk glowering and, at my appearance, upped his glower by a couple of glooms.

'You've only got that job on a temporary basis,' he snapped. 'So don't bugger it up for me when I take it over.'

This didn't call for a reply so I ignored him and said to Des, 'Planning a holiday then, Des?'

He grinned amiably. 'No no, dear boy, far from it. One of my jobs, the steelworks reclamation site at Grimthorpe, requires my presence for a couple of days. CONDES is too stingy to pay for a decent hotel, namely one with a health spa, golf course and a bit of fishing, so I have to cover that myself.'

'Jesus, it's a tough life for some,' I murmured, and began to unroll the bypass drawings.

David Nairn had done a very good job of planning the route and I spent the next few days working through his reasoning. Approximately three-quarters of it ran through not very distinguished farm land and the remainder through park land. He had avoided where possible dividing up farms, and yet curved the road round the slopes and down the dips in such a way that it would blend into the rolling landscape of the area. Although there would almost certainly be some objections to the route, there was nothing particularly controversial about most of it that I could see at first glance.

The tricky bit was going to be the Shering Valley Bridge and dealing with the route through Hickling Edge. I studied the contours on the survey once again. The proposed road levels to produce an economic design for the Shering Valley Bridge would make crossing Hickling Edge difficult. I looked up Ivan's costing report. He had assumed that the road would traverse Hickling Edge through a deep cutting and estimated accordingly. I checked the levels again and paused thoughtfully. This would have to be an enormous cutting, a gigantic slash through the chalk which would stand out for miles as a hideous white scar on the landscape. That could be a huge problem at a Public Enquiry, and possibly have political implications as well. I wondered if Ivan had considered tunnelling through the Edge, and if so why he had rejected it.

'Des,' I asked, 'has the firm got a computer whizz or a special section that can handle requests for supplementary information taken from survey CDs?'

'Indeed we have, dear boy. One Dennis Menzies is hot stuff at that sort of thing. What exactly do you want?'

Pointing to the drawings on my desk, I told him. 'It's the Kingscastle bypass survey drawings: they're contoured but the information that the contours were plotted from must be on a CD somewhere. I want to see a longitudinal cross-section along the centreline of the proposed route.'

'Then Dennis the Menace is your man. He lurks in a temple of electronics closeted away in a corner of the ground floor.'

'Thanks.' I made a note of the reference numbers on the survey drawings and set off downstairs to find Dennis Menzies.

He was a cheerful, open-faced chap about my age, but the black, wire-framed granny glasses and long brown hair framing a pale face gave him the look of a boffin. I introduced myself and we shook hands. I explained what I wanted and asked him if he could do it. He grinned. 'Piece of cake,' he said. 'We have a programme that does exactly that, I can't do it today but I'll run it for you tomorrow afternoon.'

I was slightly puzzled by his reply. 'Hasn't anybody else asked for this information before now?' I asked.

He scratched his chin. 'Yes, I think we did a few alternative longitudinal sections for Dave Nairn before he left, but I don't think we did one for this route.'

Now I was really puzzled. How on earth had Ivan managed to do his costing without that information?

*****

At about the same time, down in the West Country Major Sir Fistulas Withers Bt; MBE [Military] of Wither's Hall, Kingscastle, marched out of his bathroom with his crop-cut bristly hair still damp from his shower and wrapped in a khaki dressing gown with major's crowns on each shoulder. His monthly appointment was today. With a surge of anticipation he surveyed the uniform that his man, Percival, had laid out on the large four-poster bed. He noted with satisfaction that it had been carefully sponged and pressed; that the badges gleamed with polish and the black shoes shone like glass. The hat with its badge and ribbon had been brushed so that not a fleck of dust showed. That was as it should be; he didn't tolerate any slackness in his form of dress.

It was a bit of a struggle pulling on the underwear. He must be putting on weight, he would have to have a word with cook about stodgy food again, and if she persisted in the high calorie diet she must be feeding him she would have to go.

He examined himself in the full-length mirror. Perfect!

The dark blue St Ursula's blazer was a little tight around the waist but the prefect's badge, house captain's badge and first eleven hockey badge shone on the lapels. The gym-slip hung in neat pleats exactly to his knees and the thick stockings showed no unsightly folds or creases. He put on the straw hat with the St Ursula's crest on the front to complete the picture. Then he took it off again and laid it to one side. It wouldn't do to be seen wearing that hat in his car. He eased a finger round his waistband; those blue serge knickers were tight, Percival would be visiting the school outfitters again for a larger size.

Percival was waiting at the door with the long blue raincoat and helped him put it on. He then opened the back door of the Jaguar with its tinted windows so that the Major could slide in.

Percival dropped him off round the corner from his destination and was told to be back in exactly one hour. 'And don't be late, damn you, or I'll have your guts for garters!'

He rang the bell and went straight into the house, hanging his raincoat on a peg in the hall. With mounting excitement he climbed the stairs and knocked on the door.

'Come!' barked a woman's deep voice. 'Ah, Withers, I was expecting you! So you've been a naughty girl again, have you? Well, don't just stand there, come in and close the door.'

'Yes, Miss Stern,' he replied timidly.

*****

The hot weather continued for the rest of the week and on Satur-

60

day morning I wandered down to the local Waitrose to do some shopping. My flat was a one-bed 'bijou' residence, according to the estate agent who sold it to me, on the second floor of Palmerston Mansions – one of a long row of Victorian apartment blocks that fronted Prince of Wales Drive, Battersea. My neighbour, who lived opposite, was a nice old stick – a Mrs Aberdeen – who had unfortunately damaged her hip in a fall a few weeks ago so I always called to see her each morning to make sure she was OK. On Saturdays she gave me a shopping list so I could combine her weekly food shopping with mine.

I dropped her goodies off, stroked the Reverend McCavity her cat (so called because he was black with a white ring of fur round his neck), dumped my carrier bags in my flat then hopped on a bus to Chelsea.

I strolled into the Frog, bought myself a pint of Ruddle's Best Bitter and found a table out in the courtyard. The wisteria was in full bloom, the scent was gorgeous, bees hummed amongst the lilac-coloured flowers and life felt good that lunchtime. I thought about cars. Now a decision had to be made about what sort of car I should get. A bright red two-seater convertible Ferrari or a low-slung Italian racing blue Maserati? Dream on, Moon! But definitely not a Volvo; Ivan had a Volvo, I'd seen him getting into it one evening but that was not for me. Something sporty but not flashy; discreet, but making a statement that here was a man of the world who didn't care about show. One thing it must be – and that was cheap! That meant it would have to be pretty old if I was to afford it.

The next person to arrive was Tony Scales and he appeared carrying two pints of Ruddle's, one for me and one for him. He sank half his pint in one pull and sat back with a big sigh.

'Christ, I've had a bad morning, Marcus. They brought in this young kid, a girl who'd had half her face chewed off by a bull mastiff. She'd spent months in hospital having reconstructive surgery and then the mother's boyfriend, pissed out of his brain, punched her in the face because she was crying and smashed her mouth in. I managed to put it back together but it took me four hours in the theatre, and then I had her shipped by ambulance to the Royal Dental Hospital. The poor kid had nowhere else to go, the cops had carted off the mother and boyfriend to jail so she couldn't go home. In any case, she needed keeping under observation for a few days. What'll happen to the poor little soul I don't know, probably get taken into care but she faces a grim future.' He turned to me and shook his head sadly. 'There are some right bastards around these days, Marcus, sometimes I envy chaps like you who just deal with mechanical and technical things, not people.'

'Cheer up,' I said supportively. 'Just think what she would have been like if you hadn't been there to help.'

'Yeah, I suppose so, but it makes you think.' He finished his pint just as more of our group arrived.

After they'd settled down with their drinks I asked, 'Has anybody got a good contact with a trustworthy second-hand car dealer?'

Bob Barclay guffawed loudly. 'I should think the answer's no. You've used one adjective there that I think ensures that'll be the reply.'

I acknowledged my mistake. 'OK, does anybody know of a decent garage that sells reasonably reliable second-hand cars?'

'What sort of car are you looking for, Marcus?' The questioner was Martin Holmes, a colleague of Bob's in 'City Houses'.

One had to be careful here, the slightest hint of something a bit flashy or pretentious would bring weeks of ridicule down on one's head. Choosing my words carefully and casually, I floated out, 'Oh, something cheap and old that I could do up. I've always fancied those nineteen fifties little MGs.'

I held my breath but I'd pitched it right and got interest rather than abuse.

'The Midgets? Those tiny two-seaters? How tall are you, over six feet? They'd be too small for you, your head would touch the roof, you'd be better off with something like the TF,' suggested Martin.

He was right; I wouldn't be able to squeeze my six foot two into one of those with any degree of comfort. So I pondered on the idea of the TF. The price could be the problem.

'If I could afford it,' I murmured. 'How much are they?'

Nobody knew, but Pete suddenly piped up, 'There was one advertised in last night's *Evening Standard*. I need a new set of brake linings for my car and was browsing through the ads to see if I could get a set on the cheap when it caught my eye. I think I've still got the paper in the car. Hang on and I'll go and get it.' And with that he shot out of the garden gate to return a few seconds later with the *Standard* clutched in his hand. We spread it out and sure enough in the 'Small Ads' there was an MG TF for sale, 1964, low mileage in British Racing Green at 'Country-wide Car Sales' in Streatham. No price was quoted, which was a problem.

'Get *Glass's Guide*, that'll give you the full range of prices for that sort of car depending on its general condition and mile-age,' suggested Martin.

I made a mental note to do just that, asked Pete if I could keep his paper and bought the next round of drinks.

'Do you need a car for your job now?' asked Tony.

I explained about the Kingscastle bypass and said I would be visiting Kingscastle fairly frequently.

'Well keep your eyes open and if you see any potential de-velopment sites, let me know,' interjected Bob. 'Martin and I are seriously thinking of branching out on our own. I've pinpointed a couple of possible developments but a nice little supermarket site in a country town would be right up our street – and give your firm a juicy design contract.'

I pricked up my ears at that; if I brought in some work to CONDES it could be a career enhancer.

We finished our drinks and went for a quick Thai meal be-fore the four of them went on to Richmond in Pete's car to play five-side football in the Leisure Centre, and I headed first for a bookshop to get the most recent *Glass's Guide* and then for 'Countrywide Car Sales' in Streatham.

The bus dropped me within two hundred yards of 'Country-wide Car Sales' and I wandered casually by the lot, feigning total indifference as I cast a critical eye over the used cars parked on the forecourt. Triangular, coloured plastic flags fluttered on strings stretched across the display and brightly painted banners proclaimed 'CAR OF THE MONTH', 'BARGAIN OF THE WEEK' and 'GREAT PRICE REDUCTIONS'. The used cars seemed quite decent, there didn't appear to be any old bangers amongst them, but there again there wouldn't be on the forecourt display from anyone who called himself a professional car sales-man.

A soft voice at my shoulder murmured, 'Can I be of assis-tance, sir?'

I turned round, startled. So much for my feigned indifference, it had been penetrated easily by some hawked-eyed salesman and I had been targeted as a possible 'mark'. It was somewhat disconcerting to find that the initiative had so easily been trans-ferred from me to him. This was not going to be quite as simple as I thought. I cursed under my breath again, realising that I had now just made mistake number two: I had hesitated, whereas I should have replied off-handedly, 'No, just browsing.' So he knew I was interested in something. Fortunately he didn't know what, so I had an advantage there. I breathed normally again.

'Would it be the 1964 MG TF that has brought sir to us?' the man murmured again.

I was thunderstruck; absolutely pole-axed. All my careful de-fences had been stripped away by this mind-reading magician, this psychic seller of motors. There was no point in putting up pretence any longer; it was going to have to be a face-to-face slugging match about the price if I liked the car, and I had a nasty feeling about who would win that as well. Now there could be no pretending that it was another car I was interested in, no casually remarking 'Oh I see you've got an old MG over there; just a passing interest but how much are you asking for it?' None of that kind of negotiating, I had been sussed out from the beginning right down to my socks. But I had to know, I had to find out how he did it.

'How on earth did you know I might be interested in the MG?' I said with astonishment.

He smiled. 'You've got *Glass's Guide* with yesterday's *Evening Standard* sticking out of your pocket, and the MG is the only car we've advertised in the *Standard.*'

I let out my breath. Thank God it was as simple as that, I wasn't dealing with some alien with powers beyond my conception after all. I felt a bit better.

'All right,' I acknowledged irritably, 'I am interested in it but only at a decent price. Can I see it?'

'Of course,' he replied. 'It's inside the showroom. Please follow me', and he set off towards a glass-fronted shed at the side of the lot.

I was still somewhat nonplussed because he wasn't at all what I expected a used car salesman to be like. He was small, smartly dressed in a blue suit and striped tie, he had a round smiley face, neat black hair cut short, and wasn't in the least pushy. He spoke quietly with only a trace of a South London accent. However, I remembered my father remarking one day, 'All good con-men wear ties' so I was on my guard.

The car was, as advertised, in British Racing Green with a canvas top, and looked in reasonably good condition. The body work had the odd scrape and small dent but the tyres had plenty of tread. There was no price sticker on the windscreen, which worried me. I'd checked in *Glass's Guide* to get some idea of its value but, as Martin Holmes had told me, it depended on the condition of the car and the mileage it had done.

'It's got a current MOT certificate valid to the end of the year,' he said, adding, 'It was owned by an elderly vicar's wife who only drove it to church on Sundays.'

'The church must have been a bloody long way from the vicarage,' I observed drily. 'It's got fifty thousand miles on the clock!'

He grinned again. 'Just joking, just joking; it was actually owned by a sports car enthusiast who traded it in, in part ex-change for a second-hand Jensen. It's in very good nick for its age. Have a look under the bonnet.'

'It said "low mileage" in the *Standard*.'

'For a car of this quality and age fifty-thousand *is* low mile-age, sir,' he replied without batting an eyelid.

I checked it over and it looked in good shape to me. The en-gine was immaculate, which presumably gave an indication of the care the previous owner had lavished on it, and the leather seats were showed no sign of cracking and were polished to a shine. The clutch, brake and accelerator pedals were worn but not badly.

With him beside me I took it for a short test drive and the engine purred beautifully. There were a few rattles in the body-work and the canvas hood was a bit draughty but the brakes were positive and the clutch smooth. Overall it would suit me perfectly – if I could afford it.

We arrived back at 'Countrywide Car Sales' and climbed out of the car. There was a pregnant pause as each of us waited for the other to make the first move. I lost.

'Suspension seems a bit soggy,' I ventured.

'Always was on this model. They tightened it up on the MGB.'

'It needs some attention to the bodywork.'

'Classic cars always do.' He tapped the bonnet with his hand. 'All original, you know. None of this is faked up with fibreglass and paint. This is just as it left the factory in Coventry. A little gem; you don't get many of these on the market these days in their original state.'

'Alright,' I said in desperation, realising that I was losing this battle to an expert.

'How much are you asking for it?'

'Six grand.' He paused. 'I think for you, a man who is obvi-ously a classic MG lover, a person who would give this motor the tender loving care it deserves, I could go down as low as that.'

I gulped; this was the top of the range figure in *Glass's Guide* and I was hoping for something around four to four and a half.

He saw my hesitation. 'I'll throw in a tank full of petrol,' he added.

'You'd have to throw in the whole of Shell Oil squire, I can't afford six thousand pounds! I'll give you four.'

He took my arm. 'Why don't we go into the office and discuss it over a cup of coffee.'

He switched on an electric kettle and made us a couple of cups of instant whilst I chose the less rickety of the two chairs available for visitors.

We haggled for a few minutes and I think he eventually realised that I wasn't joking when I said I couldn't afford more than four and a half, the frayed shirt collar and scuffed shoes proving a final clincher. We eventually settled on five.

'Done!' I said as we shook hands on the deal and I could have sworn I heard him mutter, 'You have been'; but his face maintained its cherubic look so I didn't like to say 'Pardon?'

We signed the documents and I wrote out the cheque. I expected to drive the car away there and then, but he was too canny for that. He'd had a few rubber cheques in his life and made the excuse that he wanted to give the car a final service and put in fresh oil and my free tank of petrol. It would be ready for collection next Wednesday – time for my cheque to clear, I realised.

So it was with a muted song in my heart and a saggy spring in my step that I caught the bus back to Battersea, now the proud owner of my own head-turning, bird-pulling, jazzy green sports car.

The boys were already well into their first pints when I slid the car onto a yellow line outside the Frog the following Saturday.

'So what's with you, Marcus, strolling in here looking as cheerful as a dog with two dicks?' boomed Bob Barclay.

'I want you to know that I've just made the transition from pedestrian to motorist by acquiring a car. Not just any car but a two-seater, soft top sports car. It's an MG TF in British Racing Green.'

'New?' somebody said.

'Don't be daft, on my pay! No, of course it's not new, it's 1964 but it's in good nick, I've driven it.'

'Parked outside is it?' said the same voice that I now recognised as belonging to a trainee merchant banker called Brian de Ennis Holgrave, who was a bit of a car nut.

I was beginning to wish I hadn't mentioned the car when Barclay added, 'Is that the one in *The Evening Standard* that Pete mentioned? It sounds a serious crumpet-puller. Can we assume that from now on you're going to be prowling the streets in this hot rod of yours, frightening the life out of the young virgins in the West End?'

I just laughed that off and said, on the strength of my newly elevated status, that I would buy the next round of drinks. The cries of double scotches and large gin and tonics were ignored.

'Five pints, Jessie, of the usual.'

Whilst I was sipping my pint I reflected on Bob Barclay's comment. I was twenty-five years old; I'd had a few girlfriends, a lot of fun – although I don't think their fathers would have seen it that way had they known how much – but nothing serious. After Polly Power there had been no particular individual girl, we tended to knock about in groups and it would be the same fifteen or twenty people, boys and girls, that went to the parties and discos, met in the Frog, visited each other's flats, played football in the park and got pissed together. There would be the odd coupling up but most people felt like me, that it was too early to make any sort of firm commitment. Life was for living, and trying to make your way in this world was hard enough without having to consider somebody else as well. There would be time enough for settling down in the future, so have as good a time as you could until then. At least that was what I told myself.

'You've suddenly gone all quiet,' Pete Smallwood observed. 'Is it the shock of having to pay for a round of drinks that's done it? If so we'll let you buy a few more for the peace it brings.'

I grinned. 'No, I was just reflecting on girlfriends. Do you realise that in our group there's only Fullerton who's got a steady girlfriend and that's Fleur.'

Pete raised an eyebrow. 'Buying this car of yours hasn't suddenly made you go all horny, has it? The throb of a mighty engine, the feel of supple leather on the seats, the fingers of the wind caressing your hair. I can see it now: Dick Dastardly roams the road in his leather helmet and goggles, the terror of Battersea maidens.'

I laughed it off – but it did make one think.

CHAPTER FOUR

On the following Monday, in the drawing room of Withers Hall, Major Sir Fistulas Withers Bt; MBE[Military] was not having a good morning. In fact he hadn't had such a bad morning since Tubby Braithwaite fed him a bad oyster at Bertie Steggles funeral.

Slamming a copy of the Department of Transport's glossy brochure outlining the new proposed route of the Kingscastle bypass on to the tooled leather top of his desk, he was choleric with rage. Stamping round the room, kicking the head on the tiger-skin rug savagely in the teeth and swearing at the frowning portraits of his ancestors suspended round the walls, he seethed.

Two items had arrived through the letter-box that morning. The first he opened was a reply to a shooting invitation he had issued.

It read:

Andrew Witham MP

The House of Commons
Westminster
London

Major Sir Fistulas Withers Bt.
Withers Hall
Kingscastle
Wilts

My Dear Fistulas,

There are two reasons why I haven't responded to your invitation to shoot at Withers Hall on the fourteenth with a corresponding invitation to shoot the grouse on Slatterthwaite Moor.

The first is that one low fast Slatterthwaite grouse is worth at least five of the fat old 'turkeys' that you trundle over the Withers' steppes, and the second is that Anthony Molestrangler has told me that your port isn't worth crossing the road for.

I trust you will understand.

Yours ever
Andrew.

The second was the Department of Transport's glossy brochure setting out the draft route for the Kingscastle bypass.

Benevolence and goodwill to all men were totally alien to the Withers' heart at that moment. His heart, normally of stone, was, after reading both of these documents, more akin to a volcanic bomb: hot, hard and steaming.

In truth, he was another who had never been a happy soul since the day he first saw light of day in the main bedroom of Withers Hall some sixty wet Februarys ago. The midwife, having forgotten her forceps, had to improvise rapidly with a pair of barbeque tongs when Lady Withers' nether regions refused to eject the nascent and as yet un-named off-spring further than his head. The improvised surgery with the barbecue tongs had left Withers with one ear higher than the other. Cook had sterilised the tongs by boiling them in a large copper bowl. Unfortunately they were only just out of the bowl and still hot when they were used to grasp Fistulas' head, causing him to take his first deep intake of breath and howl long before anybody could slap his bottom – a trauma which probably accounted for his unusual desires in later life.

His father had viewed the new infant with distaste; said he didn't like the look of him; said that he reminded him of a long pipe-like ulcer he had seen in the intestines of an afflicted cow the previous week; and forthwith named him Fistulas.

If prep school was agony, the minor public schools to which his parents sent him were infinitely worse. Although he grew his hair over his lopsided ears, the nickname 'Loppylugs' followed him throughout his school life.

Not being a particularly clever child and not very well physically co-ordinated, scholarship and games were beyond him. The only thing at which he was even reasonably competent was organisation. His desk was neat and tidy, his locker the same; his bed space immaculately set out with his bed made with hospital corners. He achieved some recognition for this and was made milk monitor in his classes and armoury organiser in the Combined Cadet Force – for which he was elevated to the rank of corporal.

His life changed. For the first time ever he had some authority, he could shout at and bully the more junior members of the Corps whilst toadying up to those above him. This he did with a savagery that reflected all the years of humiliation and scorn he had suffered up to that point. The two stripes on his sleeve showed to the world that he was a person with status and he revelled in it. And so the bully was formed.

A career in the army followed naturally. He scraped three 'C' grades for his A-levels and these, together with his Certificate 'A' in the CCF and the fortunate fact that his father Sir Wilberforce Withers broke his neck in a riding accident, thus passing the Baronetcy on to young Fistulas, were sufficient to get him into an Officer Training Unit. There was some discussion at his medical examination about whether he was fit for service in the forces because of his lopsided ears, but he pointed out that his eyesight was 20/20; he didn't need to wear spectacles and the remainder of his head was so shaped that a hat could sit squarely on it, so there shouldn't be a problem.

The army rapidly assessed young Withers' capabilities. He was the smartest cadet on the passing-out parade. His boots shone like glass, the toe caps gleaming from evenings of spit and polish, his brassware scintillated in the sun and his blancoed belt and gaiters were devoid of a single blemish. Notwithstanding that, he passed out bottom of the list of those who were commissioned and was posted as a Second Lieutenant in the Royal Pioneer Corps.

He was taught how to dig latrines, put up tents, lay dirt roads, set up cook-houses and the many other essential but dull tasks which fell to the lot of that worthy body in supporting the fighting units.

Always immaculately turned out and meticulous in insisting that those under him were the same whatever the tasks in hand, he was not a popular soldier. Lacking any warmth or charisma that would have given him some bond with his soldiers and fellow officers, he obtained no pleasure or satisfaction from his job whatsoever. He spent days drawing up programmes, schedules and plans for camp sites, road layouts and latrine locations, most of which were ignored by both those senior to him and those below him. A late addition to the Second World War, he could be said to have had a 'good war' insofar as he didn't get killed or wounded. He was commissioned in time to join the invasion of Italy and he and his platoon dug latrines all the way up the east coast of that country from Messina to Turin. He then formed part of the second wave of forces that crossed the English Channel to liberate France, and dug more latrines from Caen to the Rhine.

In all that time he was only shot at once – by a drunken Scottish Pioneer in a bar in Maastricht. The bullet just grazed his earlobe. If his ear had been in its rightful place ten millimetres lower, it would have taken half of it off.

In his thirty-five years' service, his modest organisational skills managed to get him promotion twice – initially to First Lieutenant and then to the rank of Captain. He was made a Major and given the MBE just before his retirement, more as a gesture of sympathy than recognition of his latrine digging or leadership qualities.

But in Kingscastle he was known as 'The Major', and he milked that rank and his title mercilessly. Even the retired Colonels in the British Legion and the local Brigadier who ran Kingscastle Cricket Club deferred to Major Sir Fistulas Withers up at the Hall. Life was easy. The tenants paid their rent or were turfed out on their ears; there was hunting and shooting in the cool seasons and Ascot, Wimbledon and Henley in the summer.

Then the hammer blow fell: the Kingscastle bypass proposals. There had been talk about such a road for years but nothing had ever come of it until the days of the big traffic jam.

He was all in favour of the first proposal which put the new road south of the town, as far away as possible from his estate. He got a bit twitchy when it was moved north and was pleased to see that it avoided his property. And now it had been changed again. The bad news had dropped through the letterbox that morning. The glossy brochure posted to every dwelling in the town must have cost an arm and a leg. Now it looked much more serious; money had been spent on surveys, traffic management reports, budgets and the other myriad things necessary to prepare for full approval and work to commence.

'And the swine want to put their damned road right through my north pastures and Peterson's Piece now!' he stormed at the world in general. 'Over my dead body they will! Any snivelling pen-pusher that sets foot on my land to build a road will get a charge of buckshot up his arse and damned quickly too! Blasted socialists; all commies, the lot of them; should be taken out and shot, and would be if I had my way!'

He picked up the brochure again and a heading caught his eye.

Public Enquiry.
A Public Enquiry will be held in Kingscastle Town Hall in October this year on a date to be arranged. All organisations and people who wish their views to be taken into consideration are requested to send a written statement in triplicate to the County Council Offices in Trowbridge. Statements using obscene language or politically incorrect verbiage would not be accepted.

There was a lot more guff about volumes of traffic in Kingscastle, air pollution, noise, deleterious effects on old buildings, pedestrian hazards, cancer rates and other bullshit designed to gull the gullible into thinking that the bypass would be a God-send.

'All bollocks!' he shouted. 'A load of rot!' and rang the bell for his man.

The butler/valet eased quietly into the room, fully aware that his master was operating on an extremely short fuse – a not uncommon thing for the Major – so, apart from awaiting instructions, he stood silently by the door.

'Whisky and soda, Percival, a large one and be sharp about it!'

'Very good, sir.'

The butler shimmered out of the room as silently as he'd entered.

After a stiff whisky and soda, Withers' fulminations died down to be replaced by some careful analysis. The Major was not an imbecile and, having exhausted his rage at the Government, the County Council, The Kingscastle Borough Council and the Parish Council, he realised that if he wanted to retain his estate in its present pristine condition, rage and bluster were not going to triumph over cold-hearted Whitehall bureaucracy. Careful planning and low cunning were called for. He scratched his chin and thought for a few minutes. This was a knotty, complex problem and his limited number of brain cells threw up one realistic conclusion. He couldn't do it on his own.

His first thought was that the local populace must be stirred into action – but how? A planned campaign was what was required and that had been the Major's speciality when his unit was sent to dig latrines in the Falklands. He had planned a string of latrines from Goose Green to Stanley and the fact that the Paras had ignored totally his carefully planned, slow build-up strategy of moving forward but keeping within running range of the advancing latrines, and gone ahead on their own initiative and recaptured the island in a tenth of the time he had laid down, was irrelevant. His plan was masterly and would have worked to perfection if they'd followed it. It would have been his military swansong.

He went to his desk and sat there behind the triangular oak name board which bore, in black lettering, the title Major Sir Fistulas Withers Bt., MBE[Military]. He took a pencil from the inkstand and a piece of paper from a drawer. He wrote in big letters at the top *STOP THE BYPASS*.

That being done, he sat back and contemplated his work so far. Very satisfactory, he decided, a very catchy title, something to build on.

It didn't occur to him for one moment that most people in Kingscastle might regard the building of the bypass as a blessing. He just assumed that if he didn't want it then neither would anybody else, and those that objected to his way of thinking would just have to learn to toe the line.

He began to make a list. His tenant farmers in the north pasture would naturally do as he told them, as would his gamekeepers in Peterson's Piece. His father, Sir Wilberforce Withers, had invested shrewdly at the beginning of the Second World War and acquired many properties at knockdown prices scattered round the town. The tenants of these would likewise do as they were told. This would provide him with little cells of protest that could be made to grow and spread by word of mouth like some laboratory culture. He would draft out wording for some carefully phrased pamphlets. Most people were just like sheep; if they saw a passing bandwagon with their neighbours aboard they wouldn't hesitate to jump on it, regardless of the argument. He vaguely recalled the protest group that formed to object to the southern route, what was it called – Preserve Our Heritage or something like that? A right bunch of namby-pambies they were – but they had got the route changed, damn them. That was the source of his current trouble. He hadn't appreciated the significance of their success until now. Well, they could be reactivated with him involved, not just involved but directing it now under the new banner of STOP THE BYPASS.

A long letter in the *Kingscastle Bugle*, the local paper, would be the way to kick-start this. Stir up a bit of controversy; get one of his ex-army chums to write a reply supporting him, stirring up matters further. It would be easy to galvanise the citizens of Kingscastle to rejoin the protest group. They were British, for heaven's sake, and any hint of an imposed threat to their *status quo* would automatically get right up their noses – if it could be presented in that way. It wouldn't exactly bring them out manning the barricades with pitchforks and scythes, they weren't like those snail-eating, garlic-munchers across the Channel, who seemed to be able to stop everybody crossing their territory except the Krauts; but deep resentment at the idea of being ridden over roughshod by somebody – anybody, for that matter – would burn in their British bosoms, and this could be harnessed for his purpose.

He made a note to get the editor of the *Bugle* round for dinner one evening together with the local MP. What was the darn feller's name? He tapped his teeth with his pencil, trying to recall the MP. Poncey type, keeps his handkerchief up his sleeve; wears scent and purple shirts with button-down collars… He caught sight of the letter from Andrew Witham and that jogged his memory. Molestrangler, that was it: the swine who had spread rumours about the quality of his port. He jotted that down as well. He thought again. Then there was that blessed woman Lady Mountdurand. Although Withers couldn't stand her, the jumped-up aggressive harridan, he recognized her ability to make trouble and he reluctantly acknowledged that she did carry some clout amongst some sections of the community, so she would have to be included.

The second line of attack would be the written objection for the County Council. That would have to be carefully phrased and he would need some expert advice on how to approach those paper-pushing wallahs in Trowbridge. Finally he would organise a public meeting in Kingscastle Town Hall to assess the strength of opposition he could muster, and galvanise the local populace into action.

*****

A monument to Victorian propriety, the brick and stone Kingscastle Town Hall, with its pseudo Doric portico, lichen-stained stonework, echoing tiled-floor corridors smelling of polish and Jeyes Fluid and its gloomy lofty ceilings, had housed many different functions in its life. However, stimulated by the Major's letter and pamphlets and articles in *The Kingscastle Bugle*, this was the first time that the feathers of the yeomen and burgesses of Kingscastle had been ruffled sufficiently to consider a major civic protest since 1692, when Old Mother Haggerty was charged with witchcraft. The authorities had strapped her in the public ducking stool, immersed her in the town pond and, when she drowned, said that it proved she was innocent. The local populace said they'd got it wrong; she was definitely a witch because Mary Walturtle's baby had been born with an eight-inch penis and now the whole town would be cursed for ever unless some serious rectification was offered.

After some debate they decided to cut off the Squire's genitals and boil them in oil as a placatory offering, and all, except the Squire, felt much better for it.

Withers' meeting was held in the Council Chamber in the middle of June, and by two o'clock, the start time, all the seats including the gallery were filled. Latecomers had to stand round the walls. The dais had been moved back and replaced with a baize-covered table bearing five names under a crudely painted banner proclaiming 'STOP THE BYPASS' in pillar-box red. The four names stencilled on stiff card read 'Anthony Molestrangler MP'; 'His Worship The Mayor Councillor Cobbledick'; 'The Reverend Percy Furrow' and 'Lady Hortense Mountdurand'. The fifth name in the centre of the table, that of Major Sir Fistulas Withers Bt. MBE[Military], was painted in black on a triangular oak block.

So, under the chairmanship of the Major, the meeting was called to order with a few bangs on the gavel borrowed that morning from Heckinbottoms the Auctioneers. The pulchritudinous Mrs Evadne Stoate sat at a side table, ball-point poised and note-pad open ready to take the minutes.

The Major rose to his feet, shuffled the notes clutched in his hand and noisily cleared his throat. A voice called out 'Get on with it. We haven't got all day!'

Withers scowled angrily but stuck to his script. 'Mr Mayor, Lady Mountdurand, Mr Molestrangler—'

The voice called out again, 'Yes, we know who you lot are; it's on those bloody great name cards in front of you! Get to the point!'

'The point…' said Withers angrily, abandoning his prepared speech for the moment, '…the point is to stop this outrageous bypass which the Government is trying to force on us, riding over the wishes of the people of this town.'

'Why?' called another voice.

'Why what?' snapped Withers.

'Why should we stop the bypass? We've been asking for one for years now to free up the town centre from being permanently snarled up with traffic.' The speaker was a spikey-haired, burly young man in a bomber jacket and jeans. Withers didn't recognise him and, irritated at having his carefully crafted opening speech interrupted, he replied testily, 'I'm coming to that if you'd give me chance.'

'Well get on with it then!' shouted the first voice.

The Mayor, used to controlling unruly Councillors in meetings, decided that he should step in. He rose to his feet and held up his hands.

'Ladies and gentlemen, order please! You'll all get the chance to put your point of view so let Sir Fistulas make his statement and then we can get down to the real business.'

He gestured to Withers to carry on.

Withers, flushed at being patronised and relegated to the overture, gave the Mayor a savage glare. Molestrangler suppressed a grin whilst Lady Mountdurand tried unsuccessfully to identify the sources of the heckling. Withers turned again to the audience, who were still restless.

'This bypass has been foisted on us by this arrogant Government without any consultation with the honest townsfolk of Kingscastle. We have had no opportunity to advise on the route it will take, the disturbance its construction will cause us, or the effect it will have on the glorious landscapes for which our lovely town is justly famous.'

He was careful not to mention that the leafy acres surrounding Withers Hall, his ancestral home, lay squarely in the proposed path of the three-lane dual carriageway – a fact of which the rest of the attendees at the meeting were not generally aware: to them it was just nice tree-dotted landscape.

The last point was a good one, however. Kingscastle was well known for its beautiful countryside and the locals were very conscious of this. Withers had attracted their attention and the meeting quietened down. He was shrewd enough to sense that he was on to something and continued to elaborate on that aspect and ram home the message that an unfeeling, insensitive Government didn't care one jot for the feelings of the hardworking, honest folk of Kingscastle. They could either like it or lump it.

'Construction traffic will roar through the town centre, shaking our ancient buildings to the core, causing irreparable damage with no compensation to the unfortunate owners. You will have to foot the repair bills yourselves. The town centre will become a virtual no-go area for us. For the old and infirm who want to buy their weekly supply of the basic necessities of life; for young mothers who need clothes for their children; for hardworking housewives seeking food for their families. At night gangs of drunken navies will roam the streets so that we will be afraid to venture out after dark.'

He sensed a degree of scepticism creeping over his audience due to these gross exaggerations, so he quickly switched back to the environment.

'But that will only last a few years. Oh yes, we could perhaps accept that on a temporary basis, unpleasant although it will be. But our countryside, our beautiful countryside, the heart and lungs of our community will be despoiled for ever. The fresh air, which is our God-given right to breathe daily, will be polluted by the dust and dirt stirred up by their machines. The cancerous fumes belching out of their bulldozers could harm the future generation of citizens of our town. A scar of horrendous proportions will disfigure the woods and hills and particularly our famous feature, the picnicking spot that we love, Hickling Edge, which lies right at the centre of this outrageous proposal formulated by a bunch of uncaring Whitehall bureaucrats.'

The fact that Withers had never been on a picnic in his life and that Hickling Edge was in the centre of his estate never occurred to the audience. They were relating what he had said to their own memories of sunny days humping baskets to the top of the Edge, stretching out on rugs, eating jam sandwiches and hard boiled eggs and fending off the wasps and flies. Anger that this could be taken away from them by an unfeeling Government began to stir.

'What can we do about it?' called a woman from the back of the chamber.

'Bugger all!' shouted an anonymous voice that came from what was now apparently a group of young people, including bomber jacket.

Withers seized on the opportunity. 'That's where you're wrong. There's a lot we can do about it if we all act together. The voice of the people will be heard!'

'All we've heard so far is your voice and bloody boring that is,' called out another voice from the group. 'What do other people think?'

The Mayor interjected again, attracting another icy glare from Withers, who reluctantly resumed his seat. 'Can we have some questions from the floor please? Raise your hand if you wish to make a contribution.'

Withers grudgingly handed over the taking of questions to the Mayor and Molestrangler, both of whom were very fond of their own voices, and let the discussion flow around him. What Withers didn't appreciate was that he had plucked a very strong and deep-seated chord amongst the bulk of the audience, and all the heckling had done was to swing the audience's sympathy towards him. They didn't analyse his flaky arguments but looked inwards to the pent-up resentment at being ridden over rough-shod and unconsulted by faceless bureaucrats that his arguments had engendered.

The comments from the floor were thus mainly supportive of positive action. The few dissenting voices, who pointed out that the town had been petitioning for a bypass for years and had made the *Guinness Book of World Records* for the worst traffic jam in history, were shouted down.

Eventually the question of organisation came up and Withers realised that everybody was now looking at the platform and the platform were looking at him. Decisions were not his strong point and he was acutely aware of the fate of the last Squire who had made the public decision to duck Old Mother Haggerty; so he did what he usually did when something tricky had to be decided – he decided to propose that several committees would be formed to coordinate the various different aspects of the protest.

The Mayor started to climb to his feet but Withers beat him to it by the simple expedient of using the Mayor's shoulder to lever himself upright, thus forcing the Mayor back down into his chair.

'To sum up, this meeting has been called to decide what positive steps we, as townsfolk, can take to stop the construction of this eyesore which will despoil our landscape.'

Withers rambled on for a few minutes, ramming home the message about noise and dust pollution; construction traffic 'thundering past our ancient buildings'; more crime in the area; 'the vivid scar' which would be 'slashed across our lush acres'; and everything else he could think of that would firmly establish concern in the normally passive bosoms of the townspeople.

When he finally paused to glance at his notes, a distinguished middle-aged woman, smartly dressed and with a neat hairdo, stood up and said in a quiet voice, 'Aren't we getting way off the point, Chairman?'

Withers tried to cut her off but was stopped by the Mayor, who sensed that what she was going to say was important. She continued.

'We have been campaigning to have a bypass for ten years now and at long last the Government has agreed to provide one. Now you are proposing to campaign to reject it? I agree that to cut through Hickling Edge would be an environmental disaster, so shouldn't we be campaigning to have the road moved so that it doesn't?'

Other voices joined in to support her with calls of 'Stupid sod, Withers' and, from bomber jacket, 'That's what I was say-ing earlier, Loppylugs', until the Mayor hammered with the gav-el to quell the noise, leaving a scarlet-faced Withers wondering how his nickname had become known.

'Let's have a show of hands then. All those who want the bypass but want it moved raise your hands.' A forest of arms rose up.

'All those who want to stop any bypass?'

No more than half a dozen hands rose.

The Mayor turned to Withers and said loudly, 'It appears that the general feeling is to campaign to get the bypass moved. I think that we should change our slogan to MOVE THE BY-PASS, don't you?'

Withers was now caught between agreeing to a sensible proposal – which, as far as he was concerned, was fine because it would save his estate – and looking a first-class lemon for not thinking this through in the first place. He sat there silently with his metaphorical thumb up his bottom and his mind in neutral, so the Mayor continued diplomatically.

'I therefore suggest...' he wasn't going to *decide* either '... that we form certain committees, each of which will have a specific task that, when all are put together, will form the thrust of our protest.'

He then outlined what they would be. The 'Traffic Committee' would collect information on dust, noise, contractor's traffic, night working and increased crime. Father Macnamara, priest of St Cridoc's Catholic Church, volunteered to organise that. He thought it was appropriate as Saint Cridoc was a Dorset man who, in the sixth century, had indirectly become involved in transport when he splinted up an angel's wing after the unfortunate aerialist had had a mid-air collision with a low-flying griffin, crash-landing spectacularly in Cridoc's runner-bean patch. Cridoc had cleared an area for a runway so the angel could make a running take-off with his splinted wing. It was almost certainly the first 'Short Landing and Take-Off' in history and for this service he had been made a saint.

The 'Wildlife Committee' was to be chaired by Mr Robin Threadle, the Royal Society for the Protection of Birds representative. The 'Marching Committee' had Harry Bell, the local Scoutmaster, as Chairman – a short, stocky, energetic man with calf muscles like piano legs and very tight shorts the contents of which were a constant source of interest and speculation by Brown Owl and the Girl Guide troop.

Finally the 'Publicity Committee' would have Mrs Gloria Withington-Lombard as its Chairperson. She was also Chairperson of the Kingscastle branch of the Women's Institute and a formidable *Grande Dame*. They would organise the design and printing of leaflets, petitions, posters, banners, placards, T-shirts and other publicity vehicles for the protest marches that the Marching Committee were going to organise.

Overall MOVE THE BYPASS would be controlled by the 'Finance and General Purposes Committee', the chairmanship of which was not immediately settled. The Mayor, sensing a potential hot potato, ruled himself out, leaving it to a clash of heavyweights between Major Sir Fistulas Withers, who saw his authority gradually slipping away, Anthony Molestrangler the local MP, and Lady Hortense Mountdurand, the widow of Sir George Mountdurand, a local benefactor whose bronze statue graced the public lavatories in the High Street. Sir George had snuffed it years ago in a hunting accident. A hunt saboteur's pedal-cycle ran over his gouty foot and the resultant apoplectic fit resulted in a massive heart attack which did for him on the spot.

Molestrangler fell at the first fence when Hortense Mountdurand pointed out that he would be far more effective working inside Parliament than spending weeks down in Kingscastle chairing a committee and neglecting his official duties to the electorate. The field was thus left clear for the battle of the giants between Sir Fistulas Withers, whose estate would suffer most if the by-pass went ahead as currently proposed; and Lady Hortense Mountdurand, who regarded herself as Queen Bee of Kingscastle. The latter, adopting a little psychological warfare, took a razor-sharp pruning knife from her voluminous handbag and kept rubbing her thumb along the cutting edge of the wickedly hooked blade, doing twisting, cutting motions in the air, and then flicking her cigarette lighter on and off as the discussion grew more heated. Eventually Withers managed to shut the vision of Old Mother Haggerty and the Squire's fate from his thoughts and carried the day by pointing out that the protest group was his idea and all the best contacts were his – but with an ominous warning ringing in his hairy ears from his Vice-Chairwoman that he'd 'better not make a bugger of it, or…' The pruning knife was brandished again to emphasise the point.

The meeting then broke up into groups as the various committees recruited members and arranged to assemble throughout the following week.

CHAPTER FIVE

I was reading through Ivan's cost studies when Angela stuck her head round the door and said, 'I still haven't got that other file back from Ivan yet, he must have put it in his desk.'

'What other file?'

She came into the office looking puzzled. 'You remember when you asked me to collect all the files on the Kingscastle project, I told you that one was missing? I said Ivan had kept it? Well he still hasn't returned it.'

I frowned. I remembered the occasion vaguely, but I probably wasn't paying much attention to what she was saying that day because she had been wearing a rather low-cut blouse – which I remembered vividly, or rather its contents.

'Oh…ah!' I stammered. 'He's out at the moment but I'll ask him for it when he gets back.'

When Ivan came in after lunch I tackled him about it. He reacted irritably but a wary look came into his eye, which I just put down to his normal truculence.

'What for? Why are you making such a big issue about it? It's not important, just some scribblings of Nairn's.'

'Well I'd like to read it so can I have it please?'

'Look, Moon, the Kingscastle bypass is my project, you're only involved as a temporary assistant because I'm tied up with something else at present, so don't forget it. Anyway, I'm going to see Hugo to get this cleared up. You're not competent as a roads engineer, I am, and the sooner you get that into your skull the better.'

'Hang on, Ivan,' I protested, 'I've never claimed to be a roads man. Hugo had made it perfectly clear to me that the road is yours and I'm responsible for all the bridges. I've been asked for ideas but that's what Civil Planning Team Two is for, is it not? Now can I please have David Nairn's report?'

For one moment I thought he was going to refuse but then he took out his key ring, which was attached to a chain on his belt, and unlocked a drawer in his desk.

Christ, he had it locked away! As he was away for the next two weeks he obviously didn't want me to read it. It seemed very weird. He'd been picking at me ever since I'd arrived and for the life of me I couldn't understand why. He was surly to Des but with me it was something deeper. He couldn't possibly think I was lusting after Awful Agatha, could he? I decided to have a quiet chat with Des when Ivan was out of the way.

The file he handed over was a thin file, no more than a few pages and, from the reference number on the cover, written by David Nairn and typed by Angela. This must be the history that Hugo had casually referred to.

I took it from Ivan with a curt 'Thank you', adding, 'Is there anything else in your drawer that I should know about?'

He glared at me furiously. 'You just keep out of my desk, Moon, it's private property and I'll sue you for trespass if you so much as lay a finger on it.'

'What the hell are you on about, Ivan? I've no intention of going through your desk, I just want all the relevant information on the Kingscastle bypass. So is there any more or isn't there?'

'No there isn't,' he said unconvincingly, avoiding my eyes. 'What there is is in that file.'

'Thank you! That's all I wanted to know.' And I took the file and returned to my corner to read it through. Ivan wasn't at his desk next morning, Des had mentioned that he was taking a few days off 'trying to sort out his problem.'

The file started off with some photocopies of newspaper cuttings about the great traffic jam. I could see why the locals wanted a bypass but it had taken that disastrous episode to galvanise the Government into action. The good folk of Kingscastle had petitioned for years for a new road and had celebrated when they were finally told that they were going to get one. They were all for it.

The next phase of its progress came in the selection of a suitable route. David Nairn had worked out a route passing to the south of the town that didn't take up much good agricultural land. However, it would cross the water meadows of the River Shering, a habitat for water-birds where the very rare pied-billed grebe had been seen twice in the past ten years. Not only did this arouse the ire of The Royal Society for the Protection of Birds, but it would allegedly spoil the famous view of the old Town Church of St Peter Within–the-Walls with its lopsided spire – a view once painted by John Constable. Dave had added in brackets *'Not very well as he was only eight years old at the time.'* This aroused the wrath of the locals who thought it would damage their tourist trade. A 'Save Our Heritage' protest group had been formed and put considerable pressure on the local politicians and their MP and, as a result, we had been asked by Kingscastle Borough Council if we could come up with other ideas because the locals were now against the bypass.

So David found what he considered a less controversial route to the north of the town and this received popular acclaim. However, in order not to be controversial it was necessary to locate it a long way round to avoid the beautiful Shering Valley and Hickling Edge. The locals were now all for it again.

But when this was put to the Highways Agency of the Department of Transport and Communications, they were not. They said it would be unnecessarily expensive and they weren't prepared to waste tax-payers' money just to make a few yokels happy. They didn't exactly put it in those words but that was the strong message.

So David revised and shortened the route, which brought the road much closer to Kingscastle, and this in turn presented the problems of crossing the Shering Valley and driving through Hickling Edge with a deep cutting. That was the current draft scheme in the hands of the Department, which had been made public for comment but giving no details.

So far, apart from a few fulminating letters in the local press speculating on what might be proposed, nothing had resulted from this but I now knew why Hugo's smile had been slight and his comment when I asked if there were any problems: 'Not yet.' Thanks, Hugo!

This took me back to thinking about Ivan. Why didn't he want me to see this file? I couldn't see that it put him in a bad light anywhere. All it did was forewarn me that it was a sensitive issue and would have to be handled delicately. Was that it? Did he want me to go in like a bull in a china shop and make a fool of myself? He wasn't senior to me, although he thought and acted as though he was; we were equal Senior Design Engineers but if he wanted to lord it that was up to him. This was about the fourth or fifth time he had tried to stitch me up with the firm in some way or other. Well I didn't like that sort of atmosphere in the office but there didn't appear to be much I could do about it at the moment, although he was starting to get up my nose.

Putting that on one side for the present, I returned to the engineering aspects of the road. I was not too unhappy about crossing the Shering Valley – a well designed bridge could add to the landscape – but Hickling Edge was a problem. From the contours and the level of the road it would have to be a very deep cutting which would leave an enormous and highly visible scar. Being raw chalk and fairly steep-sided, nothing would grow on it to disguise it for years.

The more I studied the proposed route, the more obvious the solution to Hickling Edge appeared to be to drive a tunnel through the Edge rather than excavate the deep cutting in it.

There would be an immediate transition from the Shering Valley Bridge straight into the tunnel. The impact on the environment would be minimal. It would be the cost that could be the problem, although I couldn't find any reference to tunnels or cost comparisons in Ivan's report.

I couldn't discuss it with him now because he was away, as Des had mysteriously put it, 'trying to sort his problem out'. He wouldn't be drawn into expanding on this, which only served to increase my curiosity. Hugo had said something similar.

However, I needed some expert advice if such a major change was to be considered so I went to see Hugo.

'Look, Hugo, I appreciate that the road is Ivan's responsibility but you've asked for ideas about Hickling Edge and, as Ivan's away, I haven't been able to discuss it with him; but I think there's something we should examine.'

After explaining about the tunnel, I asked him if we had a tunnelling expert in the firm but he shook his head.

'No, but if you give me a day or two I'll look into it. I think Geoffrey Arbuthnot might have a contact that could help. I agree it's well worth checking out.' He paused and then asked, 'What are you going to do about the site investigation?'

I told him I was intending to go down to Kingscastle first thing next week.

'Geophysical Drilling have already done some preliminary work, David Nairn lined them up. I was going to tell them what we needed for the Shering Valley Bridge. I suppose, if tunnelling is a possibility, they'd better take some deep bores along the line of that as well. When Ivan's back he can go later to sort out the site investigation for the rest of the road.'

Hugo raised a warning finger and with a grin reminded me, 'I told you that Geoffrey doesn't like to waste company money on expensive hotels so before you go to Kingscastle, don't forget to ask Angela to find you a bed and breakfast for a couple of nights.'

'OK, I'll ask her straight away.'

When I got back to the office Des was thumbing through the pages of that week's *New Civil Engineer.*

'Keeping up to date, dear boy. Finding out who's doing what, for whom and why.'

That reminded me of something. 'Des, why do you think Ivan was so touchy about his desk?'

'Don't know. Perhaps that's just Ivan; he's such a grumpy sod about most things.'

'Hmm… I suppose so.' But I wasn't convinced.

I worked late that evening and just before I left the office, I wandered across to Ivan's desk and tried the drawers. There was nothing of interest in the ones that were open, but the top right-hand drawer, the one from which he had taken the file that David Nairn had prepared, was still locked.

I recalled the shifty look on Ivan's face when he denied having any other information, so I pulled the drawer immediately underneath the locked one right out of the desk. Feeling underneath the locked drawer, I discovered that the bottom of the drawer was constructed with two sheets of plywood side by side with a small gap between. By pushing up one of the sheets I found I could slide it over the other one and leave a gap in the bottom of the drawer. With two fingers I manoeuvred something that felt like a booklet out through the gap and it fell into the bottom drawer. Feeling around further, I discovered there were three or four similar booklets but nothing else.

I picked up the one I had extracted and grinned with surprise. The cover showed a guy in a leather mask tied to some kind of wheel. *Bondage for Boys* was its title and, flicking through the well-thumbed pages, I saw it was full of kinky sex photos. So that was what Ivan was hiding – porn mags. Well, well! I wondered if Awful Agatha was in on it as well.

I pushed the magazine back, eased the plywood back into position, replaced the second drawer and went home to Palmerston Mansions to face yesterday's cold, left-over spaghetti Bolognaise with an extra insight into Ivan's character.

A couple of days later Joanna, Arbuthnot's secretary, phoned me to tell me Mr Geoffrey wanted to see me at eleven-thirty and to bring all the information I had on Hickling Edge up with me. There wasn't very much: the proposed line of the road and a longitudinal cross-section, some geological information and a couple of preliminary test bore results. I took them up as requested and was shown through into Arbuthnot's office. A small elderly man with a heavily tanned face and twinkling eyes was there with him, sitting in one of the visitors' chairs looking very relaxed.

'Ah, Moon, I want you to meet an old friend and colleague of mine. This is Sir Gordon Proctor, you'll recognize his name no doubt.'

He was right. Gordon Proctor and Partners were a very well known consultancy who had been the consulting engineers for the tunnels on the new Western high-speed link. I shook hands with him with interest. Although of slight build, his handshake was firm and cool, and his dark eyes alert and penetrating with laugh lines wrinkling the corners.

'How can I help you, young man? Geoffrey tells me that you're one of his bright young engineers, ladder material. It's good to know that the future of the profession is secured indeed.'

'I must put in for a raise then,' I replied with a grin, and began to spread out the drawings.

Proctor chuckled. 'I've set you up there, Geoffrey.'

'No you haven't,' was the terse response from a grim-faced Arbuthnot.

I winced. Oh, shit, why couldn't I keep my big mouth shut!?

A quick change of subject was necessary so, turning the drawings so Proctor could see them properly and putting my finger on Hickling Edge, I said, 'Sir Gordon, we're thinking of putting a tunnel through that chalk feature from here to here.' I hoped the 'we' would get support from Arbuthnot but he didn't comment.

Proctor checked the length of the piece I had indicated, screwed up his eyes for a moment, and pulled his nose with his right hand. 'It would be better to keep the carriageways separate and put twin tunnels through there,' he said. 'It could be cheaper and, more importantly, safety wouldn't be compromised.'

I watched this with interest. Screwing up one's eyes and pulling one's nose to arrive at a decision was a completely new engineering technique to me. It must stimulate the brain cells. It could be worth giving it a try. In private first and, if successful, run it publicly. Marcus Moon's New Structural Analysis System: Screw and Pull. It was usually the other way round in my brief experience of life.

I must have drifted away and given a secret smile at the thought because there was a quiet cough and I noticed Geoffrey and Sir Gordon looking at me quizzically.

'Do you follow the reasoning?' Sir Gordon murmured. 'You seemed to get lost a little there, if I may say so.'

'Oh yes, perfectly. I was just imagining the effect of a major traffic accident in a single tunnel,' I replied, covering up hastily.

'Precisely! What's the sub-strata?'

'The ground is hard chalk.' I showed him the geology. He looked it over carefully for a couple of minutes.

'With flints?'

'With fossils.'

'Ah, good ground for tunnelling.'

'Could you give me some idea of the cost per metre of constructing such tunnels?' I ventured. This was the crunch and the main purpose of the meeting.

He jotted some figures down on a piece of paper that Geoffrey handed him.

'I've covered both single bore and twin bore concrete lined tunnels,' he said, passing it to me. 'The figures include everything down to the finished road, which is presumably what you need for comparison purposes. Naturally they're approximate but I think you'll find not too approximate.' He beamed at Arbuthnot. 'And now, for my fee for that piece of valuable advice, Geoffrey is going to buy me a splendid lunch at the Dorchester,' he said, rubbing his hands together in anticipation.

'I'll knock the cost of it off your bonus,' murmured Geoffrey, giving me a wintry smile.

So Geoffrey had a sense of humour after all – or I hoped he had! Also, it was nice to learn that I might be getting a bonus – reduced or not!

There were no flies on Sir Gordon; he knew exactly what I wanted the information for. It would be well worth keeping in touch with him – I could learn a lot.

That afternoon I sat at my desk with the drawings and calculated the costs of the huge cutting across Hickling Edge and the cost of putting twin tunnels through it using Sir Gordon's figures. I got out Ivan's calculations. My figure for the cutting came within five per cent of his so we were obviously on the right track with those. The tunnels came out at twenty-eight per cent more. Hmm! I screwed up my eyes and pulled my nose for a minute or two but no brain-waves flooded in so I wrote off the Proctor method of brain stimulation. I was out of my depth at the moment with this higher figure. Hugo would have to be consulted.

He was signing some letters and put down his pen when I tapped on the door.

'Come in Marcus, What can I do for you?'

I explained about the difference in the figures and asked whether I should forget the idea of tunnelling. Hugo scratched his forehead and frowned.

'You've just done a straight comparison of cost for that small section of the bypass?'

'Yes.'

'What if we take the total costs of the road as a whole with the cutting and with the tunnels? How would that look?'

Using Ivan's figures, it came out that the difference was now only three point nine per cent higher for the whole road with tunnels.

Hugo scratched his ear but I wasn't falling for that again. He said reflectively, 'I agree that the tunnels are a much better solution. It's a question of whether the Department is prepared to pay the extra to avoid an environmental problem.' He paused and made a decision. 'I would say that if the very strong anti-road feeling about Hickling Edge increases, then we must go with the tunnels.'

'Thanks, Hugo, I'll work it up a bit further then.'

Angela intercepted me in the corridor on my way back. She had contacted the local Kingscastle paper, *The Kingcastle Bugle,* and got them to fax over a copy of their 'Accommodation Available' ads.

'I've picked you out a nice place to lay your head,' she told me. 'It's one of the few that looks interesting. A Mrs Tripp, who claims to provide home cooking and all services. When you've fixed a date to go down there I'll give her a call to let her know when you'll be arriving.'

I nodded abstractedly, took the piece of paper on which she had printed Mrs Tripp's address and slipped it into my pocket.

A drive down to Kingscastle in the MG would be a nice break from the office and give the new car a good run out – well, the car was new to me. Spending a couple of days in the glorious Wiltshire countryside, getting a few signatures and watching some holes being bored; eating some home cooking for a welcome change, and maybe sinking a pint or two of local Wiltshire ale in the pub listening to russet-cheeked farmers comparing the fat-stock prices – marvellous!

This was civil engineering at its most civilised! What could go wrong?

'Have you got a girlfriend, Marcus?' Des Doubleday enquired casually as I handed him a cup of the structural engineers' coffee before taking a sip of my own.

'No, not at the moment.' I'd only just had the damage Polly Power had done to the flat door repaired and didn't want a re-peat. 'And you, are you married Des?'

I wasn't sure if it was a sensitive subject but he just gave me a lop-sided grin and said, 'Yes and no.' I waited to see if there would be a follow-up to that enigmatic reply and there was.

'Four times, dear boy, four times. Been in and out of churches like a fiddler's elbow; and twice to the same woman.'

'So hope didn't triumph over experience then in your case?' I prompted.

A faraway look spread over his face and his eyes seemed to focus on some distant spot on the chipped paintwork by the notice board as the synapses in his brain put together his memories.

'Lust,' he murmured. 'The first marriage to Jennifer was based entirely on lust. Be warned, dear boy, never marry for sex alone, it doesn't last.' He grimaced. 'In my case it only lasted two weeks. My second wife was one of Jennifer's bridesmaids and I began to fancy her at our wedding. Two weeks later I phoned her and that was that.'

'So the second time you fell in love?'

'Oh yes, I always loved Angeline. Still do, as a matter of fact. The problem was she didn't love me. That marriage lasted three years until we both ran out. I ran out of money and she ran out of the house. She went to live with the guy who came to fit our new kitchen. That's the second lesson, dear boy. Never get a randy kitchen-fitter, bastard didn't even do a good job – on the kitchen that is, not Angeline; he did a good job there, alright! Bloody dishwasher leaked and none of the unit doors ever fitted properly.'

'I'll bear that in mind if I ever have a wife and a tatty kitchen.'

He gave me a pained look.

I waited and he returned to his contemplative mode.

'Three years! Three years of enforced bachelorhood without a decent shag. My clothes were in tatters, they'd been through the launderette so often that they could have walked there on their own – and then the firm sent me as Resident Engineer on the Burwick to Brough Head main drain in Orkney. I only did a six-month tour but it felt like six years – Bloody Orkney! You know what they say about Orkney?'

'You mean you started to fancy the odd sheep after a couple of months?'

He gave a snort of dismissal. 'No, you idiot, the rhyme the soldiers made up about it during the Second World War when they had the misfortune to be stationed there?'

'I wasn't born until sixty-seven,' I reminded him.

'Well it went something like this.' He screwed up his eyes and recited:

'The bloody roads are bloody bad
The bloody folks are bloody mad
They'd make the brightest bloody sad
In bloody Orkney.

Everything's so bloody dear
A bloody quid for bloody beer
And is it good – no bloody fear
In bloody Orkney.

No bloody sport, no bloody games
No bloody fun; the bloody dames
Won't even give their bloody names
In bloody Orkney.

The bloody flicks are bloody old
The bloody seats are bloody cold
And you can't get in for bloody gold
In bloody Orkney.'

He gave a rueful grin. 'So do you imagine I had a raving time then, smothered with girlfriends, rocketing around that island in my souped-up, scarlet sports Jaguar, scarf flying, careless laughter echoing from the surrounding bogs? No bloody fear! A battered Land-Rover that couldn't pull a dead sheep out of a ditch, let alone classy crumpet, was my mode of transport! The soldiers hit the nail on the head! Was it any wonder I married Barbara, the first girl I found back in London who was prepared to buy me some new underpants?'

'No, I suppose not,' I murmured, still in a daze, thinking about Des's Orkney adventure. A snug-fitting pair of Calvin Klein's didn't seem to me to be a sound basis for a long-lasting relationship, and I said so.

'It wasn't,' he groaned. 'I kept thinking about Angeline: and, as if directed by the fickle finger of fate, I went to a drinks party in Putney one evening and who should be there but her, looking just as I always remembered her in my dreams. The kitchen-fitter had been given the shove two years ago and she'd been in Australia since then and had just got back. The upshot was that we decided to give it another go, so I moved out of Barbara's flat and in with Angeline.'

'Taking your pants with you, I suppose. What then?'

'Still there, dear boy, still there! Settled on the nest like a contented cockerel. You must come and have dinner with us sometime, but for God's sake don't mention it to Ivan.' He glanced at Ivan's empty desk and shuddered. 'He'd want to bring Awful Agatha and the thought of the pair of them in an enclosed space…!' He left the rest unsaid but it was clear that they were not close friends. 'Besides, I don't suppose Ivan wants reminding of Orkney, that's where his current trouble started.'

I was intrigued, and as Des was in a talkative mood, I gently pressed him to elaborate. 'Hugo mentioned Ivan had a problem…' I let the question hang.

Des sat back in his chair.

'Ivan took over from me as Resident Engineer on the big drain and somehow got himself shacked up with a sheep-farmer's daughter. A great big hefty, hairy, smelly creature she was, infamous throughout the islands; randy as a sow in heat – and very similar in behaviour but not as attractive. She was regularly screwed rotten by half the Russian fishing fleet when they put into Stromness, and Ivan thought it was love! Anyway, she's claiming he left something behind when he departed and it's now two years old and wants its daddy.'

'A paternity suit?'

'You've hit the nail on the head. With her track record it could be one of hundreds, but as most of 'em are fishing somewhere in the Barents Sea these days, well out of lawyer range, Ivan is an easier target. He's fighting it in the Sheriff's Court in Kirkwall with blood tests, but the first lot weren't conclusive so he's asked for the new DNA tests. These can't be done in Orkney and she refused to give samples for tests in Glasgow until it was pointed out to her that unless Ivan could be positively identified as the father there would be no money. That's why he has to keep shooting off for a few days.'

Not an apt choice of words under the circumstances, I thought.

'What about Awful Agatha?'

'She's standing by him at present. She says she believes him.'

'Do you?'

He gave a broad grin and a noncommittal shrug of the shoulders.

'Is that why he's such a grumpy sod?'

'Good heavens no, dear boy, he's naturally a grumpy sod! He's been like that ever since he arrived here. I think it's ambition, it's eating at him inside. He thinks everybody's trying to do him down and deprive him of his rightful place. You particularly! He sees you as a real threat to his progress up the CONDES ladder. Me, he's written off as a has-been so he doesn't see me as an obstacle. He doesn't realise that he's already in his rightful place, in my opinion.'

I was astonished. 'Me! Why am I a threat to him? I've never tried to denigrate him, I'm happy doing what I'm doing. The chasm of responsibility is far too wide for me to try to jump it and, present company excepted, there are too many shits on the other side for me to want to join them in any case.'

I scratched my head. Still, it explained Ivan's attitude to me but it might be necessary to discourage him from carrying it too far. I'd think about it.

'Does the whole office know about Orkney?'

Des shook his head. 'Apart from Hugo and Agatha, I don't think so, although some wit sent him a Father's Day card a couple of months ago, which sent him berserk. I've told you in strictest confidence because you must be beginning to wonder why Ivan kept disappearing and it was better that you knew the true reason rather than speculate. So keep it under your hat.'

CHAPTER SIX

It was early morning when I turned the MG into Albert Bridge Road and crossed the bridge on to the Embankment. It was too early to check on Mrs Aberdeen so I decided to phone her on my mobile a bit later.

There was a film of mist hanging over the river and the portents for a stunning July day looked promising. I headed west to make the M4 before the heavy morning traffic built up. The canvas top of the car was folded down; the radio was playing Elton John, the sun was shining, the 747s droned overhead on their way to disgorge hordes of tourists and immigrants into Heathrow, and contentment filled the Moon chest. The only problem nagging at the back of my mind was: why was Ivan so hostile? As far as I was aware I hadn't done anything to warrant his aggressive behaviour but he seemed to want to denigrate me at every opportunity. The thought that he was jealous because of 'Awful Agatha' crossed my mind again. Come to think about it, she wasn't exactly friendly either. Looked at me with a face like a horse collar whenever we encountered each other – which was as infrequently as possible, if I could arrange it. Des thought it was because he saw me as a threat to his progress, but there was no reason why we both couldn't move up in the firm if we were good at our jobs.

Coming down from the elevated section, the M4 opened up into three lanes and I was able to put the pedal to the metal and wind the car up to seventy. Any faster than that and bits of what passed for the trim tended to flap about. I turned off at the Swindon junction and made my way through the rolling hills of Wiltshire along the Kingscastle road. I hit the traffic jam about half a mile short of the suburbs and began the slow crawl towards the middle of the small town. After last year's fiasco the authorities had tried to control the traffic flow so I had to follow a one-way system through some hasty diversions avoiding Fore Street. The temporary traffic lights and mini-roundabouts only seemed to add to the congestion in the side streets. The heat of the morning added to the frustration of the lorry drivers trying to manoeuvre their vehicles round tight corners. No wonder they needed a by-pass.

I turned off the main road with relief and asked a girl pushing a pram if she knew where Roseberry Avenue was. Fortunately she did, and said it was quite close. She gave me precise directions how to get there.

Roseberry Avenue was in a quiet leafy suburb of Kingscastle, one of several identical roads consisting of small detached and semi-detached houses all built in the thirties to three different styles. Bow fronted windows and mock Tudor gables were common to all but some had detached garages, some had garages attached and some with garages attached had a fourth bedroom built above. Driving slowly, I scanned the gateposts and door architraves for number 43, 'Viva Espana'; and there it was – obviously the home of a family who took their holidays on the Costa del Sol.

It was the left-hand house of a pair of semis, both decorated the same way but Number 43 had the attached garage and the fourth bedroom. It faced south, the front garden was tidy and full of flowers; the house itself looked cheerful. The space directly outside the house was occupied by a little Ford so I pulled in further down the road. Thus it was with a degree of optimism that I heaved my bag out of the passenger seat and pushed open the front gate. The door chime played the birdy song and the door was opened by an attractive woman, aged about thirty-five to forty, at a guess. Tall, dark hair tied back, tanned face and arms and a smile that extended from her wide mouth to her guileless brown eyes.

'You must be Mr Moon,' she said. 'Your girl phoned to say you were on your way. I'm Mrs Tripp but you can call me Susan.'

'And you can call me Marcus,' I replied and we both laughed.

'Well, that's got that out of the way. Come in and I'll show you your room. You're staying with us for a couple of nights I believe?'

I nodded. 'Yes, I should get everything done in that time.'

She set off up the stairs, me following. There were some black and white photographs of a woman in a variety of sexy poses lining the staircase but it wasn't those that my eyes were focussed on.

Mrs Tripp – Susan – had a very nice pair of legs, a pert little bottom and a neat slim figure. The back view was as encouraging as the front. I wondered where Mr Tripp was and what he did, apart from go on holiday to Torremolinos – and her. Lucky swine!

My room was the one over the garage. It was bright and airy with a double bed, wardrobe, chest of drawers and a small desk-cum-dressing table with a chair and a desk light. She noticed my enquiring look.

'My husband used it as an office,' she explained, 'but now our guests use it. The bathroom is just across the landing but I'm afraid you'll have to share it with my daughter. She's at work at the moment, teaches aerobics and things at the local Leisure Centre. I've made a pot of tea if you'd like refreshing after your journey.'

She turned with a smile and left me to unpack and take a view of my new situation.

So, a nice-looking landlady, a daughter who must be nineteen or twenty at the most, a husband who used to use my room as an office but clearly didn't any longer – interesting.

It didn't take me five minutes to unpack my limited kit and I went across the landing to the bathroom for a wazz and to dump my sponge bag. More interest awaited me there in the shape of a couple of very skimpy thongs and a largish bra hanging on a line over the bath. Obviously not Susan's so they must be the daughter's. Hmm! There were three other doors leading from the landing but they were all closed.

'Your tea's ready, Marcus,' she called up the stairs.

'Be right with you.'

On my way down the stairs I glanced at the photographs again and did a double take this time. They were of Susan Tripp but taken maybe ten years ago, wearing very little and posing provocatively. She was clearly proud of her body.

Over tea and Hob Nobs I got a full run down of the Tripp family history. Lionel Tripp had done a runner a few years ago with 'some floozy he met at marriage guidance' and he and Susan had been divorced rapidly thereafter. 'He wasn't much anyway,' she told me, 'when the bugle sounded the boys stayed in the barracks most of the time.'

'Really,' I murmured, slightly embarrassed at this public exposé of Lionel Tripp's inadequacies. 'If you have a daughter he must have been on parade at least once,' I observed.

'Oh yes, when we were just married he couldn't get enough. Anyway, I'm not sure that Tracey is his.' She hesitated, and I thought she was going to say more but changed her mind. I wondered if she was thinking of giving me a list of the possible runners and riders but it seemed tactful to get off the subject for the time being so I switched to asking her about her daughter.

'Tracey's a lovely girl, you'll like her. Very athletic, been captain of hockey and tennis at school.'

She reached behind her and hauled out a school photograph of a girls' hockey team in short skirts with Tracey sitting in the middle of the front row, legs apart showing her knickers between meaty thighs and towering at least six inches above those on either side.

'Not somebody to get into a fight with,' I observed.

Susan gave me a sharp look and I realised that that was not exactly the reaction she had been hoping for.

I drained my tea cup, made the excuse that I'd better go to the site compound and make my presence known, and got up to leave.

'Dinner's at six-thirty, it's steak and kidney pie tonight – a welcoming treat as you've not visited us before,' she said as I wandered into the hall, adding, 'I'd better give you a door key then you can come and go as you please. But give the bell a good ring before you come in so's I know you're here.'

That seemed a bit odd but if that was what she wanted, it was OK with me.

When I got to the car, standing beside it was a florid, cardigan-wrapped, bushy white moustache wearing a scowl. As I approached, fumbling in my pockets for the key, he said gruffly, 'Is this yours?', pointing to the car with a stabbing finger.

'It's not for sale,' I said cheerily, 'but a good offer could tempt me.'

He blinked, and his rheumy eyes swivelled round like two bits of frog-spawn in a jam jar.

'You can't park there,' he continued.

'But I have! Are you saying it's illegal to park on this road?'

This caused him to thrust out his bottom lip and, by ejecting air upwards from his mouth, fluff up his moustache.

'Residents parking only, son.'

The last thing I wanted was to get into a hassle with the self-appointed traffic warden of Roseberry Avenue on my first day so I thought I'd better explain the situation – not that it was any of his business but purely to keep the peace. Or so I thought.

'I'm only here temporarily for the bypass,' I told him. 'I'm visiting Mrs Tripp at number 43.'

Now can you see anything provocative or volatile in that statement? No! Neither could I – but Colonel Blimp could. He went a deep puce and spluttered angrily, 'That damned woman! I know what you're up to, don't think I don't! No moral fibre in you people these days! And that damned woman has no right! No right at all to go against the wishes of the respectable people round here!'

I started to explain that the bypass would free up the town centre from its current snarled up traffic situation and make life a lot more pleasant for the townsfolk, but he wasn't having any of that.

'Oh, so you're to do with the blasted bypass as well!' he raged. 'We don't want it there, you know! I'll tell you this; you'll only despoil my countryside over my dead body! Don't give me all that nonsense about benefit, you think you can come here cut great gashes in our landscape, dig up our woods and trees, our fields and footpaths, our gates and...' He spluttered, struggling for the right word, so to be helpful I added '...stiles?'

I thought it was a nice choice of word, combining the rustic feel of a dowelled, moss-covered, wooden fence and step, with his picture of mooing cows chewing cud over farm gates, but all it did was send him even more apoplectic. Giving my tyres a savage kick, he stormed off down the road in high dudgeon shouting that I hadn't heard the last of this.

Blow me, I thought, I seemed to be able to upset people with the most innocent of remarks these days. If I said 'Good morning' somebody would snap, 'Who asked you for a bloody weather forecast!' And why did dudgeon have to be high? Could you storm off in low or medium dudgeon? Scanning Blimp's retreating back, bristling like a porcupine, I didn't think he would be in for an man-to-man discussion about that at present.

So what had he got so wound up about? I'd read in David Nairn's report that there was a protest group about the bypass but that wasn't extraordinary these days; there were protest groups about everything. In fact I wouldn't be surprised if there wasn't a protest group about protest groups. Anyway local opinion seemed to swing first one way, then the other. It seemed somewhat over the top to attack me when he had no idea what, if any, my role was in 'despoiling the countryside'.

To get to the site investigation contractors' compound I had to drive straight through the centre of Kingscastle and this partly answered my question. There were some 'Move The Bypass' posters calling people to sign a petition in the Town Hall plastered on some walls; the same message was on banners strung across the High Street. I noticed a few women on the street corners handing out leaflets, all wearing sashes saying 'Move The Bypass', so clearly Kingscastle itself was working up some steam about the new road – or at least some of the populace were. One could never be sure how many, because those in favour often found it wisest to keep their heads down when there was likely to be violent opposition, and a brick through your window could be used to emphasise their argument. But 'Move it'? Where and why? were the questions that came to mind. It had to go either north or south of the town, and according to Dave Nairn they didn't want it south and now apparently they didn't want it north either. So what else was there? Over the town or under the town – neither was a realistic option. Well the Department of Transport wanted it where it was proposed at present and that was what I was going to work on.

Geophysical Drilling Limited's site compound was discreetly located in the middle of a wood with a hardcore track leading to it off a country road.

The site was fenced with razor wire and there was a uniformed security man on the gate. I made myself known and the security man shouted towards a site hut, 'There's a chap here says he's from Insulting Services. Shall I let him through?'

A young man about my age came out and called, 'Mr Moon?'

'Yes,' I said, and the young man waved me through. We shook hands.

'I'm John Bailey, the site agent. You've come about the deep boring we have to do for the Shering Valley and Hickling Edge?

We should be able to start that on Thursday if you've got the permissions?'

'I'm going to see the main landowner this afternoon,' I replied, 'but I don't anticipate any problems.'

He gave me a wry look but didn't comment. We went into the site hut and he showed me the line of the proposed route pinned to a board on the wall. I could see that about half of the road had been coloured green. 'That's where we've completed our test bores so far,' he explained. 'We have about another two weeks' work on this area here.'

He pointed to a section at the opposite end of the route from the green colour. 'And then we have to do the middle piece.' He indicated the stretch winding through woodland, which I knew contained the bridge site and Hickling Edge.

From the tone of his voice and the grimace on his face it was clear that all was not well with the middle piece, so I asked him.

He explained. 'The Shering viaduct would cross a heavily wooded valley in the grounds of Withers Hall, and then pass through the Edge. The Hall is a Georgian pile constructed in the late eighteenth century to house the Withers family, who apparently made their fortune in the slave trade, and Withers Woods are part of the ancient English forest of oak, beech, ash and alder that covered the whole area at one time. The present occupant of the Hall is a Major Sir Fistulas Withers, obviously an ex-military man. He's the main objector to the bypass because a large stretch of it would cross his land.'

As far as John Bailey could determine, Withers had persuaded the honest citizens of Kingscastle to support his objection otherwise he would put their rent up or throw them out into the street.

'He can't do that!' I exclaimed.

John Bailey grinned. 'No, that was a bit of an exaggeration, but I suspect that it's not too far from the truth as most people I've spoken to can't wait for the bypass to be constructed.'

'So he's being a bit difficult, is he?' I asked.

'Well he did threaten to set the dogs on one of our drilling teams when he thought it was drilling too near his boundary. So we've waited for you guys to come and sort it out and get the permissions signed.'

'I'm only doing the deep borings for the bridge site and Hickling Edge,' I told him. 'Somebody else will be dealing with the road across his land.'

I glanced at my watch; there was no time like the present, I thought, so I decided that my approach would be brisk and business-like because, as an ex-army man, Withers wouldn't appreciate any waffling about. Bailey gave me directions to Withers Hall.

The gates to the Hall were very imposing: large bath stone gate-posts with carved stone griffins on top. The wrought iron gates were wide open and I could see the Hall at the end of a long drive flanked by beech trees.

Concentrating on what my approach would be, I reached the front entrance rather quicker than anticipated. The MG did a racing turn and slid to a stop on the gravel in front of the imposing portico, leaving a long skid mark and a cloud of dust that hung in the still air.

Firmly grasping the folder containing the blank permits, I sprinted up the half dozen steps and hauled on the polished brass bell pull. Give them a minute, I thought, the chap might be in the bath; although it was three-thirty in the afternoon, you never knew with these aristocratic coves.

I was just about to give the bell another tug when I heard a key being turned in the lock and the door swung open to reveal a lofty man in a dark suit, white starched shirt, black tie and waistcoat. So he wasn't in the bath after all. Adopting what I thought was a brisk and businesslike approach, I began: 'Good Morning, sir, what a magnificent house you have here and so beautifully kept. I have with me…' And I produced my folder.

Before I could continue he snapped, 'The tradesmen's entrance is round the back' and began to close the door. Instinctively I thrust a foot forward to block that manoeuvre and stammered, 'No, no, you've got it wrong. I'm not selling anything, I just wanted to talk to you about the proposed bypass.'

I saw hesitation in Lofty's eyes as they flickered from my intruding foot to the folder in my hand and to the MG in the front drive, revealed in all its dusty splendour at the end of a nasty skid mark now the cloud had settled. He knew the Major was actively involved in trying to get the bypass moved and assumed that I was delivering something to do with that.

'You'd better come in,' he adjusted smoothly, stepping aside to let me enter. But that was all he was going to permit. 'Wait here.'

He eased off round a sweeping staircase, leaving me standing in a large hall with paintings of eighteenth sailing ships hung round the walls; Withers' slavers, I assumed, plying their trade from West Africa to the Americas. I was thinking that the elegance of the ships belied the misery of their cargoes when he materialised again at my elbow.

'The Major is not available,' he said, looking down his nose, 'so you can leave whatever it is you've brought with me.' He held out his hand.

This confirmed my suspicions, this snotty beanpole wasn't the householder then, he was a flunky. That changed our relationship immediately.

'Look here, my man,' I began, 'I'm not delivering anything. My name is Marcus Moon and I want to talk to the Major on a very important matter, so will you kindly inform him that I would like to see him?'

I held his gaze until he lowered his.

'I'll see if he is available now,' he murmured and floated back behind the staircase. It took longer this time before he reappeared.

'The Major will see you now, Mr er…er…'

'Moon,' I helped out.

He gave a sniff of disdain and murmured, 'Please follow me.'

I walked through into a bright sunny room where a stocky, elderly, erect man with a short back-and-sides, a highly-coloured complexion and a bristling white moustache stood with fierce eyes fixed on my entrance.

'A Mr Moon to see you, sir.'

I knew at once I was in trouble. You know how you have this immediate feeling that the relationship coming over the horizon is not one that will burst with spring-like enthusiasm into the darling buds of May. Here, awaiting my petition, stood a classic 'hostile'.

He had all the attributes. A retired military man who used his lowly rank; a florid face with a knotted forehead; glaring eyes with no particular reason to glare; a road-kill hedgehog haircut and – the final give-away – the precisely trimmed bristly moustache like a hairy caterpillar glued across his top lip.

'Well?' he barked. 'Are you from the printers?'

I cursed John Bailey under my breath for dropping me in it and wondered how to make the right approach.

'Get on with it man, I haven't got all day!'

'I'm from Consultant Design Services,' I opened up with, but this just produced a blank look and a bristling of the eyebrows, so I hastily added, 'We are the consultants to the Department of Transport for the new bypass.'

The glare intensified and the face grew redder. 'Are you, by God?' he ground out ominously.

I plunged on. 'So I wondered if you would be kind enough to give us permission to drill a dozen test boreholes on your land in the Shering Valley and across Hickling Edge? We need the information to design the foundations for the bridge for the new road. It's very important because the type of subsoil could dictate the form of the bridge and we've got to find out how far down we have to go before we can reach good ground for the piling,' I babbled nervously.

I watched with awe as his face inflated like a puffer fish, the eyes protruded, his fists knotted, and his whole body shook with incandescent rage. Sensing that I wasn't going to be offered tea and cake, I eased round towards the door where Lofty was still hovering.

'GET OUT! GET OUT OF MY HOUSE, YOU IMPERTINENT SWINE!' he shouted, showering spittle all over the place.

'Percival, damn you, where's my blasted shot-gun? Go and fetch my gun now, man – and put number seven shot in the chambers!' he barked, waving frantically at the hovering butler.

Blood and sand, I thought, I'm out of here fast. That sounded definitely like a 'No' to me, and two barrels full of bird-shot travelling in my direction at 1200 feet per second was sufficient incentive for me to take his 'No' as confirmed and make myself scarce as speedily as possible.

'I'll leave you a consent form in case you change your mind,' I gabbled hopefully, as I scattered half a dozen round the floor like confetti.

'May I show you out, sir?' smoothed Percival, but he needn't have bothered. I hit the front door in record time with the Major's voice ringing in my ears that if I or any of my cohorts ever set foot on his land again, 'I'll blow your bloody arses to kingdom come!'

Foot hard on the accelerator, I left more wheel-spin marks and dust clouds as I snaked across Withers' gravel and shot down the drive, swerving through the gates, my back prickling with nervous anticipation.

So a bit of a set-back there! It seemed as if the retired military populace of Kingscastle was not in favour of this new road. I pulled into the side of the road and phoned Hugo on my mobile.

'Are you sure you can't persuade him? Maybe you were too abrasive? Perhaps if you tried a softer approach...?'

'I can tell you once and for all, Hugo, I was not abrasive – I was most tactful and I'm not going anywhere near that madman again, he wasn't joking about his shot-gun.'

Hugo heaved a sigh of resignation. 'Well I suppose we'll have to go through all the performance of getting a court order then. I'll phone the man at the Ministry and ask him to arrange it. It's their job to sort out that sort of thing; they're used to it these days.'

I arrived back at number 43 at about six-thirty, and passed a rather red-faced man walking stiffly out through the gate. He didn't meet my eyes and hurried off down the road. Fumbling for the door key, I pressed the bell as instructed and let myself in.

I was just going up the stairs when Susan called, 'Gin and tonic in twenty minutes?'

'Yeah, oh thanks, I could do with a stiff drink. I'll just have a quick shower and be right down.'

'Would you like me to scrub your back?' she laughed. I chuckled back and carried on up the stairs.

With a clean shirt and smartish chinos, I presented myself in the sitting-room where there was a nice large frosted glass of G and T awaiting. If this was being in digs, it seemed to me to be the dog's whiskers: not at all what I'd expected but very acceptable all the same. Susan came in carrying a similarly frosted glass and wearing a tight red dress, very low cut and very short. A little pulse started to beat in my head. Well, you never know if your luck might be in.

'Dinner in half an hour, I hope you like steak and kidney pie, it's homemade.'

We chatted about the day. I didn't mention my encounter with Fistulas Withers, but I told her about Colonel Blimp getting shirty about my car being parked in the street and his comments about the proposed bypass.

She snorted angrily. 'He's always been a pain in the arse ever since he moved in. Regards himself as everybody's keeper round here and is always sticking his nose in where it's not wanted. Some folk are against the bypass but I think most people want it. The middle of the town is a nightmare, always congested with through traffic, and the shopkeepers I've talked to can't wait for it to be built. However, there's always a few who'll object to anything and usually they're the ones who make the most noise.'

Perfectly normal harmless chatter, you would think – and you'd be right. Susan disappeared into the kitchen and a few minutes later called me through to the dining room. I noted that there were only two places set. She saw me looking at the table and said, 'Oh, Tracey's out this evening, some party, she won't be back until late so we're on our own.'

The steak and kidney pie was well up to expectations, and the treacle pudding that followed it oozed golden syrup from a light sponge that melted on the tongue – so it wasn't the cooking that had caused Lionel to be up and away with his 'floozie', as Susan put it

'There's a good programme on the telly at nine,' she murmured. 'It's a thriller about this woman who has three husbands and decides to kill them off one by one. So we could watch that first. They all die in agony – poisoned!'

I thought that there was a little too much relish put into that last sentence, so maybe Lionel had made it out of the front door just ahead of the arsenic. I was thinking about that so I overlooked the 'first'.

I wasn't averse to spending an hour or two in front of the box. Susan told me to take the remains of my wine and go and sit in the sitting-room while she made us both a mug of cocoa. That should have tipped me off as well! Coffee, tea – no problem; but cocoa, in a mug, implies a cosy intimacy – at least it should have done. I wasn't all that chuffed about drinking cocoa but she was trying hard to be nice so I let it go.

I repaired to the sitting-room as she called over her shoulder, 'Switch the telly on. You press the button on the left.'

I'd noticed, when we were having our G and Ts, that she had a good-sized television, a thirty-inch screen at a guess, so I duly pressed the button on the left-hand side and the screen flickered into life. The furniture was arranged in such a way that the only full-on view of the screen could be got by sitting on the deep leather two-person sofa directly in front of it. The two smaller armchairs were placed at an awkward angle. I hesitated for a second, but the sofa had a small side-table which would be convenient for resting my wine glass or mug, so I sat on it.

Susan was soon back carrying a tray with two steaming ornamental mugs and two balloon brandy glasses.

'I hope you like brandy,' she murmured, 'I've got some good stuff Tracey brought back from Marbella last year.'

Well I was willing to give anything a go if it had alcohol in it so I said, 'Sure thing!'

She poured out two generous measures and came and sat next to me, handing me one.

We watched *Three Into One Won't Go* and sipped our cocoa and brandy. I became aware of a warm thigh pressing against my leg. She smelt nice, shampoo and faint perfume, magnificent cleavage. The TV droned on, a head leant on my shoulder and a hand slowly came to rest on my knee.

Bloody hell, I realised, I think she's trying to seduce me. It was a very tricky situation we had here. Me, a young professional engineer trying to make his way in the world; trying to steer the narrow path of respectability between corruption and moral turpitude on one side, and penury and disgrace on the other; now faced with an unanticipated choice of 'Get thee behind me, Satan' or falling into a pit of lust and lechery the like of which I had the feeling would be way beyond anything Horse Power could've mustered up.

Well there was no choice, was there? If my wit and charm was proving to be irresistible, who was I to deprive the world in general, and Susan Tripp in particular, of the benefits of my body? In for a penny in for a pound. *Wallop!* I dragged her across my lap and gave her full mouth-to-mouth resuscitation.

The next minute we were rolling about on the rug in a passionate embrace. I didn't find out if *Three into One* went but I can tell you that one into one certainly did!

Some time later, shagged out but much more experienced, I was soaping her down under the shower in her bathroom when we heard the door-bell ring and the front door open and close.

'Ah, that'll be Tracey, she's early!' Susan exclaimed. 'Never mind, too much excitement wouldn't be good for you for the first time.' She rinsed me down and handed me a towel. She didn't exhibit any urgency which puzzled me. I would have thought that a daughter catching her mother *in flagrate* with the lodger might be embarrassing all round.

She sensed my nervousness. 'It's OK, Tracey won't come upstairs.'

While I was getting dried she collected my clothes then ushered me out of her bedroom with a quick peck on the cheek.

'I hope you enjoyed that,' she whispered and closed her bedroom door. I stood there nonplussed for a moment, bollock naked with an arm full of clothes, ears tuned for footsteps on the stairs, and then nipped to my bedroom thinking about her strange choice of words. What 'first time' – and what had that to do with Tracey?

Next morning it was as if nothing had happened. I felt a frisson of disappointment that my sterling efforts of the evening went unacknowledged. Susan served up the orange juice, poached eggs on toast and coffee without the flicker of an eyelid. When I attempted to speak, she shook her head warningly. I realised why when Tracey came in from the next room. This was my first sighting of the greater stuffed Tracey bird and it was very interesting. She was nothing like her mother and the school photograph hadn't done her justice. She was a big girl: meaty, muscular and bounding with health. A full-lipped mouth and round soft eyes set in a friendly face. Brown hair tied back in a pony-tail.

'You must be Marcus,' she said in a deepish voice. 'Mam told me about you.'

I gave Susan a quizzical glance..

'Only nice things,' she added with a warm smile.

My mind slipped back to the bra and thongs hanging on the line over the bath and I responded by returning her smile and offering my hand – a gesture I regretted a few seconds later as I tried to loosen up my crushed knuckles.

'You work at the Leisure Centre your mother told me, as an aerobics instructor.'

'I do general fitness as well; take them for circuit training, press weights etcetera. I only do four days a week, Wednesday's my day off. What do you do, Marcus?'

Your mother for one, I was tempted to reply, but the recollection of that vice-like handshake rapidly put paid to the idea of any sort of flippant answer.

'I'm trying to organise permissions for somebody to come and take geological samples for bridge foundations along the line of the proposed bypass. I'm not having much success so far,' I added ruefully. 'Your Major Sir Fistulas Withers told me in no uncertain terms to bugger off and threatened to shoot me if I so much as set foot on his land again.'

Tracey shot a glance at her mother. 'Did you know about this, Mam?'

Susan shook her head. 'It's the first time Marcus has mentioned it; he did come home looking a bit gloomy yesterday so I tried to cheer him up.'

And very successfully too, I recollected. I could do with a bit more cheering up if that was the treatment.

It was a thought I would come to regret some time later.

'So what are you going to do today?' asked Tracey.

'I've got some other landowners and tenants to see and as far as Withers is concerned we've just got to wait until we get a court order. That'll delay everything. You know how slow the courts are these days.'

Tracey frowned thoughtfully. 'A lot of us want this bypass, you know, it's only one or two people like Withers who don't want it on their land and they carry a lot of clout with the more gullible here. I might be able to help you in that direction.'

I noticed Susan start and look slightly nervous as I looked questioningly at Tracey.

'We know Withers,' she said. 'I sort of act as his trainer. I can't stand the man personally but he's a regular. Give me your form and take me up to the Hall this evening after work and I'll see what I can do.'

Susan visibly relaxed.

I didn't think there would be much Tracey could do but if she thought she could persuade the intransigent Major it was worth a try – as long as I kept out of shotgun range. So I agreed.

It was a warm summer evening and she was waiting outside Kingscastle Leisure Centre at six o'clock as I pulled up in the car with the top down. She was still dressed in what I assumed were her work clothes of tight sweat pants and a baggy track-suit top with the letters KLC across the chest.

We drove out to Withers Hall. I told her about the Shering Valley Bridge but I couldn't get her to tell me what she had in mind, she just talked about her fitness regime at the Leisure Centre.

The car slid to a standstill outside the Hall gates, that was as far as I thought it safe to go.

'How come you think you can talk the bastard round when he got so aggressive with me?' I asked.

She gave a tight smile. 'All I can say is that Fistulas is a naughty boy and I'm certain he wouldn't want the world to know about it.'

She wouldn't say more but climbed out of the car and strode purposefully up the drive with my release form grasped firmly in her large fist. I saw her ring the bell, the door open, and then she disappeared inside the Hall.

Ten minutes later she emerged and walked jauntily back to where I was waiting in the car at the side of the road.

'There you are, sunshine,' she announced and tossed the paper into my lap. Sure enough it had been signed by Withers and witnessed by a John Percival – who I assumed was the butler.

'How on earth did you manage that?' I gasped. 'I didn't think you'd come out alive.'

'I told you, Fistulas has been a naughty boy, a very naughty boy indeed, and I showed him a few pictures on my cell phone that could make it onto the front page of the *Kingscastle Bugle* if he was going to be difficult. Now, Mr Moon, it's a lovely evening and you're going to take me to the Coach and Eight at Little Worsely and buy me a dinner and a beer as a reward before you get the next instalment! I'll direct, just keep going down this road until I tell you where to turn.'

That was all I could get out of her. Had Withers been touching up some of the girls at the Leisure Centre, including Tracey? I was intrigued but prepared to settle for the signed release form, so I didn't persist with my questions.

We had a good pub dinner and a couple of beers in the very pleasant country hostelry on a ridge overlooking the Shering Valley as night fell.

'Isn't your big bridge site somewhere near here?' Tracey asked with a quizzical smile, the implications of which escaped me at that moment. When I confirmed that it was, she said, 'Let's go and look at it. I've taken all this trouble to fix it for you, so I think I'm entitled to a look.'

'But it's dark! You won't see much at this time of the night. Why don't I take you up there in daylight?'

'It'll be more interesting in the dark than back at Viva Espana,' she said with a giggle. 'The sky's clear and there's some moonlight, it's not pitch black. Come on!' And with that she climbed into the passenger seat and folded her arms decisively.

Now these things don't have to be spelt out to me in letters ten feet tall. The thought of thongs and big tits lodged in my memory bank sprang to the fore, so I started the engine and drove to the track in the woods that led to the bridge site. Parking the car behind some bushes so that it was concealed from the track, we brushed our way through the trees down the slope to where I wanted the test bores drilled. There was a nice little hollow full of dry soft leaves screened by thick undergrowth, and somehow we ended up in it. My brief attempt at explaining the science of soil mechanics was stifled by a great set of moist lips and fingers tugging at my belt.

I was just working my way to unfastening her bra when I felt something sharp sticking in my side. It felt like a stone. I quickly rolled her over and pulled it out of the ground. A quick glance at it in the faint light showed it to be curiously shaped, so without thinking I stuck it in my jeans pocket and got down to the serious business of slowly undressing the voluptuous Tracey.

A very exciting ten minutes passed and we were just getting down to the main event when I heard the snap of a twig close by. I froze immediately. Fortunately she wasn't a moaner and remained quite still when she sensed that I had.

'What's the matter?' she whispered.

'I think there's somebody further up the hill! Listen!'

Sure enough we heard movement and then people moving through the wood above us. We lay still. The rustling stopped and a male voice said, 'Stumpy, I think this is the place.'

Another voice replied, 'Yeah, the ground seems quite soft so digging tunnels here shouldn't be too much of a problem. Also it's well hidden from the road above and the track. We could easily work here without being detected. It'll take at least couple of months before any work can start on site so we've got plenty of time if the bloody Enquiry goes against us.'

'Of course it fucking will; it's all a fix, innit?' the first voice said scornfully. 'Those bastards have got it all tied up, haven't they? We should start as soon as we've got a group together so that by the time the contractors move in we'll have a good network set up.'

A third voice, a woman's, added, 'We haven't got a bloody chance, the whole thing's a set-up. The only hope we've got of killing this fucking road is to make it so expensive that they have to cancel it. We're doing the tunnels and the trenches; Newbury Mary says her team will do the tree houses and spike the trees. The bovver boys will sort out any contractors with a bit of monkey wrenching on their plant when they do start. There's not much else we can do.'

'What about people like gamekeepers?' asked the voice identified as Stumpy.

'Nah, there's no pheasants in these woods; they're all over on the other side of the valley. If we kill a few of those dickies over there before we start, the sodding 'keepers will spend all their time protecting the rest against poachers. Anyway, the ponce up at the Hall has been banging on about this road. He wants it even less than we do.'

The voices began to fade as they moved away up the hill until there was the sound of vehicle doors closing and the murmur of a departing engine. Tracey started to pull me towards her again but I held back. For me the moment had gone.

The moonlit bonk – the romance of two white bottoms winking in the silvery beams of old lunar filtering through the flickering foliage – had lost its attraction. Hordes of environmental protesters rampaging through the woods had put paid to that. The evening was ruined; Stumpy and his mob had become my least favourite people at that moment with the disruption they had caused already, let alone what they were planning for the bypass. And what was that about 'the ponce up at the Hall', by the way? None of it made much sense to me but it was too much of a distraction.

Tracey conceded that the moment had passed, fastened her bra and put her top back on.

'Let's go back to the house,' she said. 'It's more private there anyway and there's all the gear.' As we scrambled back up the hill to where the car was hidden I thought, what gear – and what about Susan?

'What about your mother?' I asked.

'Nah, you're out of luck there, she's got an out-call this evening I think.'

I blinked at this. It wasn't quite the reply I was expecting.

We drove back to Roseberry Avenue. There were no lights on in the house so my hopes rose as Tracey fitted her key into the lock and rang the doorbell.

'Just in case,' she giggled.

A funny feeling was beginning to spread through my bones about Viva Espana, a sensation that all was not as it seemed. Tracey switched on the hall and landing lights and started to lead me up the stairs. The black and white photos of Susan on the flanking walls took on a new significance.

'We'll go in my bedroom,' she murmured, 'unless you want to go in the schoolroom?'

My throat went dry. 'What schoolroom?' I asked shakily.

She threw open one of the doors that had always been closed when I was first upstairs, and there inside I could see a few old school desks with chairs; some shelves with tattered books; a blackboard on which somebody had written some simple sums and a rack on the wall with what looked suspiciously like canes, straps and whips hanging from it.

'What's that for?' I said inanely, because it was now pretty obvious what is was for.

Tracey giggled again. 'That's where all our naughty boys and girls go. Are you a naughty boy then?'

'No I am not!' I snapped as the whole thing suddenly dawned. 'So you and your mother actually run this...this...' I couldn't think of the right word. 'Business enterprise' didn't seem to fit; you could hardly put Viva Espana in the same commercial bracket as General Motors or Shell Petroleum. 'Organisation' wasn't suitable either, because obviously there wasn't any, and brothel conjured up images of Turkish tarts and cheap perfume.

Tracey looked astonished. 'You're pulling my leg! You mean you didn't know? You really didn't know? Bugger me; we thought you'd booked in here especially for a two-day course with a bit of variety. You really didn't know we're Behavioural Therapists? I'm Ms Stern, the dominatrix, and Mam's the straight one. Mam gave you the first treatment last night just as a warmer-up, and I was supposed to give you the full treatment tonight, that's why she went out. When you were disappointed that she wouldn't be here I thought you wanted a threesome. I was going to phone her, she'll be waiting down at the pub after she's finished her home visit.'

I was speechless; stunned into incredulity. So my great seduction scene the previous evening, fuelled by steak and kidney pie, had all been a set-up. It wasn't my wit and charm that had seduced her, it was me that was being processed as phase one of a commercial deal! That really boosted the old self-confidence, that did!

Tracey looked up wistfully at me. 'We like you, you know, you're a nice guy and we don't get many of those in here. Most of 'em are the same as that bastard Withers with his dressing up as a schoolgirl, and he really gets it.'

I winced as I thought of the big muscles in her strong right arm. It served the sod right. I hoped she drew blood.

'Oh – so that's how you persuaded him to sign the consent forms.'

She laughed 'Of course! He wouldn't want that to get out, would he?' She put a hand on my arm. 'I don't suppose you'd like to finish off what we started in the woods without the school room? I could let you have it at more than the usual discount.'

I shook my head. Enough was enough for one evening. I needed time to get my head round all this.

'No thanks, that's very kind of you but I think I'll turn in. I've got a long day tomorrow.'

'Well maybe another time,' she replied, looking slightly crestfallen.

She closed the door on the schoolroom and turned to her bedroom. I wished her good night and, with a faint feeling of regret, went into my bedroom. In spite of what she was and did, I couldn't help but like her, she was naturally friendly; but if the boys in the Frog and Nightgown ever got even the slightest whiff of what had gone on here I'd be doomed.

As I lay awake trying to restore some of my battered self-confidence, I began to wonder about the discount. Was it two for the price of one? Get one now, get one later? Or ten per cent off for the over sixties on Wednesdays, like B & Q?

It was while I was turning this over in my mind that I had a brilliant idea. It came in a flash and I examined all the implications but couldn't see a flaw. That didn't mean there wasn't one – Moon plans often produced unforeseen flaws – but this time I just knew this Moon plan could be a winner.

'Yes!' I exclaimed. It was countermeasures time!

I turned over and slid off to sleep with a big smile.

The next morning over breakfast I told Susan Tripp that my colleague Ivan Masterland would be coming to stay for a couple of nights sometime soon and could she book him in for the same room. She gave me that wide-eyed look and a strange smile and said there wouldn't be any problem. Trying hard not to laugh, I told her he'd definitely want the full service. She said that in that case, I should sort out the details with Tracey.

Finishing my coffee, I went upstairs to pack my bag. I met Tracey on the landing.

'Before I go, can I have a word with you about a friend of mine who's coming to stay?'

'Business or pleasure?' she asked.

'Oh, for you business, for him transportation into the wonderful world of ecstasy.'

'We don't do drugs!'

'Forget that: come out to the car with me and we'll sort out the details.'

I wanted to get back to London before lunch and this meant an early start. As I was saying a tongue-in-cheek thanks and goodbye to Susan, she said, 'What about the bill?'

I replied offhandedly, 'Oh, just send it on to CONDES marked "For the Accounts Section". They pay promptly.'

'Shall I just put it down as "Extras" then?'

'Extras?'

Her face took on a businesslike look. 'Yes,' she replied. 'It's sixty pounds a night for dinner and the room, and we usually charge a hundred and forty pounds for the extras. Staying guests get a twenty per cent discount but as you didn't use our services last night, you can have it for half price.'

My self-confidence took another nosedive.

'Ah!' I replied thoughtfully, thinking 'Skin' Flint in accounts would not be happy about seventy pounds for 'extras'. He'd be even less happy if he knew what the extras entailed! Then I suddenly remembered Bob Barclay asking me to keep an eye open for possible development sites.

'Put it down to "Providing Advice about Local Development Sites",' I told her with a weak smile.

Business completed, Tracey followed me out to the car, which gave me the opportunity to begin setting up Moon Plan A.

'Tracey, there's one other very important thing,' I told her. 'This guy Ivan, who's coming to stay for a couple of days, is an old friend. It's his birthday soon and I want to give him a surprise treat.'

'What sort of treat? Do you mean a "business" treat?'

I took her by the arm; I could feel her biceps rippling under my hand. I was starting to feel sorry for Ivan already.

'Well, he did confide in me that he loves a bit of bondage, particularly being dressed up in leather or rubber, but he's had very little opportunity, he's too shy to go to a club or whatever. Have you got any of that kind of gear?'

She nodded. 'We've got all kinds.'

'He told me that his greatest fantasy is to be awakened in the night, dragged out of bed by a beautiful woman, gagged, dressed up, tied up and then given a really good flogging. He said the thought of that really turns him on. He dreams about it all the time.'

I alleviated my conscience by thinking that he might well have done, judging by his porno mags. I let the question hang in the air.

Tracey caught on immediately. 'You mean you'd like us to do that in our professional capacity?'

I didn't want to over-egg the pudding so I replied, 'Well I'm sure it's what he'd really enjoy.' I could see her turning over the idea in her mind, so to encourage her I added: 'He's a bit thin and hairy, like a human spider. He's one of those grumpy, bad-tempered little sods ....chaps, who can take a lot of pain, but beneath all that he has a heart of gold. You'd be doing him a big favour.' I held my breath wondering if I'd blown it.

She made up her mind; I think she liked the idea of getting a feeble male helpless in the dark and whacking the daylights out of him.

'But who's going to pay for this? We'd charge at least a hundred and fifty pounds up front for that sort of service.'

I gulped, not being experienced in these matters. It sounded a lot of money to me; more than I expected. I hadn't considered this aspect of Moon Plan A. Obviously Ivan wasn't going to cough up a hundred and fifty crisp ones up front for something he didn't know was coming – and would be even less likely to if he did!

'I will, it'll be my birthday treat for him,' I explained. 'But what about the discount?'

'OK,' she acknowledged, 'let's say a hundred.'

I accepted that. 'Don't forget, it mustn't leak out otherwise it'll spoil his fantasy. It's got to be a surprise birthday treat so I'll give you the money now.'

I sighed as I peeled the notes from the thin wad in my wallet. It was going to have to be beans on toast for the next week or two at the Moon residence I thought, as I handed over five twenties. However, I was going to ensure that I got my money's worth.

'He likes it laid on really hard,' I emphasised as I slid into the driver's seat of the MG. 'Remember that!'

Tracey took a card out of her purse and handed it to me. 'In case you change your mind and want to book an appointment for yourself,' she said with a cheeky grin.

It read 'Miss Stern – Behavioural Therapist' and gave a mobile phone number. I slipped it into my jeans pocket.

I started the engine and drove off with a satisfied grin on my face. That should settle Ivan's hash for a few months. Moon Plan A had been set in motion.

I drove first to Geophysical Drilling's compound to give John Bailey Withers' signed permission to access his land, and confirmed the positions of the test bores for the bridge and tunnel.

'How did you manage that?' he exclaimed with surprise. 'I assume it's safe for my guys to go on his land now.'

'No problem,' I smiled cheerily. 'It's all a matter of personality, you know. Some of us have it and some don't. After we'd had a little chat I think he saw the futility of his objections.'

Disbelief was written all over Bailey's face but the paper he held in his hand contradicted his thoughts and he just shook his head.

I made it to the office by twelve-fifteen. Neither Des nor Ivan were in, so I had half an hour's peace to write up my report for Hugo before going down to the canteen for a quick lunch. On the way down I passed Angela in the corridor.

'How were the digs in Kingscastle?' she asked curiously. There was no guile in her eyes, so it didn't seem to be a loaded question.

'Great! The food was good, the room was comfortable and the landlady very accommodating.' I grinned at the thought. 'By the way, what made you pick Mrs Tripp's place?'

She shrugged. 'I don't know, it just sounded more interesting than the other ads. I think it was the home cooking.'

'It was certainly interesting,' I replied with a straight face. 'And her steak and kidney pie was superb.'

'In that case I'll definitely book Ivan in when he goes down there,' she said with a slightly puzzled frown.

To cement the arrangement I told her, 'I've already mentioned it to the landlady so she'll be expecting your call.'

'You seem remarkably pleased with yourself today, Marcus,' Angela remarked, looking at me questioningly, but I just strolled on with fingers crossed.

That night when I undressed and emptied the pockets of my jeans as usual, amongst the handkerchief, coins and keys was the sharp flat stone that had been frustrating my access to Tracey Tripp's tits. On closer inspection there was a glint of metal showing at one corner. I tossed it into a drawer, intending to examine it later, and then forgot all about it.

CHAPTER SEVEN

Mrs Gloria Withington-Lombard's 'Publicity Committee' met
in the sumptuous lounge of the Withington-Lombard's large
mock Tudor house on Blueberry Hill to review the situation
the Wednesday after the Town Hall meeting. The house commanded a fine view over the rolling countryside. Gloria was a
thin, ascetic-looking *grand-dame*: swept-back, thick silver hair
immaculately coiffed; parchment-like skin drawn tightly over
a fine facial bone structure; piercing blue eyes and a voice that
could slice cucumbers razor thin. She had assembled a formidable group of women to form her committee.

Tea and scones were served by Gwendoline, the maid hired
for the day from Betty's Cake Shop in the High Street.

Mrs Royce, well-fed, rosy and jolly, the wife of a prominent
local farmer, said wouldn't it be a good idea if they did something like the Railston Women's Institute and produced a topless
calendar? She would be happy to take part as it was for a good
cause, as long as it was discreet. They could use fruit and vegetables to hide any naughty bits.

Miss Pring, who was deputy director of Social Services at
the Town Hall, observed acidly that they would need a couple of

very large melons to conceal what Mrs Royce had on offer.

Mrs Royce retorted that two glacé cherries would do for the skinny Miss Pring.

'A stick of celery would hide all of her' chuckled Mrs Hartley.

'You keep out of this!' snapped Miss Pring. 'You'd need a cabbage to cover your big mouth.'

'Cucumbers,' murmured Shirley Williamson dreamily. 'Lots of cucumbers and bananas.'

Mrs Craddock, the greengrocer's wife, cut in sharply, 'Yes, we all know what you've been up to ever since your old man ran off with the vicar's bit of stuff. Disgusting I call it!' She paused and glanced round the room. 'Has anybody seen her around, by the way?'

There had indeed been no sign of the dark-haired, sloe-eyed Mrs Furrow, formerly Ong Wan Koon of The Pussy Club, Bangkok. The Reverend Percy Furrow, meek and mild vicar of the local church, had met her whilst on a cut-price trip to the Far East that he had won as first prize at the Town Fair the previous year for looking most like his dog – a Shih Tzu. He had flown back to England three weeks later, with a big smile, a pale face and a brand new bride.

'She wouldn't dare show up,' observed Mrs Craddock. 'Besides, she only knows three words of English and two of those begin with F. Mind you, she would add some glamour to a calendar if we were to do one,' she added thoughtfully as she tucked into her third scone.

The leather-jacketed, short-haired Ms Deakin, deputy head-mistress of the local comprehensive school, fingered her moustache and observed with a wistful smile, 'I wouldn't mind seeing her in the buff.' But then she remembered with bitter disappointment that she had been lining up the vicar's wife herself before Doug Williamson slid in quietly and beat her to the punch, and her face hardened.

Mrs Withington-Lombard sensed that the meeting was sliding from her grasp. She reluctantly eyed up the last scone with cream and strawberry jam, and then rapped smartly with a teaspoon on the side of her china cup.

'Ladies, ladies, please!'

The room quietened immediately. You provoked the Chairwoman of the Women's Institute at your peril if you wanted to be in the running for a prize at the next Town Fair. Mrs Royce recalled getting only 'Third prize without Rosette' for her baked ham with honey and cloves two years ago for interrupting Mrs Withington-Lombard as she read out the minutes of the last WI meeting. That humiliation had lasted a whole year before she received slight forgiveness by being awarded the crocheted traycloth 'Blue Ribbon' the following June.

Mrs Withington-Lombard began. 'Let us concentrate on the job in hand first. Mrs Royce's idea of a calendar is a good one and we will follow that up later.' She bestowed a beam of approval on Mrs Royce, who nearly wet herself with pleasure at having her acceptance back into the fold so publicly acknowledged. Mrs W-L continued: 'Our job is to produce the placards, pamphlets, letters, etcetera to create the maximum impact on the Government to get the by-pass moved away from Hickling Edge. Now, has anybody got any other ideas?'

Ms Deakin, still smarting as she thought of how that swine Doug Williamson had spiked her guns over seducing the vicar's wife before she had a chance, transferred all her anger to men in general.

'They're bound to send people to Kingscastle; why don't we capture them, strip them, tar and feather them and send them back with notices fastened to their chests saying "Move the By-pass". It's a surefire way of delivering placards, and bound to get attention in the national press and TV.'

'Yes, that's a brilliant idea,' Miss Pring chipped in, and Mrs Williamson backed her up.

Mrs Withington-Lombard turned the idea down flat. 'I don't really think so, Ms Deakin; wouldn't that be common assault? We could be in serious trouble if we physically attacked somebody, particularly if they were from the Government. No, we have to stick within the law.'

Miss Pring and Mrs Williamson were also seriously off men at that moment; well, Mrs Williamson was – Miss Pring, like Ms Deakin, had never actually been 'on men', either physically or metaphorically. Their disappointment was obvious and they looked at each other and then across at Ms Deakin, who just smiled knowingly.

Mrs W-L continued. 'Our banner and poster campaign doesn't seem to have made much impact; there's been a few letters in the

Bugle but nothing in the nationals or on the TV. Molestrangler raised the matter in Parliament but it only produced the usual smooth evasion that all would be made clear at the Public Enquiry. That's due to start in October, by the way.' She glanced down at some notes. 'Harry Bell has had the most impact by blocking the A399 with tractors for an afternoon until the police threatened to arrest them all. He tried to organise a couple of busloads of locals to go to London and march down Whitehall – we had the placards printed for them, but at fifteen pounds a head for the coaches to transport them, nobody turned up on the morning so he had to cancel it.'

She pursed her lips in a gesture of disdain. 'Robin Threadle managed to get a letter into *Country Life* pointing out that the shooting of pheasants and partridges along and close to the new road in the forthcoming shooting season would be severely disrupted for years to come. Foxes, deer, badgers and other mammals would flee the area never to return, and the habitat of the lesser warbling marsh bobbit, one of only six in the country, could be destroyed when any ponds where they nest are drained. Not unexpectedly, this didn't galvanise the nation either.'

She paused thoughtfully. That scone with the cream and strawberry jam still lay untouched.

'The Major has organised another MOVE THE BYPASS meeting at the Town Hall next week, so I suggest we wait and see if a concerted plan emerges from that before we do anything more, unless anybody has any other suggestions?'

Miss Pring, Mrs Williamson and Ms Deakin, glanced at each other again and shook their heads.

'I declare this meeting closed then,' Mrs Withington-Lombard announced, just as Mrs Craddock reached over and whipped the remaining scone on to her plate, unknowingly condemning herself to frosty isolation at the next Women's Institute meeting and only a 'Commended' for her roly-poly pudding at the next Town Fair.

*****

It was unseasonably cold for early August when the undercarriage of Loganair flight LOG 392 from Inverness bounced on the runway at Kirkwall. All the oil rig workers were muffled up against a biting wind that whistled in across the North Sea, but Ivan was dressed in summer gear for appearing in court. It was his fifth visit to the granite slab that housed the Orkney courtrooms, and he hoped like hell it would be the last.

On the walk to the terminal the wind sliced through his Italian cotton suit like a knife through butter. The warmth of the small building was a welcome relief. His overnight bag appeared as the last one on the carousel and by then the few taxis had all been taken. He glanced around nervously. On his last visit to Orkney, Maira's father, a very large, muscular, craggy-faced sheep farmer, had threatened to 'rip yerr fuckin' heed off, yerr Sassenach weasel' if he didn't do 'the reacht thing' and walk his daughter up the aisle 'the noo'. Ivan had thought it safer to stay overnight in Inverness this time, and he intended a quick, anonymous run from the airport to the court in Kirkwall, undetected by deranged fathers.

Today was the day when the DNA results from the tests in Glasgow would reveal the truth about Maira's off-spring, and it cannot be said that Ivan was over-confident he would get the thumbs up, even though the odds were stacked in his favour.

He decided that rather than take the bus, he would wait until another taxi turned up. It was a long wait and, as a result, he was stressed up to the eyeballs, and only just made it in time for the hearing.

As he entered the small courtroom, flustered and out of breath, he saw there were only a few spectators, most of them gaining some respite from the wind outside. But he was conscious of all eyes following him as he took a seat on a bench at the front next to his very relieved advocate.

Two of the pairs of eyes were distinctly hostile and, glancing round, he was aware that just across the aisle were a scrubbed-up Maira, clutching a very ugly looking infant, and her father, scowling ferociously. The infant was being held in a prominent position to emphasise its presence and, with a spurt of alarm, Ivan noted that it had an uncanny facial resemblance to him. He looked again to make sure. Its dark hair had been combed forward like his, its eyebrows were black – and was that a trace of a black beard and moustache? There was certainly a dark shadow under its snotty nose and round its chin that gave the impression of hair.

The pathologist from Glasgow was called to give evidence and it was with enormous relief that Ivan heard him state categorically that there was no correlation between Ivan's DNA and that of Maira's 'wee wain' and thus Ivan was definitely not the father.

The angry sheep farmer was not pacified at all by this and leapt to his feet, shouting, 'Aye but the snittelling Sassenach bastard was co-habiting wi' ma wee girl, leading her into wicked ways. He should be forced to wed the poor destitute thing. Who will tend the wee bairn noo?' And he gesticulated towards Ivan, clenching his huge fists.

The Sheriff pointed out that it was not the responsibility of the court to force people to marry each other; that was a private matter between the parties.

'Aye,' growled the farmer, glaring at Ivan and stabbing a finger the size of a haggis towards him. 'Well, we'll be havin' words aboot that afterwards, make no doot about that, yer weaselly clootie!'

There being no other points at issue, the Sheriff ruled that the child's father was a person or persons unknown. The irony of the plural escaped everybody, especially Ivan, as other matters intruded in his brain now.

The court cleared and Ivan faced a quandary. He had no doubt that that ogre of a farmer and his equally fearsome daughter would be lying in wait outside the courthouse door: his flight back to Inverness wasn't until 3.30pm, and that meant he had three hours to kill. He thought of asking for police protection but rejected that idea, assuming that the police would naturally side with the local man. The only thing he could think of was to lock himself in one of the cubicles of the court lavatories and wait the time out. He slid out into the entrance hall and went down a corridor to the gents'. Slipping into a cubicle and bolting the door firmly, he sat down on the toilet lid to think about his next step.

It was quiet, but he suddenly realised that he could hear voices from the street outside. By standing on the toilet seat and easing the small window open further, he could just see the entrance steps to the court. The farmer was waiting there with Maira and the child, accompanied by another equally large hairy man. He heard the hairy giant say, 'He's no come oot this way. The bastard must have got awa' from the back. The next flight to 'Ness isn't till three-thirty so let's grab him at the airyport.' And the four of them set off round the corner.

That threw Ivan into a panic. There was no way he was going near the airport now, and he certainly didn't want to stay overnight in a small place like Kirkwall, where he would be easy to find. Then he remembered from his original sojourn in Orkney that there was an afternoon ferry from Stromness to Scrabster on the north coast of Scotland – if he could get to Stromness in time. He waited as long as he dared and then made a quick dash from the court main entrance to the taxi rank. He heard a bellow of rage from way down the street and saw the farmer break into a clumsy gallop, but by then he had the taxi door open and had piled in, gasping, 'Stromness please, as fast as you can!'

Orkney taxi drivers don't shoot off like a rocket with wheel spin and burning rubber and the farmer was barely ten metres away when the driver eventually managed to stir the gear lever into first gear and eased away from the curb. Fortunately the road led downhill and so the taxi gained speed rapidly, leaving the farmer shaking his fist and mouthing curses.

'Noo where is it ye want to gae so quick? The airyport?'

'No, no, the ferry at Stromness.'

'Och ye should ha said so, it's the other way.'

Ivan was just about to berate the man for his stupidity when he recognised the lifeline.

'Can you turn round without going back through the town?'

'Och aye. But it's a longer way roond to Stro'ness. It'll cost ye more.'

'Well do it then, I'll pay the extra.'

The taxi driver wasn't that stupid either. His narrow eyes gleamed at the thought of the extra money he could make by running this Sassenach round the country lanes.

Ivan sank back in the seat. That should fool the farmer and his tribe, they would be convinced he was heading to the airport and would rush off in the opposite direction from Stromness. He relaxed for the first time that day, until he realised that he'd left his overnight bag with all his kit, including his air ticket to Inverness and on to London, at the courtroom.

He cursed under his breath, but there was no way he was going back into Kirkwall. He was off the hook at long last and, provided he made the ferry in time, he doubted very much whether

Maira or her fearsome father would cross his path again. He patted his pocket to make sure his wallet was safe and breathed a sigh of relief when he felt its bulk.

Agatha would naturally forget all about this baby drama now he had been proved innocent. It would never be mentioned again and their engagement would survive.

How little Ivan knew about women!

*****

I was just enjoying a bit of peace in the office, with Ivan away sorting out his problem and Des presumably drowning a few flies in the waters round Grimthorpe, when Hugo strolled in carrying a piece of paper.

'Ah Marcus, the very man!'

Now I can detect a nasty, cunning plan concealed in somebody's treacly voice at ten paces, when they are about to dump a piece information on me that isn't calculated to light up my day – particularly when they're carrying a piece of paper. My antennae told me that 'Ah Marcus, the very man' was the precursor for such a dumping. But there was no escape, so I waited apprehensively.

'The Ministry have just phoned to say that they're getting worried about the increasing pressure coming from this MOVE THE BYPASS protest group.'

'Are they?' I said innocently. 'But what's that got to do with us?'

'I'm glad you asked me that because there's to be a public meeting tomorrow morning in Kingscastle Town Hall at ten-thirty, and they want somebody who knows something about the bypass to go and answer any technical questions that may arise – unofficially, you understand. It might take the pressure off them because they feel that misunderstandings have crept in about the proposal.'

I cast my mind around desperately for who else could go but it was clear that there were only two people – Hugo or me. And it was even clearer which of the two it was going to be.

'It'll be a doddle,' he grinned. 'Just answer the questions in your normal calm logical way and you'll have no problems. I'll leave some briefing notes, and I've asked the design office to do a couple of presentation drawings if you need to explain anything. I'll let the Town Clerk know that you're coming.'

With that he patted me on the shoulder and pushed off. It was the pat that finally convinced me. It was the sort of encouraging pat you gave somebody when you told them to keep their chin up just before they had their leg cut off without anaesthetic.

*****

Miss Pring was attending a meeting with other council officials to decide how many extra staff they needed to take on to implement their efficiency programme when the message came through that the Ministry were sending somebody to the MOVE THE BYPASS meeting at the Town Hall the following day. She hurriedly excused herself for a minute and rushed to her office to telephone Ms Deakin at the school. Unfortunately Ms Deakin was teaching at that moment so Miss Pring had to leave a message for her to ring back. She hesitated about phoning Mrs Williamson. Ever since her husband had run off with the vicar's wife, she had been a bit peculiar. There was nothing for it, however; Miss Pring had no choice because time was short.

It turned out Mrs Wlliamson was at home so she was given precise instructions about what to get. Tar was very unlikely to be available at such short notice so Mrs Williamson was told to buy as much black treacle as she could. Also, if she didn't have any feather-filled pillows or duvets, she was to find someone who did, or buy some. That being settled, Miss Pring returned to her meeting.

'Still having trouble with the old waterworks, Marilyn?' murmured the Borough Engineer as she resumed her seat. 'It's your age, you know. You can get those absorbent pants these days; they've got elastic round the legs so it doesn't trickle down! They can hold a couple of pints, apparently.'

She flushed scarlet and hissed savagely at him, 'No I'm not! – and you can shut your revolting face for a start, Peter Ashman!'

For the rest of the meeting she seethed quietly, torn between devising some form of revenge on the BE and anxiety to get the meeting over so she could start planning their attack on the Ministry's man.

Miss Pring was definitely off men now. The Borough Engineer, not having been struck down by a lightning bolt from above or consumed by the fires of hell from below, and thus surviving unpunished, had ensured that.

At a break between lessons, Ms Deakin returned the phone call to a still furious Miss Pring, who updated her on the situation.

'What we need is something to tie the swine up with. He's hardly going to stand patiently by while we cover him in treacle and feathers, is he?'

Ms Deakin was caught in two minds. She had a solution but wasn't sure about advancing it.

'I think I might be able to lay my hands on a set of handcuffs and a gag.'

I'll bet you can, thought Miss Pring, probably fur-lined if I know you. But she just said,

'Great, bring them along to the meeting at my house at six-thirty this evening. I'll get some rope and a bag for his head. We can use the Williamson man's van. He's still shacked up some-where with Mrs Furrow so there's not much he can do about it, and Shirley won't mind.'

Ms Deakin smirked. 'Are we going to strip him naked?' she asked hopefully.

*****

I'd collected all the stuff I'd need – drawings, my notes and Hugo's brief – and made an early start, planning to get to Kingscastle well before ten-thirty to assess the lie of the land. I pushed a note under Mrs Aberdeen's door saying I'd look in when I got back that afternoon and went down to the car.

There wasn't any problem with the traffic and I arrived in Kingscastle with time to spare. I squeezed the MG into a slot marked 'Reserved for Social Services' next to an old white van bearing the logo 'D. Williamson, Builder', and wandered into the Town Hall. All the seating had been set out in the hall itself and there was a long table on the platform with name cards in front of each chair. I noticed with a shiver that Major Sir Fistulas Withers MBE [Military] was to chair the meeting.

A quiet voice from behind me asked, 'Can I help you?'

I turned and beheld a spruce man of medium height with an enquiring look on his round and pleasant face.

'I'm from CONDES, the consultants for the bypass. I was asked to attend to answer any technical questions that might arise.'

'Mr Moon, is it?' He offered his hand, which I shook. 'I'm the Town Clerk. Richard Alderson. Your Mr Elmes phoned me to say you'd be representing the Ministry, and he asked me to arrange some boards for you to pin up drawings.'

I had noticed that there wasn't a named place for me on the platform. 'Where do you want me to sit?' I asked.

He pointed to the side of the stage where there was a sort of wooden box with a rail round it, and a microphone. I noticed, with a feeling of doom, that it looked as though they'd borrowed the dock from the local magistrates' court for the occasion. Obviously the platform didn't want me anywhere near them in case violence broke out and missiles were thrown. Thanks again, Hugo!

'Come into my office and have a cup of coffee. I'll get Jack to pin up your plans – I see you've brought some.' He pointed to the roll under my arm.

I followed him through a side door and into a comfortably furnished room that appeared both busy and neat. Mr Alderson looked as though he was on top of his job.

'We want this bypass, you know, the town needs it. We're being strangled with the traffic and it's affecting business,' he murmured with a frown. 'There's just a strong objection from certain quarters that's swung a lot of the locals against it.'

'Sir Fistulas Withers?'

He gave a quiet smile. 'Just so.'

Coffee arrived and he poured me a cup. We chatted about the need for the road and he gave me a full account of last year's shambles when the big 'artic' got stuck on the corner. The building work to repair Norfolk and Chance's office had only just been completed, and Mr Norfolk and Ms Golightly from 'Mother Wouldn't Like It' boutique were suing everybody in sight.

We could hear the sound of feet, voices increasing and the scraping of chairs as the hall filled up. Richard glanced at his watch.

'We'd better go now. Good luck!'

'Isn't it "Break a leg" that they say in the theatre?' I replied with more confidence than I felt. In fact a broken leg at this moment seemed preferable to facing Withers and his cohorts. To my surprise and relief, nobody took much notice as I climbed up into my box. Jack, whoever he was, had pinned up the large-scale coloured up drawings showing the route of the proposed road and the outline of the land take required. The audience chatted amongst themselves, leaving me to scan the contents of the high table.

They looked a formidable bunch: Withers was seated in the middle between a *grande dame* who went by the name of Lady Mountdurand. Her huge liver-spotted wattles were festooned with gold jewellery. On his other side sat an aristocratic looking long-nosed body in a purple shirt with his handkerchief stuffed up his sleeve. His name card read 'Anthony Molestrangler MP'. There was a chap who looked like a small dog wearing a clerical collar (I couldn't read his name), and at the end nearest to me another *grande dame*', one Mrs Withington-Lombard, a thin ascetic looking woman with blue gimlet eyes.

Withers rapped on the table with a gavel and eventually managed to get the hall to quieten down.

'We are gathered here this morning...'

'Yes, we know why we're here, Loppylugs, get on with it!' Shouted a familiar voice.

Withers glared in the direction of the heckler. 'Any more of that and I'll have you removed from the building.'

'You and whose army?' was the unabashed reply.

I brightened up; perhaps this wasn't going to be as bad as I'd anticipated. A punch-up between the audience and the platform would distract any attention that either of them might focus on me.

Withers ignored that and ploughed on. He introduced the top table, which produced some more heckling, and then pointed ominously in my direction.

'We have forced the Government to send a representative down to Kingscastle today to account for their outrageous behaviour, and there he stands before you. We asked for the Secretary of State himself, or at least a top civil servant, but they have seen fit to add more insult to injury by sending some junior engineer who goes by the name of Moon.'

All eyes swivelled towards me, perhaps more with interest than hostility, so I just nodded and gave a smile as tight as I hoped my sphincter was.

Withers then gave a rambling discourse about noise, dust, lorry traffic, crime, air pollution, all building up to what he clearly considered to be his trump card: the hideous damage that would be caused to the landscape, especially Hickling Edge.

'A vast slash through this beautiful and historic feature!' he emphasised. 'The pride of Kingscastle, land for which our ancestors gave their blood, sweat and tears; all would be ruined for ever if this monstrous road was permitted. To propose such a thing is an insulting outrage; to force it upon us without consultation is a contemptuous kick in the teeth. So what are we going to do about it?'

'Fuck all!' shouted another voice.

Withers ignored it, he was in full flow. 'I'll tell you what we're going to do about it. We're going to act – and that minion can take back to the Ministry the information that we aren't going to take this lying down.'

The heckler called out, 'No, the reporter from the *Kingscastle Bugle* is doing that.'

This did galvanise the audience to chuckle, but there were also nasty glances thrown in my direction with a few fingers pointed and angry mutterings.

I stood up. Strangely, I had a microphone and Withers didn't; perhaps Kingscastle criminals were softly spoken. So when I said, 'Mr Chairman, I think I should say something at this time to correct a misapprehension that everybody here seems to be under—' I blanked him out.

Withers interrupted me. 'I haven't finished yet so sit down until you're invited to speak!'

'Let him speak,' shouted the heckler. 'He's got to be a bloody sight more interesting than you!'

Other voices joined in, in support, and so I continued to stay on my feet. I turned to the audience.

'We are *not* proposing to put a vast slash through Hickling Edge, as your Chairman claims. There won't be a cutting. If you look at this drawing here,' I pointed to the boards, 'you'll note that the line of the road where it encounters Hickling Edge is dotted.'

I liked a bit of drama, and as I had the audience's full attention now, I paused to bestow a smile upon Withers.

'You see, Chairman, we are acutely aware of the environment and the damage to it a deep cutting would inflict, so we're proposing to put the road in twin tunnels through Hickling Edge. The tunnel portals will be slightly recessed into the hill so, apart from motorists actually travelling along the bypass, nothing will be visible from either side and the scenery will be preserved. Kingscastle will have the bypass it so desperately needs and wants and your landscape will be unspoilt. The other big advantage of tunnelling is that the amount of excavation, and thus the number of lorries using the roads during construction, will be substantially reduced – as will pollution from noise, dust and mud.'

Withers stood there with his mouth open, his main argument destroyed. There was an audible sigh of relief from the audience and then a babble of voices as everybody started talking to each other.

The first heckler called out, 'So what have you got to say about that, Loppylugs?'

'But what about my land?' shouted Withers, going red in the face and banging on the table with his gavel. 'It's still going to cross my land!'

But he had lost his support. Even the top table could be seen to distance themselves from him.

Lady Mountdurand, still miffed at being outmanoeuvred for the Chair of the Finance and General Purposes Committee, snapped, 'Well, it's got to go somewhere and hidden in your woods is as good a place as any!'

Withers threw in his last argument. 'The Shering Valley? What about our beautiful valley?' he cried.

That produced a momentary lull in the chatter so, speaking into the microphone, I said that we were very conscious of the beauty of that valley. The bridge across the Shering Valley will be designed in full consultation with the Kingscastle authorities, I assured them, and should enhance the landscape rather than destroy it.

The smiles returned to all the faces, except Withers', who slumped back in his seat, defeated.

'That seemed to go quite well,' the Town Clerk observed as I unpinned the drawings. I nodded and gave him a weak smile. The feeling of triumph was beginning to diminish as realism crept back into my mind.

Meanwhile. the three witches – Miss Pring, Ms Deakin and Mrs Williamson – seeing their treacle and feathering plan in ruins now, slid out of the hall in disappointment, climbed into the white van and drove away.

As I drove back to London the uncomfortable feeling in my water grew stronger. Maybe I'd over-egged the pudding a bit in my enthusiasm to wrongfoot Withers – well quite a lot actually. The proposed tunnel solution seemed to have been embraced as a *fait accompli* saviour by the townspeople, whereas it was still only a proposal. None of the 'powers that be' who would make the final decision, had agreed to driving tunnels under Hickling Edge. Most of them were not even aware of the idea.

My only hope was that Ivan would go along with it.

CHAPTER EIGHT

On Wednesday morning as I went up the stairs to the first floor, I passed Awful Agatha coming down. I said hello but she cut me dead. What was all that about? I thought as I wandered into the office. Des looked up from doing *The Times* crossword and greeted me with a broad grin.

'You're in deep shit, dear boy, right up to your chin.'

'Well, don't look so cheerful about it! What's the problem?' I said nervously, racking my brains to se if I'd committed a homosexual act or had sex in the office – or, even worse, committed a homosexual act in the office. As far as I could recall, I hadn't.

'Ivan's back from Orkney. He's solved his problem, he's definitely not the father of the infant and he's really pissed off with you; in fact he's stormed along to see Arbuthnot to make an official complaint.'

'Why Arbuthnot?'

'Hugo's at that Concrete Society conference for the whole of this week.'

'Complaint about what?'

'About you arbitrarily changing his road scheme whilst he was away.'

'But I haven't! It's exactly the same as it was when he left it.'

'No it ain't! The line might be the same but you've put it in tunnels through Hickling Edge and removed his cutting.'

'Yes, so it's a better design. It's quietened down the protest movement and should give the Ministry an easier ride through the Public Enquiry.'

'He don't think so, dear boy. Mind you, I've got to agree with you – it's a much better solution but you've trampled all over his pride. I told you he was ambitious; he thinks you've done it deliberately to show him up. He wants the firm to fire you.'

'Stupid sod! I did no such thing. I didn't even think about that. Anyway, I discussed it with Hugo and he sort of said go ahead.'

'Well I just thought I'd warn you.'

'So what now, Des?' I asked nervously.

'Arbuthnot's no fool; he's going to consider what's best for the project and for CONDES, whatever Ivan says. I should just wait. What's a seven-letter word beginning with P for "In the dock or in the hotel"?'

'Pillock' was the word that sprang to my mind, but Des suddenly cried, 'Ah, Portman!' and pencilled it in five across.

I sat at my desk chewing a fingernail for a few minutes and then the phone rang. Joanna just said, 'Can you come and see Mr Geoffrey immediately, Marcus.' It wasn't a question.

I trooped up the stairs and along the corridor to Geoffrey Arbuthnot's office. Joanna ushered me through with a sympathetic smile. Arbuthnot was sitting behind his desk twiddling a pencil and a pink-faced Ivan, pulsating with visible rage, sat rigidly on the edge of one of his guest chairs. Arbuthnot motioned me to the other one. There was no beating about the bush, it was straight in.

'Masterland tells me that Elmes made him responsible for the road on the Kingscastle bypass and that you've deliberately changed his design whilst he was away to show him in a bad light.'

I looked at Ivan, astonished that he would say that to Arbuthnot. Was that really how he saw it?

'That's not so, sir,' I replied, 'I changed the cutting through Hickling Edge into twin tunnels because I thought it was better both aesthetically and environmentally. I discussed it with Mr Elmes and, if you will recall, got some advice from Sir Gordon Proctor about tunnelling costs.'

Arbuthnot nodded. 'But let me ask you three questions, Moon. The first is: do you confirm that Elmes appointed Masterland here as the engineer in charge of the road.'

'Well yes, sir, he did.'

'The second is, are twin tunnels cheaper than a cutting?'

'Well no they're not, but—'

'No "ifs" and "buts", Moon! The third question is – has the client, in this case the Department of Transport and Communications, approved the idea of tunnels?'

My heart sank. 'Well no, the tunnels are more expensive but—'

'Just answer the questions!'

I sighed. 'No, sir, the tunnels are more expensive. They add about four per cent to the cost of the bypass; and yes, the fact that we were looking into tunnelling has been mentioned to the Ministry but they've not specifically been asked to approve it yet.'

Arbuthnot put his fingers to his lips. 'You are aware, are you not, that CONDES only employs the best people? You are also aware that it is a policy of this firm to give our senior engineers responsibility for deciding the design parameters on the projects they are given – subject to approval by a partner? And finally, you are aware that Masterland has been given the responsibility for the road and so it's up to him to decide whether or not to incorporate tunnels or a cutting, and not up to you?'

I nodded miserably. 'I suppose so.'

'So you should not have changed the design while he was away and without his approval. Fortunately no harm's been done, except to Masterland's blood pressure, and I trust that the matter is now settled. I emphasise, however, that your action in this matter verges on the edge of being unprofessional and we do not condone such behaviour in this firm, so please make sure it doesn't happen again. You are a bit of an oddball, Moon. I shall be keeping a close eye on you in future; a very close eye.'

We walked back to our office, Ivan strutting along with a broad smirk on his face, and me with my future prospects hanging by a thread as well as an awful sinking feeling about the consequences arising from what I had told the public meeting in Kingscastle - of which Arbuthnot was blissfully unaware.

I turned to Ivan. 'Look, Ivan, I'm sorry if you think I was trying to up-stage you but that wasn't the case. I thought twin tunnels were the best solution in view of the strong strength of local feeling against the potential damage to the environment a cutting would cause. I did discuss it with—'

He cut me off there savagely. 'I don't care what you or the local yokels thought! It's my project and I make the decisions, so just mind your own business and stick to the bridges in future.'

After that he refused to talk to me, and when I tried to explain about the public meeting he just put his hands over his ears and chanted 'La la, la la, la la.' So I left him to it.

He changed the route through Hickling Edge back to a deep cutting.

When Hugo got back, I took him my design for the Shering Valley Bridge to see what he thought about it. He looked at it carefully and then said, 'I like the form, very elegant, but it's a bit thin for heavy motorway traffic, isn't it?'

I could see his point because it wasn't the normal motorway bridge; but then it wasn't intended to be. I explained my thinking.

'From an aesthetic point of view I've tried to make it appear as slender as possible so that it enhances the landscape rather than intrudes upon it. I've managed to keep the depth down by using a form of cross lattice post-tensioning.'

Hugo frowned. 'That something new, isn't it? I've not heard of that being used for bridges.'

'I've run it through the computer twice and then independently. I asked Dennis Menzies if he would check it out. All three answers were almost identical, it does work.'

Hugo smiled. 'OK then, but I want to check it too. However, for the time being you can go ahead.'

*****

Doctor Charlotte Prinknash – Charlie to all who knew her – stripped off her blood-covered surgical gloves and dropped them into the bin for disposal. She undid her face mask, took off the close-fitting cap that hid her lustrous hair and put those in the laundry bag.

It had been a long hard morning in theatre; she had done three appendicectomies and assisted at two gall bladders. She took a refreshing cup of coffee from the machine in the ladies' locker room and then, dumping her surgical scrubs, had a quick shower and dressed.

'Doing anything tonight, Charlie?' called one of the other members of her team.

'Well, I've been invited to a party this evening but I'm not sure. What I need is a good night's sleep at the moment.'

'Yes, me too,' said her friend Anna with a rueful smile. 'What's wrong with people these days? We seem to be doing more and more ops. The NHS is certainly getting their money's worth out of us.'

Charlie grinned. 'Old Thorogood nearly had one of your fingers off when he cut out that big stone. I've never seen one that size before! Anyway, let's go and get some lunch before doing our ward rounds.' And they both set off for the canteen.

Charlie Prinknash, budding surgeon and talented artist, was the middle child of Sir David and Lady Angela Prinknash of Prinknash Keep, Gloucestershire. She was certainly not your typical well brought up young lady of the shires. Her mother had determined that Charlie was not going to attend one of those upper class girls' schools where they turned out ladies with an accent that could incise glass, a vocabulary like a drill sergeant and the voracious appetites of a black widow spider. Charlie, her elder brother and younger sister had gone to Stroud Grammar and, through dedicated teachers and hard work, had made it to top universities. They now earned their own living.

The working day over, Charlie drank some more coffee and debated whether or not to go to this party. She had been invited by one of the other doctors to join his group but although she knew he fancied her, she didn't fancy him.

'Oh come on,' she said to herself, 'don't be such a misery, it'll do you good. It's Friday, give yourself a break, and you never know – it could change your life.' She gave a sceptical smile.

*****

'Jenny Twentyman is throwing a big "bring a bottle" party tomorrow night in The Golden Monkey in aid of something or other. As it's August and a lot of people are away, she's looking for some spare men. Can any of you come?'

The question was addressed by Pete to the four of us gathered round the bar of the Frog and Nightgown. Tony looked at me and I looked at Bob Barclay, and then all three of us looked at Robin Fullerton. Fullerton worked for a public relations company and spoke in the jargon of PR, which caused ridicule to be heaped on his head in the Frog.

'Run it up the flag pole and see if Fleur salutes it,' murmured Tony ironically. Fullerton looked nervously at the ceiling – a man caught on Morton's Fork. If he said he'd have to ask Fleur, he would suffer even more scorn and derision; but if he said yes, he'd have his balls torn off if Fleur disapproved. He decided that scorn and derision was a safer option.

'I'd love to but Fleur and I have been invited out to dinner that evening.'

It was a good try on the spur of the moment, but nowhere near good enough.

'Oh, who by?' enquired Pete innocently.

'Er, the Millingtons. It's his birthday.'

'Aren't they away skiing?' murmured Bob, who didn't even know any Millingtons, let alone where they might be on Friday evening.

'No no, they get back today,' Robin said desperately.

'Where did they go?' I asked. 'I heard it was Zermatt.' I didn't know any Millingtons either.

'Only for the first week, they went somewhere else for the second.'

'Cloud cuckoo land perhaps!' grinned Bob. 'Come clean, Fullerton, you've got to get Fleur's permission, haven't you, before you can commit yourself?'

Fullerton flushed angrily and snapped, 'It's different for a modern couple, there has to be trust and frankness on both sides. You lot wouldn't recognise either if they ran over you in the street.'

'Well, are you on or aren't you?' asked Pete, who had been waiting patiently for an answer.

Jenny Twentyman always threw a good party, lots of booze and pretty girls in summer dresses, so three of us nodded acceptance. Bob added, 'Fullerton will let you know if Fleur says he can come out to play, but it'll only be after he's done his homework and tidied his room.'

Friday evening duly arrived and I scanned my somewhat limited wardrobe for some gear to impress on the girls at Jenny's party that here was a trendy, dynamic young professional going places.

I'd forgotten to do my laundry that week so had to settle for a clean denim shirt. My chinos weren't too bad but the only pants I had that were wearable were the bright orange ones with a blue Donald Duck on the rude bit – thirty pence from the Oxfam shop given to me by my sister as a joke. Still, nobody would see them and even if I got lucky, they could make a talking point if we ran out of anything else to say.

So, suitably attired and clutching my bottle of Pontefract Chardonnay – £2.99 from ASDA – I caught the bus to Fulham and the delightful Jenny's party.

The place was half full when I arrived. I could see Pete chatting to a busty bird in a low red top (he always went for the 'well built' girls), but of Barclay and Fullerton there was no sign. I put my Chardonnay on a side table with half a dozen others of a similar pedigree, scanned the other bottles of undrinkable plonk, grinned, and went to the bar to order a pint of best bitter ,taking stock of the talent on show. There were the usual leggy girls in tight jeans or short skirts gesticulating with elegant fingers to emphasise a point they were trying to make. One or two were holding those long thin cigarettes. I knew half a dozen or so and smiled when our eyes met.

The party hadn't warmed up yet and 'Jim Peete, The Disco Beat' was just setting out his stall of strobe lights and hot music. Barclay turned up about five minutes later but there was still no sighting of Fullerton.

'Fleur won't let him out!' chortled Pete.

We joined a few others that we knew at a table close to the dance floor, the disco opened up, the drinks flowed, the finger buffet disappeared in a flash and the chat got louder. I grabbed Kiki Heatherington – she was the best looking bird in our group – and we hit the dance floor running. Eventually Bob decided that I was hogging the best crumpet and came to cut in.

As I was leaving the crowded floor, I collided with the back of a girl with the most beautiful shining dark hair. I hadn't noticed her when I came in as I surely would have done if she'd been there; she must have been one of the late arrivals. She was dancing with a tall thin guy, who muttered something. I didn't notice what because when she turned round to apologise, the world stopped. If the back view was great, the front view was stunning. Two of the most beautiful violet eyes set in a concerned oval face. Our gaze locked for a couple of seconds before other dancers jostled between us.

'Er, sorry!' I stuttered.

'That's OK, it was our fault,' she smiled before turning back to her partner.

Now this must sound pretty dull to you and I can understand that, but to me it wasn't. You know how it is? Somehow you just know. It doesn't take a week, a day or an hour; it can happen in an instant – and it had just happened to me. All that stuff about a knowing glance across a crowded room – all balls, I had maintained – until then. There had been an instant and reciprocal attraction in that single moment. A fusing of minds, as if my thoughts were her thoughts and vice versa.

I took a deep breath to regain my equilibrium. 'Say, who's that superb girl with the dark hair?' I asked the others at the table but by then she had been swallowed up by the crowd on the dance floor so my question remained unanswered.

I saw her again a few minutes later when I went to the bar but she was laughing with a big group at a table on the other side of the room and didn't see me. I couldn't get her out of my mind as the evening progressed and resolved that this encounter must be followed up. But as usual, as the evening progressed we got more and more pissed, and talked each other into doing more and more ridiculous things. Somebody dared Pete to drink a pint up his nose through a straw, and we collapsed with laughter when he snorted and choked, spraying beer all over the place. Marian, whose chat-up line to girls he fancied was 'I'm a stocking salesman but I'm going up the ladder fast', balanced three wine glasses on top of each other on his nose.

Then Barclay said, 'Do you remember Marcus's famous Moon Pivot? I'll bet a quid he can't do that now in the state he's in.'

Well, a challenge is a challenge to a well-smashed Moon and so I was right up for it.

'Right,' I slurred. 'Anybody else want to put a quid on it then?'

A forest of hands went up.

'Thou of little face…faith,' I corrected hastily. 'Somebody bring me a pint then.'

The Moon Pivot consisted of spinning round on one heel only, doing a complete rotation, whilst balancing a full pint of beer on one's head without falling over, stumbling or spilling a drop.

Yes, I know what you're thinking, and if somebody else had claimed they could do it I would have been the first one out with my money at evens. But pride is pride and we all know what pride cometh before – and this was no exception apparently.

I say apparently, because what happened to me after that is hearsay. The last thing I remember was balancing the pint on my head, lifting one leg and starting to spin before being rammed hard in the back by a beefy shoulder, presumably belonging to an out of control dancer.

My next recollection was of a splitting headache and, on separating the eyelids, beholding, not twelve inches from my own sandpapered eyeballs, a pair of the most beautiful deep violet eyes. What's more, they were filled with concern and set in a face that would have launched a Trojan war. There was something very familiar about that face but in my befuddled state I couldn't place it.

I made a big effort and glanced around. This was certainly not my flat or a hospital. I lay in a big double bed in a cheerfully decorated little bedroom with sunshine pouring through the window. The realisation that it was daylight dawned only slowly, as did the fact that I was in bed and she was not.

'Put that bloody sun out and come to bed!' I croaked, but it was just bravado. I couldn't have raised a smile.

She chuckled and that sealed matters there and then. It was a delightful chuckle, throaty yet light, which showed beautiful white even teeth and crinkles round her eyes.

'You'll live,' she smiled but I wasn't listening; by then I had been well and truly hit with the velvet hammer. I was in love.

Waves of nausea flooded over me and I sank back on the bed and closed my eyes. I had never felt so contented in my life.

When I awoke again, the sun had gone from the room. I heard the rattle of crockery and somebody singing softly. The headache had abated to a bearable throb. Had I been having a wonderful dream? I wondered. But somehow I knew it was all true. Touching my forehead, I could feel a large lump just above the right eye, which appeared to be covered with a substantial plaster. Flakes of blood adhered to my fingers so I must have been cut as well, and the lump felt very tender and sore when I pressed it.

Gingerly I climbed out of bed to discover two things – both very disconcerting. The first was that I had been stripped right down to the bright orange Donald Duck pants; and the second, discovered on looking in the dressing-table mirror, was that I looked like shit. Pasty face with two eyes glowing like hot coals in the snow, a large, blood-soaked white plaster which couldn't quite conceal a red and purple bruise over my right eye. Somebody, presumably my as yet nameless angel of mercy, had washed off as much blood as they could but dark brown encrustations had formed in the creases of my eye sockets, giving me the appearance of 'the Ghoul from the Grave'.

I heard that chuckle again at the door and whirled round, a manoeuvre which set my head spinning and my eyeballs rotating in what seemed like different directions. She was standing in the doorway watching me. I hastily grabbed for the duvet to cover up Donald Duck. It didn't seem the right time to open up a conversation about him, and I cursed my failure to do the laundry.

She grinned. 'A bit jazzy those! Are they standard engineering kit these days? Anyhow, I'm not worried if you're not. I'm a doctor, I've seen much worse than that!' She paused and looked at me quizzically. 'You don't remember me, do you? Charlotte Prinknash, we were at uni together for a short time but you were much too senior to talk to a mere "fresher" in those days.'

The penny dropped. I remembered her now, Charlie Prinknash. She had been an ethereal figure that appeared in my final year. I had admired her from afar but afar was as close as I got in the short time our residences coincided. She was reading medicine and moved in totally different circles from the engineers.

'Marcus Moon,' I croaked and held out my hand, giving her another flash of the orange knickers.

'Yes, I know who you are: I remember you. You were the one who was sent down for a month for shaving all the fur off the Vice-Chancellor's poodle and painting it in Arsenal colours.'

'Doncaster Rovers,' I corrected her without thinking.

'Ah yes,' she murmured softly. 'It was that that upset him the most.'

I groaned inwardly. Bringing up my student misdemeanours didn't seem the most auspicious way to start a relationship. She must think me mad, stupid or irresponsible.

'I didn't know he was a Liverpool supporter,' I said weakly. 'Anyhow, my Rovers support has waned these days since they were relegated.'

'That's OK; I don't have a dog, so there won't be a problem if you have an irresistible urge to do it again.'

She gave me a smile, not just any old smile but a full, look-straight-into-your-soul, affectionate-but-concerned, through-the-corneas smile. I got back into the bed, laid my head on the pillow and closed my eyes, a man at peace.

184

When I awoke the next morning, she brought me a cup of tea and explained that at Jenny's party she had heard a crash and then somebody shouted for a doctor. Smallwood was too pissed to do anything, so when she came over and saw that it was me who had split his head open on the edge of a table and was leaking blood all over the place, she thought it quicker and safer to get me to her house, which was just round the corner from the Golden Monkey and where she had her medical kit, rather than wait hours for an ambulance and go through all the drama of Accident and Emergency at Chelsea and Westminster Hospital. Bob and Tony had carried me there and helped undress me.

She allowed me to stay in the spare bedroom for another two days until she was satisfied that there was no concussion, keeping me gently at arm's length.

However, when I left by taxi on the Tuesday evening to go back to my flat with confirmation that it would be alright to return to work at CONDES on the Wednesday, she gave me a full-face, open-lips kiss that certainly wasn't a 'Goodbye, it was nice to know you but…' brush-off.

I arrived at the office late on Wednesday morning, playing the wounded soldier, determined to milk the sympathy to the maximum. Fortunately the bruising hadn't spread to give me a black eye, but all the girls in the office, except Agatha, still tutted over the big piece of plaster and made a fuss of me. Angela even brought me my coffee, much to Ivan's disgust.

'Women aren't men's chattels, you know,' he said waspishly.

'Well, yours certainly isn't,' I replied with a grin, which produced more teeth-gritting and jaw-clenching. 'What do you mean by that?' he snarled. It was widely known that Agatha was still giving him a hard time over his Orkney affair. She had remarked very pointedly that whether or not the baby was his, the fact that he had been in the frame at all meant he must have, as she put it, 'had relations'.

'Oh, nothing,' I said airily, thinking of the contrast between Charlie and Awful Agatha.

Des just grinned and murmured with deflating accuracy, 'Pissed again, I suppose?'

I returned to Charlie's a week later so she could remove the three stitches with which she had sutured the wound, and took her out to dinner. She told me she was an Assistant Surgical Registrar at The Royal Free Hospital. I said I had no problem with that as long as she didn't regale me over dinner regarding ferreting about in somebody's intestines. The coffee we had afterwards in her little house in Fulham was the best coffee I'd ever had – it came with a lovely, warm, cuddly armful of Charlie. We arranged to meet to go to the cinema on the following Tuesday. I can't remember anything about the film but if life was good before, it was ten times better now.

Three weeks later, I got tired of having to return to Palmerston Mansions for clean clothes and moved into the little house in Fulham permanently.

A few days after I returned to work Ivan didn't show up in the morning and Des didn't know where he was either. I nonchalantly asked Angela if she knew anything when she brought in the post.

'Yes, he's gone down to Kingscastle this morning to sort out the boreholes for the rest of the road,' she said. 'I've booked him in those digs you recommended. Mrs Tripp said they were looking forward to having him.'

The casualness disappeared in a flash to be replaced by an Olympic-winning boggle. Boggling was not something I had practised in front of the mirror but from the look on Angela's face, it clearly wasn't necessary. I managed to gargle out, 'Say again?'

'Ivan's gone down to Kingscastle. Why, is there something wrong with that?'

With an effort, I hauled my jaw up from the floor as the brain kicked in. Oh, Christ has he? I started to smile and had to bite my lip. I'd forgotten all about Moon Plan A, Mrs Tripp and her House of Pain after my bollocking from Arbuthnot. Ivan and I hadn't spoken since that incident; not that that would have changed anything. Well, it was too late now even if I wanted to - and I didn't. Moon Plan A had launched itself down the slipway of its own accord and was going to hit the water. The rest was in the hands of the gods, or rather Miss Stern and Susan.

'You look surprised,' observed Angela. 'Is there a problem?'

'No no,' I replied airily. 'When's he due back?'

'Tomorrow I think.'

Somehow I don't think he will be, I thought, trying not to laugh.

Even Des was intrigued enough to put down his crossword.

'You look pleased with yourself.'

I just passed it off with a shrug. 'No, it's nothing Des, it's just my usual chirpy nature shining through in these dark days of gloom and despondency.'

Leaving a couple of mystified people staring at my back, I turned to my PC, thinking that if something did happen, the most important thing would be for me not to tell anybody about it apart from Ivan. That would give me some leverage. I was certain that Ivan wouldn't either. But I would know and he would know and he would know that I knew. So that should keep him off my back in future. A satisfactory solution to an unsatisfactory situation.

And then I had a better idea!

Somewhere in the back pocket of my jeans lurked the card Tracey Tripp had given me. I felt around and pulled it out. It was a bit dog-eared, having been through the wash, but still legible. 'Miss Stern – Behavioural Therapist. For Appointments Phone 09934 5239871'.

Impatiently I waited until Des slipped out of the office for something, and then rapidly dialled the number, keeping my fingers crossed that somebody would answer. After a couple of rings Susan Tripp's voice said, 'Hello, can I help you?'

'It's Marcus Moon,' I whispered. 'You remember I ...er... stayed with you a couple of weeks ago? Are you free to talk?'

'Oh, hello, Marcus, how nice to hear from you. Are you coming to visit us again? I believe your friend's arriving today to stay with us, a Mr Masterland – the one we've arranged a treat for.'

'Yes, well it's about that that I'm phoning.'

'Oh dear, he's not gone off the idea, has he? Tracey would be so disappointed; we've got all the equipment ready.'

'No, no,' I said hastily, 'far from it. He was only talking to me about his fantasies again the other day. In fact, secretly I think he'd appreciate some record of the event.'

I'd remembered Tracey had taken photos on her mobile of Withers, the ones that had persuaded Withers to sign my permit to take borings on his land. Trying to keep my voice as level as possible, I continued.

'I just wondered if Tracey could take a couple of shots with her mobile – at the height of the action, say – so he can refresh his happy memories when he looks back in the future so to speak?'

I sucked in air through my teeth as though I'd just remembered something. 'There is a small problem though; I've just realised that Ivan's computer automatically erases any e-mails it considers might be junk, so if Tracey could e-mail them to me I can make sure he gets them. It'll be a nice surprise when he gets back to the office.'

I held my breath, thinking it *would* be a surprise, although I doubted that Ivan would see it in a very 'nice' light!

Susan gave a chuckle. I think she sensed something was up but had obviously decided that no harm would be done if they went along with this.

'Sure, I'll ask her to send them early next morning so that you'll have them ready for him when he gets back.'

I gave her my e-mail address, said I hoped to see them both soon and put the phone down. There was no chance of that, but business is business.

Arriving early next morning full of eager anticipation, I was partly deflated and partly elated when Awful Agatha put her head round the door as soon as I'd arrived, and announced that Ivan had phoned in to say that he wouldn't be in for a couple of days, he was suffering from a stomach upset. I bet he was, and other complaints on top – or should I have said 'on bottom!' I grinned to myself, switched on my PC and logged on to my e-mails. My heart jumped; amongst the new and old jokes there was an e-mail from trastern@cort.net which looked very promising. I was just about to open it when, totally out of character, Des strolled in, right on time for once.

'Bugger me, Des; are you off colour this morning?' I observed, glancing at my watch.

'Joys of Spring, dear boy, joys of Spring! Felt the old sap rising, so fettled up Angeline, had breakfast at the local greasy spoon and here I am, ready, willing and able *'to tote dat barge and lift dat bale'* for the benefit of CONDES.'

I blinked at this surfeit of information.

'You haven't heard then?' He raised an eyebrow in my direction.

'Heard what?'

'There's a meeting of all Partners and Associates in Geoffrey's office at nine-fifteen. God, I'm late, must rush.'

'About what?' But my question was too late, he'd gone.

He was back in less than an hour with a satisfied smile on his round face. 'Hugo's got it; I thought he would.'

'Got what?' I cried. 'For heaven's sake, Des, what the hell are you talking about?'

'So sorry, dear boy, of course you wouldn't know. Our venerable senior partner, Geoffrey Arbuthnot, is retiring in three months' time, his health isn't too good. Hugo's going to take over as Senior Partner. We were all asked to consider and approve this. Very democratic; and it was unanimous. Even Hamish Robertson and Ewen Jones agreed. Hamish is nearly as old as Geoffrey but I thought Jones might fancy the job, but he didn't.'

On reflection, I felt pleased about this. I had always liked Hugo Elmes; he was a good boss and a very clever engineer, and my unfortunate escapade with Ivan and Arbuthnot might be forgotten with the latter's departure. It seemed a good choice to me in my lowly situation, but more to the point, I was dying to see what 'trastern@cort.net had sent, and couldn't wait for Des to push off somewhere so I could open the file. I hadn't thought it through at that stage.

There were two photos, both slightly blurry, but there was no doubt about the people involved. The first quite clearly showed Ivan dressed in some kind of shiny tight-fitting black suit like a wet suit. He was blindfolded. Standing beside him was a grim-faced Miss Stern in black corselet, stockings and bending what looked like a wicked cane with both hands. The second picture showed Ivan in his black suit, standing in the schoolroom by himself with a background of instruments of punishment. I was disappointed that there wasn't an action picture but nevertheless these would be fine. I started to laugh and quickly ran off a print of each on the office printer before Des returned.

He came in just as I removed the last print from the tray.

'What's tickling you then? Have I missed something?'

I passed it off by replying, 'No, no, it was just a thought' and quickly slid the two pictures out of sight into one of the Shering Valley Bridge folders.

On Thursday morning Ivan was at his desk when I arrived. To my astonishment, he was all bright and perky; he even wished me 'Good morning' with a twist of his mouth which I took for a smile, and did the same without comment for Des when he showed up fifteen minutes late. Des glanced at me and raised a questioning eyebrow but I just shrugged.

At coffee time nobody made a move so eventually Des grumbled, 'I suppose I'd better get my own coffee then.'

'Get one for me while you're at it,' I added. 'One sugar!'

He flashed me a look.

'And me,' echoed Ivan.

After Des had trudged reluctantly out of the door, Ivan slipped out of his chair, made sure the door was firmly closed and came across to me. I waited apprehensively.

'Hey, Marcus, that was some digs you recommended.' He gave me a knowing nudge. 'They really give you the full treatment, don't they? Did you get the—'

I cut him off there. My mind was spinning and I wanted time to adjust to this unexpected situation.

'So you had a good time?'

'Yeah, brilliant. That Tracey bird, Miss Stern she calls herself, is something, isn't she? She really turned me on. We must make a few more visits to Kingscastle, eh?'

This was not going as I anticipated. What was worse, he was assuming I was a fellow traveller down the masochistic road, which I certainly was not, and I didn't want that reputation. It was time to put the mockers on that immediately.

I gave a puzzled frown. 'You went out with Tracey? What was it you said she calls herself – Miss Stern? Why would she do that?'

Doubt flickered across his face. 'You know – the old school room?'

My face was expressionless as I replied, 'I most certainly do not know. What the hell are you talking about? Have you been up to something naughty then?'

I waited, unmoving. I think that was the moment when the last vestiges of whatever faith Ivan had in human nature fell away. He paled and stood there dumbstruck, realising that maybe he had said too much.

'Is this something Agatha should know about?'

That stopped him in his tracks. He glanced round nervously as if she could be within earshot and grabbed my arm, but before he could say any more, Des arrived juggling three cups of coffee.

Des raised an eyebrow.

'So you two are talking again are you? What's brought that about?'

I looked squarely at Ivan. 'Ivan was telling me what a good time he had down in Kingscastle…'

I let the sentence hang there. Des shot Ivan a glance and Ivan hastily shuffled some paper on his desk and didn't elaborate. But the message had been delivered.

I gave him my 'right, you nasty little shit, I've got you where I want you' smile. At least that was what it was intended to be but, as it was the first time it had been tried out on a human, it might well have looked as if I was suffering from severe constipation. I had tried it on Mrs Aberdeen's cat, The Reverend McCavity, back in my block of flats but he'd just looked at me with his usual contempt and proceeded to lick his balls. Ivan didn't go that far but I noted a flicker of fear in his eyes as it finally sank in that we were not, after all, companions in S & M and he had said more than he should have.

The photos I decided to keep in reserve. Only thing was, I forgot that I'd slipped them into a Kingscastle file.

*****

The test bores at the bridge site showed hard chalk six metres down, ideal for good foundations. Those along the rest of the proposed route were also encouraging. It looked as though all the material that needed to be excavated for cuttings could be compacted and used to build up the embankments. This would be a huge saving in cost and considerably reduce the amount of heavy lorry traffic on the public roads – traffic that might have been needed to take away and dump spoil and bring in fill from surrounding quarries: a big plus for the Department of Transport in their evidence at the forthcoming Public Enquiry.

Hugo confirmed that he had approved the design principles for the Shering Valley Bridge, so for me, it was all systems go.

*****

The news that that the route across Hickling Edge had been changed back from twin tunnels to a deep cutting, and therefore that would be included in the scheme with which it was intended to proceed at the Public Enquiry, was greeted with incandescent fury in Kingscastle. If they were unhappy with the scheme before, they were incensed at being misled, and the action committees of MOVE THE BYPASS had been revived with much more determined enthusiasm.

Gloria Withington-Lombard, the Chair of the Placards and Posters, got together with Harry Bell of the Marching Committee to organise banners and placards for protest marches and demonstrations. It was decided, as time was short, to abandon the nude calendar as a fund-raiser and concentrate on putting collecting boxes round the town. Harry Bell pointed out that there was very little time to build up a nationwide movement and so whatever they did would have to be sudden, dramatic and spectacular if they were going to get a positive response with national media coverage sufficient to embarrass the Government into changing the route and this was not going to be easy.

Protest marches were held in Kingcastle, blocking the A399 road for hours; police had to be bussed in from Devizes, Trowbridge and the surrounding area. This infuriated the citizens even more, scuffles broke out and arrests were made. The Government didn't bat an eyelid.

The Marching Committee then organised a mass visit to Whitehall with busloads of protesters, farm lorries, tractors and trailers loaded with farm muck, turf and slurry and even the odd combined harvester. But the police were alerted and managed to seal off the M4 just outside Newbury where traffic could be easily diverted. This enraged the Kingscastleians even more, and the lines of shield-bearing coppers in full riot gear, with masks and batons in formation at their road block of cars and vans, were pelted with the contents of the trailers.

The national media had a bean feast with it but treated it all as a joke. When the riot police were pelted with muck on the M4, pictures of policemen and vehicles covered from head to foot in cow shit provoked national laughter, the point that the demonstrators were trying to make was lost. 'MAN URE FILTHY' screamed *The Sun,* and ' PLOD CLOD' printed *The Mail* over the picture of policeman with a lump of turf stuck to his helmet.

However, this made no difference. The Government saw no reason to change the line of the road.

*****

Being the one who had expounded the tunnels solution and thus the person who had, however unwittingly, misled and tricked the good folk of Kingscastle into relaxing their guard, it was with a certain amount of trepidation that I found myself on the Ministry's team specifically to explain about the Shering Valley Bridge at the Public Enquiry. This had all the makings of a quick termination of a promising career – and possibly a young life, if it went pear-shaped.

Ivan was going to be questioned about the selected route for the road. The timetable prepared by the Inspector holding the Enquiry required him to give his evidence at an early stage; I was on much later, when the details of the bridge across the Shering Valley were to be outlined.

I wondered if wearing a wig and a false nose might help.

CHAPTER NINE

It was with some trepidation that I phoned the Kingscastle Borough Engineer and suggested to him that, if he was free, I would come down to Kingscastle the next day to discuss our proposals for the Shering Valley Bridge. There was a certain amount of caution in his voice when he agreed.

'You're not very popular in Kingscastle, you know. The locals think they've been seriously conned by the Government and it's you that they blame. They haven't got round to burning effigies of you yet but I wouldn't turn up on bonfire night if I were in your shoes. You'd better park round the back and use the rear entrance to the Town Hall. My office is on the first floor.'

I gulped, racking my brains for some alternative but nothing came to mind – and I had given an undertaking to discuss the design of the bridge with them so I didn't want there to be another reason for Arbuthnot to roast me. It was fixed I would be there at ten-thirty and would do as he suggested.

Charlie wondered why I was distracted when I got home that evening. I explained about the Borough Engineers comments and burning effigies. She was quite concerned. 'They wouldn't do that - would they?' I thought it unlikely but that night I was beset by vivid dreams about hemp rope and lamp-posts, baying mobs and limbs torn off, so it took a bit of will-power to press the foot on the accelerator and turn the steering wheel of the MG towards Kingscastle next morning.

I didn't realise it but Lady Luck was smiling on me, the day I rang the Borough Engineer to fix the appointment happened to be a day on which Miss Pring, Deputy Director of Social Services, was away on an 'Assertiveness Course for the Managerial Female' and thus didn't learn of my forthcoming visit until that morning.

Taking back roads to avoid the town centre and wearing a scarf wrapped round the lower part of my face together with a baseball cap pulled well down over the eyes, I eased the car quietly into a place next to the rubbish bins in a secluded courtyard at the rear of the Town Hall. Still dressed like that, I slipped up some back stairs to the first floor. All seemed quiet so, holding the bundle of drawings in front of my face, I scanned the name plates on the doors until I found a door with a plaque that read 'Secretary to the Borough Engineer'. I was just going to knock when a voice behind me said loudly, 'Ah, Mr Moon, there you are. Please go in and go straight through into my office.'

Straightening up sharply, I spun round to see if anybody else had caught my name but the Borough Engineer just grinned cheerfully and said, 'Would you like tea or coffee?'

'Er, coffee please, one sugar,' I mumbled through the scarf as we passed through the secretary's office.

He nodded to a middle-aged woman, who I presumed was the said secretary and who was eying me with undisguised hostility, and said, 'Same for me, Mrs Pritchard' as we walked past her pristine desk into a large pleasant room.

'I'm Peter Ashman,' he said, shaking my hand. 'So you managed to get here without being lynched then?'

It was said in jest…well, I assumed it was. I gave a nervous smile and said, 'So far so good.'

I spread out the sketches for the bridge and explained the thinking behind them. After looking at them carefully, Ashman made one or two comments, mainly about landscaping, but seemed very pleased with the modern structural form we had proposed to span the valley and how we had blended it into the contours. He thought we should open up the site a bit more so the bridge could be seen.

'It's a very elegant and impressive structure and would complement the view down the valley,' he observed. 'Yes, definitely this will add to our landscape, not take away from it.'

I agreed that we would arrange for this if we got approval at the Public Enquiry.

'Ah yes, of course, there's that. You realise that the Council will oppose the location of the bypass as is currently proposed? We're obligated to do so by our members.'

I just nodded noncommittally, not wanting to comment on the location of the road and finished my very bitter coffee. Obviously no sugar had been added.

The BE gave me a steady look. 'So what happened to the tunnel scheme then? We were very happy with that so why was it dropped?'

I explained that although we thought the tunnels would be the best solution, they were only a proposal and in the end the Ministry had decided they would be too expensive. A small white lie to get me off an uncomfortable hook.

'Not as expensive as moving the road further away,' he pointed out.

I gave a weak smile of acknowledgement and that was all. I was on difficult ground here. If we continued on this line and it got back to CONDES that I'd discussed the road again it could be more than just a bollocking. Having my whole future put in jeopardy by Geoffrey Arbuthnot was quite sufficient for me already, so I clammed up.

Ashman gave a sympathetic smile. 'I know you have to present the Ministry's case at the Public Enquiry next month, that's what you're paid for, but the people here aren't convinced.'

I nodded and explained that the road had been taken out of my hands. I was just responsible for the bridges now. A chap called Ivan Masterland was our senior roads man.

Peter Ashman scratched his chin. 'Do you think he would come and talk to me about the landscaping treatment? It's one of the things the Council is concerned about and if we can resolve that it'll be one less contentious point at the Enquiry.'

'I'll tell him,' I responded, and left it at that.

I donned my disguise again, shook his hand, said I'd send him copies of the final designs for the bridge and slunk back through the secretary's office. This time there were two women glaring at me. The new arrival was a thin, sour-faced woman with greyish hair tied back in a bun, round wire-framed spectacles perched on a pointed nose and a mouth that was pursed like the rear end of a plucked chicken.

I heard her say in a low voice, 'Yes, that's definitely him.' Their eyes followed me as I made for the door. As I was fumbling with the door handle the BE's secretary murmured, 'I knew he was coming yesterday Marilyn, I rang your office but you were away on some course or other.'

Now what? was the first thing that came into my mind. Were alarm bells going to ring throughout the building, a siren sound to tell the population of Kingscastle that the devil incarnate was loose amongst them or what? It was a very uncomfortable feeling.

In the event nothing happened, and I drove out of Kingscastle unmolested – I admit rather faster than I entered and with frequent glances in the rear-view mirror!

I reported to Hugo the gist of my meeting with the Borough Engineer and said that if he was happy with that I would develop the bridge design in more detail. I also mentioned that Kingscastle seemed very wound up about moving the road to avoid Hickling Edge.

'Yes, I've seen the television but they're not really making much impact.' He sucked air through his teeth pensively. 'It's a pity about the tunnels, that could have avoided all these problems but we have to accept that they would add to the cost. We can't avoid that. Well, it's out of our hands now. The Highways

Authority and the Department of Transport have nailed their colours to the proposed route mast, and we're stuck with putting forward the best case for it at the Public Enquiry.'

Ivan had been very subdued since we had had our little conversation about Miss Stern and had made no attempt to make further trouble for me. Awful Agatha had continued to give him a hard time since his return from Orkney, with a very strong warning not to step off the straight and narrow again. He had even been civil to Des and asked his advice on one or two matters relating to the road.

As we were supposed to be working as a team, when I got back from Kingscastle I told Ivan what had transpired at my meeting with the Borough Engineer and that the BE would like to discuss CONDES' landscaping ideas for the road.

To my astonishment Ivan was back with his rude, grumpy uncooperative attitude. He was dismissive of the whole idea about explaining his landscaping proposals but grumbled that he supposed he'd better go and talk to the Borough Engineer as I'd set him up. I shrugged and gave him Peter Ashman's secretary's phone number so he could make an appointment. He stopped me as I went to walk away.

'By the way, Moon, I've been thinking.....' I refrained from comment and he continued. '....it's just your word against mine, you realise that? And as you were the first to go to the Tripps, people will be more likely to believe me than you if tales get around about you-know-what.'

He had a good point, or he would have had if I didn't have the photos. But I was cheesed off with the whole thing. It was ridiculous.

'Look, Ivan, why don't we just lay off this competitive hostility? You're good at your job and I'm good at mine. Why don't we just leave it at that and concentrate on our work? For some reason I don't understand, you don't like me and I certainly don't like you, but that's no reason why we can't work together.'

He looked at me suspiciously, trying to work out if there was an angle, and then gave a grunt which could have been acceptance or rejection and turned back to his computer.

For a few days all seemed to be smoothed over. While it could never ever be said that he had become a bundle of fun, at least he was civil.

But all that was soon to change.

*****

The *Kingscastle Bugle*, all the nationals, BBC South West, ITV and Sky News all got the phone call and e-mail from Miss Pring. They had been covering the Kingscastle protest marches and other trouble-making events so they were up for some more promising copy like truffle hounds under an oak tree.

The Volvo swung into a vacant car space outside to the Town Hall. Ivan stretched his cramped limbs after the drive, turned off the engine, gathered up his briefcase containing his notes and landscaping ideas, including the deep cutting through Hickling Edge, and eased out of the car. He gave a dismissive sneer at the 'MOVE THE BYPASS' banners festooning the front of the building and turned to lock the car door. He didn't pay any attention to the battered old white van that moved out of a space further along and reversed almost up to him.

The next thing he knew was that a large bag had been dropped over his head, his arms seized in a strong grip and wrenched round behind him where his wrists were handcuffed together.

'What the hell do you think you're doing...' was as far as he got before he was lifted off his feet and felt himself dropped on to a metal floor, heard the slamming of the van door and the roar of an engine as his enclosing coffin accelerated away.

He started to shout 'Help, help!" but then a cloth was thrust through the bag into his mouth and fastened there with tape. Somebody sat on his legs whilst they were tied together. He sensed from the smell and feel of things that his captors were women, and for a few moments he thought it was Mrs Tripp and Tracey who had devised another way of giving him a treat. A muffled voice said, 'Get his trousers down!' and hands tugged as his belt to loosen it. He began to get excited. There was a dismissive sneer as his trousers and pants were lowered as far as the bonds round his ankles would permit.

'A good job starving Africa doesn't depend on a meat and two veg like that!' said another woman's voice, sounding disappointed.

'Get his tie and shirt off as well.'

Ivan's tie was undone and his shirt ripped open, buttons flying in all directions, before being pulled down his arms as far as the handcuffs.

This definitely wasn't a Tripp treat, he realised with increasing horror; this was being done with serious intent. Terror surged through his body, panic set in and he began to thrash about desperately.

'Sit on his feet, Shirley, I'll hold his head whilst we cover him.'

He felt a heavy body drop on his legs and hold them tight and an equally firm grip on his head. He tried to bite the hands that held his head through the bag, but with the gag still wedged in his mouth, he couldn't do any damage.

The next sensation was a cool viscous substance being poured over his bare chest, genitals and legs, followed by something light and furry.

'Turn him over Marilyn,' instructed one of the voices and he was rolled unceremoniously on to his stomach with his face pressed hard against the metal floor. The sticky stuff was poured all over his back and thighs and then the fur followed.

'We can't do his face or feet,' said somebody.

'It doesn't matter, this looks pretty good,' said another, adding, 'Are you listening to this, arsehole? This is what happens to people who lie and treat Kingscastle people like fools. Just tell that to your Government.'

The journey continued for another five minutes, but to Ivan it felt like five hours. He wondered what they were going to do with him and also what they had done to him. Was it paint? Had he been painted almost all over? The smell was sweet rather than turpentiney. He heard a change of gear as the vehicle slowed down. He could hear other traffic noises.

The van stopped suddenly and there was a moment's silence. Cold air wafted over him as the doors were opened. Were they on the edge of a cliff? Were they going to throw him over? He wept with fear and wet himself. He tried to shout, 'No No! Don't kill me. I'm only an employee, I'm not from the Ministry.' But to no avail. The bag over his head was loosened and he was hauled up into a sitting position and dragged along the floor so that his feet dangled over the sill at the rear of the vehicle. He could hear traffic and voices clearly now. Somebody fumbled with the handcuffs and then he felt a firm push at his back, which launched him out into space.

He fell about half a metre before hitting cobblestones. Instinctively he put his hands out to protect himself as he fell. The vehicle engine roared and it shot away from the scene.

It was a moment before it dawned on Ivan that he was still alive, his hands were free and there were people round him. He quickly wrenched the bag from his head and looked round. He wet himself again with horror. He was in the middle of Kingscastle Market Place, surrounded by a cloud of white feathers drifting slowly away in the light breeze.

But that wasn't the cause of his horror. It was due to the fact that he was surrounded by a phalanx of flashing cameras, television crews and shouts from a large crowd of bystanders of, 'Serves you right, you liar! Fascist scum!' and 'Lying bastard!'

Ivan looked down. His body was thickly covered in white feathers that were sticking firmly to a layer of black tacky stuff. His trousers were round his ankles and instinctively he reached down to haul these up over his feather-covered legs and tackle – although in that respect his modesty had been preserved by the vast quantity of feathers adhering to the latter.

One or two people thought it was a publicity stunt, while others thought it was a student rag from the local agricultural college. They were all laughing and jeering.

Ivan panicked. 'Call the police!' he screamed. 'I've been attacked and kidnapped. Help me!'

Fortunately for him a police patrol car had stopped to see what was attracting the crowd, and an alert policeman, grasping the situation immediately, shot into 'Snoozeland', seized a sheet from under the nose of a protesting manager, and then ran to wind it round Ivan. They were now faced with the problem of what to do with a very pissed off and sticky Ivan.

'Throw him in the duck pond!' was a very unhelpful suggestion from a bystander. 'He'll feel at home there.'

Eventually, after the Press and TV had got more shots, the police managed to manoeuvre him through the crowd into the back of a police car, which then drove off to Kingscastle Hospital where Accident and Emergency said Ivan was neither an accident or, as he had no injuries, an emergency. Therefore he was nothing to do with them, and they had better things to do than waste time with somebody who played stupid games. The police should take him to the Fire Station and put him under a hot shower. So he was reloaded into the car and driven to the Fire Station.

After they had cleaned him up under hot showers and one of the firemen found him an old track-suit to replace his ruined clothes, Ivan regained some semblance of coherence. He was taken to the Police Station where he made a statement. Three more policemen were then dispatched to find the perpetrators of Ivan's ordeal.

It wasn't difficult – the finding of them, that is – because all three had chained themselves to railings and statues under MOVE THE BYPASS banners outside the Town Hall. Police reinforcements were summoned, and the photographers and TV crews thought it was their birthday as the three witches fought tooth and nail as they were cut loose and dragged kicking, screaming and biting to the police vans.

The national news coverage of all these events was massive and gave 'MOVE THE BYPASS' protest more publicity and support than they could have dreamed of.

*****

The phone rang on the desk of Her Majesty's Secretary of State for Transport and Communications, the Right Honourable Graham Preston MP. His Parliamentary Private Secretary Tom Froome picked it up and wished he hadn't when the scorching blast hit his eardrum.

'GRAHAM, HAVE YOU SEEN THE FUCKING TELEVI-
SION NEWS?'

'If you hold on a minute, sir, I'll put Mr Preston on.'

Graham Preston had caught the gist of the message standing
at the other side of the room talking to Sir Joseph Storey, his
senior civil servant, about the Public Enquiry at Kingscastle. He
slid smoothly over and took the phone.

'Good day, Prime Minister—' That was as far as he got.

'No, it is not a good day, Graham; it's a bloody awful day!
Put your television on and then ring me back.' The connection
was broken.

Preston gestured to Froome to switch on the large flat screen
television in the corner of the office. He watched with a sinking
feeling the camera shots from Kingscastle showing a fully feathered Ivan being discharged from an old van and tottering about
shouting 'Call the police!' He was surrounded by flash bulbs
and TV cameras and a crowd of very unsympathetic citizens.
Placards could clearly be seen in the crowd reading 'GIVE US
BACK OUR TUNNEL'.

This was followed by further shots of Mss Pring, Williamson and Deakin being cut from railings and dragged kicking and
screaming into a police van by four policemen to each woman,
screaming 'Give us our tunnel!' At least, Mss Williamson and
Deakin were kicking and screaming; Ms Pring couldn't shout
anything because she had her teeth firmly locked into PC Shayne
Connolly's calf muscle through his blue serge trousers.

With mounting trepidation Preston rang Downing Street.

'Christ, Graham, the media are after our blood!' yelled the PM. 'The Opposition are rubbing their hands with glee and those incidents in Kingscastle are just the grist that their mill has been waiting for. We've got this bloody by-election coming up in North Wilts because that stupid bugger Harrison got himself trampled on by a cow – and it's a marginal seat. We cannot allow this sort of thing. Is the feathered fellow one of your civil servants?' Without waiting for an answer, he ploughed on: 'First they want a bloody bypass and we give 'em one; now they want to move the thing all round the county and everybody is blaming us for - exactly what I do not understand. And what's all this about a tunnel? What the fuck's going on, Preston? Perhaps you would care to throw some light on the matter as you're supposed to be in charge of transport – at present?'

Graham Preston blanched at the last two words. Now was definitely not the time to throw in a light-hearted observation, so 'Perhaps we should put the road on wheels' was stillborn in his throat.

'If I may explain, Prime Minister, it appears that the people of Kingscastle are delighted with the proposed bypass and have given your Government the credit for its far-sighted wisdom.'

'Cut the crap, Graham, and get to the point!'

'The point, Prime Minister…' it was as well to keep emphasising how important the listener was '…is that the proposed line of the road cuts through a Site of Special Scientific Interest, Hickling Edge. It's also a famed beauty spot and the locals don't want it disfigured by a great gash of a cutting. That's why they want the road moved.'

'Well, why don't we move it then?'

'Cost is the main reason. We've done several alternative studies and this proposal is the most reasonable in agricultural land take and cost.'

'Is there no other solution? What's this about a tunnel?'

'I believe that the locals would be content if, instead of putting the road in a cutting, it was put through a tunnel under Hickling Edge. There would be additional cost but it would be a lot cheaper than moving the road.' *Or losing the next election*, he muttered under his breath.

'How much more?'

'We're looking into that at the moment. I'll ring you back in an hour if that's alright?'

'One hour! And find out who the poor sod wearing the feathers is, that's going to need smoothing over.'

The call was terminated and Preston mopped his brow as he put down the receiver.

Sir Joseph Storey gave a wintry smile.

'When I spoke earlier to Molestrangler, the Kingsforest MP, Minister, he told me that he thought our consultants had done a scheme for tunnelling. He said one of their chappies had shown a proposal for driving twin bores under Hickling Edge at a public meeting and it had gone down very well with the local populace. You may recall I mentioned it to you but you dismissed it.'

'Yes, that's all very well, but if it's going to cost an arm and a leg, we don't have the funds, and that tight-arsed bastard Brown at the Treasury won't give this department another shekel.'

212

Sir Joseph smiled again. 'Leave it with me, Minister,' he soothed and made to leave.

'We've only got an hour, don't forget!' cried Preston in desperation.

Sir Joseph summoned some minions and within minutes he had on his desk all the information he needed about CONDES. He punched out the phone number.

'Sir Joseph Storey, Department of Transport speaking, may I talk to Mr Geoffrey Arbuthnot about the Kingscastle bypass please?' There was a short pause, then: 'Mr Arbuthnot...?' Sir Joseph introduced himself and briefly outlined his reasons for calling. 'And I understand that your firm has done a study for tunnelling under Hickling Edge as an alternative to a deep cutting?'

Arbuthnot gulped. Storey seemed to know more than he did about the Kingscastle bypass, but he was an old campaigner.

'Yes indeed, naturally we look at all solutions to provide our clients with the best possible service.'

'In that case, can you tell me the extra cost, if any, of tunnelling against a cutting? Incidentally, I take it that the unfortunate person who was feathered is one of your staff?' Without waiting for a reply he continued, 'The Prime Minister wishes to extend his deepest sympathy for that unfortunate occurrence.'

Arbuthnot blinked at these two blockbusters. He hadn't the faintest idea what Sir Joseph was talking about. The news about the 'unfortunate occurrence' had not reached him yet, nor did he have the slightest idea of the extra cost. But he knew a man who did.

Arbuthnot was left with his finger in his ear and his mind in a whirl. Cornered, he needed to buy some time.

'Thank you, Sir Joseph, if you can give me ten minutes I'll get the relevant file.'

The intercom buzzed on my desk and I picked up the handset. I immediately recognised the voice and the peremptory tone.

'Moon! Come and see me now, and bring all the Kingscastle files with you.' That was it.

Now what? Had my conversation with the Borough Engineer been sneaked to Arbuthnot? Was this the chop? Was he going to take the bridges from me? Well, if it was either I wasn't going down without a fight. If he wanted a bloody argument then he was going to get one!

Grabbing the pile of Kingscastle files, I strode out of the door like strife before Jerusalem: up the stairs, into Joanna's office and straight through into Arbuthnot's just as her phone rang.

'Right...!' I said, dumping the files on his desk and leaning over it '...what's your problem?' Arbuthnot's eyebrows shot up nearly to his hairline, he reeled back and, from the look of stunned astonishment on his face, I calculated that perhaps I'd got this wrong, so I hastily added '...and what can I do to help?'

'That's a bit sudden isn't it, Moon?'

'Well you emphasised "now", sir, so I dropped everything to get here as quickly as possible.'

It sound feeble to me but he seemed quite impressed. I heaved a sigh of relief. So it wasn't going to be the chop after all.

He put his fingertips together and leant on his desk. 'I've had a phone call from a senior civil servant at the Department of Transport. They're interested in the idea of tunnelling under...' he glanced at his notes '...Hickling Edge, and want to know what extra cost it would entail if it was implemented.'

'It would add three point nine per cent to the total cost of the bypass, approximately seven hundred thousand pounds.' I had the figures fixed in my mind.

'Are you certain?'

I told him I had used Sir Gordon Proctor's figures and my calculations were in the file. Arbuthnot flicked open the top folder with a casual finger and nearly had a coronary. It happened to be the Shering Valley Bridge folder. His eyes bulged, his normally pasty face turned deep pink and strangulated gargles came from his throat.

My first thought was that he was having a seizure, and if he was 'mouth to mouth' was definitely out and chest compressions would be in; but then he jabbed with his finger at the first entry in the folder. I didn't think my calculations could be that far out so I leaned over his desk to have a look. Lying on top were the two pictures of Ivan Masterland in his latex suit at Susan Tripp's House of Pain!

Arbuthnot was virtually speechless; obviously Mrs Arbuthnot was not into flagellation, so clearly this was something of a surprise to him.

He looked up from the file totally bemused, and in a dazed sort of voice repeated, 'Three point nine per cent on the total cost, approximately seven hundred thousand pounds?' I nodded, the brain racing in top gear.

'Sorry sir,' I said as casually as I could. 'Masterland was showing me those pictures of a fancy dress party he went to – vicars and tarts, I think it was; said it was far too racy for him. He must have slipped them into this file by mistake.'

I quickly closed the Bridge folder and whipped out the Costs file, opening that at the pages relating to tunnelling. Arbuthnot looked at them distractedly, probably wondering about the religious beliefs of vicars who dressed from head to toe in shiny black latex and wore blindfolds.

When he had pulled himself together and satisfied himself that the figures matched what I had told him, he nodded. 'Moon, do you know anything about an unfortunate occurrence in Kingscastle?'

My heart nearly stopped. I knew about a few unfortunate occurrences in Kingscastle but I wasn't sure how he knew, or which one he was talking about.

I was saved by the sudden interruption of Joanna, who burst into Arbuthnot's office gasping, 'Ivan Masterland's been attacked in Kingscastle wearing feathers! Apparently it's all over the news! The police have just phoned to say that he's unhurt, they've managed to get all the treacle and feathers off him and have arranged a driver to bring him and his car back here.'

I glanced at Arbuthnot. He was sitting back in his chair, eyes closed, his hand on his forehead, fingers massaging his temples. This latest news must have been the final shock to his system.

First there was Masterland photographed in tight black latex; then the same employee is all over the news wearing feathers. He must have thought it was all too much and didn't seem to have anything to do with Civil Engineering as he recalled it. I imagined the poor bugger thinking: it wasn't like this when Brunel and Telford were in their prime.

'Is that all the information there is?' I asked with interest. 'Is it on the telly?'

Joanna shook her head. 'I don't know, I suppose it must be, but that's all the police told me.'

Arbuthnot pulled himself together; he had to phone Storey back urgently. Perhaps by the time he'd finished his call the other horrors would have evaporated.

Dismissing me with a wave of his hand, Arbuthnot picked up his telephone. I gathered up the files and strolled out of the office past a puzzled Joanna, to whom I gave a grin.

'I think Mr Geoffrey would appreciate a strong cup of tea as soon as possible after he's finished his call.'

*****

Sir Joseph Storey received the information that tunnelling would only add around three quarters of a million to the overall cost of the bypass impassively. As far as his Department was concerned, that was peanuts. He sat there for a moment tapping his teeth with his gold pen while he considered how to use this information to the best advantage – to him, naturally. He decided that if he persuaded the Minister to set up a study group to examine road pricing in general over the whole country, he could add five hundred people to his Department. Yes, that would be the price for getting his Minister out of the Kingscastle mire.

'Three quarters of a million!' Preston spluttered, half choking on his morning tea.

'Don't worry, Minister, I can find that in our budget, but I do think it advisable to form a small study group to examine road pricing so that we're not caught out in the future – with your permission of course. Shall I get our press office to draft out a release about the change?'

Preston agreed wholeheartedly. It would get him off the hook. While the press release was being drafted, he phoned the PM and got clearance for the tunnel on the basis that no extra funds would be needed from The Treasury.

The draft release prepared by the Ministry Press Office under the direction of Sir Joseph read:

'Having been advised by his civil servants, Graham Preston, Secretary of State for Transport and Communications, has decided that the Kingscastle bypass shall pass under the famous beauty spot and Site of Special Scientific Interest, Hickling Edge, in twin tunnels.'

Preston balked at this. *No way Jose.* He wanted a hundred per cent of the credit, he didn't want to share it with the Civil Service. Sir Joseph smoothly suggested that if he was not happy with it they could release his earlier comment when told about tunnelling.

'What was it, Tom, you must have it in your notes?'

Tom Froome flipped over a few pages of his notebook and then read out. '*...if those fucking locals think we're going to spend a fortune on tunnelling under their blasted hill they've got another think coming.*'

But Preston was a shrewd politician and Storey had to defer to him in the end. The headlines next day read.

'*Minister Intervenes to save Countryside.*

The Right Honourable Graham Preston MP, Secretary of State for Transport and Communications, has personally intervened to instruct that the new Kingscastle bypass be put through twin tunnels under Hickling Edge in order to preserve the views of this famous landmark for the people of this country. Hickling Edge is a Site of Special Scientific Interest and the Minister emphasised that it was vital for his government to ensure that the country's heritage is protected from the ravages of developers and their ilk. The tunnels will be incorporated in the Department of Transport and Communication's case at the Public Enquiry to be held in Kingscastle next month.'

*****

The news about Ivan had spread like lightning round the firm and when I got back to my office, Des was hopping about with glee.

'Is this your doing?'

'No it isn't, it's nothing to do with me whatsoever!'

He looked at me sceptically. 'You don't seem over upset by the news.'

'Neither do you. Capering about like Felix the Cat.'

'He's really going to be pissed off with the world now, so we'd all better watch out.' Des chuckled again. 'I can't wait to see the telly tonight or the papers tomorrow morning. It's certainly brought the MOVE THE BYPASS protest to the nation's attention.'

It had certainly caught the Minister for Transport's attention and I was gratified next morning to read in the *Telegraph* that he had now accepted that a tunnel solution was a better bet for Hickling Edge and, presumably, his chances of being re-elected at the next election. That headline on page two was a follow-up piece to the front-page picture of Ivan covered in white feathers with just his dark head and his dark feet free. I bought copies of *The Mail, The Sun, The Mirror* and *The Times*. They all used roughly the same partial long shot of Ivan standing in Kingscastle Market Square. *The Mirror* and *The Sun* had a close-up of him tumbling out of the back of a white van as well. I cut out all the pictures and was just about to drop them in a drawer when something on the long shots caught my eye. Behind Ivan was a row of shops with Boots and W H Smith prominent but between them was a gap, obviously the unit there had been demolished but clearly it was a prime site. There was a sign fastened to the hoarding but it wasn't clear; the cameras were focussed on Ivan, not the background. I could make out a short word and then a slightly longer word. Could it be a 'For Sale' notice? How to check without driving all the way to Kingscastle? I did think of asking Ivan if he'd happened to notice it while he was in the square but I thought it was a bit provocative.

He didn't show up for work that morning anyway, Hugo came in and told us that Ivan had become something of a celebrity and the press were clamouring for his side of the story.

'What about the effect on CONDES?' Des asked, but Hugo seemed quite relaxed about that.

'There's no such thing as bad publicity,' he grinned, 'as long as they spell our name right.'

As the next day was Saturday I decided to forgo my usual lunchtime at the Frog and Nightgown and drive down to Kingscastle to check out that site. Stalls had been set up in the Market Square and it was thronging with people. I parked in the Town Hall car park, no longer worried about my safety, and wandered through the crowd to where Smiths and Boots were located. It was a 'For Sale' sign on the vacant site, and it gave the name and phone number of the estate agents handling the sale. The sign looked new and I could hear sounds of a digger working behind the hoarding. I rang the agents on my mobile, hoping I hadn't had a wasted journey. No, they said, demolition was just being completed, the site was still for sale but they had had a lot of enquiries. Well, they would say that. I arranged to call in and get the particulars.

Anderson, Casely and Pearce were just round the corner and Mr Anderson, a rubicund cheerful soul, told me that it had only come on the market three days ago but it would have a much higher value if the bypass went ahead and got rid of the terrible congestion in the town. He said the owner wanted a quick sale and if he got the asking price they wouldn't go to auction. He obviously thought the forthcoming Public Enquiry meant that there was still some considerable doubt about the bypass. I didn't disillusion him. I thanked him for the information and told him that a colleague of mine would be in touch.

As soon as I was out of earshot of the agency I rang Bob Barclay on his mobile. He was with the boys in the Frog.

'Bob, you remember asking me to keep my eye open for a possible development in Kingscastle? Well, I think I've found you a site. It's a cracker, right in the Market Square between Boots and W H Smith. If you're interested I should get yourself down here as soon as possible.'

There was a sharp intake of breath. 'Are you sure, Moon? It's not one of your shitty spoofs again, is it?'

'No it isn't, you ungrateful bastard, and for your scepticism there'll be a substantial finder's fee.'

'You've convinced me now!' he laughed. 'I'll be down there this afternoon. Will the estate agents be open?'

I told him they would (I had seen their closing times on their door), and that I'd meet him outside the Town Hall at two-thirty.

CHAPTER 10

Jessie, the well-built barmaid at the Frog and Nightgown, brought the tarnished silver ice bucket over to our table and turned the bottle of Dom Perignon 1986 round so that Bob could read the label.

'Just the job,' he pronounced, rubbing his hands together as Jessie made short work of the gold foil, wire and cork.

This was not the usual Saturday group; the people gathered round the table in the Frog that evening were only Bob's close friends: Tony Scales with his girl friend Simone. Pete Smallwood, Bob's partner Martin Holmes and me with Charlie. We were celebrating the setting up of Barclay Developments Limited and the acquisition of its first site – a small supermarket in Kingscastle.

Bob raised his glass.

'Here's to Marcus, who found the site at great personal risk to life and limb. Not his, naturally, but one of our feathered friends.'

We all toasted Ivan and hoped that eventually he might moult.

When the champagne had been demolished – which didn't take long – we piled into a couple of taxis and shot off to The English House for a special dinner at Barclay's expense.

Next morning I went to see Hugo to see if the design of a small supermarket was of interest to CONDES and he enthusiastically confirmed that it was.

'Great oaks from little acorns grow, Marcus.'

I didn't mention Ivan and his press coverage.

'How are things in Civil Team Two these days?' It was just tossed out casually but Hugo's sharp eyes scanned my face. Ivan's return to work after his feathering had provoked a lot of controversy. There were those who thought it couldn't have happened to a more deserving person – those tended to be the ones that knew him. There were those who just thought the whole thing very funny, generally the structural engineers who thought most things in life were funny. There was Awful Agatha, who said it was disgusting and was cloyingly sympathetic to her man; and there was Hugo, Des and me who, although we'd had a laugh at his appearance in the media, were worried about the effect it might have on his state of mind because we had to work with him.

Ivan had taken a few days off, and when he returned to the office he was much more introverted. It seemed as if he expected that everybody was going to point him out and laugh at him. Des and I both told him we were appalled that he should have been subjected to that ordeal and that if he wanted more time off we would cover for him. Of course, being Ivan, he took this the wrong way and accused us of trying to use his embarrassment as a means of taking over his work and diminishing his position.

'What position?' we echoed together.

Then he said to me through tight lips, 'I haven't forgotten that it was you that sent me to Kingscastle.'

'Don't be ridiculous, Ivan, I did no such thing; I just told you that the Borough Engineer wanted to discuss the landscaping of the bypass. I didn't know what you were going to do, or when; or even if you were going to go down there, so don't blame me for what happened. It could just as easily have been me!'

Little did I know the truth of that but I don't think Ivan was convinced.

I shrugged my shoulders at Hugo's question. 'We're getting on well with drafting the tender documents for the bypass so if, or rather when, we get the go-ahead everything is on programme, so no problems there.'

'That's not what I meant.'

I knew it wasn't what he meant, and as the senior partner elect it was his job to know the state of morale and cooperation within the company. But I didn't like being put in the position of office snitch.

'Look, we're professional engineers, Hugo, and we're all doing our jobs to the best of our ability. We don't have to have friendly personal relationships to do that, although it would be more pleasant if we did,' I added wistfully.

He nodded. 'OK, as long as it doesn't affect our work. By the way, well done about the supermarket.'

*****

Major Sir Fistulas Withers OBE [Military] nibbled the top of his Mont Blanc pen as he sat upright at his desk trying to cudgel activity in his brain. He had a double problem: if he wanted his evidence to the Public Enquiry to be taken seriously he had to submit it to the Authorities in Trowbridge in writing at least two weeks in advance. The problem was he knew those pen-pushing wallahs in the County Council would just file it amongst the rest of the petitions from the idiots and half-wits he assumed would be objectors, and do absolutely nothing about it. He also realised that if he really said what he felt about the snivelling weasels hiding behind their shield of bureaucracy in their steam-heated offices with their inflation-proof pensions who were proposing to ride roughshod over his civil rights, they would chuck it straight into the waste basket.

His second problem was what to do in addition in order to make an impact. More nibbling of the Mont Blanc continued. The only things these days that seemed to make any form of impact with the Government was civil disorder, marching, rioting, stone-throwing, battling with the police. Pictures of horses rearing with hooves flailing, tear gas billowing, police in riot gear clubbing down elderly ladies, crowds machine gunned, babies being eaten alive... He checked himself; it was a very satisfying thought but his imagination had been running riot. However, it was clear that some form of public troublemaking was required if attention was to be drawn to his argument. The problem was he didn't know how to organise it.

Those three women who had treacled and feathered that fellow from the Ministry had certainly attracted national coverage, but he didn't want to spend the next two years doing jankers in one of the Her Majesty's prisons.

In the old days he could have arranged a battalion of Pioneers, with shovels and buckets, marching shoulder-to-shoulder through Kingscastle singing their marching song, 'We're going to dig latrines and stick it up the Marines', but those days were long gone.

A stiff whisky and soda was called for to stimulate the few brain cells he had, and when Percival shimmered in with the 'bracer', Withers stopped him leaving by asking, 'Percival, do we know anybody who could make trouble?'

'Trouble, sir?'

'Yes, trouble, Percival. Marching, rioting, chanting, blocking-the-road sort of trouble.'

The butler looked perplexed. 'If you could indicate in which direction you would like to focus this "trouble" sir, I will give it some thought.'

'The Public Enquiry, man, what else? That's what I want it to focus on. I want to ram my argument down the Government's throat and the more publicly the better. It's the only way, Percival, the only way!"

'Very good, sir.' And Percival silently shimmered out, still bemused.

Fifteen minutes later there was a gentle knock on the drawing room door and Percival eased in with a discreet cough.

'Yes, what is it, Percival? I'm trying to put together this damned document which nobody will read anyway, so make it snappy.'

'Something has occurred to me which may be of assistance, sir. You will recall the telephone conversation you had some months ago with a gentleman who went by the name of Stumpy. He spoke to you in connection with STOP THE BYPASS?'

Withers shook his head. 'Can't remember the fellow.'

'If I recall, sir, he was proposing to take some physical action on your property to prevent the road being built and wanted your cooperation.'

Withers screwed up his face thoughtfully. 'Yes, I do remember something of the kind, now that you come to mention it, but what has that to do with making trouble?'

Percival blinked, thinking that it should be obvious even to a lobotomised goldfish, but wisely, he kept both his thoughts, and thus his job, to himself.

'Well, sir, I would suggest that Mr Stumpy probably associates with the same lower social classes as those who form the gangs of hooligans and ne'er-do-wells that we see frequently on television demonstrating and attacking the police. Perhaps contact with him could be of assistance to you?'

'By God, Percival, you could be right – but how do I get hold of him?'

'Leave it to me, sir, and I will make enquiries.'

After three days of head-scratching, pen-chewing, re-writing and Scotch-drinking, Withers surveyed his statement for the Public Enquiry with some satisfaction. There was no attempt at logical argument or statistical support; he had simply condensed his thoughts so that now they consisted of a series of bullet points, military fashion:

1] Don't want it across my land.

2] Will ruin the shooting estate.

3] Will be an eyesore.

4] Will cause a lot of disturbance with dust, noise and pollution.

5] Will cost a lot of money that could be spent on hospitals.

(He rather liked that one, it was a telling point. He gave a grim smile. *I bet they've not thought of that in Whitehall; it could rock the politicians back on their heels.*)

6] Won't sell land for it.

7] Will go to The European Court for Human Rights.

He didn't actually know what The European Court for Human Rights was, but thought that the threat of it would put the shits up the politicians as well.

Yes, he thought, that should do it, cut out the waffle and drive his point well and truly home. He rang the bell to summon Percival.

'What do you think of that eh?'

He handed him the draft. Percival scanned it quickly.

'Very good sir, but if I might make an observation, what exactly is the point you are trying to ram home?'

'To get the bypass either stopped or moved, man, isn't it obvious?'

Percival coughed gently. 'To you and I, sir, yes. But I think you should spell it out clearly in your statement. You know how these clever lawyers can twist words.'

Withers frowned as he acknowledged that Percival had a point and added to his bullet points:

8] Should be cancelled or moved elsewhere.

He printed off the statement, folded it, put it in an envelope and told Percival to address it to the Inspector at County Hall, Trowbridge and send it first-class.

Then a thought struck him so he called Percival back, slit open the envelope, added his name and address and signed it.

Percival hovered, giving his usual discreet cough that signalled he wanted to attract attention. Withers looked at him irritably.

'What now?'

'I have located Mr Stumpy, sir, as you asked. Do you wish me to do anything further?'

Withers certainly did but he hadn't thought it through yet so he replied, 'Just give me the address.'

'It isn't an address, sir; it's a mobile telephone number. Apparently Mr Stumpy is of no fixed abode.'

'Well, leave it on my desk; I'll deal with it later.'

The more Withers thought about it, the better it became. There would be nothing in writing to connect him to any incidents, and Percival could get Stumpy to make all the arrangements. No doubt Stumpy would need paying in cash, so there was some risk there, but if he could agree that it would be half up front with the other half on completion, it would both increase the incentive and halve the risk. The difficulty was that Withers had no idea what was required to make sufficient trouble at the Public Enquiry to ensure that his complaints were advertised to the country in general and the Government in particular. He would have to rely on Stumpy's advice for that – which left everything open-ended.

'What you need for that, squire, is three charas of the lads to pack the audience. I can get you two from Swindon and one from Bath and they'll bring all the banners and stuff – but it ain't going to be cheap.'

'How much?'

'Let me see. Thirty lads on each bus: it's a ton a day per head, that's three grand; plus another grand for the bus hire and exes: say twelve grand total.'

Withers nearly choked. 'Are you telling me it would cost twelve thousand pounds for a couple of hours' trouble-making? That's damned outrageous, daylight robbery! You must think I came over on the last boat, I'm not going to pay that!'

'It's up to you, squire, if you think you can do better elsewhere then fuck off and try, but that's the going rate for Rent-a-Crowd.'

Withers knew he was over a barrel and gritted his teeth. 'Alright, but it's half up front and half when your people have torn the place apart.'

'Cash,' said Stumpy. 'We don't do cheques.'

Withers thought about that, he didn't want Stumpy seen turning up at the Hall.

'My butler will meet you in The Royal Oak in Kingscastle Market Place tomorrow night at seven o'clock with the first payment. He'll give you instructions about the date, time and place.'

'And he'd better be there with the bloody second payment before the charas leave after they've done their stuff squire, otherwise…!' The threat hung in the air.

*****

The Public Enquiry into the Kingscastle bypass was scheduled to be held in Kingscastle Town Hall under the direction of the Department of the Environment's inspector, a Mr Gilbert Bowman. All parties who had submitted written objections, and had not withdrawn them, were advised by letter, and notices were prominently displayed around the town.

Major Sir Fistulas Withers Bt. MBE [Military] opened his letter and gave a snort of disgust as he read that in view of the small number of written objections, he would be given the opportunity to expound his case immediately after the Highway Authority's Consultants had explained the detailed design of the scheme. The estimated time when he would be called was two o'clock on the second day, immediately after lunch.

'Going to ruin my blasted lunch!' he fumed. Well, he was going to give that Government lackey Bowman something to think about. If they thought they could buy his land they were wrong; he had already made that perfectly clear by kicking those surveyors they sent to negotiate with him out of the front door on their arses.

His lawyer, the spineless wimp, had advised him to negotiate to get the best price – otherwise, he warned, the Government could acquire what they needed by issuing a Compulsory Purchase Order and just taking it.

'A few charges of buckshot are what they'll get if they set foot on my land, Compulsory Purchase Order or no,' Withers had told him.

Now he had an ally in Stumpy, who would make sure that the Major's point was well and truly made. Withers smiled with grim satisfaction.

*****

To my relief, although I would attend, it was decided that Hugo would present the technical evidence on behalf of the Department of Transport at the Public Enquiry. Ivan refused flatly to show himself in public in Kingscastle, and my piece, the Shering Valley Bridge, was no problem for Hugo, who was a specialist bridge engineer himself. He asked us both to write a brief summary of our reasoning for the choices we had made, and Ivan had to swallow his pride and explain about the twin tunnels under Hickling Edge. I printed mine off my PC and got the engineers running the CAD program to produce coloured pictures of the

Shering Valley Bridge from various strategic view points to illustrate that it fitted into the environment, and then left the whole lot for Angela to mount on stiff card and pass on to Hugo.

He was scheduled to speak after a woman from the Highways Agency presented their statistical case for constructing a bypass round Kingscastle. She would provide all the traffic information and future traffic forecasts, outline the current situation in the town and explain how it would be significantly improved. Hugo would explain why it would be built at that particular location, how the sensitive areas of the Shering Valley and Hickling Edge would be treated, how nuisance from noise and dust would be controlled, and the other steps that would be taken to minimise inconvenience to local people and businesses during construction.

There didn't seem to be anything controversial in any of that and I wasn't sure why my presence in Kingscastle was required. I got a vague impression that perhaps I was being roped in as a bodyguard in case the locals changed their minds yet again, deciding that there was something else they didn't like and put their objections to Hugo in another unusual but forceful way.

'Shall I bring my Under Thirteen House Boxing Certificate to brandish and frighten them off, Hugo?

He gave a weak smile and changed the subject. 'We'll have to stay somewhere overnight. What about that place you stayed at? Could they put us up? I heard that she's a good cook.'

I gave a start, I was hoping I'd heard that correctly and flashed Hugo a nervous look to check. There was no duplicity in his

234

manner so I spluttered something about only having one room with a single bed, and suggested that Jane book us both into the Royal Oak Hotel in the Market Place – 'It's much closer to the Town Hall,' I told him.

I also suggested that I went down to Kingscastle the day before for two reasons. The first, to see what the set-up was for the Enquiry; and the second to check out the foundation sites at both ends of the Shering Valley Bridge. All the test bores had been done and they showed hard chalk four metres down, but I wanted to get a feel of the locations. The Hickling Edge end I had not seen at all, and the Withers Woods end only sketchily, being otherwise engaged in pale moonlight whilst on top of Tracey Tripp – not the most reliable way of checking out a site, if much more pleasurable. I chuckled at the thought of Geoffrey reading an imaginary soils report that said: '*The bearing capacity of the ground was ascertained by driving Tracey Tripp into it with repeated thrusts.*'

It was a lovely morning when I set off for Kingscastle at six-thirty. In the clear night the first frosts of autumn had brushed the grasses and trees, diamonds sparkled all round in the bright early sun. I registered at The Royal Oak, confirmed Hugo's reservation and wandered across to the Borough Engineer's office for a chat. His secretary was still chilly but brought me a coffee with sugar in it this time. The BE said that they had one or two minor points to raise about disposal of earth, and mud on roads, but nothing serious.

I drove out to the spot in Withers Woods where I'd parked before, strolled down through the Shering Valley, crossed the river over a footbridge and made my way to the bottom of Hickling Edge. It was quite an escarpment, a lot higher and steeper in close up that it had appeared from a distance. It would be an interesting transition from the bridge straight into the tunnels. There didn't appear to be any obvious problems on that side of the river so I wandered back to the leafy hollow where Stumpy and his cohorts had frustrated my attempt, as I thought at the time, at seduction.

It was very quiet in the woods, there was no wind and the warm air was still. Then I heard a noise, I couldn't be sure but I thought I heard a soft mewling sound somewhere off to my left. Normally this would just have been dismissed it as one of the many woodland sounds, a bird or a small creature, but something made me turn off the track and investigate. Under a tree I found a small dog of indeterminate breed – indeterminate to me, that is – lying on its side in obvious distress. The reason for its distress was abundantly clear. Its front driver's-side paw was wedged tightly between the roots of the tree. The poor creature had gnawed on its own leg to try to free itself and was now lying at an awkward angle, utterly exhausted with pain and fatigue.

I reached out to see what was holding the paw and if I could free it but the terrified animal bared its teeth and gave a threatening growl. You couldn't blame it! Hunting around, I found a broken branch that looked fairly strong then I took off my thin, lightweight jacket and wound it round my left forearm. Approaching the dog, I offered it my protected arm and made what I hoped it would interpret as friendly soothing noises.

It didn't! It roused itself sufficiently to seize the arm in its teeth – teeth that were sharp and strong enough to go right through the jacket and into my arm. I winced but the dog hung on so I was able to wedge the branch against the root and ease the paw backwards so that it was released. I could see the problem; there was a squashed piece of metal gripping the paw just above the foot. The dog must have put its foot into the hole between the roots and forced it through the metal band; it then couldn't pull it out. I eased the band open, slid it off the paw and dropped it in my pocket. The dog gave a yelp of pain and let go of my arm. It just lay there exhausted with a pleading look in its eyes. It seemed to know that it was I who had helped it but it didn't know what to do next. Get it to a vet, was my thought. The paw had started to bleed again so I wrapped my handkerchief tightly round it whilst the dog just lay there patiently.

'Come on, Nipper, you poor little feller, let's get you out of here and that leg attended to.'

I scooped him up in my arms and made my way back down the track to where I had parked the car. Using my jacket as a bed, I made the dog as comfortable as I could in the foot-well of the passenger seat and set off back towards Kingscastle.

The first person I saw as I entered the outskirts was an elderly lady walking with a large dog, a Labrador at a guess. She would be likely to know where the nearest vet was, so I pulled up alongside her and wound down the window. Fortunately, she said, the nearest vet was only a couple of hundred yards away. She gave me precise directions and told me the vet's name was Mrs Chynoweth and she was very good.

There was a small car park at the side of the surgery with two other cars in it, so I parked in a slot and managed to lift Nipper out without hurting him. I carried him into the waiting area, where two people sat looking daggers at each other: a small boy with a white mouse that was running up and down his arm and round his neck, and a starchy looking lady with a large Persian cat on her lap that had its fur raised and its eyes fixed rigidly on the mouse. I explained the circumstances of Nipper's injury to the receptionist and she immediately went in to speak to the vet. Mrs Chynoweth was a large, kindly looking lady in a white coat. She had that manner that animals seem to sense is for their benefit and they relax in her presence. Nipper, who had been trembling and whimpering as I talked to the receptionist, immediately calmed down when Mrs Chynoweth took him from me and carried him into her surgery. She laid him on the table and unwound the handkerchief. Gently taking the paw in her gloved hand to examine it, she drew in a sharp breath.

'Nasty damage but not too serious, it will heal in time,' she murmured as she carefully cleaned the wound.

This was good news for me but even better news for Nipper, although he wasn't aware of the alternative.

'Fortunately the bone isn't broken,' she said. 'I think I can stitch the wound and save the paw. Do you know who he belongs to?'

I shook my head. Mrs Chynoweth reached over and turned the collar on his neck round so that we could read the small brass label riveted to it.

'His name is Ben and he lives at 24, Mayfield Avenue. Do you know where that is?'

I shook my head again. 'I'm a stranger round here.'

'It's not far away. I'm going to have to put him to sleep to do the stitching and then he won't be able to walk on that leg for a few days. Can you take him home?'

I nodded and said I'd wait.

She smiled. 'You'd better let me have a look at that arm of yours before you go as well, it looks like quite a deep bite mark you have there.'

I glanced at the puncture wounds on my arm where Ben's sharp teeth had bitten through my jacket and she was right, they did look a bit sore with a slight oozing of blood.

'I don't think he's got rabies,' she grinned, 'otherwise we might have to put you down instead!'

Half an hour later, with my arm dressed by Mrs Chynoweth and a still woozy Ben curled up back in the foot-well of my car, I set off to follow the directions she had given me to Mayfield Avenue, the home – although I wasn't aware of it at that time – of Mrs Evadne Stoate. Mrs Stoate, it turned out, was not one of life's optimists.

I left Ben in the car; I thought it might not be wise to turn up at the front door with the family pet mutilated and semi-conscious in my arms. Walking up the uneven path to the door, I rang the bell. There was a short pause and then the door opened as far as the security chain would allow.

'Excuse me, madam…' I began. 'Do you happen—' I was cut off at that point by a powerful voice.

'Whatever you're selling, young man, I don't want any, so bugger off!' And the door started to close.

'No, no, you don't understand!' I cried hastily. 'I'm not selling anything, it's about your dog, Ben.'

With that there was a rattle of chain and the door swung right open to reveal a large woman in middle age, I guessed, wrapped in a floral dressing-gown. She had thick grey hair held back with a hair-band and her red face was screwed up into a scowl. Hands like a grab dredger started to reach for my throat.

'What have you done with my Ben, you swine? Her scowl grew even more ferocious as some recognition appeared in her eyes. 'You're the bloody council's dog-catcher, aren't you? There's that shifty look about you. You've taken him, haven't you? Well, if you've hurt him I'll rip your bloody head off here and now, you cruel bastard!'

It was not difficult to tell that she was not best pleased with her local council's approach to animal welfare and, although somewhat nettled at being identified as the council's dog-catcher, I thought it prudent to step back quickly out of grab range.

The first thought that came into my head was – '*A good decision, Marcus, to leave the dog in the car.*' Standing there clutching a badly damaged, semi-conscious dog in my arms would have taken some explaining, and I didn't think I would have been given much time to outline my case before becoming head-less in a very painful way.

'Madam, I assure you that I'm not from the council and Ben is quite safe,' This was gabbled out rapidly. However it seemed to pacify her slightly and she lowered her hands. 'In fact I have him with me in my car.' I gestured towards the gate. Her scowl changed into a puzzled frown. I continued: 'I found him in Withers Woods, he's – erhm, resting at the moment.'

'Oh my poor darling!' cried Mrs Stoate and, brushing me aside, she swept down the path like the four furies, wrenched open the passenger door of the MG and beheld the curled up, doped up, bandaged up and fed up form of Ben lying on my jacket. He gave a little whimper of recognition as she cradled him to her ample bosom, making cooing noises and showering kisses on his head.

It must have dawned on her at that point that, although Ben was by no means his normal, perky, woofing self, he had been well treated, and that I, standing there jacketless and with a bandaged arm, having delivered him to her door, so to speak, must have had something to do with the well treating. Consequently Ben was deposited back on the passenger seat and before I could turn, I found myself taking his place, clutched headfirst between her enormous breasts, held there helplessly by two meaty arms the size of York hams. Oh Christ, I thought, I hope she doesn't start kissing my head as well!

'Thank you, thank you!' she cried. 'I was so worried about him, he's been missing for three days. I thought the council's dog-catchers had taken him. What happened?'

241

I think she realised that in the position I was held I couldn't reply to this, so she released me, picked Ben up again and said, 'Come in and tell me all about it. I'm Mrs Stoate, by the way, but you can call me Evadne.'

Her house was the left-hand one of a pair of semi-detached in a street of semis. Inside it was immaculate. She deposited Ben in a neat little basket in the corner of the kitchen with the word 'BEN' stitched into his blanket so, if he had a sudden memory loss, he could tell it was his.

He licked her hand as she put him down.

'I'll make some tea,' she said. 'You go and make yourself comfortable in the sitting room.'

I gave a slight shudder. This had an ominously familiar ring to it and, if I was right, then it would have to be stamped on as soon as possible. I looked round carefully. A large silver photo-frame on the mantelpiece contained the black and white photo of a couple at the door of a church. In a white wedding-dress and three stone lighter was Evadne. Presumably the man grinning inanely by her side, was Mr Stoate, but there was no sign of a male presence in the room. Lionel Tripp sprang to mind but the thought was so awful that I wiped it out immediately.

Evadne brought in two steaming mugs of tea and sat down on the sofa. I had taken the one- person armchair.

'Now tell me all about it,' she began.

I gave her an outline about finding Ben trapped in a tree root, taking him to the vet and what Mrs Chynoweth had said about his paw not being broken but requiring rest to give it time to heal. She listened in grim silence until I had finished. I fished the offending piece of metal out of my pocket and gave it to her. She looked at it closely.

'It seems to be a bracelet of some sort that's got squashed, and it's quite heavy.'

It was covered in soil so she took it to the kitchen and rinsed it off under the tap. When she came back she was quite excited.

'It's very pretty, and look, it's got some sort of little stones round the edges. It's a pity it's all squashed.'

I took it from her; it was indeed quite heavy and, cleaned up, looked as though it could be valuable. I handed it back to her.

She frowned. 'Somebody must have dropped it accidentally; I'll take it down to the Police Station as soon as Ben's fit to walk to see if someone's reported it lost.'

She dropped it into a Winston Churchill Toby Jug on the mantelpiece.

Mrs Stoate had been so overjoyed at getting Ben back and talking about the bangle that it only now suddenly seemed to occur to her that she was entertaining a complete stranger in her house wearing a dressing-gown. I wasn't too happy either, as her gown had slipped open to reveal a meaty thigh and it was clear that she wasn't wearing much underneath it. She blushed and pulled the gown more tightly around her.

'I'll just go and put something decent on but take your time with your tea,' she said, disappearing out of the door. She was back in a couple of minutes wearing a jumper and slacks and looking more comfortable. I felt the same – the Tripp females had made me twitchy.

She looked at me quizzically. 'I've seen you somewhere before haven't I, what's your name?'

'Marcus Moon,' I replied noncommittally.

'You're not from round here are you, Marcus?'

'My home town is York but I live in London now.' I could see the next question in her eyes.

'If it's not a rude question, what's a chap from London doing wandering in Withers Woods?'

Well there was no point beating about the bush so I told her. 'I work for the consulting engineers who are designing the proposed new bypass and I was reconnoitring the site of one of the bridges. I'm here to help in case my boss needs support giving evidence at the Public Enquiry that starts tomorrow.'

I waited to find out if she was a pro or an anti as far as the bypass was concerned.

'That's where I've seen you! You spoke at that public meeting in the Town Hall and told us about the tunnels.'

She suddenly found herself faced with a dilemma. She had been an anti simply because she didn't like change. She had joined Withers' campaign because of the vague feeling that any change would not be beneficial to Kingscastle, but without giving much thought as to the pros and cons of that specific proposal. She had never liked the arrogant and self-centred Major ever since he had given Ben a kicking under the table when Ben peed on his shoes at a STOP THE BYPASS meeting. Now she felt positively hostile towards him because Ben had been injured in Withers Woods.

'Do you think it would be good for the town if it went ahead?' she asked tentatively. 'It will ruin vast expanses of our beautiful countryside and cause an awful lot of mess, noise and disturbance, won't it?'

I gave her as truthful a reply as I could. 'The answer to your main question is that you'll be surprised how much the town will benefit from the removal of all the through traffic from its narrow streets. More shops will open, business will thrive, people will be able to walk about with being choked by fumes and dust and the whole place will lighten up. That's the benefit.

'However, there's no doubt that there'll be disruption for two years while the new road is being built. You'll have some contractors' traffic passing through the town, some of the countryside will disappear under tarmac and concrete for ever – but less than you imagine. Landscaping will soften the impact, and large parts of the Withers Estate, which are private now, will be visible to the general public. Most of the new road goes through that one ownership, you know. We sent him a copy of the draft route; it's by far the cheapest solution.'

I raised a questioning eyebrow at the expression on Evadne's face.

'We didn't realise that!' she exclaimed. 'Withers has never mentioned that to the committee. He's being telling everybody that it would take land from hard-up farmers, tenants and small-holders. That's what he led everyone to believe. No wonder the swine has got this protest group together! He's just looking after his own interests, and he doesn't give a hoot about the town!'

Glancing at my watch, I said I'd better be going, thanked her for the tea, expressed the hope that Ben would shake off his ordeal quickly and stood up to leave.

Evadne said, 'I don't think I've thanked you enough for saving Ben. Without you he would have died the most awful death and he's all I've got since Mr Stoate passed away last year. Please come and see me again the next time you're in Kingscastle – if you can spare the time.'

I'm sure it was well meant so I murmured my thanks, scratched Ben behind the ears as I passed through the kitchen on my way to the door, and received a little chirrup of recognition.

'He likes you,' commented Evadne as she showed me out.

So he bloody should, I thought when I examined my chewed up, blood-stained, dog-haired jacket after I climbed into the MG. A hundred quid at Austin Reed that had set me back. I hoped that the Royal Oak could get it dry cleaned so that it would be at least presentable for the Enquiry next day.

*****

The Public Enquiry opened in Kingscastle Town Hall on Wednesday 28th October, presided over by Mr Gilbert Bowman. MA[Cantab], C.Eng, FICE, Dipl.TP. The first day was a non-event. Ms Margery Glazebrook from the Highways Agency gave her evidence in a concise and prim manner. Most of it consisted of statistics: traffic flows past, present and estimated, cost benefits to the nation, reduction in road deaths and injuries and waffle of that ilk. Nobody questioned it when invited to do so, nobody mentioned political expediency, and nobody mentioned the by-election in North Wilts.

Hugo was called up to the rostrum next to address those who had managed to remain awake. He explained that we had examined routes both north and south of the town and the southerly route had not been welcomed as it destroyed the water meadows of the River Shering and the historic view of the town church as painted by John Constable. Two northern routes had been examined and the one chosen was substantially cheaper, it would be quicker to construct and would cause less disruption to the local populace. There were two major problems that had to be overcome: the Shering Valley and Hickling Edge. Hugo told the Enquiry that CONDES appreciated that these were very sensitive issues and, after discussions with the Kingscastle authorities as promised, a design for the Shering Valley Bridge had been agreed and some views of it were pinned up on the wall behind the inspector.

'Now for Hickling Edge,' he said with that disarming smile of his. 'Yes, that has been a problem…' There were a few guffaws from the sparse audience. '…but the Ministry has dug into their pockets and found the necessary cash to cover the cost of driving twin tunnels under the Edge and thus preserve the unique landscape of this feature.'

'How long will it take to build this road?' a woman asked.

Hugo smiled again. 'If the road is approved following this Enquiry then it could be completed two and a half years from the date of the approval.' Although he didn't mention it, that would be about the time the next General Election was due so Hugo was using that to push the Government for a quick approval.

There being no other questions, the Inspector adjourned the hearing until ten the next morning, when landscaping and security would be presented.

Next morning Hugo and I had the full English West Country Breakfast together in the oak-panelled dining room of the hotel, me with unabated enthusiasm and him with a guilty conscience.

'Don't you dare mention this to Emily,' he warned me. 'Otherwise your progress upwards in consulting engineering will come to a juddering halt.'

Well, it was nice to know that I was progressing and it was upwards so, with a mouth full of Wiltshire sausage and egg, I shook my head, confirming acceptance of the situation.

Mr Bowman gave a final glance at his watch as the minute hand reached ten o'clock and called Giles Fotheringham, the Highways Agency's landscape specialist, to give his evidence.

Hugo gave me a nudge. 'There's a lady over there trying to attract your attention.'

He pointed across the hall to where, with a start, I saw Susan Tripp wiggling her fingers in the air and staring in my direction.

My heart gave a jolt. Oh ah, this was going to be a bit tricky. I put the brain into overdrive and ended up with mental wheelspin – I got nowhere. A half-hearted wave back was my only response.

'A friend of yours?' Hugo asked.

'Sort of.' I tried to sound offhand.

'The great cook?'

I still wasn't sure if he was taking the piss so I just nodded and fumbled in my case for something to distract him. I gave him the soils report. He took it with a frown.

'I've already got a copy of that,' he said, and gave it back to me.

'Sorry,' I apologised, but it achieved its object, it got him off the subject of Susan Tripp. It was a temporary reprieve.

Fotheringham was followed by Group 4's security expert, who outlined the measures they would take to prevent any disruption and vandalising of the contractor's plant if the road went ahead. Bowman adjourned the Enquiry for a one-hour lunch break and said that the afternoon would be given over to local people who had submitted written objections, before he took any final statements.

Hugo and I were pushing off to The Swan for a pint and a sandwich when Susan cut through the few spectators and buttonholed me just before I could escape through the door.

'Hello, Marcus, you're a naughty boy, you haven't been to see us lately!' She looked towards Hugo questioningly so I had to do the introductions.

'This is my boss, Hugo Elmes, Mrs Tripp,' I told her, putting as much steel into my voice as I could and fixing her with a warning glare. 'This is Mrs Tripp, Hugo; she's the lady who looked after me when I came to do the soil survey permissions.'

'Pleased to meet you, I'm sure, and you must call me Susan.' She gave Hugo her warm smile.

Oh please God no, I was thinking, but Hugo didn't appear to sense any undercurrent and reciprocated the warm smile.

'We're just going to The Swan for a bite to eat, why don't you join us, Susan?'

My heart sank further. Please say 'no' I prayed.

'I'd love to, thank you.'

She walked beside Hugo, chatting. 'We've also had the pleasure of putting up your Mr Masterland, he's been to see us a couple of times but Marcus has only stayed the once.'

I was torn between speculating on what that randy little pervert Ivan had been up to with his secret visits that he hadn't mentioned, and what she was going to drop out next. Fortunately Giles Fotheringham hove in sight and asked if he could join us for lunch. I could have kissed him!

At our table, the waiter asked what we would like to drink. Susan said, 'A large gin and tonic', adding, with a glance at me: 'Brings back memories.'

Hugo raised an eyebrow questioningly and I squeezed everything together tightly. Before she could say any more I gabbled, 'And what will you have, Giles?'

He ordered the same and then the focus was on Hugo. He forgot his implied question temporarily and ordered a pint of bitter.

'Same for me,' I said, adding hastily, 'I heard a funny joke the other day. This man was waiting at the bus stop when the bus came. It was full so the driver told him to wait for the next one. "How long will it be?" he asked. "Twelve and a half metres, same as this," cracked the driver!'

I laughed heartily at my own joke but nobody else laughed and, surprised by this sudden change of subject, they all looked at me as though I'd gone nuts.

Hugo murmured, 'Really!'

It achieved its object though, and Susan's reference to the G and T was forgotten.

'It all seems to be going smoothly,' Giles observed, getting us back to the Enquiry.

'Have you heard any stories about what's likely to come up this afternoon?' asked Hugo, still looking at me as if he was wondering whether to phone for the men in white coats.

I was puzzled as well. That guy Fistulas Withers, who had made such a song and dance about the bypass previously, had been ominously absent from the proceedings so far. It was his land that was going to be taken one way or another, yet so far not a cheep from him.

Susan observed, 'Well, I've heard something. I understand there's something in the wind but what it is I don't know.'

I didn't like to ask her how she knew; it was better to keep well away from that subject!

As we walked back to the Enquiry after lunch, I noticed three coaches parked in the Town Hall car park, two from Swindon and one from Bath.

When we retook our places in the Town Hall just before two o'clock, it was obvious that something was in the wind. Whereas the seats had been sparsely occupied for the first one and a half days, they were now packed by a noisy crowd of youths, some in hooded jackets and T-shirts and others in anoraks. All had bags and bundles of something.

I noticed Withers sitting in the front row clutching some paper.

The Inspector's eyebrows shot up in astonishment as he beheld this mob when he entered from the Mayor's parlour. He rapped on the bench for silence and an anticipatory hush fell over the crowd. He glanced at his notes, shuffled his papers into a different order and, for some reason known only to him, moved Withers' contribution to later on.

'Mr Robin Threadle from the Royal Society for the Protection of Birds, please.'

Withers half stood up and then sank back in his chair with a look of surprise on his face. There was an ominous growl from the crowd at this.

Even before he opened his mouth, Robin Threadle, representing the RSPB, gave the impression of a man who had just been hit over the head with a sock filled with wet sand. He was a thin, weedy-looking man of about forty-five. Thinning hair was combed down all round the sides and back of his head like a well-used mop and his spectacles perched on the end of a pimply long nose. He launched into his contribution in a high-pitched, squeaky voice.

'I want to tell you about the warbling marsh bobbit and its little nests,' he began nervously. 'It can only mate once a year…' He was cut off at that point by a heckle from the audience.

'I bet that's more than your missus does!'

'With you, at any rate!' somebody else called out.

Another loud voice shouted, 'We don't give a fucking monkeys about some fucking warbling bobbit, so get off the platform and let the nob speak.'

Threadle looked even more stunned when Major Sir Fistulas Withers then took the opportunity to stand up again and shout, 'Objection, Your Honour! I was supposed to be on first thing this afternoon, I've got some very important points to make – more important than some damned bobbit!'

There was a growl of support.

The Inspector looked over his spectacles, clearly annoyed at these interruptions. Everything had gone smoothly so far and he was probably anticipating getting home in time to watch an early programme on the television about wine-making in the Dordogne or some such thing.

'And you are?' he snapped.

'Major Sir Fistulas Withers and it's my land that you lot are trying to steal for this blasted road.'

'Well this is not an American courtroom, sir, so please sit down. There are one or two people scheduled to give evidence before you. You will be called when it's your turn.'

The ominous growl grew louder but the Inspector seemed impervious to its significance.

Hugo muttered, 'There's going to be trouble here.'

Another loud voice called out, 'Go on, kick him of the stage, yer great Nellie, and give the Major a chance. It's his land you're stealing.'

Other voices joined in, shouting that the Major should speak and some banners were unfurled, done by a badly briefed sign-writer, which read 'HAND SOFF WIT HER SHALL'.

Threadle faltered under this barrage and looked hopefully towards the Inspector for guidance but Mr Bowman, who must have at last realised that real trouble would break out if he didn't accede to the crowd's demands, stood up, waved Threadle away from the rostrum and shouted into the microphone, 'I call Major Sir Fistulas Withers.'

Cheers mixed with catcalls followed this announcement and the crowd quietened down expectantly while Withers took to the rostrum.

The problem was he didn't have much to say. He just read out in a loud hectoring voice eight bullet points, and then stopped. Everybody waited, expecting more.

The Inspector took off his spectacles and looked hard at Withers. 'Is that it?'

The crowd grew restless; they'd probably expected some verbal fireworks in which they could have joined. Withers stood there nonplussed and then apparently decided that he'd better say something more so he started to read out his bullet points again. The Inspector interrupted him before he'd got halfway through.

'Yes, yes; you've said that before and made your points. If there's nothing else you can add please go and sit down while I call the next person.'

I guessed Withers felt he was being dismissed without his points being given the weight they deserved, so he clung to the rostrum and started again to go through his list.

Meanwhile the Inspector had called out, 'Miss Golightly please.'

Now Ms Golightly of 'Mother Wouldn't Like It' boutique was a lady whose build belied her name. She lumbered purposefully up to the rostrum like a Challenger tank moving across Salisbury Plain and waited for Withers to move. He didn't and glared at her intimidatingly. She glared back.

'Move it, buster!' she demanded, gesturing with her meaty thumb.

'Thank you, Sir Fistulas,' snapped the Inspector.

'I haven't finished making my points yet,' he rapped back.

'Let him finish,' somebody in the mob shouted and this was taken up by other voices.

'Go on, Major, you tell 'im, the snotty bastard. You're entitled to 'ave your say.'

Fists were brandished and youths began to stand up with a loud scraping of chairs, and wave banners.

'Sir Fistulas, if you don't sit down I'll have you removed by the stewards.'

'What bleedin' stewards?' jeered "rent-a-mob". 'Go on, send 'em in, we'll wait for 'em.'

At this point Ms Golightly finally seemed to lose patience with standing there in front of the rostrum, so she reached over to try to seize the microphone from Withers' grip but he refused to yield. The two of them wrestled with each other until Ms Golightly, being a good sixty pounds heavier and six inches taller, managed to topple him off the rostrum. Whereupon he rolled on the ground on his back, still clutching the microphone, and dragged Ms Golightly on top of him. Not a wise move under the circumstances! The photographer from *The Kingscastle Bugle* seized his moment and got a few good shots of Withers, purple in the face and flat on his back with Ms Golightly spread-eagled on top of him, skirt round her waist and a face-matching purple thong (from her range of 'Knickers and Bras for the Imaginative Girl') displayed in such a way that no imagination was required.

Rent-a-mob loved it.

'Give 'im one, fat arse, show the randy little sod.'

'Go on, Major, now's yer chance, make yer point to 'er.!'

The whole place now erupted in chaos and the rotten fruit and vegetables that the mob produced from their bags and bundles were hurled at all and sundry, but particularly the unfortunate Inspector. Hugo and I slid out of our seats and made for the door. We made it but not before a squashy pear hit me right between the shoulderblades of my freshly dry-cleaned jacket. Hugo and Susan Tripp remained unscathed and we stood and watched as the police arrived to be greeted by even more rotten fruit. Realising that they were heavily outnumbered, they radioed for back-up but in the five minutes it took to arrive, things got really lively. The Inspector gave up banging with his gavel and shouting for order and, deciding discretion was the better part of valour, crawled under his desk and huddled there to avoid most of the missiles. The few ordinary spectators reached the exits splattered with fruit and eggs. With them out of the way, one group, presumably the 'lads' from Swindon, thought it would be more exciting if they took on the other 'lads' from Bath and a struggling melee developed in the middle of the Hall. Ms Golightly managed to wrench the microphone from a crushed and almost asphyxiated Withers and levered herself to her feet using Withers' face to assist her. She was promptly hit in the eye by a ripe tomato and collapsed back on to the unfortunate Major.

The back-up police reinforcements arrived and waded into the melee but by now both the missiles and the protestors were exhausted. A few of the more aggressive lads were seized and marched out cheerfully between two coppers to the waiting vans and the rest retired wearily back to their seats, bloody, smelly but unbowed.

The Inspector emerged from under the desk and surveyed the carnage. The police chief inspector suggested that it might be wise to call an adjournment for an hour while some semblance of order was restored. The mob, on hearing this, must have decided that they had done what they had been paid to do, and pushed off *en masse,* I assumed to some pub to get legless.

Stumpy slid into the Hall and helped Withers lurch to his feet. He hissed menacingly in the Major's ear, 'Your bloke had better be there with the folding stuff, otherwise this lot will take the town apart, and we all know who would be responsible if that happened!'

Withers was totally bemused, he didn't know whether it was Monday, raining or breakfast time. One eye was weeping from Ms Golightly's fingers being stuck in it; his jacket was torn and covered in rotten fruit, and his breath rasped from lungs crushed by fourteen stones of floppy female. He had a strong feeling that the proceedings had not gone as he had hoped and his brilliant bullet points had not been forced home into the Inspector's brain by either his oratory or the crowd's vociferous support. That big fat woman had ruined it; if she hadn't interrupted just when he was ramming home his message, all would have gone well. And where was she anyway? He'd give her a piece of his mind! He glared round savagely but Ms Golightly had staggered to the ladies' to remove an eyeful of tomato puree and repair her make-up.

Withers suddenly became aware of the proximity of the threat. Stumpy – at least he presumed it was Stumpy, as they'd never met – was waiting for confirmation that his deal would be consummated and was clearly getting nervous that an answer had not been forthcoming.

'Well, squire, is he?'

'Oh yes, yes, Percival will be there!'

'He'd better be or I'll be back!'

The Major tottered to a chair on the front row and slumped in it, defeated.

Hugo decided that there was no point in the two of us staying on for the rest of what obviously was not going to be a very interesting conclusion now that all the excitement had finished, and we headed to our respective cars. Fortunately we had checked out of the Royal Oak in the morning; the sounds of singing, swearing and breaking glass coming from the Highwayman Bar were clearly audible in the car park.

As we walked Hugo said casually, 'Susan seems a very nice woman.'

'Really?'

'I think she took a fancy to me,' he murmured with a wistful smile.

'Shall I include that in the top-secret file to go with the full English Breakfast then?' I ventured.

'One all,' he replied with an oblique grin.

CHAPTER 11

Paul Harris, a gangly senior structural engineer from Structural Team One, wandered into the office when we were all present. He was carrying a bag and a notebook.

'I'm collecting for Geoffrey's leaving dinner; it's twenty-five quid a head, fifty if you're bringing a partner. We're holding it at The Royal Garden Hotel on 26th November, it's a Friday so you can sleep it off on Saturday morning. You've seen the notice on the notice-board, I assume.'

Ivan asked if the secretaries were going and was told that they all were. He gave a weak but relieved smile, which was immediately wiped off his face when Paul said, 'Agatha said you'd take care of her contribution.'

Des asked if he'd take a cheque and was told it was cash only. I found a few notes in my wallet which, with some loose change, managed to add up to fifty quid. (I'd mentioned the dinner previously to Charlie and she said she'd be delighted to come and meet my friends and colleagues.)

Ivan, with a face like a fiddle, fumbled reluctantly in his wallet before handing over a pristine red fifty.

The evening of Arbuthnot's leaving dinner arrived. Charlie had bought a new dress, a little violet number that matched her eyes. Her dark hair shone, she wore a small gold and amethyst brooch given to her by her grandmother and, apart from the fact that I thought her cheeks could do with pinking up a bit, she looked stunning. My solution to that was simple: regardless of her cries of 'my hair; my dress; my make-up; my nails!', a good rogering rectified the cheek situation. As a consequence, we were one of the last arrivals at the pre-dinner drinks.

I introduced Charlie to Geoffrey and Mrs Arbuthnot, and got a brief handshake from each while they looked over my shoulder to see if the next guest was more important – or, in the case of the diminutive, hatchet-faced Mrs Arbuthnot, under my armpit. They were followed in the receiving line by Hugo and his wife Emily. I liked Emily Elmes instantly. She had a wonderfully genuine smile, a slightly oriental look and beautiful skin; black hair that framed her face, and a gentle, nicely modulated voice. She and Charlie chatted together for a couple of minutes. The other two partners, Hamish Robertson with his lady, and Ewen Jones, who was single, both drooled over Charlie and, apart from a brief handshake, ignored me. We moved on to join a group from the first floor. The men spent far too long kissing Charlie's hand as their eyes absorbed her superb figure, shown off to its best advantage by the low-cut dress (uncreased – we had got it off before the pinking up).

We then joined a cheerful group from Civils One, more introductions all round. The banter was relaxed and the champagne flowed until I noticed a distinct change in the atmosphere and one or two people started to drift away from our group. Turning round, I beheld the cause. Ivan was standing just behind me, casting his aura over the proceedings – but he wasn't looking at me, it was Charlie he had in his sights, and the look on his face was pure lechery. She didn't notice, she was chatting to another girl about the latest fashion in shoes, but I did. As soon as he realised he'd been spotted, he became sleazy charm personified.

'Oh hi, Marcus, and is this gorgeous little creature your *current* squeeze?' he oozed, putting stress on the word 'current'. He turned to Charlie. 'Hi, I'm Ivan, you must have heard of me, I'm the leader on the Kingscastle bypass project that Marcus is helping me with.'

Charlie knew all about Ivan – well not quite all, the Tripp saga was an event about which a clam would be considered voluble compared to me – but she was much too polite to tell him to fuck off so, with a cool look, she just said, 'I'm Charlotte – and would you mind removing your nose from my cleavage.'

Ivan was unabashed and, forcing a cheery wave, said, 'We must get together sometime, see you later.'

'Not if I see you first,' she muttered to his retreating back. She turned to me. 'So that's the odious Ivan that you've been telling me about, is it? I see what you mean now, but he's stopped his funny business – hasn't he?'

I frowned. 'I'm not sure. He's been remarkably cocky over the last couple of weeks so I'm watching my back carefully. I don't want another roasting from Arbuthnot for something Ivan has set up.'

I got us another couple of glasses of champagne and went over to look at the table plan. We were on the same table as Des Doubleday and his wife Angeline, and Angela and her boyfriend, who was the size of a furniture van – so that ruled out any thoughts of hanky panky there – if I was contemplating the same – which I wasn't but which in all honesty I had in the past. The other six guests were Dennis Menzies and his partner George – a surprise there – and two guys from structural engineering with their wives. Ivan, I was pleased to see, was on another table with Awful Agatha.

The food was excellent and we were just in that lull between the end of eating and the inevitable speeches when I had a higher calling and excused myself to go to the gents'.

As I came out, a policewoman in uniform emerged from the ladies' at the same time. I did a double take. She seemed a very unlikely policewoman: heavy make-up, bright red lipstick and a large bust that strained her white blouse, so much so that her red bra was visible between the second and third buttons. She gave me smile and touched my arm.

'Are you at the Arbuthnot party, dearie?' she said in a voice that sounded like two cicadas mating.

I nodded.

'Which way is it?'

It took a second or two for realisation to arrive.

'Are you a Strippergram?

'How could you tell?' she pouted, smoothing down her tunic with a meaty hand. 'I'm supposed to be realistic.'

'For whom?'

I just couldn't picture Geoffrey Arbuthnot receiving one of these, particularly with the redoubtable Mrs Arbuthnot by his side.

The 'policewoman' fumbled down her front; obviously what was hidden down there had become lost in the vastness of her cleavage. Eventually she produced a damp piece of paper.

Unfolding it, she read out in a sing-song voice.

'I am a present to Mr Geoffrey Arbuthnot from his friendly tunnelling engineer Marcus Moon.'

'WHAT! Here, give me that!' I snatched the paper from her hand and looked at it with horrified eyes. It did indeed say precisely that – and the handwriting was familiar.

'Where did you get this from?' I demanded.

'Ooh, don't get your knickers in a twist, dearie. It came from Mr Moon, the man who phoned the agency to make the booking, he sent it.'

'Has he paid for you?'

'Oh yes, cash in advance – but they normally give me a big tip after I've performed as well.'

'Do they indeed? Well there's obviously been a mistake here. You see, *I* am Mr Moon and all this is news to me. I think you've been misled. You were actually booked by a guy called Ivan Masterland and clearly he's got our names mixed up – silly man! I think we'd better put that right quickly. Look!'

I took the piece of paper and scratched out my name and the word 'tunnelling' so that they weren't legible, then I wrote

IVAN MASTERLAND in clear capitals above it and offered it back to her. She hesitated and gave me a cunning look.

'It don't bother me who booked me, dearie, I've been paid to perform and perform I will, but I could be persuaded to change the script.' She gave a sly wink.

I got the message instantly. I slid two ten pound notes from my thin wallet and handed them to her with the paper. Bloody Ivan was costing me a fortune.

'The party's in the Tulip Room, second on the right. I should give it five minutes.'

I watched while she stowed the paper and notes away in Cheddar Gorge and then rejoined our table with nervous anticipation. Charlie shot me a glance; she sensed that something was in the wind but I couldn't say anything.

It seemed a long five minutes before the double entrance doors suddenly burst open with a crash that got everybody's attention. There she stood in all her glory: hat and tunic on; notebook in hand, pencil poised.

'May I 'ave your attention, ladies and gen'lemen please? Is there a Mr Geoffrey Arbuthnot present in the room?' she boomed.

A sudden hush fell over everybody. Geoffrey put up his hand nervously as though he was at school and Matron had just asked which boy hadn't washed behind his ears that morning. His voice quavered.

'I'm Geoffrey Arbuthnot. Is there something wrong, officer?'

The 'policewoman' advanced towards him menacingly. I glanced expressionlessly at Ivan; he was staring at me with a big smirk on his face.

'Do you know that your car is so badly parked that it's blocking all the traffic in the street outside, Mr Arbuthnot?' She moved round the side of his table. 'And that is an offence under Section One of the Road Traffic Act, punishable by severe embarrassment.'

As she said this, she pulled a small tape player from her pocket, set it on the table and the beat of 'The Stripper' echoed round the room. She whipped off her hat to reveal long bleached hair that cascaded round her shoulders; stripped off the tunic and ripped open the Velcro strips that held together her white blouse with the false buttons. She then shimmied to the music right up to a paralysed Geoffrey, wobbling her vast, barely contained tits under his nose. She dropped her skirt and clad only in red bra, red knickers and grip-top stockings, plonked herself heavily in his lap, which must have caused his legs to creak under the strain. Finally, she planted a big red lipstick kiss right in the middle of his forehead. I looked across at Ivan again; he was wetting himself with delight.

She fumbled in her bra and pulled out the piece of paper. The room was still stunned to silence. When the music stopped, she read out in a squeaky voice, 'I-am-a-present-to-Mr-Geoffrey-Arbuthnot-from-his-friendly-engineer – Ivan-Masterland.'

All heads spun round to look at Ivan. He went white with shock; his jaw nearly hit the floor. He leapt to his feet, shouting, 'That's not right. Not me, you stupid cow, it's from…' He stopped, realising that he was saying too much. '…somebody else,' he added hastily.

Fortunately for him a much bigger distraction was taking place at the Arbuthnot table by then and most people's eyes and ears returned to focus on that. Mrs Arbuthnot had recovered from her paralytic shock and leapt into action. A small, wiry, sharp-featured woman with a determined jaw, she seized the stripper by the arm and forcibly dragged her off Geoffrey's knee, shouting, 'How dare you, you brazen hussy! Leave my husband alone, I don't care if you are the police, I shall report you to your superior. My husband knows the Chief Constable of Surrey at the Golf Club, and he will hear about your outrageous behaviour, have no doubt about that. Get out immediately! GET OUT!'

The stripper looked round with a puzzled expression and, apparently realising that matters had gone beyond her normal hilarious receptions, began to gather up her discarded clothes.

'They usually give me a tip,' she proffered to the table at large when she had managed to shake off Mrs Arbuthnot's arm. The only response she got was Geoffrey muttering, 'But we didn't come by car, we had a taxi.'

In all the hubbub, I noticed that the stripper had dropped the piece of paper with her greeting written on it, so I slipped out of my chair, strolled across and put my foot on it. By dint of shuffling, I managed to move it to one side where I could pick it up un-noticed – or so I thought.

The evening livened up considerably after that. Hugo made an excellent witty speech which was both funny and affectionate. Ewen Jones sprayed spittle over all those within a two-metre radius and Geoffrey, quite recovered from his ordeal, made a very moving speech about the history of Consultant Design Services. He hoped it would go from strength to strength under its new senior partner and hoped that he wouldn't lose touch with all the good friends he had made in consulting engineering. There was no mention of the Strippergram. The drinks flowed, the disco played, we all danced and everybody – except Ivan, I'm sure – had a good time until midnight.

For the next couple of days Ivan was very quiet. He couldn't say anything without admitting that he had been trying to set me up, nor could he prove that I'd switched the script, but he brooded on it, and I knew that wasn't the end of the matter.

Charlie slit open the envelope whilst we were having breakfast. She slid out a printed card and quickly scanned it.

'What do you make of this?' she said in surprise passing over the card.

It was an invitation to a drinks party at Ivan Masterland's flat in Wandsworth in a week's time. It was specifically addressed to 'Dr Charlotte Prinknash'. It didn't include me and it didn't say 'with guest'.

I raised a quizzical eyebrow, not quite sure what to say next. Three thoughts sprang to mind: 'Stupid bugger'; 'You seem to have scored a hit with Ivan'; and 'Well, are you going to go?' I settled for the non-controversial second.

'He hasn't invited you,' she teased with a cheeky grin. I produced the third alternative.

'I'm thinking about it.' The grin widened. So I gave her the first thought!

'Me or him?'

'Both of you!' I laughed, and grabbed hold of her to give her a good truffling. When I put her down she said, 'That's a bit odd, isn't it? Deliberately leaving you off the invite?'

'That's Ivan. He couldn't take his eyes off you at Geoffrey's leaving dinner – until he found out that he'd booked the stripper! Then he had to go and change his trousers.'

'Metaphorically, of course.'

'Well I presume so!' We both laughed. 'So what *are* you going to do?' I asked.

'Ignore it, I think that's the best thing, otherwise he'll suggest alternative dates or something like that and we'll be into a long rigmarole of correspondence.'

Three days later, when Charlie came home from the hospital after her late shift, she told me that Ivan had tried to phone her but as she was in the middle of surgery, fortunately she couldn't take the call.

'What's he up to?' she asked.

I was getting really irritated with Ivan. He behaved normally – well, normally for him – at the office and never said a word about Charlie. But Awful Agatha must have sensed that her hold on her future meal ticket might be loosening and so kept coming into Civils Team Two office, much to the annoyance of Des.

'He's got the hots for you,' I replied. 'A quite understandable feeling,' I grinned wolfishly at her. 'After Geoffrey's dinner, most of the office and particularly the randy structural engineers, feel the same way. But Ivan's beginning to make a nuisance of himself, whereas that's my prerogative.' I gave her an evil grin.

'No, Marcus, no!' She held me off with one hand. 'I've had a long hard day; anyway it's your turn to put out the rubbish.' And with that she gave me a push towards the little kitchen and locked herself in the bathroom.

Ivan didn't let up and now began to send Charlie e-mails as well as trying to phone her at the hospital. She didn't reply to any of them.

Then she got yet another e-mail from him, this time suggesting that they go out for dinner at The Golden Deer, a very expensive restaurant just across the road from the Royal Free Hospital's main entrance.

'He's bloody well harassing me now,' she said angrily. 'Will he never realise that I don't want to go out with him, I don't want to hear from him and, with the exceptions of your company events, I don't want to see him again.'

She was now very angry and beginning to brood about it, which was unusual for her. I didn't like her being put in that position so I decided once and for all it was time for a showdown with Ivan.

Next morning I made a point of arriving at the office early, which provoked some unjustified comments from Sue on Reception – 'Is your watch gaining?' – and Hugo halfway up the stairs – 'Couldn't sleep, eh?'. But I wasn't in a mood to exchange banter, having worked myself up into a froth in anticipation of confronting Ivan, so I just gave a weak smile.

Of course, I'd chosen the morning when he was out on another of his sites and so I had to contain my anger until after lunch. Even Des noticed that all was not love and affection in the Moon bosom.

'What's up with you, get out of bed on the wrong side?'

'Don't you start! I've enough on my plate with bloody Ivan – when he condescends to get here.'

'Ah! Very understandable! Would you like me to make myself scarce or can I stay and watch the feathers fly?'

That forced a grin out of me. 'An appropriate analogy as far as Ivan's concerned, after his experience in Kingscastle, but please yourself.'

Ivan came in after lunch all strutty and pleased with himself as he dumped his briefcase on his desk. Containing my annoyance, I strolled over to him.

'A word in your shell-like, Ivan, if you please.'

'I'm busy at the moment, Moon. Can't it wait till later?' It was a surly brush-off but he didn't meet my eyes and turned to fiddle with the catches on his briefcase. That was the last straw.

'No it can't wait "till later", you nasty little creep!'

I grabbed his thin shoulders and turned him to face me; he tried to draw back apprehensively.

'What the hell do you think you're playing at, sending all those letters and e-mails to Charlie? And pestering her with your bloody phone calls? Can't you get it through your skull that she's not interested in you and she doesn't want to hear from you or see you?'

The apprehension was suddenly replaced by a smirk. 'Oh that's what this is about! Getting all sensitive, are we, Moon, all touchy? A bit jealous, eh? Not so sure of yourself, are you now? I think she really fancies me, I saw it in her eyes at Geoffrey's do. If she doesn't want me to contact her, then why hasn't she told me so herself then?'

I exploded with scornful laughter. 'Because she thinks that if she does it might just encourage you to persist in harassing her! And as far as fancying you is concerned, don't flatter yourself, a concupiscent blind wombat wouldn't fancy a creep like you, so lay off! That's your last warning!'

In spite of the smirk still pasted on his face, I saw a flicker of fear in his eyes.

'Well, if you really want to know, I don't fancy her in any case, she's not my type, too stuck up for me,' he riposted. He shook off my arm and turned back to fiddle with his case.

I decided to leave it at that for the sake of our working relationship and returned to my desk. Des was grinning like a Cheshire Cat.

'That seems to have set out the position quite clearly,' he observed, 'so now we can get on with our work.'

I must admit I felt a lot better for that. I had certainly cemented Ivan's enmity now, but then I suppose I always was a threat to his ambitions, so it was much better to have it fully out in the open. If we were going to compete for whatever it was Ivan imagined we were competing for, then it was better that this was widely known so that any mischievous underhand sleights would be taken for just what they were.

Anyhow, the outcome, much to Charlie's relief, was a complete cessation of Ivan's harassment.

A few days later I was asking Des's advice about post-tensioning anchorages when Ivan slid into the office. He headed straight to his desk without making eye contact with either of us or saying a word. Des looked at me and gave a shrug of dismissal but I felt a little shiver of apprehension. The bugger was up to something.

About half-past-ten Joanna stuck her head round the door and said 'Marcus, Mr Geoffrey would like to have a word with you.'

The shiver of apprehension returned but this didn't sound too bad: it wasn't a peremptory command, it was more like 'come along for a chat'. What about I couldn't guess, unless all my skeletons had fallen out of the cupboard and I was simply being lulled into a false sense of security. So it was somewhat nervously that I tapped on Geoffrey's door and was bidden to enter.

He was not normally affable, so when he began by saying, 'Take a seat, Marcus – you don't mind if I call you Marcus, do you?' I blinked. Was I being softened up? I sat down warily on the edge of the chair but he took my agreement for granted and continued.

'You're aware that I'm retiring next week and that Hugo Elmes is taking over as senior partner. A very sound and capable engineer – he came as a junior engineer when my father was senior partner, you know.'

'No, sir, I didn't know that.'

Geoffrey's eyes took on a faraway look and he steepled his fingers together, resting his elbows on the desk.

'Oh yes, my father and David Dingwall started the firm way back in the thirties. It was called Consultant Design Partnership then. David was knighted when he became President of the Institution and eventually became Lord Dingwall of Wallsend.'

'Fascinating, sir – and what happened to your father?'

Geoffrey shook his head sadly. 'A tragedy it was, a tragedy! He shot himself in the foot with a poisoned dart while he was experimenting with a blowpipe in Brazil. It was given to him as a mark of respect by one of the tribes up the Amazon for whom he'd designed a water supply system. He thought there was an obstruction in the pipe and blew down it to clear it.'

'Painful, I would think, sir, you can't be too careful with those things.'

'Painful! It was fatal. He was dead in twenty minutes.'

'I see what you mean, sir, tragic. Always look before you blow. A lesson for all of us.'

Geoffrey perked up. 'On the brighter side, I took his place in the partnership. Did you ever read my paper on the syphonic action of sewage under self-generated gas?'

I shook my head.

'It was a masterpiece. I read it before the whole Institution.'

'Really? Well, as my father always said, there's nothing like getting in first.'

'No, Marcus, you misunderstand me. I presented it in front of a large audience at the Institution. It went down very well thanks to a tip my father gave me just before he left for South America.'

He paused expectantly. I fed him the line. 'And what was that, sir?

'Always leave an exciting piece of information to the end. Send 'em home wanting more.'

'And what was it you left to the end, sir?'

'I told them that the inverted syphonic action could be utilised to accelerate the flow by as much as a third!'

'I bet that had them leaping out of their seats.'

He shot me a sharp look. 'This was the Institution of Civil Engineers, Marcus, not one of your young people's pop concerts. No, a gratifying round of applause at the end was my reward.'

'They were pleased it was over, were they, sir?'

But he wasn't listening; he was back there in the hall, basking in his moment of professional fame. He brought himself back to the present with a shake of his head.

'Of course, I shall be very sad to cease being active in the profession but I'm satisfied that in Elmes, Robertson and Jones we have a first rate management team and in one or two of our young engineers, somebody to follow in their footsteps – provided they keep their noses clean – if you follow me?'

I did follow him all too well, but I wasn't happy where he was going. The shrewd brown eyes fixed on my face.

'Masterland tells me it was you who arranged for that policewoman at my leaving dinner…'

I felt my face freeze with shock. That slimy snake! I swore violently under my breath. I'd been right all along – it was a set-up! So this was going to be the *coup de grâce*. After lulling me into a false sense of security with his reminiscences, the cold-eyed assassin was going to terminate my career with a final stiletto through the heart.

To my astonishment, Geoffrey carried on. '…and I thought that was very funny indeed,' he said, breaking into a chuckle. 'Very, very funny: needed something like that to put a bit of life into those proceedings, it was getting too much like a blasted wake for my liking.'

He gave a quiet smile and, leaning forward, said *sotto voce,* 'Of course, Mrs Arbuthnot doesn't approve of that sort of thing so I had to play it down; but it was just what was wanted to give the party a boost. A piece of initiative there – I'm very grateful to you, young man!'

While I was trying to digest this swing in my fortunes, he gave a puzzled smile, pursed his lips and shook his head. 'A policewoman, of all people; who would have thought it?'

By this time I wasn't sure where I was or what I was doing. The adrenaline had been pumping round in so many directions that I had no idea what the expression on my face must be. Fortunately, Geoffrey may have been getting overexcited with his thoughts of big-busted policewomen in red knickers so the subject suddenly changed again.

'I saw your design for the Shering Valley Bridge the other day – first rate. I'm sorry if I was a bit hard on you over the tunnelling matter but Elmes tells me you're an oddball so I don't expect it did you any harm. Well, it's all settled now, thank goodness. You'll understand that I have a lot of people to see so I just wanted to wish you all the best with your career and say goodbye.'

He stood up as a signal for me to go but I was now thinking of something else.

Oddball! That was twice he had referred to me as an oddball, and now Hugo had done so. A brilliant, out-of-the-box, laterally thinking, talented engineer would perhaps have been over the top but I could have lived with it. But 'oddball'? That had a touch of insanity attached to it that I found disturbing. Was I being categorised as the company imbecile? Mad Moon, the barmy bridge man?

I was thinking about this when I realised that Geoffrey was now standing up, offering his hand with a puzzled expression on his face, as if wondering why I wasn't taking it.

Springing hastily to my feet, I gabbled out, 'Oh sorry, sir, thank you very much and I hope you and Mrs Arbuthnot have a long and happy retirement.'

I tottered out of the office with his bemused eyes following me to the door, thinking, *Oh God; I'd only confirmed the crackpot image yet again.*

Still, on the plus side, bloody Ivan's little snitching stunt had backfired. Geoffrey had enjoyed the Strippergram – despite – or maybe because of – being convinced she was a real policewoman.

* * * * *

The timing for the building of the bypass that Hugo had given at the Public Enquiry obviously alerted the politicians; the Inspector's report was approved by the Secretary of State in record time and CONDES was instructed to invite bids for the construction, on behalf of the Department of Transport. Invitations to apply were advertised in British and European journals as required by European Union regulations.

After numerous checks, meetings and reports we were told that the contract had been awarded to MacLowland Limited. Hugo breathed a sigh of relief. They were a very efficient outfit, you could be sure you got a pound's work for your pound from them.

Hugo called a meeting of all parties in our offices. It was held in the big conference room on the top floor. Ivan and I, plus Adrian Shaw, Deborah Mason and Jack Bradley, who were to be the Resident Engineers on the road, the Shering Valley Bridge and the tunnels respectively, trooped up there at the appointed time. Jane, Hugo's secretary, produced a couple of pots of coffee and handed these round whilst introductions were made. The MacLowland top man, Mulluc McLowland, a dapper and brisk

Scot, introduced his team and then we got down to business with Hugo chairing the meeting.

His first point was to emphasise that the object of all parties was exactly the same. It was to get this road built on time, on cost and to the standards specified. Therefore whatever cooperation Macs needed from us they would get and CONDES expected the same from Macs. This was accepted without question.

Hugo's second point was a very important one. He emphasised that it was CONDES' job to design the project but it was Macs' job to build it. It wasn't up to CONDES to try to tell them how to build it, it was Macs who were the experts on construction and therefore it was their responsibility. However Health and Safety laws did require CONDES to bring to Macs' attention anything that they felt was abnormal. Therefore CONDES required to be kept informed about construction intentions such as the temporary works to support the big bridges during construction. This also was accepted without question.

Macs said that they wanted to use sub-contractors for certain specialist work and handed over a short list of their proposals. I noted that for the Shering Valley Bridge foundations they wanted to use a specialist piling firm, Rock Solid Substructures Ltd. We had no problem with them; they had done work previously for some of Hugo's bridges.

Deborah Mason, who was one of my bridge design team, asked about site accommodation. Macs' Site Manager explained where they would put their main construction camp but there would also be a secondary camp close to an existing road near the Shering Valley. This would serve both the tunnels and the valley bridge.

*****

The e-mail arrived on Stumpy's laptop just as he was bedding down in his squat in Salisbury. It was from his contact in the Highways Agency to tell him that a contract had been signed for the construction of the Kingscastle bypass, following the Minister's acceptance of the Inspector's recommendations and the issue of invitations to tender. He immediately alerted the rest of the group and warned them that they didn't have much time so they'd better start planning first thing next morning. He also e-mailed three other groups round the country who were protesting about genetically modified crops in Norfolk, nuclear reprocessing in Cumbria and cutting down trees in Devon, with the same information. The latter was the most likely one that would join up with his group. Newbury Mary's team were tree-house specialists whose skills had been honed at the old cruise missile protest camp at Greenham Common and they had already said that clearing the trees on Withers' estate to make way for the road was 'shaving Mother Earth's pubic hair'. Stumpy thought he could certainly count on them to make their share of trouble.

Stumpy was an old hand at road protests. His nickname was 'The Mole'. He and his team could dig a maze of tunnels in such a short time that the Viet Cong would have stood back open-mouthed with admiration. On the Winchester bypass it had taken the authorities two months to extract him and his mob from their burrows in such a way that they didn't infringe their human rights. Ideas like putting a bag of cobras down there were ruled out as a consequence. Stumpy knew exactly how far he could play it right up to the limit of the law and public sympathy.

Next morning he telephoned Sir Fistulas Withers.

'So they're going ahead with it then, squire, what do you want us to do?'

It was a rhetorical question because Stumpy was going to do it anyway but he wanted Withers' support to avoid getting, as Withers put it, 'a charge of buckshot up the arse of any damned trespassers on my land'.

'Who the hell are you?' was the testy response to his question.

'It's me, Stumpy. You remember, I organised your support at the Public Enquiry and we talked a few months before that about stopping the bypass? I said we could make it so expensive to proceed that there was a good chance they'd scrap it?'

Withers gave a shudder at the recollection of the Public Enquiry. Ms Golightly's bodily imprint, floppy warmth and hairy chin were still firmly locked in his mind.

'Ah yes, Mr Stumpy; so what are you going to do? You're the experts at this sort of thing. Use explosives? Mortar the site camp? Kidnap the contractor's men? I've got some old hand grenades you could use.'

'Nah, nothing like that, squire, they'd slam us in the pokey if we did that. No, it's much more subtle. We just put ourselves in the way and make it so they can't move us. After a bit they'll have to give up. Holding up construction will cost 'em too much bloody money, but we could do with some help.'

Withers coughed violently. 'So you want more money, is that it?'

Stumpy laughed. 'Well a few quid wouldn't go amiss, you're right there, squire, and some food would help; but the main thing is we need is wood. Planks of wood – a lot of planks in fact. Normally we'd nick it from building sites – take old scaffold boards, hoardings, etcetera – but it'd be less risky if you could provide some. We need it for the tree-houses and for shoring up the tunnels, see.'

Withers didn't see; he'd no idea what Stumpy was talking about. Tree-houses? Tunnels? Were they going to live up in the trees and why would they need wood for the Hickling Edge tunnels? Still, Stumpy sounded if he knew what he was doing. Then it dawned on Withers, as a constructor of latrines all over the world, that what they were going to do was burrow underground on the route of the road. The tunnels would need shoring up and that was what the wood was needed for. This sort of thing was right up Withers' street, organising a temporary camp to dig holes. His mind began to click into gear: what would they need, where could he get it, how to deliver it…?

'Are you still there, squire? I thought we'd lost you for a minute.'

'Ah yes, Mr Stumpy, and I would be obliged if you would call me Major,' Withers said testily. 'Now this sort of thing is my speciality, you know. When I commanded the 4th Platoon of the 2nd battalion of the Pioneer Corps in Kota Bahru back in '74, I built a camp in two weeks for a battalion of sappers; showed those damned insurgents a thing or two, I can tell you! Then in 1978, I think it was, I built a camp for four hundred men in Al Barwa, Iraq in less than ten days, on shifting sand. That was where Sergeant Kosmicky fell into the big latrine when the sides collapsed as he was having a dump. That caused a bit of a stink – but not as much as Kosmicky did when we dug him out.' He chortled at the thought. 'Then in 1982, in Novo Slobograd…'

Stumpy covered his mobile, raised his eyebrows and turned to the others. 'Fuck me! We're going to have to fight our way round the fucking world before this dickhead comes up with something useful.'

He spoke into the phone again and cut Withers off.

'Yes, squire, that's very impressive but can you get us the wood?'

Withers glared at the phone, angry at being cut off before he could impress upon these ruffians what an important fellow he had been in camp building and latrine digging. However, he needed these people if he was going to prevent the bypass being built so he bit his tongue, swallowed his irritation and said that he would arrange for a good supply of planks. He had just demolished an old barn and the wood was available whenever they wanted it.

Stumpy gathered his team, joined by Newbury Mary's tree protesters back from Devon, and briefed them on what was required:
saws, axes, shovels, hammers, nails, big iron spikes, tarpaulins,
tents, stoves, fuel, food and a myriad of small items to set up
camp. This would have to begged, borrowed, scrounged, stolen
and, in the extreme, purchased, all in the next few days.

The two groups had available two large battered vans and,
with the Major's connivance, were able to shift all their gear and
themselves deep into Withers Woods with arousing the attention
of the authorities.

They set to work immediately in the area that they had previously reconnoitred.

The Save the Trees mob lopped branches, strung ropes and
built their tree-houses so that they were only accessible by ladders which could be withdrawn upwards in an instant should
the authorities appear. Another team spent time driving the big
iron spikes deep into all the trees on the path of the road that
were scheduled for felling. These would rip the teeth out of any
chainsaw, reducing it to scrap metal when the contractor tried to
cut them down.

Stumpy's men dug. They burrowed like frenzied rabbits, digging and shoring and constructing a small settlement underneath
the ground, all the rooms linked by tunnels. At one point they came
across a small deposit of scrap metal. Stumpy picked up a piece; it
looked like a badly rusted iron hasp from some sort of container.
He threw it on the pile of earth outside the tunnel together with the
rest of the mud-covered scrap and they carried on digging.

*****

The first design meeting for Bob Barclay's supermarket project was called for ten-thirty on Tuesday morning. Hugo decided that, although normally this would be a job for the structural engineers, I should go as Bob was my contact.

Barclay had rented a set of offices in a modern block just off St James Street in the West End. I took the bus along the Kings Road and walked down to the new offices from Piccadilly. A nice shiny new plate in the entrance hall read 'Barclay Properties Limited – Second Floor'. Sprinting up the stairs and through the glass entrance door, I beheld a very attractive, very well-stacked girl smiling from behind a reception desk. Considering Bob only had one project as far as I knew, it was an impressive entrance.

'You must be Marcus,' she smiled. 'I'm Jemma. Mr Barclay's waiting for you in his office.' She pointed at a door leading from the reception. 'Would you like coffee?'

'Er, coffee with milk and one sugar please.'

I went through the door she had indicated, to be confronted by another equally attractive girl sitting at a desk with a PC and various wire trays of documents. She too stood up and offered her hand.

'I'm Jane, Bob's PA. Go straight through, Marcus.'

Through yet another door into a nicely furnished office with an executive desk, chairs and a small conference table all in light oak. Barclay was standing by the window chatting to a small guy I judged about the same age as me but with long fair hair that hung down past the cut-away collar of his velvet jacket, and designer stubble on a podgy, serious face.

'Ah, Marcus, this is Perseus Rixon, my architect. Perse, this long lugubrious streak is Marcus Moon, my engineer.'

Rixon scanned me dispassionately with his dark eyes and gave a dismissive sniff. 'I've never heard of him,' he said in a round plummy voice. 'I don't like working with people I've never heard of. I'd like to bring in my own engineer and I don't like being called Perse either, Bob – it's Perseus.'

Bob raised an eyebrow. 'Well you'd better start liking working with Marcus because he's the one who found the site and brought the job to us – Perse.'

That reduced Rixon to a pink-faced silence. So far I hadn't said a word. I turned to Bob.

'How come you've got those gorgeous girls in your office, Robert, where did you get them from?'

'Careful selection, my lad. The theory is simple: it's easier to teach somebody to type than to teach them to grow tits.'

Rixon cut in. 'I don't like that sort of talk Bob; it's not funny. It's politically incorrect, sexist and demeaning to women.'

He went to the head of the table and sat down. He was obviously getting pissed off at being ignored and cleared his throat noisily, glancing at his watch. 'Can we get on please? I've got a busy day ahead.'

Bob smiled at him. 'No you haven't. This is your first job. And before you go any further, that's my seat at the head of the table; I'm chairing all my consultants' meetings, so shift yourself somewhere else.'

I thought Perseus was going to argue but the look on Bob's face persuaded him otherwise. Whilst a red-faced Perseus reluctantly moved to a chair at the side, Bob turned to me.

'I met Perse when I was working for City Houses. He's a bit of a prick but underneath it all he does have some good design ideas. He's just set up his own business – The Perseus Rixon Group of Designers. Have you heard of them, Marcus?'

I shook my head.

'So you're even then. Perse, he hasn't heard of you either so let's get down to business.'

We all took seats, me opposite Rixon, and Martin Holmes joined us a few minutes later, with Jane to take notes.

'What about a Quantity Surveyor?' I asked.

Bob said, 'I assumed CONDES would be the services engineers and the QS as well. Is that a problem?'

'Not at all.'

I saw Rixon start at the name CONDES. So he had heard of the firm. Well, that wasn't surprising really because they were quite well known. It might come in handy at some time or other.

The Perseus Rixon Group of Designers, which it rapidly became clear was Perseus Rixon plus two other dogsbodies, had done a detailed survey of the site and produced an outline scheme which, to give him credit, was a good one. Bob said he had interest from both Waitrose and the local Co-op as tenants, but Waitrose were the front-runners and had provided a detailed specification of their requirements, which Bob had passed on to Perseus. Structurally it didn't present any problems as far as I could tell.

While Perseus was doing his presentation, I studied him. It became abundantly clear that a sense of humour had been omitted from the Rixon genes and replaced with a thin shell of prickly defensiveness that hid something. What, I wasn't sure. One thing I was sure about was that if he didn't come up to scratch with Bob Barclay, he was going to have a hard time.

'Do you want a clear span, Perseus, or can you accept a central row of columns?'

It was the first time I'd spoken directly to him. I think he realised at that point that business was business and nobody was fooling about now.

He didn't answer me but looked at Bob.

'The rent per square metre is the same but what will be the effect on the cost?' Bob asked.

Again Perseus didn't answer but this time looked at me.

'Structurally not much different, but a clear span will mean a much larger volume to heat and light and therefore the mechanical and electrical equipment will cost more and it will cost more to operate.'

'A central row of columns then,' decided Bob.

Perseus pulled a childish face and pouted. 'Architecturally and aesthetically I need a clear span. It gives me more scope to express the subtleties of the form so that the building cries out to world saying, "Here I am: enter me to experience your dreams".'

Bob and Martin looked at each other in astonishment. Bob spoke first.

'For Christ's sake, Perse, it's just a big shed, not Miss United Kingdom in a swimsuit. I'm not going to submit it for the Royal Institute of British Architects prize of the year. It's a frame with some cladding round it and a smart front. Your job is basically to make the smart bit as smart as possible as cheaply as possible.'

Perseus looked as if he'd just been struck by lightning – well, I suppose he had in a way, Barclay was not known for mincing his words and the sheer commerciality of his brief had shocked young Rixon. I wondered if he would resign, flounce out of the room, nose in the air, tossing his long hair back disdainfully in a gesture of disgust. That's what they do in Victorian melodramas but obviously Perseus was not widely read, so no such luck. I could sense trouble ahead though; he was going to try to pull something.

We got down to discussing the details and at twelve-thirty Perseus went back to his office to produce drawings and specifications.

'Come on, Marcus, let's have a glass of wine and go do Giuseppe's, I'll treat you to lunch – do me a favour though and keep an eye on that bugger. I don't want him wasting my money trying to make a name for himself.'

CHAPTER TWELVE

Mrs Stoate carefully checked Ben's damaged paw and was gratified to see that it had completely healed. He wagged his tail, licked her hand and gave a little whine as he had when he was hurt. That drew her attention to the Winston Churchill Toby Jug on the mantelpiece where she had put the bangle that had trapped Ben's paw. A pang of conscience nipped her. That bangle might belong to somebody who treasured it as a memento from a loved one. She really must take it to the police station and hand it in. So next morning she had her hair done at 'Crimpers', finished her shopping at 'Gupta's the Grocers' and carefully crossed the road to Kingscastle Police Station with Ben trotting alongside. Cuts in the police budget had forced a lot of small police stations in the area to either close or only open for a few hours a day, but Kingscastle was fully manned twenty-four hours a day seven days a week.

Sergeant Bulstrode, the desk sergeant, put his mug of strong tea down on the scarred mahogany counter, smiled and said hopefully, 'Hello, m'dear, be you comin' to report a mass murder then?'

Mrs Stoate lifted her cavernous handbag on to the counter and fumbled around, finally pulling out the gold bangle. She showed it to the sergeant who gave it a quick look and raised a questioning eyebrow.

'Ben found this in Withers Woods, Sergeant, some time ago but as he'd hurt hisself I couldn't bring it straight in. It looks quite valuable so as soon as he was better I thought I'd hand it in to see if anyone's reported losing it.'

'Ben bein'?'

She laughed. 'Oh, Ben's my dog, it got stuck on his paw.'

The sergeant weighed it in his large hand and examined it more carefully. 'Heavy innit! Could be gold, I suppose. I'll look in the book to see if anyone's asked about it.'

He thumbed through a fat ledger on the desk and shook his head.

'No, m'dear, there's nothing in here. I'll just enter all the details, date, time an' everything, and if nobody claims it, it's yours after three months.'

He squinted at Evadne with a flash of recognition.

'It's Mrs Stoate, innit? I thought I recognised you. Ee, we've had your old feller in here a few times of a Friday night. A bugger he was, alus getting drunk at the Ferret and Firkin and wantin' to sleep it off in one of our cells. Haven't seen him in a while, how is he?'

She looked downcast. 'He's been burnt, I'm afraid.'

The sergeant looked concerned. 'Oh dear, not badly, I hope?'

Mrs Stoate gave him a wry look. 'They don't bugger about with 'em in Kingscastle Crematorium, y'know, Sergeant!' A little bit of moisture crept into her eyes. 'All I've got now is Ben here.'

She pointed to the dog who, having exhausted all the interesting smells of vomit and urine, had curled himself up under a bench and was having a quick scratch at an irritating flea.

The sergeant took down all the details, laboriously writing them into the ledger with a ballpoint pen that he kept licking through force of habit, and then put the bangle into a plastic bag and sealed it.

'Give us a call in three months, m'dear, and we may have some good news for you,' he told her with a kind smile and a blue tongue.

The bangle lay in its bag on the counter and was still there when, a couple of minutes later, the Reverend Percy Furrow called in to see if he could pin a hand-painted poster about the Town Church Jumble Sale on the notice board outside the Police Station. The poster had been done by ten-year-old Jimmy Steggles, who'd won the Montdurand Primary School Jumble Sale Poster Competition.

The Rev. Percy was an amateur archaeologist and the bangle caught his eye. He turned it over in his fingers.

'That's unusual! Early Anglo-Saxon if I'm not mistaken, Sergeant. Where did you get it?'

The sergeant explained its origin and that it had been found by a dog in Withers Woods. The Reverend Percy screwed up his eyes thoughtfully.

'Do you mind if I get the Senior Archaeologist from Shering-ford University to have a look at it? It could be quite rare and valuable so I should keep it locked up. That shouldn't present you with any difficulties in this place!' He tittered at his witti-cism.

The sergeant scratched his head. 'Well, I don't see no prob-lem about that, vicar, as long as he don't take it away, but I'll have to clear it with the superintendent.'

Bounding with enthusiastic energy, a bearded, tousle-haired, fresh-faced and sandalled Dr Justin Postlethwaite showed up two days later with the Reverend Percy, and got even more ex-cited than the vicar when he studied the bangle.

'By all the saints, you were right, Percy, this is a classi-cal piece of Anglo-Saxon jewellery! Eighth or ninth century, I would say. You see the traces of enamelling? Where exactly was it found and have any other pieces turned up?'

Percy and the sergeant both shook their heads.

'Nobody's brought anything like that in to the station afore as far as I know, sir,' said the sergeant thoughtfully. 'What should we do now?'

Postlethwaite stroked his chin.

'As I think it's gold, the first thing is to notify the local Coro-ner. We're obliged by law to do that just in case it's a genuine artefact. Then we should go and examine the site where it was found.' He turned to the sergeant. 'You say a woman brought it in – what did you say to her?'

The sergeant scratched his head. 'Just the usual – if nobody claims it in three months, it's hers.'

Postlethwaite shook his head. 'I don't think so. If it's what I think it is, it'll belong to the Crown. It's very old and will be a museum piece. She might be entitled to a small reward but that's all.'

Mrs Stoate got the phone call from the police as she was doing a spot of dusting before lunch. She wasn't able to add much more to the information that she had already provided. Sergeant Bulstrode told her the bangle was very old and would probably go into the museum and she might get a small reward. She told him that there was nobody in Kingscastle who knew exactly where the bangle had been found except Ben, and he wouldn't be much help. Then she recalled that a young chap called Moon from the consultants on the bypass had been the one to rescue Ben, and so it was likely that he would remember where he'd found the bangle.

The phone rang on my desk and Sue told me that a Sergeant Bulstrode of Kingscastle police wished to speak to me.

'What have you been up to, Marcus? Have you been a bad boy?' she giggled.

It's strange, isn't it, when the police contact you, you always think that one or other of your sins has caught up with you. Some people blurt out things like, 'Is it about parking my car on the zebra, officer? I was only there for two minutes.' Or: 'If it's about last night, officer, she swore blind she was eighteen.'

'Just put him through, Miss Johnson,' I replied primly.

'Hello?' I said questioningly, but I couldn't help thinking about the Tripps; parking; speeding; what I'd told the public meeting in the Town Hall; Ivan's problem and a whole range of other what might be considered slightly dodgy activities.

'Is that Mr Marcus Moon?' The voice was authoritative and gave nothing away.

'Could be, why?'

'And you are the gentleman who found Mrs Evadne Stoate's dog in Withers Woods?'

That sounded better. 'Yeerrs.'

'Can you tell me exactly where you found him, sir?'

'Well, it was sometime ago but I do remember the spot, as it happens, because it's close to where we're going to put one of the big foundations for the Shering Valley Bridge.'

'Is that where the protest camp is?'

'I don't know about that, there wasn't a camp there when I found the dog. Why, what's this all about?'

'Well, sir, it appears the bangle that you took off the dog's leg is a rare piece of jewellery and the university archaeologists want to examine the site to see if anything else can be turned up.'

Oh oh! Hang on here, I thought. That rang alarm bells. The last thing the Ministry would want was the whole multi-million pound bypass project delayed while some students truffled about with trowels, brushes and string, digging up some cracked pots and old arrow heads.

I fobbed him off by telling him I expected to be back in King-scastle shortly and I would phone him beforehand with the date so that I could show whoever it was where the dog had been trapped. That seemed to satisfy him.

I spoke to Hugo about this but he didn't seem overly concerned. It wasn't our problem, he said, so I let it go.

*****

By now all parties involved in the bypass, including the Government, were aware of Stumpy and his gang of protesters. The argument revolved around who was responsible for sorting out the problem and getting them off the site. Withers had been served a Compulsory Purchase Order with a plan showing the extent of the strip of land the Government was acquiring compulsorily from him, so it was assumed that it was the Government's responsibility to move the protesters as Stumpy's camp fell within that area. MacLowland Limited were establishing their main construction camp but were being held up by the tree protesters at the site of the secondary camp for the Shering Valley Bridge and the Hickling Edge tunnels. CONDES' problem was that Stumpy's tunnels were right on the spot where the huge piled foundations and thrust block for the springing of the east end of the Shering Valley Bridge was to be located.

Rock Solid Foundations Limited had turned up with their piling rig but had not been able to gain access to the site either because of Stumpy's efforts. From our point of view there was also concern that these may have resulted in undermining the area for the foundations.

Hugo got the phone call from Macs just as he was leaving the office on Friday night, looking forward to a relaxing weekend playing golf. Ivan and I had been working together on the bypass project for some time, not in mutual harmony and affection but in a sort of cool truce to get the job done – as Des put it, 'to ensure that the finished road level at Ivan's tunnels and your bridge coincide.' He didn't think travellers would appreciate lugging their vehicles up or down a flight of steps if the finished levels were different.

Hugo called us both into his office.

'I'm sorry to mess up your weekend but we have a problem at Kingscastle. Can the two of you get down there tomorrow morning and check out if these protesters have done any serious damage that will affect the east part of the road and the Valley Bridge foundations?'

Ivan said it was no problem for him and so I had to pretend it wasn't for me either. In fact, for me it was a crucial weekend. I was intending to go with Charlie to Prinknash Keep to meet her parents for the first time – an event for the boyfriend akin to swimming with hungry tiger sharks or tight-rope walking over Niagara Falls.

Charlie and I had planned to go down to Gloucestershire to meet David and Angela Prinknash together so I would have somebody to hold my hand. Now she would have to go on her own by train. More to the point, so would I, except that now

I would go on by car from Kingscastle. This did have a small advantage; it meant that I wouldn't have to put up with Ivan's miserable moaning on the journey down and on the way back. We'd have to go in separate cars.

I rang Sergeant Bulstrode and told him I would be in Kingscastle next day and if he'd like to arrange for somebody to meet me at the bridge site around eleven o'clock, I'd show them where I'd found Ben.

Ivan and I parked our cars on the country road next to a van that had 'University of Sheringford' painted on the side. A tousle-haired, brown-bearded chap in a Levi shirt and brown corduroys was smoking a cigarette and leaning on the van. He introduced himself as Doctor Justin Postlethwaite and said he was the senior lecturer in archaeology at the university. He shook hands with both of us. Ivan's handshake was brief and included a barbed comment that he hoped Postlethwaite wasn't going to waste everybody's time by bringing in a bunch of hairy-arsed students for a 'jolly' in the countryside and hold up the road construction. Postlethwaite looked surprised at this but didn't respond.

As we walked down the hill through the woods towards the protesters' site, he said quietly to me, 'Your friend's a bit touchy, isn't he?'

I gave him a sympathetic grin. 'He's not my friend, we just work together on this project, and Ivan's like that with everybody. I wouldn't worry if I were you.'

298

There were a few tents and old chairs scattered round a wood fire. About a dozen people in black balaclavas were milling around with shovels and bits of wood. As soon as they saw us they shot down their tunnels like meerkats at the flick of a hawk's wing.

I looked round at the tunnel entrances and at the vast amount of excavated earth scattered about.

'Bloody hell, they've certainly made a mess of this! How deep do you reckon they've dug?'

Ivan tugged at his beard and scowled. 'No more than two to three metres, I would say, otherwise they'd be into the water-table.'

I agreed, thinking that shouldn't cause us any problem; the pile caps and thrust block were much thicker than that. It was the nuisance factor of the diggers being there that was important. Still, that wasn't our business to resolve. Ivan bent down and picked up something from a pile of earth. He rubbed some of the mud off with his fingers.

'Hey, what do you think this is?' he said, showing me a small triangular piece of dull yellow metal with some scratches on it.

I took it from him. 'Gosh, it's quite heavy. Do you think it's gold?'

He snatched it back. 'I found it first!' he snapped, and pushed it into his pocket.

Postlethwaite came over. He had heard the exchange. 'Can I see that please?' he asked.

Ivan reluctantly took it out of his pocket and handed it over.

'Don't forget, I found it – and he's a witness.' He pointed at me.

There was a gasp from Postlethwaite and we turned to look at him.

'My God, if this is what I think it is—.' He stopped suddenly.

'What?' exclaimed Ivan, his moustache bristling with curiosity. 'What do you think it is?'

Postlethwaite didn't reply directly. 'Let's have a look round. Where exactly did you find this?'

Ivan looked suspicious. 'Why? What is it? Is it valuable?' Greed shone in his eyes. 'I found it so if it's valuable, it's mine!' And he grabbed it from Postlethwaite's hand.

'Where did you find it?' Postlethwaite insisted.

Ivan pointed to a pile of excavated soil at the side of a tunnel. We walked over to it and scrabbled about but all we turned up was a badly rusted piece of iron, which Postlethwaite examined carefully. He looked thoughtful. 'Whereabouts did you find the dog with the bangle on its leg?' he asked me.

I pointed further up the hill. 'About twenty metres up there.'

I showed him the tree root and he put his hand into the hole and felt about but there was nothing else. Nor could we find anything else of interest to him in the vicinity.

'A rabbit or something must have dug it up from somewhere around here,' he murmured thoughtfully.

I could see the archaeologist in him was very excited but he suddenly clammed up. He turned to both of us and said, 'Look, will you do me a favour and not say anything to anybody about this for the time being? This could be an important archaeological site and until we've checked it out more thoroughly, I don't want hordes of people coming up here with spades and metal detectors wrecking whatever there is before we've had a chance to examine it. That lot...' he pointed at the tunnellers '...could have damaged some things already.'

Ivan frowned. 'Why, what do you think it is? Will there be a reward? If so, don't forget who found it first, I don't want you claiming you did, Postlethwaite. Just remember that.'

Postlethwaite glanced at him distastefully but replied casually, too casually I thought: 'It could be the site of an early English settlement. The huts would have been made of wood and straw so there'll be no trace of them now. But we could find cooking pots, pieces of old weapons, crude crockery fragments, things like that.'

I nodded acceptance and said we wouldn't say anything about the site. But our prime objective was to get the bypass built and we didn't want it held up. Postlethwaite acknowledged that.

The troglodytes still hadn't emerged from their underground lair so we pushed on back up the hill along the line of the proposed road.

Not more than thirty metres away, we came across the first tree-house. The ladder had been pulled up and cautious faces looked down on us from forty feet up a large tree. All the lower branches had been removed so there was no way of climbing up. I could see two more similar houses in trees further along.

'What do you think they're doing, just being awkward by being in the way?' Postlethwaite asked.

'No, not just that, they've probably been spiking the trees as well,' snarled Ivan. 'They're trying to make as much a nuisance of themselves as they can. They're professional troublemakers and all living on handouts from the State – that's you and me,' he said angrily.

We walked back to our respective cars, not overly concerned about the protesters' activities; their removal was for the authorities to sort out.

I shook hands with Justin Postlethwaite, who said he'd be in touch, and climbed into the MG. Ivan just returned to his car and departed without saying a word.

As soon as he couldn't be overheard, Postlethwaite whipped out his mobile phone and I saw him talking animatedly into it as I turned the car round to head for Gloucestershire.

I was still intrigued by Ivan's find. Postlethwaite hadn't asked to keep it, which puzzled me; maybe he didn't want to draw too much attention to it. More likely he didn't want to get into an argument with Ivan. I wondered if it was valuable and if so what Ivan intended to do with it.

I followed Charlie's directions to Prinknash Keep and arrived at a pair of open wrought iron gates fronting a long curving drive flanked by chestnut trees just coming into leaf, with parkland on either side. I knew Charlie lived on an estate and that her father was a baronet but I hadn't expected something quite as grand as this. The MG swung into the drive, my apprehension increased the closer I got to the house, until by the time I reached the front door I was in a cold sweat.

It wasn't a particularly big house – rambling perhaps was the best word to describe it – but the old bath stone of the main building radiated a mellow warmth in the late afternoon April sunshine. Immaculate beds filled with brightly coloured flowers – pansies, wallflowers, and tulips were just the ones I could recognise – surrounded the front and the one side I could see. It was very impressive.

What would her parents make of me? I wondered. Here I was, a Yorkshire lad, down from t'north, entangled with their daughter and obviously giving her one, as they say (well more than one, and frequently). I just prayed that subject wasn't going to arise on my first visit.

I humped my bag out of the boot and up the steps to the large front door. I wasn't sure what to expect after my encounter with Withers' butler at Withers Hall but I decided I wasn't going to be overawed by another one. Be firm and masterful, that was the plan. I rang the bell.

The door opened and I beheld a tall, aristocratic looking chap in a dark suit with an expressionless face.

'My name is Marcus Moon, my man,' I said. 'I'm a guest of Dr Charlotte Prinknash for the weekend.'

I held out my bag for him to relieve me of it – which he did with what I thought was a glazed look.

'Come in,' he murmured, 'and follow me.'

I followed him through the hall into a bright sunny drawing room where Charlie and another woman, with a strong facial resemblance and the same dark hair and violet eyes, were talking in front of a large fire with a carved wooden overmantel bearing a shield.

Charlie's eyes lit up when she saw me. 'Oh goody, you've made it then, I was getting worried. I see you've met Daddy already.' She pointed at my bag carrier.

I froze. Oh shit, off to another bad start!

'I'm sorry' I gargled. 'I thought…'

I saw a twinkle in his eye. He put down my bag and held out his hand. 'David Prinknash,' he said with a smile.

'Howdydo, sir.' I managed to say. 'I'm Marcus.'

'Yes,' he said. 'You've told me that already.'

The lady came over, smiled and shook my hand. 'I'm Charlie's mother Angela.' Then she turned to her husband and said, 'Well don't just stand there, David, get Marcus a drink, he's had a long drive, I'm sure he could do with some refreshment.'

'It'll be a John Smith's Brown Ale then, will it? Theer's nowt like it,' David said, mimicking a Yorkshire accent. His eyes twinkled again, taking any sting out of his joke.

'Touché, but no zurr thank ee. I'd be likin' a flagon of yer home brewed Gloucestershire zider, pressed by yer own feet, if that be possible.'

We both started to laugh. The two women just looked at each other with raised eyebrows and shrugged.

'Men!' said Angela.

'Children!' said Charlie.

'Get him a white wine, Daddy, one of your decent Montra-chets, not that stuff you give the vicar to get rid of him.'

We were soon joined by Charlie's younger sister Emily, who was another cracker. Slim boyish figure, tanned face, mischie-vous eyes with laugh lines and dressed in riding kit. She took more after her father than her mother with short, light brown hair, but she did have her mother's violet eyes. Charlie had told me that she tested sports cars for a living.

'Is that your TF outside? She's a beauty and in good nick for her age,' Emily said with interest. 'I wouldn't mind a go in her one day – if Charlie isn't jealous,' she chuckled.

In the end four of us had the excellent white wine and Sir David Prinknash had his usual scotch and soda. They were very easy to get on with and after a few minutes of nervous discom-fort I soon found myself embraced in the general conversation. They were very interested in what was happening in and around Kingscastle and particularly in the protest camp and the tunnel-ling. David said that the whole area was a treasure house of ar-chaeological remains, there was no telling what the road might turn up. Stonehenge and Avebury were the best known places, he said, but there were burial mounds and other ancient sites of worship all over that part of England.

'There must be hundreds of things buried or lost in the past that haven't been found yet. It's only with the advent of met-al detectors and enthusiastic amateurs that more stuff is being turned up now since the end of the Second World War. More valuable artefacts have been found in the last forty years than were found in the previous thousand. Tons of things must have been destroyed under the plough in the past.' He shook his head resignedly.

'Have you found anything at Prinknash?' I asked.

He shrugged. 'We haven't looked, but this place is very old, or at least part of it is. The first house was built here in the reign of King Edward IV and since then it's been occupied by Prinknashes, who were into just about everything from royalist plots to piracy, so I have no doubt that there'll be things like old weapons and a few skeletons buried around the place. One of Cromwell's generals, General Sir William Waller, knocked the original house down and the present house was designed by Robert Smythsen at the end of the sixteenth century.'

'That reminds me, we're putting you in the guest suite in the east wing, Marcus,' Lady Angela told me.

Emily chipped in with a grin, 'That's the haunted wing, the family sleep in the west wing. The ghost of old Sir Cedric Prinknashe is supposed to stalk the corridors of the east wing on moonlit nights, seeking out ne'er-do-wells who are out of their rooms and doing horrible things to them. He had some very nasty habits, I can tell you!'

'And the floors creak,' added David dryly.

I got the message. There would be no hanky-panky this time round. Friendly though they were, I wasn't accepted into the family to the extent that they were going to bunk their ewe lamb Charlie and me together on first acquaintance. First acquaintance with them, that is – Charlie and I were already very well acquainted in London!

We finished our drinks and I picked up my bag to go up to my room. Charlie said, 'I'll show you where it is', and Angela Prinknash called out, 'Dinner at seven, drinks at six-thirty and it's casual.'

'That's a good job,' I murmured to Charlie, 'I forgot to bring my white tie and decorations.'

My room was vast and freezing. The late April sun had gone and there was a distinct chill in the air. The walls were panelled; there was a large four-poster bed, a couple of huge wardrobes, tables, chairs and long draped curtains on either side of the window. I had a long shower in a Victorian bathroom to warm up. Fortunately there was plenty of hot water and the shower was one of those old fashioned types that really drench you rather that the modern style of prostate spray showers. I dragged a clean shirt out of my bag, gave the armpits a squirt of *Arpege Pour Homme* and read some back numbers of *Country Life* whilst I waited for six-thirty to arrive.

On the dot I strolled down the wide staircase and made for what turned out to be the library, where I could hear the buzz of conversation and the clinking of ice in glasses.

In addition to David and Angela Prinknash, there were two other people in the room. I recognised the long-nosed bloke in the purple shirt with his matching handkerchief dripping from his sleeve from my visit to Kingscastle Town Hall, but I couldn't remember his name. The other person was a tall, elegant, elderly lady with tinted hair piled on top of her head and a low-cut dress that showed rather more wrinkled cleavage than was attractive. However, her glittering emerald and diamond pendant distracted the eye from the wrinkles. So much for being casual! There was something familiar about her but I couldn't put my finger on it. Of Charlie and Emily there was no sign as yet.

David introduced me to the lady. 'This is Charlie's…er… friend…Marcus. Marcus, this is Miss Gloria Rainsford.'

'Ah!' I gently shook the delicately proffered fingers of this actress so well-known from my childhood and said how pleased I was to meet her. She had difficulty in reciprocating the feeling, it seemed to me, or maybe that was just the Botox freezing her face. In any case, she seemed to be wearing that mask actresses adopt when confronted by their scruffy, seat-buying public.

Turning to the long-nosed chap, David presented me to him. 'Anthony Molestrangler, the MP for Kingsforest. You've probably come across him in connection with the new bypass.'

I said that I had briefly shared a platform with him.

'Really?' sneered Molestrangler, flaring his nostrils suspiciously like a racehorse offered a dubious sugar lump. 'I don't recollect it. When was that?'

'The meeting in Kingscastle Town Hall chaired by Sir Fistulas Withers.'

He wasn't impressed and blew his nose loudly on his purple hanky before turning away to talk to Angela Prinknash.

This left me with Gloria, I didn't feel we had much in common but I felt it was only polite to make an effort.

I floated out. 'I remember you in *The Two Headed Baby from Outer Space*. You were impregnated by an alien. It had a three-year gestation period.'

I remembered it well. I'd gone with my friend Derek Crompton: it felt like three years sitting through that turgid film, waiting to see her squeeze out this terrible monster. We expected the heads to be side by side, bawling lustily in Kreon, but they turned out to be one on top of the other – a disappointing cinematographic trick. We felt we had been cheated out of our hard-earned pocket money.

Clearly Gloria thought it wasn't an Oscar-winner either because her face chilled over, but she was a game girl and tried to regain the initiative.

'And what are you…er…Marcus? David said you were Charlotte's friend. What does that mean?' One eyebrow was raised suggesting, as a good actress can, that dirty deeds might have been afoot.

Fifteen-all, I thought.

'I'm a civil engineer,' I replied, avoiding the tricky part of her question.

'I've never been a civil engineer,' she murmured. 'I was once a civil servant, and in *The Day the World Exploded* I was a nuclear engineer. Is that something similar?'

'Vaguely; civil engineers deal with roads, bridges and railways.'

'Did you see me in *Riding down from Doncaster?* I was at my best in that movie playing a poor, ragged but beautiful waif who meets this very rich, handsome man whilst stealing a ride in a railway train – and she marries him in the end.'

'I bet the audience didn't see that coming,' I murmured.

Fortunately Charlie and Emily arrived to rescue me at that moment, so I missed her reply.

Dinner was delicious and fairly relaxed; I was seated between the two girls and opposite Anthony Molestrangler.

'Are you for or against the bypass, Mr Molestrangler?' Emily enquired mischievously.

He was a true politician. 'Both,' he said. 'I have to reflect what my constituents want, but I can honestly say that as a result of my contacts with the Prime Minister and the Secretary of State for Transport and Communications, we managed to get the right result between us.'

'So it was all down to you? That's some achievement,' I commented. 'You must be very pleased. No worries for the next election then?'

He gave a sickly smile. 'One has to do one's best when one is placed in a position of great responsibility, you know.' And, looking down his long nose at me, he added, 'Or perhaps you don't.'

'Not me,' I said. 'I'm just a minion.'

As the apple crumble arrived, Emily whispered mischievously, 'Are you and Charlie – you know?'

'I know what?'

'You know. Doing it?'

I fixed my features into what I hoped was a disapproving look. 'You country girls are all the same, too much romping in the hay with the farmers' boys and not enough cold showers,' I grinned.

Charlie must have overheard Emily's questioning. She leaned around me and snapped, 'Shut up, Em, or we'll talk about Georgie Porgie!'

That reduced Emily to an embarrassed silence for a few minutes until she changed the subject and asked if she could take my MG out for a run in the morning.

Charlie said, 'You should let her, she'll give it a good check over, that's her job.'

After dinner, while the others were having coffee and brandies, David poured me a glass of port as we sat round the fire in the library and very discreetly started the interrogation – because that's what it was.

Well, if you were the father of a cracking-looking, talented daughter who was obviously worth a few sovereigns, you wouldn't want her throwing herself away on some gold-digging, randy wastrel from the sticks, would you? No, neither did he!

I wasn't sure which of those adjectives I should start trying to convince him I was not – if you get the idea. 'Randy' wasn't a good start, there could be difficulties if we went in that direction, so that was best left out of the conversation. David saved me from choosing by opening up with, 'Which part of Yorkshire is your home?'

'Is the accent that strong?'

'No, Charlie mentioned it!'

This gave me the opportunity to ramble on about York, my father (a bank manager), my mother (a pillar of the Townswomen's Guild), my school (a modest one, but well known for its rugby team), my only sister who, I told him, was the 'Irn Bru' arm-wrestling champion of Cleckheaton.

'Really?' David said, raising his eyebrows, and then realised that I had understood exactly what he was doing and burst out laughing.

'You had me going for a second there,' he chuckled. 'Tell me about CONDES. Even I, down here in our corner of Gloucestershire, have heard of them. I think your senior partner, Arbuthnot isn't it, is a member of my club.'

Oh lord! My heart sank. Geoffrey clearly thought I was barmy and it wouldn't do my situation with the Prinknash family much good if they discovered their baby bunny was shacked up with a fruit-cake.

'He's just retired,' I told him. 'I think the strain of running a big practice was affecting his health. Hugo Elmes has taken over as the senior now.'

I hoped that my use of words like 'strain' and 'health' might throw into doubt the veracity of any observations Geoffrey might make about my sanity – if he was ever called upon to make any.

Molestrangler and Gloria departed after coffee and cognac, and the whole family made a move to bed at ten-thirty. Goodnights were exchanged and I retired to my lonely outpost in the deserted, dark east wing.

Money hadn't been wasted on fancy electrical fittings and the shaded single forty-watt bulb hanging from its flex in the centre of the room cast the minimum amount of light round the room, leaving many dark shadows and gloomy recesses. Fortunately the bed had an electric blanket, so after a wash and teeth-cleaning, I put out the light and settled down for the night.

I must have just drifted off when I sensed the duvet on the other side of the bed twitch. I pulled it back and it moved again, yet there had been no sound. I felt a cold draught of air, then that side of the bed went down as if a weight had been lowered on to it.

I went rigid with fear and screwed my eyes tightly closed. Oh Christ, I thought, it's the spectre of Sir Cedric Prinknashe come to wreak his evil ways on my helpless and lonely body. The light switch was across the room by the door and the only light in the room came from a shaft of moonlight that filtered through a small gap in the curtains, making a shimmering patch on the carpet. I opened my eyes momentarily, only to see a dark shape looming above me. I was just tensing up, ready to throw off the duvet and make a run for the door, when a pair of soft lips pressed themselves on to mine.

Pushing her away, I gasped, 'Fuck me, Charlotte, you scared the living daylights out of me! I thought that bloody Sir Cedric had materialised to work his wicked will! How the hell did you get here? I didn't hear anything.'

She gave a low chuckle. 'There's a secret passage that was built in the reign of Queen Mary so protestant priests could escape when the house was raided by her soldiers. It goes from your room down to a door in the pantry. I came up that. Anyhow, enough of history, what are you going to do now?' She snuggled up close.

'I'm not sure I can do much after the fright you've given me! I've gone all weak and feeble.'

'I'll tell you what. As Sir Cedric hasn't showed up, I could work my wicked will on you instead,' she chuckled, reaching under the duvet.

Nothing was hinted at breakfast next morning but Emily reminded me about letting her give the MG a run. There was a twitch on her lips and a gleam in her eye so I knew she was guessing that my night hadn't been a lonely one. I reluctantly handed over the keys at this discreet blackmail.

She was back after half-an-hour and to my relief, the car showed no obvious signs of distress. She tossed the keys back to me and said, 'You've got a decent motor there, Marcus. The tappets are a bit noisy and should be adjusted the next time you have it serviced, the steering bushes need tightening and the front wheels are slightly out of balance, but apart from that it goes well.'

Charlie took me for a long walk round the grounds and we called in at the local village pub, The Prinknash Arms, for a swift drink before lunch. Emily had pushed off in her jodhpurs and hard hat to exercise her horse. There's something very sexy about jodhpurs, and I got a bruise on my arm for mentioning it.

We both had to be at work on Monday morning – Charlie had a busy day in the operating theatre and I had to report to Hugo about Kingscastle – so we set off for London after lunch on Sunday afternoon and arrived back in Fulham around six-thirty.

On the way Charlie was unusually quiet. I didn't think the visit had gone too badly after my first *faux pas* in mistaking Sir David for the butler, but she was worrying me by her silence. I had to ask, I couldn't bear the tension, and when I did she burst into peals of laughter.

'I knew you'd ask! I just knew it! You couldn't wait to find out, could you? And they say women are curious! What about men?'

'Well, how did it go then?' I enquired, irritable at being tricked.

'Well, Daddy *quite* liked you, he thought you were a bit serious and could do with feeding up.' She waited for me to interrupt but I didn't fall for it this time and let her continue. 'Mummy sort of agreed with Daddy…' I still said nothing. '…and Emily is frightfully jealous.'

'Is that it?'

'Oh, and by the way, they want us to go down there for the Bank Holiday.'

I shook my head, relieved. Women! But I must have passed muster to be invited back.

'By the way, who's Georgie Porgie?'

'Oh him? He's a boy from Stroud that we were at school with. He's always been keen on Emily but at school he was always trying to put his hand in our knickers – hence Georgie Porgie. His real name is George Grainger and he's an Olympic horseman. He and Em go off to riding competitions, jumping and eventing.'

'Do they…?

'Pah! You're worse than she is, trying to get your oats second-hand.'

'We'll be home soon,' I said with a filthy leer. 'So we'll see about that!'

Well, it was supposed to be a filthy leer but Charlie asked me if I'd got indigestion. I frowned thoughtfully; my looks, glances and leers of late hadn't been doing very well, obviously more practice was needed. I wondered if there was a book, *Looks and Leers to make Your Friends and Enemies Quail.* I'd check on the web.

*****

At Bob Barclay's weekly design meeting, Perseus Rixon said he was meeting the planning officer of Kingscastle Borough Council the following Tuesday. I said I was going down there that day as well and I could give him a lift. He hesitated and I wondered if he had come across Susan and Tracey Tripp on a previous visit and wanted to go on his own, but then he nodded and told me that I could pick him up at his office at nine o'clock.

As his office was in the East End, in precisely the opposite direction to the M4 and Kingscastle from CONDES' office, and it would mean me having to drive twice through all the morning traffic going into The City, I told him to sod off. He could either get a taxi to CONDES' offices, or find his own way to Kingscastle.

'Make your choice.'

The rules having been laid down, I waited for his answer. I hoped it would be the latter but, flushing angrily, he climbed down and said he would get a taxi.

Bob grinned. 'Have a nice trip.'

Perse turned up half-an-hour late at CONDES, didn't offer an apology, looked down his nose at the little green monster but settled himself in the passenger seat and proceeded to tell me how much carbon the car was emitting to pollute the atmosphere. Fortunately it was a nice day, and with the top down, the wind noise made it difficult to hear what he was saying, so after we hit the M4 he shut up and concentrated on trying to stop his long hair blowing about.

I parked in the Town Hall car park and went to see Peter Ashman, the Borough Engineer, to up-date him on progress on the bypass and find out if his department would have any problems with access to the proposed car park at the rear of Barclay's supermarket. After combing the wind knots out of his hair, Perse went off to have his meeting with the planners. We agreed to meet back at the car at lunchtime.

I was there first and was just debating whether to have a pub lunch at The Swan or a knife and fork roast at The Royal Oak when Perse turned up, looking very pleased with himself.

'Piece of cake,' he said. 'The Chief Planning officer doesn't know his arse from his elbow. I told him that my scheme would set the town centre of his little kingdom alight!'

I didn't like the sound of this. 'So what did he say?'

'He said he thought that the design of the front should blend in with the buildings on either side. I told him, "Get out of the past and get into the future man! Think big! Think dramatic! My design will put Kingscastle on the map".'

'So is he going to recommend to the Planning Committee that it be approved?'

Perseus shifted nervously. 'Well, we didn't actually get that far. He left the meeting suddenly after that, saying he had an urgent appointment. I was left with an assistant planner. He seemed to like my scheme so I think it will be approved.'

'Bob said you had to get definite guidance about what they would and what they wouldn't recommend. He doesn't want to be dragged into a long planning battle followed by planning appeals, you know.'

Perse bridled at that. 'I'm Bob's architect, I know want he wants better than you and I'm telling you that there's no problem!' he snapped huffily.

'OK then, as you say you're the architect, it's your balls Bob will personally rip off and feed to the piranhas if it doesn't work. I've seen Bob in action if his advisers cause him problems.' I shuddered. 'It's not a nice sight, not nice at all!'

Perse flushed but didn't reply. I turned away.

'C'mon, let's eat. The Swan do a great pint and cottage pie and I'm hungry.'

He made no move to follow me.

'Are you coming?'

He shook his head and fumbled in his case. 'I don't drink alcohol and I don't eat anything made from dead creatures. I've brought some lettuce and cucumber sandwiches with me and some mineral water, so I'll wait in the car if you don't mind.'

I shrugged, feeling relieved. The journey down had been a pain and I wasn't really looking forward to having him banging on over lunch about political correctness, sexual equality, and finally dog and cat food. ('Do you know that one third of the edible protein eaten in Europe is eaten by dogs and cats whilst Africa is starving?' he'd told me.)

'OK, please yourself,' I said and strolled into The Swan's snug and called up a pint of their best bitter.

When I emerged, still savouring the rich flavour of their cottage pie and feeling pleasantly content, I was astounded to see that where my car was parked, a crowd of excited people had gathered and were chattering away and pointing. Some blue flashing lights and the top of a police van were visible over their heads. Easing my way through the crowd, I saw two police cars and a police motorbike, and Perseus Rixon being carried bodily by four burly coppers towards the police van. They heaved him in, slammed the doors shut, climbed into and on to their respective vehicles and drove away with the lights flashing and sirens hee-hawing.

I stood there bemused.

'What's all that about?' I asked an elderly gentleman who was leaning on his stick watching.

'Do you know him then?'

'Yes I do,' I replied. 'That's my car.' And I pointed at the MG.

'They've buggered your window,' he sniggered, exposing two rows of badly fitting false teeth set in purple gums.

I looked at the car. There was broken glass all over the interior and the passenger side window just showed jagged edges of glass round the frame.

What had happened? Had Rixon gone berserk? Had he found half a caterpillar in his lettuce that had tipped him over the edge?

'I saw it all!' The old chap was grinning as though he'd something to sell. 'I were sittin' on that seat yonder havin' a smoke, you know, when it happened.'

'When what happened, for Christ's sake?'

I was getting impatient, and the crowd had drifted away by now so I was left with him as my only witness.

'Do you know how old I am?'

I was tempted to tell him if he wanted to continue adding more years to whatever age he was, he'd better start talking soon.

'Eighty?' I hazarded, pitching it low.

He grinned triumphantly. 'Have another go.'

I took a deep breath. 'This is the last guess. Seventy-six.'

'Eighty-five!'

'Well, I'd never have thought it. And you've got good eyesight?'

He nodded. 'Oh aye!'

'Well, what the hell did you see with it?'

'That young feller, he were sittin' in yon car eatin' his sarnies.'

'Yes?'

'They were wrapped in that sticky stuff.'

'Cling film, yes.'

'Well, he wound down the window and dropped it on the ground.'

I waited. This didn't seem cataclysmic so far.

'A copper saw him and come up and asked if it were his. He said it were but he didn't want it any more. The copper said neither did Kingscastle, and told him to pick it up. The feller refused, so the copper then asked him if he'd got a licence to deposit rubbish in a public place.

'The feller told him, "Why don't you stop harassing ordinary citizens and sod off and catch some muggers and burglars for a change?" He said some more about the police but I couldn't hear what it were.

'The copper then said he was arrestin' him for depositin' controlled waste without a licence. The young feller said he knew his rights and told the copper to sod off again, wound up the window and locked the car door. The copper got out his radio and called reinforcements and a whole army turned up.' The old man sucked his teeth. 'You wouldn't get the coppers to turn out like that if you'd been mugged or burgled, I bet.'

I finished his story off for him. 'So they smashed the window, unlocked the door and carted him of to the nick?'

'Yeah…you spoilt my story!'

'Sorry about that, but I was growing old too fast listening to it. Anyway, thanks for telling me.'

I went over to the car. Apart from the broken window, nothing was damaged. I cleared as much glass as I could from the driver's side and set off to find Kingscastle police station. I put the car in a visitors' space, went up the steps and into the reception where a burly sergeant was filling in some forms behind the counter.

'Yes, sir, come to give ourselves up then, have we?'

I smiled wearily. I suppose it can't be very exciting looking at miscreants' driving licences and insurance certificates all day.

'I think a colleague of mine has been brought in, he was parked in the Market Square and there was a kerfuffle about something?'

'And you are?'

'Marcus Moon from CONDES, the consultants on the bypass.'

A big smile lit up the sergeant's face. 'Mr Moon, we've spoken on the phone, I'm Sergeant Bulstrode. You're the gentleman what rescued Mrs Stoate's dog Ben when he got his leg snagged.'

I said I was, and he extended a large meaty hand for me to shake.

'That were a good deed, she were ever so chuffed.'

'I am glad; she seems a nice lady. But what about my colleague?'

'Would that be...' he glanced at a large book on the counter '...a Perseus Priapus Rixon, sir?'

I couldn't help but smile. Bob had said he was a bit of a prick but I didn't think he'd been so named.

'Yes, that's him.'

Sergeant Bulstrode drew in his breath through his teeth. I could tell the news wasn't good – for Perse that is.

'Is he a friend of yours, sir?'

From the way it was put, 'Yes' was clearly not going to do my standing with the Kingscastle cops any good.

'Good lord, no! He's just an architect that I happen to be working with.'

'An architect, is he? Well, we've locked him up, sir. He's going to be here overnight and will probably be charged tomorrow with dropping a piece of plastic wrapping in the street without a licence.'

'What's the penalty for that, ten years' hard labour?'

The irony bounced off him. 'No, sir, he'll probably get a conditional discharge. A night in the cells should teach him a lesson. We'll let him go tomorrow.'

'A pity! There is one other thing. Your guys smashed my car window – who's going to pay for that?'

Sergeant Bulstrode glanced at a form on his desk. 'Ah yes, I've got a note of that, a green MGTF, isn't it? If you'll just hold on here while I make a phone call...' And he disappeared into a back office.

He was back a couple of minutes later and scribbled an address on a piece of paper. 'If you go round to John's Garage he'll fix it for you straight away and send us the bill.'

I blinked with surprise. 'Really? That's brilliant. Thanks, Sergeant.'

'Glad to be of assistance, sir, anybody who helps Mrs Stoate is a friend of mine. A fine woman!'

I raised a questioning eyebrow and he gave a deep chuckle.

I drove the MG round to John's Garage. It was one of those old-fashioned garages in a vast shed where everything seemed to be total chaos but a buzz of activity filled the place. John himself was waiting for me, complete with oil-streaked hands, grease-covered overalls and a toothy grin. It looked as though he'd just slid out from under an old Sunbeam Talbot that had its back axles and differential hanging down.

'Mr Moon, isn't it? Steve Bulstrode told me about you. You're lucky, we just happen to have taken in an MGTF that was smashed up on the driver's side and written off for scrap a few weeks ago. One of the parts we salvaged was a passenger side window. It'll take a couple of hours to fit it and clean out all the glass from your car, so you can either sit down and read *The Sun* …' he nodded to a rickety old chair in the corner where there was a desk with invoices and a newspaper on it '…or have a run in that old Alpha over there, rather than hang about here.' He pointed to a neat-looking two-seater across the yard. 'The keys are in it – and it's insured. It's a demo car.'

Well, two hours spent driving a decent sports car in Kingscastle whilst waiting for my car to be repaired sounded a lot better than ogling a pair of oversized tits in *The Sun* for two hours, and ten times better than waiting at least two weeks for my local garage in Battersea to find a replacement window, so I took up his offer. The question in my mind was what to do with my two hours' free drive. Visit the Tripp family – a possibility, though only to find out a bit more about Ivan's activities. Deciding that was too risky, I settled on a visit to Evadne Stoate to see how Ben was.

I pulled up outside 24 Mayfield Avenue and rang the bell. Evadne answered the door with Ben beside her. He gave a little chirp when he saw me and wagged his tail.

'Marcus, what a surprise! Come in, have you got some news or something? Ben recognised you, didn't he? He's a clever boy.' She scratched his ears.

There was something different about Evadne. She seemed more comfortable and relaxed, and she was nicely dressed in a smart skirt and jumper with her hair done and make-up carefully applied.

I explained about my car and how Sergeant Bulstrode had helped out with getting the broken window repaired. There was a flicker in her eyes at his name and I remembered what he had said at the police station.

I grinned. 'I think the sergeant fancies you, Evadne, he spoke very kindly about you.'

She blushed and said hurriedly, 'I'll just go make us a pot of tea.'

325

Ben came and lay down on the hearth rug beside me. Apart from a bald patch on his leg he seemed to have fully recovered. I patted his head and he flicked the end of his tail a few times to acknowledge it.

Evadne came back in carrying a tray, on which was a sponge cake, teapot, milk and sugar, and two cups.It seemed she had decided to come clean about Sergeant Bulstrode and her voice took on a confidential tone.

'The sergeant and I are walking out these days. It all came about because of that bangle Ben found, so it's brought both of us good luck.'

'What does "walking out" mean, Evadne?'

She blushed furiously.

'Oh,' I murmured. 'So that's what it means!'

'You are awful!' she simpered, and turned away to pour out the tea.

My car was ready when I returned to John's Garage and they'd even washed and polished it. There was no point in hanging around in Kingscastle any further; Perseus Rixon had a bed for the night – an uncomfortable one, no doubt – and he could find his own way back to the Smoke tomorrow. So I thanked John enthusiastically and slipped him a fiver (which was going on expenses), receiving an oily handshake in return.

I debated whether to phone Bob Barclay at his flat or wait till the morning. In the end I decided that there was no time like the present and punched out his number on my mobile. He answered after a couple of rings so I gave him a brief resumé of what had transpired in Kingscastle. He fell about laughing.

'No, listen, Bob, there could be a problem here. It's not Perse's incarceration that worries me, Bob; it's what he said about his meeting with the planners. He's such an arrogant, conceited sod that I suspect he got right up their noses and that isn't going to do your project much good. By his own admission, he wouldn't listen when they tried to give him an outline of what they wanted to see in their Market Square and patronised them about being old-fashioned. He didn't get an answer to the question of whether they would recommend the scheme to the Planning Committee – the Chief Planner buggered off on some pretext about another meeting.'

That stopped Bob's laughter. 'Jesus, I don't like the sound of that, it's not what he was instructed to do.' He thought for a moment and then said, 'I'll phone the Planner in the morning and find out what they really want, and when Perse gets out of jail I'll have a quiet word with him. Thanks, Marcus.'

CHAPTER THIRTEEN

Stumpy had been watching the three geezers who turned up at his camp from within his tunnel and had seen the one with a face like a wet week-end pick up a piece of metal, show it to the lanky one and then put it in his pocket. He also saw the boffin's reaction although he didn't know who any of them were. When he was sure that they had gone, he crept out and scratched at the area roughly where he remembered the other bits of metal had been dumped. A lot more earth had been dumped there but after ten minutes he found a small fragment of silver with a chip of enamel adhering to it. He put it in his pocket for further investigation later.

Unfortunately for him, there wasn't a 'later'. His involvement on the site was abruptly terminated that night following Justin's phone call. At four o'clock in the morning, when they were all sleeping, a large force of police, with the assistance of hired security men and women in overalls, raided the camp. Bringing long ladders, ropes and poles, they dragged the tunnellers out of their burrows, the tree dwellers down from their eyries and carted the lot off to the police station in a couple of vans. Macs' men immediately moved in; put security guards in the woods and began to erect a security fence round the area.

On Monday morning, Dr Justin Postlethwaite turned up with three carloads of students and a van full of equipment, including metal detectors, shovels, sieves, drawing boards, tents and food. While some set up a camp, others began marking out the area into square grids using pegs and string. Over the next few days, as one group systematically scanned each grid carefully with metal detectors, a second group began to sieve the material that Stumpy's men had excavated from the tunnels.

It was on Wednesday that the sievers made their first discovery. Another badly rusted hasp and a silver triangular cheek piece from a helmet. These were carefully recorded.

By Saturday all the excavated earth had been sieved and three more pieces turned up: the base of a drinking vessel – probably a chalice – made from gold, a gold ring and a silver and enamel clasp from a cloak. All of them were covered in dried earth and were only identified after being carefully washed and cleaned in warm water using a soft brush.

The metal detector team had narrowed down their area of search to a small patch of woodland adjacent to one of Stumpy's tunnels and close to where Ben had been trapped. They recorded very strong signals from that area and started trial excavations with trowels and brushes. These turned up a gold sword hilt set with small olive-green peridots, two gold cloak torques and some loose garnets. The remainder of the site that Macs had fenced-off showed nothing of interest and was abandoned. Fortunately, the interesting area was away from the bridge foundation site and so Rock Solid Foundations Ltd was able to move in with its piling rig and begin setting out.

The whole archaeological team now began to excavate the interesting area carefully by hand. About fifty centimetres down they came across some rusty iron bands, obviously reinforcing bands for wooden chests rotted away long ago.

Macs provided them with a small generator and powerful lights so that shifts of students could work throughout the night. With huge excitement, they started to turn up the bulk of the treasure: complete gold chalices encrusted with jewels, some badly crushed but others almost perfect; six more sword hilts, the blades long gone; gold and silver candlesticks; bangles, rings, silver church plates, belt buckles, parts of helmets, brooches and, in a deeper pit alongside, six skeletons, each with the back of its skull smashed in.

Justin was beside himself with excitement, but very early on he had realised that what was being turned up was a serious major archaeological find and he needed help from the British Museum's experts. Three of their staff arrived the following day and began to classify the stuff as it arrived at Kingscastle police station in a security van. It was laid out in an interview room and, where possible, pieces fitted to other matching pieces. One enamelled plaque sent the experts into a foaming frenzy. It bore the lettering '*Aelfred mec heht gewyrcan*' – 'Alfred ordered me to be made'.

'My God!' breathed Justin. 'This really is King Alfred's lost treasure! Rumours about it have abounded, but it was just thought to be a folktale which grew over the ages because Alfred was known to have had a camp here at one time.'

The whole lot was photographed, weighed, measured, catalogued, reported to the Coroner and locked away in a vault in the NatWest Bank, Kingscastle Branch.

When it was thought that everything there was to find had been found, the whole area was rescanned to make certain nothing had been missed, but nothing else was discovered. Justin and his students returned to college and MacLowland and Rock Solid were left to get on with the road. The actual site where the treasure was found was securely fenced off and guarded until it could be decided what should happen to it. Kingscastle Council wanted to keep it as a tourist attraction, and invited ideas from the public.

Ivan and I followed the Kingscastle excavations with interest, Ivan with more than normal interest, I thought. I'd caught him looking up 'Buried Treasure' on his computer and scribbling notes, which he locked away in his desk next to his stock of porno mags.

He collared Justin Postlethwaite one day when we were making a site visit and asked him with a feigned nonchalance, 'Hey, Postlethwaite, is this stuff you're digging up classed as "Treasure Trove" or is it just "Treasure"?

Postlethwaite replied, 'You mean was it deliberately buried with the intention of recovering it later, or was it just lost?'

Ivan nodded eagerly.

Justin grinned. 'Neither. Under the 1996 Treasure Act, it makes no difference. Anything over three hundred years old with even a small amount of gold or silver in it automatically belongs to the Crown – the Government. The British Museum values it and then it'll be offered to museums to buy; and only if nobody wants to buy it will it be returned to the finder. Why?'

'Oh, nothing,' muttered Ivan. 'I just wondered.'

'What about the finder if museums *do* buy it?' I asked, noting the gleam in Ivan's eye.

'Well, usually the amount they pay can be given as a reward to be shared by the finder, the landowner and any tenant or occupier of the land. They don't have a right to it, it's just a reward, but that's what usually happens.'

The inquest on the treasure was held in Kingscastle Town Hall at the beginning of June. A large crowd turned out, most of them just to see it – the Kingscastle Hoard, as it was now called. It was likely that this would be the last time that everything would be together in one display. The press were there in force and the rows of artefacts photographed from all angles. The Coroner confirmed that it was 'Treasure', a not too difficult decision, and therefore belonged to the Crown.

Subsequently The British Museum valued it at three million pounds and several museums, including the British Museum and the Wiltshire County Museum in Kingscastle, bid for pieces. The whole lot was sold without difficulty.

The Department of the Environment announced that three million pounds were being allocated to be divided between the finder, the landowner and the tenant or occupier of the land – and that was when the fun started!

*****

Ivan burst into the office clutching a copy of *The Times*, his normally pasty face flushed with excitement. He pointed at me, saying, 'You're my witness, don't you forget that and don't try and back out because Postlethwaite was there as well.'

Des looked at me, bewildered by all this.

'What the hell are you talking about?' I said to Ivan.

'Finding the Kingscastle treasure!' he shouted triumphantly. 'I was the one that found it, remember – and I've got that piece of gold to prove it!'

Des told him. 'Slow down, Ivan, and explain yourself.'

Ivan waved his copy of *The Times* and jabbed his finger on an article on the front page.

'The Government are going to give the finder three million quid and that's me. I'm going to be rich!'

I took the paper from him and sure enough it said that the Kingscastle Hoard had now been sold to various museums, and that the Department of the Environment, although under no obligation to do so, were going to make an *ex gratia* payment of three million pounds to be divided between the finder, the landowner and any tenant or occupier of the land.

'It doesn't say you're getting three mill, and it doesn't mention your name as the finder either,' I pointed out.

A cunning gleam appeared in his eye. 'Don't forget I have proof. You're just envious, Moon, because it was me that found it and not you. I'm going to appoint solicitors to act for me and make sure I get my share.'

And with that he pushed off out to do whatever it was he was going to do in private.

Des looked at me. 'Is he right? Was he the finder?'

I rubbed my face thoughtfully. Perhaps I was envious; a share of three million would certainly have helped the Moon finances and made my bank manager less likely to treat me as an irritating nuisance.

'It's possible, Des. He did pick up a piece of what looked like gold but then Evadne Stoate's dog had already done that sometime earlier.'

And I told him the story about finding Ben and the crushed bangle on his paw. I assumed that Evadne still had it at home lying forgotten inside Winston Churchill on her mantelpiece.

When he got back to his flat, Ivan took the small triangular piece of metal that he had found in the excavated earth round Stumpy's tunnels from where he had hidden it in his sock drawer, unwrapped it from an old pair of socks and carefully rinsed it under the hot tap. The earth was deeply embedded into the decoration and he used a toothbrush to scrub it out. It definitely seemed like gold, being unusually heavy. There was some fine engraving on one side and it had four small red stones set in one edge. He wondered if it was some sort of medallion but whatever it was, it didn't matter – it was his evidence. He gloated over it. This small scrap was his key to a fortune. It was concrete evidence that he had been the first to find a piece of the Kingscastle Hoard.

The next thing to do was to establish his claim. Moon and Postlethwaite were his witnesses and they would have to make statements and swear to the date and time of his discovery. A frown crossed his face. Could they lie or refuse to do that? He didn't think so but it was a nagging thought. The sooner they made their statements the better, he decided, and it had better be done through a lawyer. The trouble was, Ivan didn't know anybody like that who he could rely on, and he was terrified of going to a strange firm and getting ripped off.

Thumbing through the Yellow Pages for Wandsworth, he turned up 'Solicitors' and worked his way down the names. He didn't know exactly what he was looking for but hoped that inspiration might be triggered off by a friendly sounding firm.

His finger came to rest on 'Claims Resolved Quickly Ltd': 'WE WIN, YOU GET THE MONEY'. That sounded the sort of thing he was looking for. Their address was on East Hill, not far from his flat. He punched out their number and spoke to a cool-voiced receptionist, who transferred him to the secretary of Mr Mark Jones, 'one of our directors'. He made an appointment to see Mr Jones at eleven-thirty the following day.

After a restless night and an anxious morning, barely containing his excitement, Ivan parked his Volvo on a yellow line in a side street close to East Hill, blasé about parking fines now he was going to be a millionaire. He walked briskly up East Hill until he found himself outside a converted shop unit with the window blanked out and 'Claims Resolved Quickly Ltd' painted in large white letters on a green background.

Inside, on a clean green carpet, was a stainless steel coffee table with two stainless steel and leather visitors' chairs; a stainless steel desk and, sitting behind it, a stainless steel receptionist with spun wire hair and a smile that looked as if her face had been opened by an old fashioned tin-opener.

'Yes? Can I help you?' It was the same uninterested cut-glass voice that had answered his telephone call.

'I'm sure you could, my dear,' he leered, 'but I've got an appointment to see Mr Jones at eleven-thirty.' Already the money was beginning to talk.

'Mr Masterland, is it?' She glanced down at her screen. 'Ah yes. Take a seat; I'll let Mr Jones know you're here.'

How she managed it Ivan didn't know, but as if on cue a dapper man in a sharply cut light grey suit, a patterned tie with a footballer's knot, narrow eyes and gelled spiky blond hair appeared, holding out his hand.

'Mark Jones,' he said with an East-end accent.

Ivan stood up and shook his hand; it was one of those sloppy handshakes, rather like massaging a bowl of tripe.

'Ivan Masterland.'

'Come on through, Ivan.'

And with his hand in the middle of Ivan's back, Mark Jones guided him past some stairs and through an office where another girl out of the same mould was painting her nails. She looked up with interest but, on seeing Ivan, went back quickly to her cuticles.

They carried on through into a small, well fitted-out office at the back of the building, away from the traffic noise of the main road.

'Well now, Ivan, how can I be of assistance?'

Ivan spread out the page of *The Times* that related to the finding of the treasure and the decision about the Kingscastle Hoard.

'I was the person who found that, and I want to claim my share of the three million pounds the Government is going to give as an award.'

Mark Jones looked hurriedly down at the newspaper to conceal the startled expression that flashed across his face.

'Why don't we sit down and start at the beginning Ivan,' he smoothed. And, taking a legal pad from a drawer in his desk, he wrote Ivan's name and address at the top.

Ivan explained about the bypass, the protesters digging tunnels and him visiting the site. He said he had noticed a glint of metal coming from what looked like a stone in one of the piles of earth and had picked it up. He took it out of his briefcase and put it on Jones' desk.

'Of course it was covered in mud then, I've washed it off and you can see that it's gold with those little jewels.'

Jones picked it up and turned it round in his fingers. 'Are you certain that this forms part of the Hoard? It couldn't be from something else could it?'

Ivan explained that a Dr Postlethwaite had been there, he was an archaeologist and he had confirmed that it was Anglo-Saxon. Also there was an almost identical piece that could be seen in the collection.

'Has anybody else claimed to be the finder?'

Ivan said nobody had, otherwise it would have been reported. He was certain he was the only one.

'Does anybody else know about this?' Jones asked. 'This man Postlethwaite must know, but have you told anybody else?'

Ivan said that a chap he worked with called Moon had witnessed him finding it as well, and that both Moon and Postlethwaite could give statements to that effect.

'But are they willing to?' asked Jones.

Ivan hesitated. 'Yes, I think so, but what if they refuse?'

'Well, we could subpoena them to appear in court – they'd have to tell the truth then. But it would be much better if they gave voluntary statements.'

Jones tried to control his excitement. His eyes gleamed as ideas raced around his brain and he rubbed his chin thoughtfully.

After some consideration he told Ivan, 'If what you say is true, I think you have a cast-iron case here, Ivan. There shouldn't be any difficulty in establishing your right to a substantial part of the award. Of course, it will require to be presented in the correct legal way, we wouldn't want any slip-ups there that could nullify your claim, would we? The sooner the better, I think, to make sure we get our claim lodged early; we wouldn't want to miss out by being too late either. I'd like to start work on this immediately…as soon as we've settled the small matter of our fees.'

He looked at Ivan, who shifted nervously on his chair as Jones mentally did an assessment of what he thought he could squeeze out of him.

'I normally require a ten thousand pound retainer to cover our initial costs and then, so you don't have to worry about costs racing away should the proceedings go on much longer than expected – as they could well do with our long drawn-out legal system…' He gave a knowing smile in Ivan's direction. '…I suggest that we take twenty-five per cent of any award that we can negotiate for you in lieu of further fees.'

Ivan gulped with shock and his jaw dropped. 'That's a bit on the high side, isn't it?' he stammered. 'Your advert says the client gets all the money if you win.'

Jones gave a sympathetic smile. This was not going to be difficult. Ivan had already unconsciously accepted the ten thousand retainer and was just arguing about the percentage.

'It doesn't say exactly that. It says if we win you get the money, and if we won, say, one and a half million pounds in this case, then you would get one million, one hundred and twenty-five thousand pounds – which is money, isn't it? In fact it's a lot of money, won by our efforts on your behalf.'

Blinded with the exaggerated figures, Ivan reluctantly agreed. The thought of over a million pounds for himself was enough; he didn't care about what anybody else got.

'I'll draft out a standard letter of appointment for us then,' murmured Jones smoothly, 'and if you sign one copy for us, and let me have your cheque for ten thousand, we'll start work as soon as it clears.'

Ivan nodded, his mind in a whirl. This was all moving a lot faster than he'd anticipated, but Mark Jones seemed very enthusiastic and thought he had a cast-iron case, so nothing could go wrong.

'There's one other thing,' Jones was saying. 'I would like Moon and Postlethwaite to come in and swear statements about the finding of the artefact as soon as possible after your cheque has cleared. Their evidence could be vital to establish your claim.'

Ivan waited while the letter appointing Claims Resolved Quickly Ltd was printed out. He scanned it briefly in his excitement, signed two copies, kept one for his records and wrote out a cheque for ten grand to go with the other copy that Jones locked in a safe. It was fixed that Ivan would try to get Postlethwaite and Moon there on Saturday.

As he walked back to where he had parked his car, he felt depressed rather than elated, but as that sort of feeling came naturally to him, he didn't examine the reason for it.

The sixty-pound parking ticket stuck on his windscreen didn't improve this feeling.

However, by the time Wednesday morning dawned, Ivan was beginning to savour his first morning as a potential millionaire with relish.

'Morning, Des, morning, Marcus, another nice day ahead of us, I think.'

Des and I looked at each other, wondering if we were hearing things correctly. Ivan strolled across to his desk and opened his briefcase. Was he actually humming a tune? It sounded like 'Who wants to be a millionaire'.

Des couldn't stand it any longer and put down *The Times*, a gesture akin to him receiving news about the imminent outbreak of World War Three.

'What's got into you, Ivan? This isn't the normal miserable, arrogant sod we've all come to know and hate.'

Ivan grinned. At least, I think it was a grin, although in Ivan's case it looked like somebody had wired a car battery to his testicles.

'Went to see a top class lawyer yesterday, one of the best in London for dealing with claims, and he told me that I had, to use his own words, "a cast-iron case". I'm going to be rich. His receptionist is a cracker and she fancies me as well.' He leant back smugly in his chair. 'He's drafting out my claim to submit to the authorities but he wants to take a statement from you, Marcus – and that poofy archaeologist bloke.' He looked at me. 'I'll give you a couple of hundred from my pay-out.'

I stared at him in astonishment. Much as it would grieve me, I would have given him, or his lawyer, a statement confirming that I'd seen him find a piece of the treasure if he'd just asked me. Yet he thought he had to offer me a bribe. I was very tempted to tell him to get stuffed, but then two hundred quid is two hundred quid to an impoverished engineer, and if that was his opening offer, I was curious to see how high he would go.

'A thousand,' I riposted.

That wiped the grin of his face. 'No way!' he snapped. 'If you don't give a statement voluntarily then the lawyers will subpoena you and you'll be forced to tell the truth in court under oath in any case.'

He had a point, I hadn't thought of that.

'Alright two hundred, but up front – now.'

He hesitated but then, deciding that the sooner it was settled the sooner he would be rich, fumbled in his wallet and handed over two hundred pounds in twenties.

'You're the witness to this, Des,' he growled at Doubleday.

'When do you want the statement?' I asked.

It was fixed that I would go to Claims Resolved Quickly's office on Saturday morning at eleven o'clock. He was going to phone Justin Postlethwaite and try to get him there at the same time.

He went out of the office to make the phone call in private. I turned to Des.

'What are you and Angeline doing on Friday night?'

He looked puzzled. 'Nothing as far as I'm aware, dear boy, why?'

'Well, it occurred to me that as you're a witness to Ivan handing over his bribe and I'm helping him out, you and Angeline and Charlie and I might go out and blow his two hundred on a fabulous evening at the Blue Angel – "Dinner and Dancing till Dawn".'

A slow smile spread across Des's face. 'A fine idea, you're on, dear boy. I'll ring her now!'

The Saturday morning traffic was heavy with all the shoppers in Wandsworth but I found a parking space on East Hill and made it to Claims Resolved Quickly's office at the agreed time to find Justin Postlethwaite and Ivan glowering at each other across the small coffee table in the reception. Whatever method Ivan had used to get Postlethwaite all the way up from Sheringford obviously hadn't gone down too well with him.

Postlethwaite greeted me with a friendly nod. 'So he's dragged you in as well has he?'

I was saved from replying by the appearance of a youngish man with spiky blond hair, wearing a flowery West-Indian shirt open to his navel, cream slacks and white tasselled loafers. He looked like the man who sets up your deck-chair on the Tangiers ferry and then tries to seduce your mother.

He must have noticed my expression because he said 'DDS – dress down Saturdays. I'm Mark Jones, by the way, Ivan's legal advisor.'

Ivan introduced us and we followed both of them through to his small office. The receptionist clearly wasn't smitten enough with Ivan to come in Saturdays and feast her eyes upon him.

'Right,' said Jones briskly. 'As I understand it, you two will confirm that Ivan found a piece of the Kingscastle treasure at approximately eleven forty-five on the morning of the 25th of March, and will sign a statement to that effect. Is that correct?'

We nodded reluctantly.

'Just to make absolutely certain, you will confirm that the piece of treasure that he found was this piece.'

He gestured for Ivan to produce the cleaned up fragment.

I confirmed that it was but Postlethwaite sat open-mouthed and didn't speak.

'Is this the piece, Dr Postlethwaite?' snapped Jones, holding it up for him to see clearly.

Postlethwaite turned to Ivan and said in amazement, 'You didn't hand it in to the Coroner? You've kept it?'

'Of course I haven't handed it over, it's my evidence, my trump card,' shot back Ivan.

A slow smile spread over Postlethwaite's friendly face. 'Bloody hell,' he murmured. 'Do you know the law about buried treasure containing gold? Do you know what the penalty is for not handing something like that over to the Coroner within fourteen days of finding it?'

The world seemed to stop as the implications of his words sank in. The atmosphere suddenly froze; everything seemed to follow in slow motion.

Postlethwaite turned to Jones. 'You're a solicitor – you're supposed to know these things. Your client has laid himself open to a fine of five thousand pounds and three months in jail for not handing that in to the authorities.' He pointed to the gold fragment.

'It forms part of one of the biggest Anglo-Saxon finds in British history,' he told Ivan. You can't just keep it! All finds, to be official, have to be properly recorded by the Coroner. I'm sorry, but as the appointed archaeologist for the dig I shall have to confiscate it and report you to the Kingscastle police. No doubt they'll wish to contact you further.'

While this was registering with Ivan and Jones, both of whom looked as though they'd been hit with a brick, Postlethwaite delivered the final kick in the balls to Ivan.

'Of course you realise that this illegal act will render any claim you may have had to be the finder null and void!'

Ivan went white with shock as all his dreams collapsed around him. He was rendered speechless. I couldn't help but feel sorry for him. It was a shame because he was good at his job but he'd brought all these troubles on himself by his view that the whole world had only one objective and that was to screw him – only reinforced by today's events.

Postlethwaite stood up, took the artefact and put it in his pocket. 'Under the circumstances there's nothing further that you can want from me so, if you'll excuse me, I'll get back to Sheringford.' He glared at Jones, nodded to Ivan, touched me on the shoulder and added, 'Maybe see you in Kingscastle sometime', then left. Nobody tried to stop him, it all rang very true.

Ivan gradually recovered his senses and turned savagely on Jones.

'You should have warned me about this, you're a solicitor and you're expected to advise me about these things! I want my ten thousand pound retainer back now, and I'm going to report you to the Law Society and claim damages for gross negligence!'

Jones was clearly equally shaken that his possible few hundred thousand pound share of the booty had, in a few seconds, gone up in smoke. But not only was he a crook, he was also obviously a pragmatist.

'Ah yes, Ivan. but there's a small problem there,' he said smoothly. 'Two problems, in fact.

'You will recall that when you signed our letter of appointment, Clause 6[c] stated quite clearly that the retainer was non-refundable. Also, there's not much point in complaining to the Law Society because I don't happen to be a member.' He gave a thin smile.

'But you must be if you're practising as a solicitor,' I said.

'Didn't quite finish my finals, mate, got chucked out after two years – and I've never claimed to be a qualified solicitor.'

Ivan sat there looking stunned. Not only had his high hopes of vast riches been shattered, he faced a possible three months in jail, a five thousand pound fine and now this slimy little flash bastard had ripped him off to the tune of ten grand with no redress. It was all too much. Years of burning resentment must have been stored away under pressure, and just when it was all about to come right for him, this cheating trickster had swindled him out of his rights.

The dam burst, a red mist seemed to fill his eyes, and he hurled himself across the desk at Jones, regardless of anything. He connected with a beautiful, swinging right-hand smack in Jones' left eye, worthy of Mohammed Ali at his best. Jones reeled back in his chair then fell over backwards with a demented Ivan on top of him, clawing and punching like a maniac. The PC and the phone crashed to the floor and the two of them rolled around with arms and legs thrashing in all directions. Ivan was making throaty animal cries and Jones screaming, 'He's trying to kill me, get him off me, for Christ's sake!'

Ivan didn't seem to be doing too much serious damage. His teeth were clamped on Jones' nose, but apart from that, they were too close together to land telling blows, so I let them roll around for a bit before I reacted. Grabbing Ivan by his collar, I dragged him off Jones and held him back for a couple of minutes while he calmed down a little. Jones staggered to his feet and backed away into a corner with his hand held to his eye, a trickle of blood coming from his nose and his flowery shirt ripped open.

'You bloody maniac!' he howled. 'I'll sue you for every penny you've got, you raving madman!' And, turning to me, he cried, 'You saw him! You witnessed him assaulting me!'

'Sorry, squire, didn't see a thing,' I said calmly. 'Apart from you tripping over the carpet and banging your head on the desk, that is.' His eye was already starting to swell up and close; it really was a good punch Ivan had landed. 'You're going to have a lovely black eye there tomorrow; I should put some ice on it, if I were you.'

There didn't seem much else I could do, so I let go Ivan's collar. 'Come on, Ivan, let's get out of here.'

I took him by the arm and led him to the door. He was shaking like a leaf but whether it was still with rage or with reaction, I didn't know.

'Where's your car?' He pointed just along the road and I could see his Volvo at the kerb. 'Are you OK to drive?'

He pulled himself together and nodded. I walked with him to his car; his eyes seemed unfocussed so I waited with him for a few minutes until he had steadied up. He fumbled in his pocket for his car keys, pulled them out and climbed into the driver's seat. After a few deep breaths, he started the engine and drove away without saying a word. I watched him go; he seemed alright so I crossed the road to the MG.

As I drove back to Fulham, I reflected with a chuckle that it had been an unexpected morning. Turning over what Justin Postlethwaite had said, I wondered if Mrs Stoate had handed in *her* piece of the treasure. I stopped the car, got her number from directory enquiries and rang her from my mobile. There was no answer, so I left a message on her answerphone and said I'd ring later.

So Ivan had laid out ten grand as a retainer as well, and been skinned for that. Heavy! Well, he wasn't going to get back the two hundred he'd given me either because that had gone last night on a great evening with Charlie, Des and Angeline at The Blue Angel.

I smothered a grin as I thought back to Claims Resolved Quickly. Well, Ivan's certainly had been – he couldn't complain about the lack of speed!

I spoke to Evadne Stoate the next morning and she told me that she had taken the bangle to the police some time ago.

'They said it was very old, Marcus, and I might get a small reward but I wouldn't get the bangle back because it would go in the museum.'

'How's Ben? Has he fully recovered?'

'Oh he's fine. I think he's enjoying the fuss people are making of him.'

Do dogs have a sixth sense? I don't know.

Ivan drove home in a daze. He just couldn't bring himself to accept that he'd been well and truly shafted. When he got into his flat he slumped in his armchair. Was it all real? Had it happened? In all the information he had gleaned about treasure, he couldn't recall anything about penalties for not reporting finds. Had Postlethwaite conned him into handing over his valuable artefact to do him out of his reward as the first finder? But Moon was a witness so Postlethwaite couldn't pull that off – unless, of course, he and Moon were in league. And what about that swine

Jones, could he be in on it as well? Had the three of them combined to screw him?

His mind was in a torment of contradictions but none of them told him it was his own fault for trying to be too secretive, too clever and too greedy. He just couldn't believe what had happened to him. One minute he was going to become a millionaire, the next he was facing penury and a stretch in Wormwood Scrubs, and it was all that bloody crook Jones' fault. It was only mildly satisfying that he had punched him in the eye and bitten his nose and, he told himself, if Moon hadn't interfered, he would have really sorted him out. His daze turned into suppressed fury – he'd sue Jones through every court in the land.

And then the reality of the situation hit him.

They wouldn't actually prosecute him, would they? After all, he didn't know that he should have reported his find, and if he hadn't flashed it about in Jones' office nobody would have known about it, would they? Then he realised that they would. That swine Postlethwaite would have remembered and asked about it.

The other thing was, he realised, he didn't have the resources to sue Jones, as Jones was clearly wealthier than him and money usually won.

'Oh God, why does everything have to happen to me?' he whimpered.

And what was he going to tell Agatha? She had already been looking in jewellers' windows, having her finger measured and asking how many carats the bigger diamonds were. He was only just getting her over his Orkney problem; she had been banging on about that for ages, in fact ever since he arrived back after his dreadful journey from Stromness, and it was only his anticipated change of fortune that had put a stopper in that.

'No smoke without a fire!' and 'If there was some doubt about the baby's paternity there must be good cause!' she'd harped on.

He was dreading Monday morning. Bloody Moon would have told the whole office about his disaster at Claims Resolved Quickly's office and people would be laughing behind his back. He put his head in his hands and moaned aloud.

On Monday morning, I did decide to tell Des about the shambles at Claims Resolved Quickly's office, because if I didn't he'd wonder what had transpired with Ivan's lawyer. He knew I was going there on Saturday morning to make a statement and I couldn't plead ignorance.

I gave him the full nine yards about Ivan's misfortune when I bumped into him at reception, and we both agreed to keep it quiet. The problem was, had Ivan gone parading his forthcoming fortune round the office? If so, we reasoned, then that was his problem to sort out, not ours.

Ivan was at his desk with his head down when we went into our office and merely grunted at our 'Good mornings'.

By ten o'clock, I was at Bob Barclay's offices for a meeting to finally agree the form of the application to the Kingscastle planners for permission to build the supermarket. Perseus had been bailed to appear at the Kingscastle Magistrates Court the morning following his incarceration. He had subsequently been given a roasting by the magistrates for dumping litter, which was followed by a Conditional Discharge as forecast by Sergeant Bulstrode. He was then given an even bigger roasting by Barclay after Bob had had a long talk with the Chief Planner, so it was expected that a subdued and penitent architect would appear at the design meeting.

Bob, Martin and I sat and waited for his arrival, chatting about friends and drinking coffee supplied by the gorgeous Jemma. It was quarter to eleven when he finally showed up, his normally pale face all red and flustered through his designer stubble, his trendy jacket undone and sweat beading his upper lip.

He burst into the room in front of Jane, apologising profusely, excuses tumbling out of his mouth at an astonishing rate. He should take lessons from Des Doubleday, I thought. Des had it off to a fine art. His excuses were put over so smoothly that he made you feel guilty for getting there too early.

Bob waved his hands downwards to calm him, and ushered him to a chair.

'Calm down, Perse, no problem, slow it up man! Jane, will you ask Jemma if she'll be kind enough to bring Mr Rixon a cup of strong tea please.'

We had already had gallons of coffee and I didn't want anything else to drink, so we waited whilst he drank his tea with a shaky hand.

When Perseus had regained his equilibrium, Bob said to him casually, 'Have you got your cheque book with you, Perse?'

Perseus frowned as the significance of the question eluded him. 'Yes, why?'

Bob ticked items off on his fingers. 'Well, Martin's and my rates are sixty pounds an hour. Marcus, being a plebeian engineer, is somewhat less expensive at fifty pounds per hour, so for the three-quarters of an hour we've just been sitting here twiddling our thumbs waiting for you, that'll be a hundred and twenty-seven pounds fifty. Being in a generous mood, I'll round it off to a hundred and twenty-seven! So if you'll just write out a cheque for that amount, payable to me, we'll say no more about it – and you can continue as my architect.'

This was all accompanied by a smile that didn't reach his eyes and a look that brooked no repudiation.

Perseus blushed furiously and had just opened his mouth, no doubt to object, when he noticed the look. So he took his cheque-book out of his case and grudgingly wrote out the cheque.

While he was doing this I was wondering what was going to happen to my thirty-seven pounds fifty worth, but Bob winked and mouthed, 'Lunch?'

I nodded with a grin. Bob called, 'Jane, ring Doctor Smallwood and see if he's free to join us for lunch today.'

Perseus perked up a little at that, he clearly thought he was going to get one of Barclay's great lunches. He wasn't – he was just going to pay for it!

Following his 'discussion' with Barclay, Perseus had totally redesigned the elevation to the Market Square to fit in with what the planners wanted and, subject to a couple of minor changes, the scheme was finally agreed.

'So are we all happy with that?' asked Bob.

With an expression on his face as if he'd licked a nettle, Perseus nodded and wisely kept his mouth shut.

However, all was not doom and gloom in his life that morning. At the end of the meeting Bob told us that he had arranged funding for the project and we could submit an interim fee account.

Slightly mollified, Perseus pushed off to prepare his bill, and Bob, Martin Holmes and I took a cab to meet Pete at The English Garden for lunch, with Perse's cheque underwriting the whole affair.

Pete was there before us, and a bottle of nicely chilled Chablis and four glasses were awaiting our arrival. He was in a good mood.

'Scales phoned me just before I left, he was cock-a-hoop – he's been appointed as a lecturer in paediatric dentistry at The Royal Dental Hospital. It's a big leg up for him. He said that the only problem is, he'll have to give up rugby; he can't afford to have his hands damaged. You can't have great knotted, mangled, trampled-on hands when your workspace is inside the mouths of small children. But as he said, it was good while it lasted and a career must come first.'

That was great news, it was something that Tony had always aspired to and we were all delighted that he had made the breakthrough. We drank more wine to celebrate his success and so it was around three o'clock when I got back to the office. I carried the roll of Perse's drawings ostentatiously through the reception in case I met one of the partners.

Apparently, Ivan had been simmering all morning. Somehow he had worked his anger and frustration round to blaming me for not telling him to take his artefact to the authorities and then for stopping him beating the shit out of that crooked weasel Jones. He was rude to everyone that day to such an extent that even Des lost his temper with him.

'Just cut it out, Ivan, or I'll ask Hugo to move you out of Civil Planning Team Two.'

Ivan scowled. He glared at me and then kept his head down for the rest of the afternoon. He left early. He didn't give any reason but just packed up his stuff and went. I heard him speak to Agatha in the corridor but didn't hear what he said, although her voice was a touch shrill.

Ivan parked the Volvo in a resident's parking spot in a quiet side street near his flat and carefully checked that all the doors were locked. Although it was getting dark, the street lights hadn't come on yet.

'Got a light, mate?'

He spun round to find two large, shaven-headed youths with tattooed arms standing behind him.

'No, I don't smoke.'

He affected unconcern as they began to crowd him against his car but they smelt the fear.

'Got the time then?'

They pressed up against him harder; he looked round for help but the street was deserted.

'I'll call the police if you don't leave me alone!' It was a cry of desperation.

'Did you hear that, Shane, we ask him for the time, nice and polite, and he wants to call the filth. I think that's insultin', don't you?'

'Yeah, and we don't like bein' insulted, do we?'

'So what have you got to say about that then, yer pasty-faced bearded bastard?'

Ivan nearly wet himself. They were toying with him and he couldn't see a way out.

'Nothing, nothing, I didn't mean to insult you and I'm sorry if it sounded like that,' he stammered, trying to move between them. But they pushed him back.

'I fink he needs a lesson in manners, Darren, Marky said he was a stroppy little sod. His Mummy and Daddy have brung him up all wrong.'

And with that, the larger of the two slammed his fist into Ivan's midriff, causing him to double up against the car.

When I arrived just after nine on Monday morning, Angela, Jennie and Awful Agatha were standing in the corridor looking grim. At my appearance, they stopped talking and three pairs of hostile eyes watched my approach.

'What's up with you three, then?'

'You know bloody well what's up! He's told the police about you so don't think you can get away with it!' hissed Agatha.

The others glared at me as well. Even little Jennie, who wouldn't normally say boo to a goose, radiated hostility.

'No, I don't know what's up!' I replied, puzzled. 'What're you talking about?'

'It's Ivan,' explained Angela. 'He's in hospital. He got mugged outside his flat on Friday night.'

'Is he OK?' I asked with concern.

'Of course he's not OK, he wouldn't be in hospital if he was OK, would he?' snapped Agatha. 'And I've got better things to do than answer daft questions from you.'

She had me on the back foot. Ivan in hospital? 'I meant is he seriously hurt?'

Angela said that she didn't think so, no thanks to me. He had some cuts and bruises but they were keeping him in for observation.

I frowned at her phraseology. There was something going on here that I didn't understand.

'What d'you mean, "no thanks to me"? I've got nothing to do with whatever it is you think it is – if you know what I mean!'

Agatha scowled. 'Well, it's in the hands of the police now so you can explain it to them. I hope they lock you up and throw away the key!'

'I don't know what the hell you're talking about, Agatha! I've nothing to explain to anybody, but if Ivan isn't coming in I'd better let Hugo know.'

'He knows,' said Angela, and they all turned away and walked into their office.

Des gave me a funny look as well when I gained our office.

'You didn't really arrange for Ivan to be beaten up, did you?' he asked as soon as I passed through the door.

The light dawned.

'Oh, is that what this is all about? Of course I didn't! Is that what people think?'

Then I realised that there must be more to this than just the normal Moon/Masterland rivalry rumours.

'Why would they think that, Des?'

'Well, apparently Ivan told the cops that he distinctly heard one of the guys that beat him up say, "Marcus said…something or other" and that they were acting on your instructions.'

'Bollocks! He's made that up.'

'Well, the cops think that if it was just a mugging, why didn't they steal anything? Ivan had his wallet and his mobile in his pocket – and they were untouched.'

I didn't like the sound of this. I couldn't imagine that Ivan himself would arrange for somebody to beat him up and hospitalise him just to get at me, but that seemed to be what had happened. No…there must be some other explanation.

For the rest of the day, I sensed people in the office giving me a wide berth. I felt like a pork chop at a bar-mitzvah. Even Hugo was chilly when he passed me in the corridor.

I was telling Charlie about it at home that evening when the door-bell rang. I opened it and beheld two people standing there: an expressionless, hard-faced man of average height and a woman police constable in uniform. I could tell at once that she wasn't a Strippergram – for a start she was flat-chested. The man flashed a warrant card.

'Mr Marcus Moon?'

'Yes.'

'Can we come in, sir?' And without waiting for an answer, they pushed passed me into the small hall.

Charlie said, 'Well now you're in you'd better sit down', and she led them into the sitting room.

'I'm Detective Sergeant Barnes and this is WPC Farrow.'

'So what can we do for you, Sergeant?' I started.

'You know about the assault on Mr Ivan Masterland outside his flat last evening?'

'It was talked about in the office today.'

'How would you describe your relationship with Mr Master-land?'

'We don't have a relationship.'

'You don't like him?'

'We're professional colleagues working together in the same office.'

'Do you get on with him?'

I looked at him keenly. 'I take it you've met Ivan?'

He nodded.

'And talked to him?'

He nodded again.

'Well in that case, you'll appreciate that he doesn't get on with anybody and neither do they with him!'

Barnes changed tack. 'Where were you last night?'

'Why? Do you think I attacked him?'

'No, but somebody arranged for him to be attacked, so just answer the question.'

'At home here all night!'

'Can anybody verify that?'

Charlie spoke up. 'Yes, I can.'

'And you are Miss…?'

'I'm Doctor Charlotte Prinknash – I'm a surgeon at The Royal Free Hospital.'

That slowed him down a bit. He changed direction again and handed me a typewritten piece of paper. I read the descriptions of two men.

'Do you recognize either or both of those men?'

I gave the paper back to him. 'No.'

'Do the names Shane and Darren mean anything to you?'

'Is that what those two guys are called?'

'Just answer my question!'

'No, they don't.'

He looked disappointed. 'We may have to talk to you again, sir, but that will be all for the moment.'

As he headed for the door, I stopped him and looked him straight in the eye, giving him the Moon pupil-penetrating, double whammy look designed to terminate any doubts hovering around in a suspicious brain.

'Before you go, Sergeant, I had nothing whatsoever to do with whatever happened to Ivan.'

It didn't work. He gave a weary smile of acknowledgement.

'They all say that, Mr Moon. I'll leave you my card in case you think of something else you might want to tell me?'

It was a question, not a statement.

I was furious with Ivan. A joke's a joke but, as Smallwood used to say, a chair-leg up your arse is furniture. I never did understand that but it seemed to fit this situation admirably.

Charlie wondered if Ivan had set this up deliberately, or if he was just taking advantage of a situation to have a go at me.

'I can't believe he'd go to such lengths with a plot, so it must be the latter,' she said, 'but it's still way over the top. The problem is defending a negative. It's difficult to prove you didn't arrange something, particularly when it's not something tangible. We must just hope that the cops catch the two guys.'

Next day the tension in the office was worse. They all knew the police had been to see me and that condemned me out of hand for a start. Only Des and, to some degree, Angela treated me normally. Des clearly didn't believe I'd had Ivan beaten up. As he said, if I wanted Ivan done over I could quite easily have done it myself because I was much bigger than him. Angela had obviously thought about it and decided that she couldn't believe I would do something like that either, although she felt sympathy for Awful Agatha as a work colleague.

*****

Detective Sergeant Barnes chewed the top of his biro. He was thinking something similar to Des but what evidence he had pointed to Moon – if somewhat vaguely. The most positive piece was Masterland's statement that the two thugs had mentioned the name Marcus. It could be another Marcus but it wasn't a common name. Also, it would be a remarkable coincidence if it *was* another Marcus when there was already one who shared the same office as Masterland and clearly didn't like him. DS Barnes didn't believe in coincidences.

But that was the problem. Moon didn't seem like the sort of person who would go to the extent of paying two thugs to beat up a work colleague just because he didn't like him. It didn't hang together somehow. There had been no suggestion of any strong motive; no chasing each other's girls; no previous violence; no debt problems; a bit of workplace competition, maybe, but they were both well thought of professionally.

Barnes shook his head. The evidence was very thin really – there was no way he could take this to the Crown Prosecution Service with a chance of a conviction. It was one person's word against another's; that was all he had.

The two attackers held the key. If he could catch them they would lead him to the purpose behind the assault. He read the descriptions Ivan had given, they were pretty concise and he had two Christian names, unless they were faked. He decided to have the details circulated to all the beat coppers in the area and see if that produced anything.

*****

'Don't forget it's casual, drinks at seven, dinner at eight,' called Des as I switched off my PC and tidied up my desk.

'So dinner's still on?' I replied gloomily. 'I was wondering if my apparent transformation into Al Capone might have given you and Angeline second thoughts.'

'Don't be daft! I know you didn't set Ivan up.' He grinned. 'It's not your style. If you were going to fix him it'd be a lot more subtle than that!'

'See you later then,' I called as he wandered out of the office.

I wasn't sure if that was a compliment or not but it cheered me up. Des might be one of the laziest people around but he was no fool. If he didn't believe the story others might start to think the same way.

Charlie and I turned up at Des's flat just after seven. There were two other guests already there. Des introduced them with an artful smile. 'Jack's a paediatrician from St Georges and Annie is a GP. I thought Charlie would be bored stiff if we just talked engineering all night but I don't give a hoot, Marcus, if you're bored stiff listening to tales of blood, guts and foul pestilence!'

'Thanks, Des, but I'm impervious to it now. Every night Charlie comes home and we have to go through what happened in the theatre that day. When you're just tucking in to lightly-grilled, pink liver with bacon, listening to a vivid description of a gall bladder being removed…well you can imagine!'

'You great liar!' Charlie punched me on the arm. 'I do no such thing.'

It turned out to be a great evening, Jack and Annie were lively company, and Des and Angeline served up some good food and wine and kept the conversation moving.

Later, over coffee, Des gave me a knowing grin. 'Tell them about Geoffrey's Strippergram, Marcus, we never did get the true story about that in the office. I know you had something to do with it because I noticed you retrieve her script after she dropped it on the floor!'

'Alright, you've got me banged to rights,' I chuckled.

So I related the whole story. This naturally brought Ivan's name into the arena and Des told everyone what the current situation was with me.

Jack came to the same conclusion as Detective Sergeant Barnes. He said that the only way to get to the bottom of the affair was to question the two louts. Then he added, 'It's obvious that somebody has organised this, it wasn't a random mugging because nothing was taken. Has Ivan upset anybody else to such a degree that they would go that far? It sounds like a revenge attack to me. Has he slapped some kid who was annoying him in the street or taken offence at something somebody said and thumped them?'

Blood and sand, of course! It came to me like a revelation from above.

'Mark Jones!' I exclaimed. 'The shyster lawyer. He's just the sort of guy to have fixed that! Why didn't I think of that before?'

They all looked at me in astonishment.

Charlie said, 'Isn't he the man who swindled Ivan out of ten thousand pounds? You told me that you'd had to drag Ivan off him before he did serious damage.'

'The very man! I'd bet a hundred quid that it was him that fixed it for Ivan to be beaten up!'

Des looked thoughtful. 'But Ivan said it was definitely your name that he'd heard…'

'Marcus – Mark? There's not much difference in a scuffle, is there? And it would be a good opportunity to land me in trouble.'

'Yeah, I suppose so. So what are you going to do?'

I took a deep breath; this could be the solution to my current situation. 'I'm going to phone DS Barnes tomorrow and give him the full story about Ivan and this con man Jones and let him sort it out.' I grinned. 'He could get three collars out of this – the two thugs and Jones.'

DS Barnes listened with interest first thing next morning when I related the full saga of Ivan and his finder's claim, and the involvement of Mark Jones.

'We'll look into it, sir. Do you happen to know where this man Jones can be found?

I told him about 'Claims Resolved Quickly' on East Hill and said that that was his office. He was purporting to give legal advice but admitted that he wasn't a qualified lawyer.

'Thank you, sir, I'll let you know if there's a development.'

*****

While DS Barnes was mulling over this new information, one of the beat coppers who patrolled North Wandsworth stuck his head round the door.

'Sarge, those two guys you asked us to look out for…I saw two men who fit that description go into the Red Lion about half an hour ago. My radio's on the blink so I nipped back here to let you know.'

DS Barnes grabbed his jacket. 'Let's go.'

*****

I got the phone call later in the afternoon.

'It looks like you're off the hook, Mr Moon. We have two youths in custody who've admitted to the assault on Mr Masterland, and claim that they were paid fifty pounds by Jones to do it. Mr Jones is helping us with our enquiries at the moment.'

'Phew, that's a relief, I can tell you. Do you want a statement from me or anything?'

'No, sir. As far as you're concerned, that's the end of the matter.'

Des was looking at me questioningly. He had heard my side of the conversation. 'Is that what I think it is?'

'Yes. DS Barnes has got the two thugs in the nick and they've admitted beating up Ivan and being paid to do it by that crooked lawyer Ivan thumped.'

Des stood up. 'I'll go and tell Hugo, there could be a bit of grovelling all round after this!' He chuckled. 'What are you going to do about Ivan?'

I grimaced. 'For want of any evidence to the contrary, I'll put it down to an honest mistake about mishearing the names.' I bit my lip. 'I wish he'd quit this hostility though – if it wasn't for that he might have got the right name in the first place. He seems to be conditioned to think that I'm a rival who's always trying to usurp his position and that I'm responsible for every ill that befalls him. I'd like to put a stop to it but he doesn't seem open to reason. Still…' I told Des '…I'll give it one more try.'

The opportunity came sooner than I anticipated.

It was Thursday before Ivan returned to work. He was sitting at his desk when I arrived just after nine, looking a picture of misery. There were two strips of plaster and visible bruises on his face, one of his eyes was a slit and turning yellow from the bruising.

Des gasped. 'Christ, Ivan, you must have taken a hammering!'

Ivan avoided looking at me directly, and when he spoke I could see that he had two broken teeth and a swollen lip, which made it difficult for him to articulate his words.

'It was that bloody crooked lawyer who put those thugs up to it! Barnes told me they'd charged all three of them.'

No apology for all the trouble he'd caused me. Still, that was Ivan.

'So how are you feeling?' I asked him.

He grimaced and scowled. 'Not too bad, it's my mouth that hurts the most, the broken teeth and a pain in the jaw when I bite on anything. They can't give me an appointment for three weeks at the dental surgeons. Bloody NHS!'

Tony Scales sprang into my mind. I didn't want to raise Ivan's hopes but I'd give Tony a ring to see if he could do anything. If he could, it might be the catalyst that fractured the hostility.

I phoned him on his mobile at the Royal Dental Hospital at lunchtime and explained the situation.

Tony said, 'But I thought you couldn't stand the guy?'

I explained about the tension that existed in the office and that this just might help ease the situation if he could help Ivan. I crossed my fingers.

He said that he'd check in his appointments book and see if he could fit Ivan in after normal working hours. He promised to phone me back in the afternoon.

'But it's going to cost you, Moon! My fee for psychiatric treatment for barmy engineers is a constant flow of Ruddle's for the next two Saturday lunchtimes.' I asked whether it was me or Ivan he was referring to.

'Both of you!' he chuckled.

I couldn't help but feel sorry for Ivan. It hadn't been one of his better weeks and it was no skin off my nose if he got dental treatment earlier.

A receptionist at the Royal Dental rang me in our office at three-thirty and said Mr Scales could see Ivan that evening at five-thirty. Could I confirm that he would attend?

'Hold on a moment,' I asked her.

I called across the office. 'Ivan, I have a friend who's a very good dental surgeon and works at the Royal Dental Hospital, he can see you at five-thirty today to do something about your teeth. Can you get yourself there?'

He responded instinctively, grasping at the offer of early relief without his usual suspicious mind questioning the offer.

'Thank God for that, I'm in agony. Tell him yes, I'll be there.'

'He'll be there,' I said. 'His name's Ivan Masterland and he'll come to the reception at five-thirty.'

But after I'd put the phone down, Ivan's normal nature kicked in. He looked at me suspiciously.

'You're not kidding are you, Moon? This isn't a wind-up, is it? Because if it is, I'll get you!'

I assured him it was genuine but he was clearly sceptical and I think the only reason he went was he was in so much pain he'd try anything.

Des observed pointedly in Ivan's hearing, 'Your friend must be going to do this in his own time staying on late with an assistant. He must be a good friend to do that for you, Marcus.'

Next morning Ivan came in to the office around ten-thirty. His face was still puffy but the strut was back in his step and his complexion had lost the greyness and lines of pain that it had yesterday.

'So you saw Tony Scales?'

He nodded. 'Yeah! But he kept me waiting ten minutes. The National Health Service doesn't teach people bedside manners, does it? There was no chat, it was get in the chair and let's get on with it. He's a bit slow, this guy you sent me to. Do you know I was in the chair for two hours? He messed about for ages taking measurements, x-rays, injections and drills before he sealed off the exposed nerves, put temporary caps on the broken teeth, and replaced two fillings that had been knocked out. He took more x-rays and said that I have a crack in the jawbone but it's not serious. He said to fix an appointment for a week's time when the swelling has subsided so he can take moulds for permanent caps – but I'm not satisfied. I'm going to see if I can find another dentist to check what he's done first, before I go. It all seemed a bit amateurish.'

Des stared at him in amazement. 'And that's it?'

Ivan looked puzzled. 'Why, what else is there?'

'Well if you don't know, it's not for me to tell you!'

Des looked at me, shaking his head with disgust. My olive branch hadn't been recognised as such.

CHAPTER FOURTEEN

Mss Williamson, Deakin and Pring were charged with aggravated assault, kidnapping and, in Miss Pring's case, assaulting a police officer and causing malicious damage to his clothing – namely one trouser leg. The teeth marks in PC Connolly's actual flesh didn't warrant a specific mention.

Apart from giving their names and addresses, none of them would say a word. They were put in separate cells and hauled into Kingscastle Magistrates Court the morning after their attack on Ivan. They all said that they would represent themselves. Ms Deakin said that they didn't want some junior legal hack screwing up their defence. They confirmed who they were. The charges were read out and they all pleaded not guilty. The Chief Magistrate, Mr Chance, a retired solicitor, gazed at them severely over his pince-nez and said he was disgusted that respectable citizens of Kingscastle could resort to such behaviour, but the charges were too serious for the Bench to deal with and they were remanded on police bail to appear at the Crown Court in Devizes. They signed the documents that would temporarily release them back into society and left the court. All this took place just before the Government's about-turn on the Hickling Edge tunnels became known.

When it did, *The Kinscastle Bugle* was on it like a ferret up a trouser leg. 'FREE THE KINGSCASTLE THREE' read the banner headline. 'Heroines who Sacrificed Their Freedom to Save Our Countryside'. The nationals picked up the story of the common citizens' struggle against a lying, unheeding Government, having to sacrifice their freedom in common cause in order to make their point. The photos of Mrs Williamson and Ms Deakin being dragged off to police vans were rehashed and spread over the front pages. There was a close up of a set of teeth clamped on a blue serge-covered leg from which the identities of the biter and bitten had been carefully cropped. The whole town picked up the theme with enthusiasm, and 'FREE THE THREE' placards and posters appeared everywhere.

'They were promised a tunnel and what did they get? LIES!' screamed the Red Tops.

Ivan intended to take the day off work to give evidence. 'I hope they give the bitches life,' he told Des savagely as he left the office the previous evening.

On the date set for the Crown Court hearing, buses filled with protesters poured into Devizes and packed the court and the square outside.

When Judge Fiona McFarland, a dour Scottish lady, gestured to the Clerk to call for quiet in the courtroom, the chants of 'FREE THE THREE' could still be heard quite clearly through the windows.

After the charges had been read out and they were asked how they pleaded, all three replied, 'Not guilty and proud of it.'

Judge McFarland began the proceedings by asking, 'Who is acting for the Crown?'

'I am, My Lady,' announced Clifford Parker QC, a smooth, sharp-faced practitioner of many years in the circuit courts. 'And my colleague is William Ball.'

He indicated a pimply youth sitting behind him with a tattered wig that obviously had belonged to someone else because it perched on his head like an abandoned puffin's nest.

'And who is for the defence?'

The bench usually occupied by the defence team was conspicuously empty.

Ms Deakin stood up in the dock and announced that she was.

'Are you sure you are happy to proceed without professional assistance, Miss…?'

'Deakin, and it's Ms, if you don't mind.'

'Be that as it may, I must advise you that I strongly recommend that you do have professional representation, Ms Deakin. You face some very serious charges.'

'No thank you, My Lady. Anything a man can do dressed like a hairy penguin, we are quite capable of doing ourselves dressed normally.'

Judge McFarland shrugged. 'Well, if you are determined, it is your right. If you are the spokesman—'

She was interrupted again by Ms Deakin. 'Spokesperson, My Lady.'

Judge McFarland gave a heavy sigh. 'I do hope we're not going to have these solecistic interruptions continually, Ms Deakin, otherwise I fear we could be in for a long day.'

That shut Ms Deakin up – she didn't know what solecistic meant!

'As I was going to say, you can come out of the dock to the defence bench if you so wish?'

Still nettled, Ms Deakin replied, 'I'll stay with my sisters if you don't mind.'

Judge McFarland sighed again resignedly. 'Very well, your fellow accused can sit with you on the defence bench but they do not have the right to speak or interrupt and you will be accompanied by the dock officers.'

After all the shuffling and place changes had taken place, the judge turned to the prosecution counsel and intoned wearily, 'Perhaps we can now proceed Mr Parker.'

The police gave their evidence quite clearly and accurately, supported by some newsreel clips of Ivan falling out of the van covered in feathers and the three women being carted off by the police with Miss Pring's teeth lodged in PC Connolly's calf muscle.

Ms Deakin, speaking on behalf of all three of them, said they had no questions in cross-examination and the police stepped down.

Ms Deakin then said she'd like to make a statement on behalf of all three of them. The judge said it was a bit irregular but if the prosecution had no objection, to go ahead.

Ms Deakin then told the court that they had been driven to take drastic action by the lies and misinformation given by the Government. The whole town was happy with the tunnel solution when it was proposed, but this had been a deliberate, cunning and calculated smokescreen to deflect the town's anger at having their beautiful countryside spoiled by a hideous slash through one of nature's natural gems. The Government had never had any intention of putting a tunnel under Hickling Edge. All they were concerned about was money. Their attitude was that Kingscastle, its environment and standard of living could go to hell if it meant that the Treasury saved a few pounds.

It was a good speech and the packed courtroom rose to its feet with warm applause. Even Judge McFarland was sufficiently moved to allow the applause to continue for a short time before bringing the court back to order.

After a couple of minutes thought she said, 'I would like to see Mr Parker and Ms Deakin in my chambers. I suggest that the jury go and get a coffee in the meantime.'

When they were all assembled, Judge MacFarland addressed the two of them. 'Look, it's quite clear what happened, that is not disputed, and they are serious offences which normally would warrant custodial sentences. However, if you and your colleagues plead guilty, Ms Deakin, I am minded to consider a lengthy term of community service in view of the public feeling and deceit which appear to embrace this case. What do you think, Mr Parker?'

Clifford Parker sucked in his breath and blew out his cheeks as he considered the proposal. He was guaranteed a guilty verdict this way, whereas although the defendants were plainly guilty, the jury might well be swayed by strong emotions, believing that the Government had deliberately lied, and acquit all three. He nodded acceptance.

Ms Deakin was not stupid, she realised that they were being offered a way out of a very nasty situation. Two years in jail would not do any of them any good, particularly as they had won the argument and got the tunnels.

'Thank you, My Lady,' she said. 'We accept and will change our plea to guilty.'

They all trooped back into court and Ms Deakin gave the thumbs up to her two worried co-defendants who had been left sitting there.

Judge MacFarland indicated that Ms Deakin should speak.

'We would like to change our plea to guilty, My Lady, but with a rider that it was all the Government's fault for the totally inept and devious way the information had been provided. If they had been open and sensible in the first place, none of this would have been necessary.'

Judge Fiona McFarland's serious face broke into a faint smile. 'A philosophy that could be well applied to most government projects,' she ventured.

The jury was discharged and the defendants given two hundred hours of community service each, with a strong recommendation from the judge that none of them should lose their jobs over this matter. Although they had gone too far, they had demonstrated a public spirit that was sadly lacking in Britain these days.

The crowd rose again and applauded them as they left the court and went outside, where they were greeted by even more rapturous applause.

Ivan was beside himself with fury. 'That's outrageous!' he raged at Clifford Parker. 'Why wasn't I called? It's all your fault – you were too weak, you gave in too easily. It's a stitch-up! Can't we appeal or something?'

Parker shook his head wearily and passed on to deal with his next case.

*****

The Government's announcement about the Kingscastle Hoard award had not just stirred up Ivan, it had galvanised Withers. He had been simmering in Withers Hall ever since the find was announced, wondering how and when to stick his oar in. No sooner had he heard the news about the award than he was on the phone to his lawyers in the City, Messrs Greybody and Droole.

'It's on my damned land,' he raged, 'so I want at least two million as my share!' he told Fortinson Droole.

Mr Droole did a rapid calculation in his head and worked out that Messrs Greybody and Droole could be on for at least a hundred thousand in fees if they played their cards right. He told Withers to send him all the deeds covering the Withers Estate and any other documents relating to the ownership of the land, together with as much information about the Kingscastle Hoard that he could lay his hands on.

Stumpy didn't get *The Times* nor did he listen to BBC radio programmes, so it was a few days before he found out about the award when he went down to Kingscastle to renew his police bail.

'Fuck me!' he exclaimed when he realised that he could well be the 'finder' since he had dug up those bits of metal. He thought he still had a bit somewhere in the squat as evidence but he couldn't find it. He also realised that he and his mob could be technically the 'occupier' of the site, and therefore come in for a double dose of cash.

His problem was, he didn't know what to do. Contacting any official body was totally alien to Stumpy's culture. He couldn't bring himself to do it. His normal contact with the police was to wear their handcuffs. He asked around the other people in the squat. One girl said she had done one year of law at Brighton before she dropped out and she would have a try at drafting out a letter to the Department of the Environment.

'Address it to the Minister,' Stumpy told her. 'We might as well start at the top.'

Both Rock Solid Foundations Ltd and MacLowland and Sons Ltd consulted their lawyers and both were advised that they had an excellent claim as occupiers of the site. MacLowland's construction contract specifically said that they would take over and *occupy* the land for the whole length of the bypass for the duration of the contract, and the Kingscastle Hoard site was certainly within that land. Rock Solid's claim wasn't quite as solid as their name implied, their rig had been parked outside Stumpy's camp, but as there hadn't been a defining fence, it could be said to be within occupancy range. Their lawyers cobbled together a case and waited.

The firms of lawyers all submitted their respective claims to the Department of the Environment and made it quite clear that unless their clients got a substantial chunk of the award, they would take the matter to court. Each had cleverly pitched their claim sufficiently high, knowing that it would be unacceptable, and each rubbed their hands together with glee at the thought of the massive legal fees that could ensue if it did go through the courts.

The Department threw Stumpy's claim straight out the door without pause for breath on the grounds that he was a trespasser, had committed criminal damage, had no evidence that he had found anything and therefore had no rights. They pointed out that he was on police bail, having been charged with trespassing and causing wilful damage to the land, and if he disagreed with their decision then it was open to him to take further action if he thought it was warranted. That was the end of Stumpy's optimistic, and ultimately brief, involvement.

'Well, it was worth a try,' he reflected sadly as his faint dreams of riches disappeared, drifting away in a cloud of cannabis smoke.

As for the claims from Withers, MacLowland and Rock Solid, they were initially rejected: Withers' on the grounds that the land was under a Compulsory Purchase Order and therefore belonged to the Government, not him; MacLowland's that they were not physically occupying the site where the treasure was found, nor were they tenants because they didn't have a lease; and Rock Solid's because they didn't have any legal involvement with the actual discovery, or the site where it was found.

The sting in the tale came when the Department of the Environment announced that, because there was no proven finder, no tenant and no legal occupier and the land was under a CPO, it was proposing to award the three million pounds to itself as it was technically the land owner.

Withers blew a fuse when he leaned of this. He raged at Molestrangler over the phone.

'Your lot are nothing but cheating, swindling, lying, conniving shysters! You take my land for a bloody pittance when I don't want to sell it; you don't hand over the money for the site because you claim the paperwork's not complete. Then, when something valuable turns up on it which should rightfully be mine, you produce some cock and bull story so you can steal it!'

Molestrangler bit his lip. This did sound very devious and might not do his re-election chances much good if Withers spread it around that he was party to it – as he surely would.

'I agree wholeheartedly, my dear Sir Fistulas. I only wish I could help but it's not in my area, you know. I'm on Sport and Leisure. Of course I will raise the matter with the Secretary of State for the Environment but it may well be that your only redress is to take the matter to court as it's a tricky area regarding whose land it was at the time of the discovery.'

'You can be sure of that, you useless, poncey, great pillock, and believe you me, this won't be forgotten when the next election comes round! You can scratch any contribution to your re-election fund from me for a start, Molestrangler!'

It looked as though the matter was going to resolve itself into a three-way fight between Withers, MacLowlands and the Department of the Environment about who got what, if anything. The media were already starting to wind up a storm about the Government cheating honest citizens out of their rights. They even hinted that the Government had known all along about the treasure and had deliberately waited until they could issue a CPO before moving in to claim the award for themselves.

The lawyers sharpened their pencils, re-booked their holidays to include luxury villas on the French Riviera, and slavered at the mouth as they clocked up the billed hours and banged in writs all over the place.

The D of E wilted under the onslaught and decided to wash their hands of the whole affair, saying that all the claims would have to be examined in the High Court. Mr Justice Column, a well-respected pillar of the Bar, was appointed to hear the case in two months' time.

*****

Sergeant Bulstrode read about this in his copy of *The Sun* whilst he was working his way through a large plate of eggs, bacon, sausage, tomato and mushrooms, cooked for him by the buxom Evadne Stoate – now sitting opposite him in her kitchen.

'Have you seen this, petal?' he said, showing her the article. 'The bloody government have nicked all the reward money for the big treasure find up Withers Woods.'

Evadne chuckled. 'Well, they would, wouldn't they! They should give it to Ben. He were the first to find it really.'

Sergeant Bulstrode looked thoughtful at her comment, wiped a piece of bread round the last remaining traces of egg on his plate, pulled on his tunic, fastened his bicycle clips, gave Evadne a peck on the cheek and rode off to the police station with the thought turning over slowly in his mind.

When he got there, he telephoned Evadne. 'I've been think-ing about what you said, Evadne. I reckon your Ben *was* the finder so why don't you have a word with Mr Norfolk and see what he says? I'll give him a ring if you want.'

She hesitated. 'I dunno, Steve, I don't want to make no fuss and I can't afford any lawyers.'

'Let me give him a call and see what he says, yes?'

She agreed reluctantly and when Bulstrode had explained the full circumstances to Mr Norfolk, the solicitor suggested that Mrs Stoate call in to see him and he wouldn't charge her if he didn't think she had a case.

In the meantime, he looked up legal precedents for people finding treasure, so he was well briefed when Mrs Stoate hove into sight the next day. She turned up with Ben in tow.

'And is this the little doggy who found the bangle?'

Gervaise Norfolk reached down to give Ben a pat. He managed to snatch his hand away a split second before Ben's teeth closed together with a snap.

'Feisty little creature, isn't he!' he said, moving his vulnerable parts hastily out of chopper range.

'He don't like suits,' explained Mrs Stoate. 'Withers up at the Hall kicked him once and he were wearing a suit. Ben's not forgotten that.'

Norfolk sat her down and asked her to tell him the circumstances of finding the bangle. He made notes as she went along.

Norfolk listened with growing excitement and when she'd finished, he said thoughtfully, 'Mrs Stoate, I'd like to take your case on. I think you have a *prima facie* case as the finder of the Kingscastle Hoard, particularly as it was you who took the artefact to the authorities and reported it. That establishes a date of the find officially. Quite clearly nobody else has made a legitimate claim, so I think you have an excellent chance.'

Mrs Stoate now looked even more worried as all the stories she had heard of extortionate legal fees flooded back into her mind.

'I can't afford no legal fees, Mr Norfolk, I only have my widow's pension.'

Norfolk smiled. He was a kindly soul at heart but he didn't like working for nothing. If he was going to take the risk, he felt he would be entitled to a reward if he was successful.

'I'll tell you what, Mrs Stoate, I'll take the case on for no fee at all but if we're successful, I'll get ten per cent of the settlement. Are you happy with that?'

When it had sunk in that it wasn't going to cost her anything, Evadne readily agreed and Norfolk said he'd confirm it in a letter.

Gervaise Norfolk was a thorough man. He carefully collected copies of all the times, dates and records relating to Mrs Stoate's bangle. He phoned me and asked me if I would give a statement because it would help. I readily agreed and he said he would draft something and e-mail it to me for me to check and modify if necessary.

Finally, when he had put together a logical and fully supported case with statements from me, Sergeant Bulstrode, The Reverend Percy Furrow and Dr Justin Postlethwaite, he submitted it to the Department of the Environment by registered post.

The timing was perfect, although he didn't know that. The politicians in Westminster were getting twitchy about being accused of sharp practice in trying to award themselves all the money; even the Prime Minister had spoken to the D of E's Secretary of State expressing concern. So when Gervaise Norfolk's carefully presented case on behalf of Mrs Stoate and Ben arrived, it was a good opportunity to get them off the corruption hook and demonstrate that the honest citizen had nothing to fear and the Government was a fair and reasonable body under the current administration.

Mrs Stoate and Ben were awarded one million pounds as a reward for being the finders of the Kingscastle Horde and for behaving responsibly by turning their find in to the authorities as the law required.

The question regarding whose land it was, and who was or wasn't occupying it, was still going on in court, and it looked like being a long drawn out affair running into tens of thousands of pounds in fees and years in the resolution.

Mac's bulldozers started clearing the route for the bypass through Withers Woods, Rock Solid bored their piles down to bedrock and Debbie Mason, our Resident Engineer on the Shering Valley Bridge, reported that work was on programme and Stumpy's tunnels had made the excavation for the big pile cap and thrust block much easier – which was far from his intention!

She also mentioned in passing that Withers was selling off plots of land in the area for housing and light industry. Greybody and Droole's rapidly mounting fees were bleeding him white, and Fortinson Droole, the senior partner, was, as a result, doing the opposite. He was buying up plots of land in Spain with his rapidly mounting profits.

I phoned Bob when I got this news and he was on to the possibilities like a shot. 'Leave it with me, old son, and if I buy a couple plots your firm will be the consultants, rest assured.'

'With Perseus Rixon?'

'Definitely not!'

*****

The headline 'MILLION POUND MUTT' caught my eye in the morning paper. I read that a Mrs Evadne Stoate and her pet dog Ben had been awarded a million pounds finder's fee for being the first to officially find and register an artefact that was part of the Kingscastle Hoard. Good luck to them, I thought somewhat enviously.

Mrs Stoate was reported as saying it wouldn't change her life, and Ben apparently just growled and sank his teeth satisfyingly into the besuited Anthony Molestrangler's ankle as he was handing over the bank draft at the official presentation in Kingscastle Town Hall.

The accompanying photograph showed Evadne, in a large feathered hat and flowery dress, beaming happily as she held one side of the draft whilst Molestrangler, wearing a smile that looked as though it was nailed to his face, held the other side.

My envious thought was mitigated a week later when an envelope arrived at the office addressed to me and marked 'Private'. I slit it open and took out a short note, which simply read:

'Thank you for what you did for Ben and me.
Yours Evadne.
P.S. Me and Steve are getting on fine!'

Pinned to it was a cheque for £20,000.

'Bugger me!' I muttered with astonishment.

Des and Ivan were watching with interest.

'What've you got there?' enquired Des curiously.

Ivan said, 'It's probably a note from some bird giving him the elbow, although why she would fancy him in the first place is beyond me.'

I put the cheque and note back in the envelope and slipped it into my pocket.

'Nothing,' I said. 'It's a family matter.'

Ivan had been very subdued of late apart from the occasional snide comment. It was either his roughing up or the possible outcome of his brush with Justin Postlethwaite at Claims Resolved Quickly. He still hadn't heard anything from Kingscastle police, but the thought of a five thousand pound fine and three months' porridge was still firmly at the front of his mind.

I wondered what else he was planning because I was certain there was something in the wind. He kept shooting sly little glances in my direction and smirking quietly to himself as he watched what I was doing out of the corner of his eye.

That was on the Tuesday. On Thursday, Dennis Menzies, CONDES' computer whiz, came into the office wearing a very worried look. He dropped a bunch of print-outs on my desk and said, 'I think we've got a major problem – or rather you have, Marcus!'

I looked at him. This was not a typical situation. To get Dennis out of his enclosed electronic environment into bright light and fresh air was a very rare and worrying event akin to a hedgehog sunbathing.

'In what way?'

He looked round to see if we were being overheard. Des was engrossed in *The Times* crossword as usual at nine-fifteen in the morning, and Ivan was feigning indifference, but obviously trying to catch every word if it was a problem for me. A prickle of unease ran down my spine.

Dennis lowered his voice. 'I've run your calculations for the bridge deck through the computer twice now and the same answer has come up. The post tensioning you're proposing isn't enough. The figures show that you need at least double that at mid span. The bridge would collapse under normal traffic loading using your figures.'

I grabbed his print-out and studied the conclusion; it looked as though he was right.

I frowned. How had this come about? Well, that would have to come later; the thing now was to correct it immediately. MacLowland were already on site working on the bridge so this could be serious. I felt I had no option but to take it to Hugo and see what he thought before I did anything.

'Come on, Dennis, we'd better go and see Hugo.'

Ivan called out, 'Made a cock-up, have you, smart-arse?'

Well it certainly looked like it, and a major one at that.

Hugo was going through his mail when I tapped on his door.

'Come in.' He raised a questioning eyebrow.

There was no point beating about the bush so it was straight in.

'Dennis has checked my calcs for the Shering Valley Bridge and it looks as though I've made a mistake. The stressing at mid span should be twice the amount that I've specified.'

Hugo looked at Dennis, who confirmed that the output data did show that. Typically Hugo, he looked at solving the problem first before allocating blame.

'Have you got a copy of MacLowland's construction programme?'

I handed him the A5 bar chart from the file and he ran his finger down the line of today's date.

'Well, it won't be too difficult to rectify, they haven't started on the superstructure of the bridge yet, but it's going to make us look stupid. How has this come about? It can only be from incorrect input data. I thought you'd double checked that, Marcus?'

'I did,' I said miserably. 'I gave it to Dennis on a CD.'

Dennis frowned and tugged his ear. 'No, to be precise, you didn't, you gave it to Angela to give to me. When she brought it down she apologised for holding on to it for a day because she thought she'd mislaid it, but then it turned up under some paper on her desk.'

'OK,' said Hugo. 'Let's go through this from the beginning and see what we need to do. Can you get the input CD, Dennis, and we'll start with that.'

Whilst he went off to get the disk, I scratched my head. I couldn't think where I could have made a mistake of that magnitude. I had been doubly careful because it was a new technique that hadn't been used for bridge deck design before.

Dennis came back with the CD and Hugo fed it into his PC. He scrolled down the data slowly and we watched carefully.

When it got to the end Hugo asked, 'Where's the impact loading for heavy lorries?'

'I put it in there, just after the maximum live load input.'

'I didn't see it!'

He scrolled back to the live loading and down to the next item, which was the braking forces, but there were no impact loading figures.

'I know I included them,' I protested. Turning to Dennis, I said, 'I gave you a provisional CD a few weeks ago when we were checking that this method of stressing was feasible. Have you still got that?'

He said he had and went off again to fetch it. Hugo tapped his fingers impatiently on his desk while we waited, and I grew more and more nervous.

When the disk arrived, Hugo fed that into his PC. The loading figures were identical. The main point, however, much to my relief, was that between the live loading figures and the braking forces were three lines of data for impact loading.

'The input from the first CD was transferred directly on to the final one so it couldn't have got missed out!' I told them. 'It's not possible.'

We all looked at each other.

'Could it be a computer glitch?

'Very unlikely,' murmured Dennis. 'I've never heard of a computer erasing three lines of data out of the middle of the input off its own bat before.'

Nobody wanted to speculate what the alternative was if that was not the reason for the error.

Hugo summed up the situation. 'Well, we've found it, that's

There Came A Big Spider

what matters. The main thing is to modify the post-tensioning schedule. Thank God we've found the problem early enough to minimise any extra costs. In fact I doubt if there will be any at this stage, so no great damage has been done. Thank you both for bringing it to my attention, and Marcus, you'll reissue the schedules and prepare a variation order to cover the extra stressing?'

'Yes, straight away.'

Dennis went back to his lair amongst the compost heap of keyboards, humming processors and printers, and I wandered back to the office thinking about two things.

Thank the lord that Dennis was so meticulous and precise in everything he did and remembered – and it would have been very easy for an experienced engineer to take the disk from Angela's desk, slip it into a PC, erase three critical lines of data and replace it under some paper.

It was an evil thing to do. There would be very little danger to the public – everything would have been double-checked again and hopefully the error detected and corrected. However the finger for sloppy engineering and incurring extra costs would be pointed at me as the person responsible for the design – as it had been.

A cold anger built up inside me. This was getting close to dangerous, and it was time to put a stop to it here and now.

I waited till Des had left the office for something or other, took the two incriminating photos of Ivan from the file where I had hidden them – the one with him wearing his bondage gear with Miss Stern standing behind him in all her glory, and the one of him in the school room – and walked across to his desk. He looked up as I approached.

'Made a balls-up of your bridge design, have you?'

I didn't answer him directly; I just dropped the photos on his desk and waited.

He automatically glanced down at them and then froze. His face went three shades whiter and then bright red and finally purple. A chameleon would have been impressed. He opened his mouth but no words came out, just a strangulated gargle.

I smiled at him. It wasn't a smile I needed to practice. It was clearly a genuine, serious, implacable smile that emphasised without any doubt, 'I've got you by the balls and you're going to stay that way for as long as it takes.'

I leant over his desk so my nose was no more than fifty centimetres from his. He couldn't move his head back further because of the wall.

'You try pulling one more stunt like that,' I said very quietly, 'or do anything in the future that I consider is likely to do me harm in this firm, and these photos go all round the office – copies to everybody here, the partners, the girls and especially Agatha.'

I didn't wait for a response, just left the pictures with him and strolled back to my desk. He was too shocked to speak.

He didn't know that those were the only ones in existence – I'd erased the originals from my inbox! The bluff made it all the sweeter.

On the last day of August, Angela came into the office and told us that Hugo had called a meeting of all the main staff, about forty of us, in his office in half-an-hour's time. Rumours of a reorganisation had been swirling about the firm for some time now and it was clear that our long-term workload was not as healthy as it should be.

When we had all packed into Hugo's office, sitting or standing where we could, he told us that he, Hamish Robertson and Ewen Jones, the three partners, had decided to reorganize the firm from top to bottom. This, he explained, was partly due to the downturn in work at home, the increasing influence and effect of the European Union, and the increase in the price of oil per barrel.

He told us that our traditional markets, the Government, the councils, large private industries and property were all suffering from the recession and we would have to start finding new markets for our consultancy services. The partners wanted the senior staff to take a bigger role in marketing these. He outlined the extra roles they wanted people to take on, with a hint of greater rewards should they be successful.

My function was to be expanded to cover large structures, both commercial and industrial, and to try to develop our business in the Middle East. I would report to Ewen Jones and liaise with David Nairn, who ran our fledgling office in the Gulf.

Ivan was given a similar brief but he would be Senior Road Engineer and concentrate on European Union work in the old Eastern bloc countries. He would report to Hamish Robertson. We would be in separate offices although on the same floor.

Des was to be responsible for dealing with the British Government's Overseas Aid Programmes and was to develop our contacts with Whitehall and the Foreign and Commonwealth Office. He would report to Hugo.

Other senior staff were given more direct responsibility for design and developing their own particular fields: water supply, sewage treatment, harbours, airports, power generation, etcetera. The old Planning Teams were abolished.

I felt as if a great weight had been lifted from the back of my neck. Ivan had been replaced by the Arabs. Yes, well I didn't know much about the Middle East at that point but I was looking forward to learning and was raring to go!

I told Charlie about the reorganisation and that I had been given more responsibility, which could lead to more pay. 'Or getting fired!' she said shrewdly,

I waved that aside nonchalantly. Moon, the international, jet-setting, businessman/engineer, has now been unleashed on the world.

'Poor world!' and 'Get ready for World War Three!' were some of the kinder comments when this was revealed to the guys in the Snug bar of the Frog and Nightgown the following Saturday.

Charlie and I were incredibly happy together. I couldn't believe my luck and I looked forward to every day with her in my life. I decided to sub-let my old flat in Palmerston Mansions and Charlie came to help me pack up my few remaining things one Saturday morning. There wasn't much, and what there was went into two cardboard boxes that would fit in the back of the MG.

She was clearing out a drawer when she picked up what looked to her like a mud-covered, flat stone.

'What on earth is this, Marcus? Why've you kept this rock? Does it have some special significance or shall I chuck it away?'

Bloody hell! Could it possibly be…?

I took it from her and looked at it. I had a funny feeling about that stone. I'd forgotten all about it lurking away in my drawer. A lot of recent history began to flash through my mind.

It had all started really with that prat Major Sir Fistulas Withers threatening to put a charge of bird shot where the sun don't shine. Then Susan Tripp and her steak and kidney pie followed by crumpet on the rug. Tracey Tripp and I rolling about at the site of the proposed Shering Valley Bridge foundations and the removal of her substantial bra being frustrated by the item I was now holding. Stumpy disturbing us – I shuddered to think what could have ensued if he hadn't! My macho jack-the-lad confidence being flattened by the realisation that I was staying in Kingscastle's number one knocking shop and my great seduction scenes were, in fact, me being set up by Tracey and her mother in a sado-masochistic commercial deal. Setting up Ivan for what I thought could be a life-changing experience for him – which I suppose it was, but not in the way I expected. Receiving the kinky photos of Ivan, which finally got him off my back. Finding Ben trapped by what was the first piece officially recorded of the now famous Kingscastle Hoard. Justin Postleth-waite's comments about the penalties for not reporting treasure. Evadne's twenty grand, which had helped us refurnish and re-decorate Charlie's little house. Bob's growing property empire. Tony and Pete's professional successes – Pete was now a junior partner in a Harley Street practice.

It was all a jumble of ifs, buts, maybes and, most important, luck in its various guises. But in the end life was good!

Charlie stood there with an expression of total mystification on her face as she beheld me seemingly float off into another world.

'Hello, hello! I'm still here! So what is it about this stone that has sent you off into a dreamlike trance, Mr Moon?'

I was going to scratch my head but stayed my hand. This was going to be tricky. Any movement or facial expression of that kind would betray a weakness. There was no way I was ever go-ing to tell anybody about Mrs Tripp and her House of Pain. If it ever got out that Marcus Moon had thought he was pulling some classy crumpet, when all along it was she who had been tempt-ing him with a free sample with the express intention of charging him for the next instalment, my friends would split their sides laughing.

The rest of the story was non-controversial and Charlie knew most of it already. The problem was, she was very bright and very observant and the slightest flicker or hesitation in present-ing the tissue of lies I was thinking of concocting would have been seized upon and used to rip my credibility to shreds in an instant, with the possible withdrawal of erotic services for an unspecified length of time.

No, the truth was better – or as close to it as I could get without actually admitting anything. It was how it was put over that would dictate the outcome.

'Well,' I began, 'it's a long and dramatic story of lust, lechery and evil intentions. It starts with this young innocent country maiden – flowers in her hair and a blush on her cheeks (you, of course, wouldn't know anything about being one of those)...' It was as well to throw in something like that as a distraction to stop their mind focusing too closely on what you were about to reveal. '...who was entranced by the wit and sophistication of a man of the world like me. The promise of a pint of lager easily lured her to an out-of-the-way pub deep in the primeval forest. There, powerful intoxicants were poured down her throat until she was desperate for sexual relief. She begged me on her knees to take her into the woods. So by the light of the silvery moon and on a bed of soft leaves, I was about to work my wicked will on her when she gave a cry of pain.

'"What is it, my little flower?" I cried, "Am I being too rough with you?"

'"Oh no kind sir," she replied. "But there's something pointed sticking in me."

'"Not yet," I murmured.

'"No, in my back, sir. It hurts."

'So, being a gentleman, I found and removed the offending item and slipped it in the pocket of my jeans to remind me of that glorious evening when she finally yielded to my undoubted charms.' I glanced down modestly at my fingernails.

'Is that it?'

I metaphorically crossed my fingers. 'It is, I confess.'

There was a pregnant silence, then Charlie sneered scornfully.

'What a ridiculous load of twaddle! I've never heard such a rambling pile of nonsense! For Christ's sake, Marcus, I asked you a sensible question and I expect a sensible answer.'

'OK,' I said resignedly. 'I was just trying to make it more interesting. I actually noticed it on the site when I caught a glint of metal on top of some excavated material, and just thought it was an unusual stone, so I slipped it in my pocket to examine later and forgot all about it.'

'Let's have another look at it then,' she said. 'I'll go and rinse it under the tap and get that caked mud off it.' And she vanished into the small bathroom.

Well, I did tell you! It's not the telling of the truth that counts: it's how the truth is told without the need for detectable deceit!

But I digress.

She came running back into the sitting area, excitement bursting out of her.

'Just look at it now! If it is what I think it is, it could be very important!'

She was right, but I knew already in my heart of hearts what it was. Now that all the mud had been washed off it was clearly a gilt cheek-piece embedded with tiny jewels from some sort of helmet. I had seen its identical twin when the Kingscastle Hoard was exhibited at the Town Hall and the Coroner was deciding its fate.

I told her this and she said, 'What are you going to do?'

With a grim smile I replied, 'Possibly three months in jail and a five thousand pound fine if anybody gets to know about it.'

'You could post it anonymously to the Kingscastle Coroner.'

'I could,' I said.

So if you're ever down Kingscastle way and you call in the museum there, see if you can spot a right-sided, gilt cheek-piece from an Anglo-Saxon helmet!